Steve Swartz

## ABOUT THE AUTHOR

NICOLA GRIFFITH is a native of Leeds, England. At eighteen she moved to Hull, where she taught women's self-defense—to groups as diverse as the Equal Opportunities Training Unit and the Union of Catholic Mothers. She was also the lead singer/songwriter for the all-woman band, Jane's Plane. She is the author of *Ammonite* and *Slow River*, and the editor of the Bending the Landscape series. Ms Griffith currently lives in Seattle with her partner, writer Kelley Eskridge. Her homepage may be found at *http://www.nicolagriffith.com*.

# the blue place

# nicola griffith

Perennial
*An Imprint of HarperCollinsPublishers*

A hardcover edition of this book was published in 1998 by Avon Books.

THE BLUE PLACE. Copyright © 1998 by Nicola Griffith. All rights reserved. Printed in the United States of America. No part of this book may be used or reproduced in any manner whatsoever without written permission except in the case of brief quotations embodied in critical articles and reviews. For information address HarperCollins Publishers Inc., 10 East 53rd Street, New York, NY 10022.

HarperCollins books may be purchased for educational, business, or sales promotional use. For information please write: Special Markets Department, HarperCollins Publishers Inc., 10 East 53rd Street, New York, NY 10022.

First Avon Books paperback edition published 1999.

Reprinted in Perennial 2002.

*Designed by Kellan Peck*

Library of Congress Cataloging-in-Publication Data:
Griffith, Nicola.
    The blue place / Nicola Griffith.
      p.  cm.
   I. Title
   PR6057.R49B58    1998                    97-44256
   823'.914—dc21                           CIP

ISBN 0-380-79088-2

02 03 04 05 06 RRD 10 9 8 7 6 5 4 3

for kelley, my pearl

I would like to thank Jan Berg, Eddie Hall, Holly Wade Matter, Mark Tiedemann, Cindy Ward, and my editors, Jennifer Hershey and Charlotte Abbott, who each in their own way helped make this a better book; my agent, Shawna McCarthy; and Dave Slusher, webmaster extraordinaire.

# the blue place

An April night in Atlanta between thunderstorms: dark and warm and wet, sidewalks shiny with rain and slick with torn leaves and fallen azalea blossoms. Nearly midnight. I had been walking for over an hour, covering four or five miles. I wasn't tired. I wasn't sleepy.

You would think that my bad dreams would be of the first man I had killed, thirteen years ago. Or if not him, then maybe the teenager who had burned to death in front of me because I was too slow to get the man with the match. But no, when I turn out the lights at ten o'clock and can't keep still, can't even bear to sit down in my Lake Claire house, it's because I see again the first body I hadn't killed.

I was twenty-one, a rookie in a uniform so new it still smelled of harsh chemical dyes. My hat was too big. My partner and I had been called to a duplex on Lavista. It was me who opened the bathroom door.

As soon as I saw that bathwater, I knew. Water just doesn't get that still if the person sitting in it is alive: the pulse of blood through veins, the constant peristaltic squeeze of alimentary tract, the soft suck of breath move the liquid gently, but definitely. Not this water. It was only after I had stared, fascinated, at the dry scum on the bar of soap, only after my partner had moved me gently aside, that I noticed her mouth was open, her eyeballs a gluey blue-grey where they should have been white.

I wake up at night seeing those eyes.

The sidewalks around Inman Park are made from uneven hexagons, mossy and slippery even without the debris of the recent storm. I walked in the road. A pine tree among the oaks smelled of warm resin, and the steam already rising from the pavement brought with it the scents of oil and rubber and warm asphalt. I smiled. Southern cities. People often say to me, *Aud, how can you stand the heat?* but I love it. I love to feel the sun rub up against my pale northern skin, love its fingers reaching down into muscle and bone. I grew up with subzero fjord winds edged with spicules of ice; to breathe deep and feel damp summer heat curling into delicate bronchioles is a luxury I will never tire of. Even during the teenage years I spent in England, when my mother decided the embassy could get along without her for a week or two and we all went up to Yorkshire to stay with Lord Horley, there was that endless biting moan over the moors, the ceaseless waving of heather and gorse. The American South suits me just fine.

Atlanta is lush. The gates and lawns and hedges I walked past were heady with the scents of trumpet honeysuckle and jasmine, the last of the pink and white dogwood blossom. By June, of course, all the small blooms would wilt in the heat, and the city's true colours, jungle colours, would become apparent: black-striped tiger lilies, orchids, waxy magnolia blossom. By the end of August, even those would give up the ghost and the city would turn green: glossy beryl banana trees with canoe-sized leaves, jade swamp oak, and acre upon emerald acre of bermuda grass. And as the summer heat faded into the end of October, the beginning of November, the green would fade with it. In winter Atlanta became a pale black and white photograph of a city with concrete sidewalks, straw-coloured grass and bare, grey trees.

Thunder rumbled to the southwest and lightning turned the clouds the pink of Florida grapefruits: a long, long wait until winter.

I lengthened my stride, enjoying the metronomic thump of boot on pavement, the noisy sky, and when I took a corner wide walked smack into a woman running in the opposite direction.

We steadied each other for a moment—long enough for me to catch the expensive scent of her dark, rain-wet hair—then stepped back. Looked at each other. About five-seven, I'd say. Slim and sleek. Face smooth with wariness: after all, I'm big; I'm told I look frightening when I want. And that made me think how fragile she was, despite the hard muscle I had felt under my hand. It would be so easy—a step, a smile, swift whirl and grab, and snap: done. I even knew how she would fall, what a tiny sound her last sigh would be, how she would fold onto the pavement. Eight seconds.

She stepped back another pace. It was meant to look casual, but I noted the weight on her back foot, the set of her shoulders. Funny the thoughts we have at nearly midnight. I clasped my hands behind my back in an effort to appear less threatening, then nodded, stepped to one side, and walked away. All without a word spoken. As I moved past the big houses shrouded by dripping trees I fought the urge to look over my shoulder. Looking back would frighten her. I told myself there was nothing unusual about a woman walking the streets at midnight—I did it—but my hindbrain was stirring.

Thunder rumbled again, and water sluiced down in sheets as sudden and cold as spilled milk, beating itself into a froth on the sidewalk. The air was full of water and it was getting difficult to breathe. Lightning streaked down to my left just a bit too close for comfort. I turned for home and started to jog. No sense drowning.

The road jumped under my feet. Transformer, I thought, but then the sound hit, batting at me from both sides like huge cat's paws. My eyes widened and promptly filled with rain. I shook my head, trying to get rid of the ringing in my ears, but the world jumped again, pavement slamming the soles of my feet, only this time the sound was as solid as a punch in the gut, and this time I recognized it—explosives. Then I was turning and running back to where I had just come from, back to the corner, towards a house unfurling in orange flame and black smoke, a brighter yellow at the center, like a gigantic tiger lily. I skidded to a halt in confusion. It's too early for lilies. . . .

I stood helpless, face getting hotter and hotter. I lifted my hand to shield my eyes but it didn't help much. I had to step back a few yards. The flames roared. People began to appear in their doorways. Blinds twitched. I did nothing. Let the neighbours look their fill; if there had been anyone in that house, they were beyond aid, and no doubt someone had called the fire department. Not that there was much point: the fire burned very neat and clean; the neighbours' houses were safe; I doubted even that the garage would catch.

It was far too good a torch to be the work of an amateur firebug who wouldn't be able to resist sticking around to watch their work, but I looked anyway. No sign of the woman with the rain-wet hair.

My hindbrain was beginning to stretch and snuff now, so I thought about that woman. What was it about her that put my senses on red alert? She hadn't done this: most accelerants had very particular scents, difficult to hide, and besides, she had been running towards the house, not away.

Sirens whooped in the distance. The police and firefighters would be all burly and adrenaline-harsh in their uniforms. They wouldn't want me there, wouldn't know how to act around me, and tonight I could not be bothered to put them at their ease just so they would call me Lieutenant out loud but wonder silently what I was doing wandering the streets alone at midnight.

The flames were dying quickly, leaving dark images like shrivelling leaves on my retina. I backed into the shadows.

I stripped off my wet clothes and sat cross-legged on the silk rug to rub my hair dry with a towel. Rain beat on the windows. Blood beat in my veins. Turning the corner wide . . .

It's a simple thing. If you walk tight around a corner, you can be surprised by anyone who is waiting on the other side. It's like sitting with your back to the door, like chambering a round and leaving the safety off, wearing a dress that will restrict your legs, or walking with your hands in your pockets: stupid. But so many people do it. Every now and again I go into a school to teach self-defence classes to young women. I ask: How many of you know which way to look before crossing a busy street? And every single hand will go up. So then I ask: Who knows the fire drill? And most of the hands stay up. Even if I ask who knows CPR, or what to do if you smell gas, there are a lot of hands. But if I ask how many know how to walk around a corner properly—or escape a stranglehold, or find out if the man behind you really is following you— they lower their hands in confusion. Yet these are all sensible precautions. It's just that women are taught to not think about the danger they are often in, or how to prevent it. We're taught to feel fear, but not what to do about it.

I'm used to people thinking I'm paranoid. I just tell them it doesn't take any extra effort to walk around a corner properly, or sit with your back to walls in strange places, because it becomes automatic, like looking left then right then left again before crossing the road, and it could save your life. It's saved mine more than once. I'm used to being the only one who believes that, the only one who takes these routine precautions.

But that woman last night had also been taking the corner wide. And she had remembered to do it while she was in enough of a hurry to run.

There was no trace of the rain when I woke next morning. The tree outside my bedroom window was golden green with sunshine and birds were singing blithely. I stood under the shower a long time, letting the water quench lingering thoughts about that house burning like a hot lily.

I have a big kitchen; square, with a terra-cotta floor. French windows open onto the deck I built last year. In summer the whole thing is in shade but when the leaves are still small with spring, sunlight shivers lightly over the planking. I took my toast and tea outside and cut up an orange while a cardinal landed on the bird feeder. Someone burnt down a house practically under my nose. My curiosity was piqued, but it wasn't my problem. My problem was to beat the morning traffic and get to the Spanish consulate in time for my nine o'clock appointment.

I ate my breakfast and thought about the second daughter of the Spanish Cabinet minister, who was coming to Atlanta for four days next week. I hoped she didn't want conversation. I dislike clients who try to be my friend. The Spanish hadn't told me, yet, the reason she was visiting. I hoped it was something boring, and safe. I like excitement but only in situations I have planned and can control. I don't like to risk my life, or anyone else's, to protect those I don't know and care about even less.

I wiped my hands on a napkin, put the napkin on my plate, carried the plate and cup into the kitchen. Napkin in the laundry, dirty dishes in the dishwasher, butter in the fridge. Orderly house, orderly life. I dressed carefully. Although Philippe Cordova would have checked me out thoroughly before calling about the job and no doubt knew I didn't need the money, it never did any harm to emphasize that fact. It saved time down the road. So I picked one of my handmade Kobayashi suits in soft grey, put gold at my ears and moussed my white-blonde hair behind my ears. Boxy European shoes. Pearl choker.

I felt sharp, rich, very good looking. It pleases me to wear silk couture and gold and pearls. I like the way it feels on my skin, the way it fits.

The jacket I wore last night was on a hanger in the bathroom, still drying. I transferred the leather fob of the car key to my pants pocket, the house keys to my jacket, dipped into the inside breast pocket . . . and found it empty. I checked again, then in all the other pockets. My wallet was gone.

I knew it wouldn't be on the table by the door, or on the dresser, or on the floor or behind a cushion on the couch, but I checked anyway. I caught sight of myself in the long mirror in the hall. I looked utterly calm. I strode over to the phone, dialed Cordova's private line at the consulate. While it rang I remembered the smell of the woman's rain-wet hair, her wary face.

"Philippe? Aud Torvingen. How is your schedule? It looks as though I'll be twenty or thirty minutes late." I didn't offer an explanation, he didn't ask. People don't, usually.

I put the phone down, breathed hard through my nose. Others hate the mess of crime, and the pain, the loss and bewilderment and anger, but what I resent is the inconvenience. Driver's license, gun permit, insurance card . . . I looked at the phone again but didn't pick it up. Something told me I wouldn't have to make all those phone calls this time, and if I was wrong, well, two more hours wouldn't hurt.

Whoever had my wallet had my address. When I left the house I set the alarm system.

Outside the birds still sang, the sun still shone. Trees shivered in a light breeze, dropping clouds of pollen. The screened porch was thick with it. My maroon Saab had turned greenish gold. It looked like a small furry hill in the driveway. I backed out into the road and left the motor running while I went back up the driveway and placed a few twigs and leaves in unobvious places. I memorized the pattern of footprints and car tires in the pollen.

The wallet was poking out from under a bush about four feet from the corner. I squatted down but didn't touch it. It was clearly visible to anyone looking. The arson inspectors would have looked.

I touched the leather gently with a fingertip. Dry. I leafed through it. Nothing missing. I tucked it away in my inside breast pocket and stood.

I have a strange kind of face; people trust me. More than that, they see in my face what they want to be there. One old man I pulled from a car wreck said I had a face like a holy angel. Some think I'm the girl next door—the way she should have been if only she didn't hang out with the wrong crowd, if she didn't drink, if she hadn't gotten pregnant when she was sixteen. Those I have killed have never expressed an opinion, though several did look surprised. My face is my most useful tool.

The uniformed officer standing by the tape around the burnt-out shell was young. He had no idea who I was. Wearing any other clothes I would have smiled and pretended to rubberneck, and he would have thought I was just like him and ended up telling me things he shouldn't have. But I was dressed for the Spanish consulate. I walked up briskly and nodded at the figure in protective gear poking about in the ashes behind a wall thirty yards away. "Who's the fire inspector?"

"Ma'am?"

I smiled pleasantly. "Bertolucci or Hammer?"

He slid his eyes sideways, unsure how to deal with this pushy civilian who was obviously more important than she seemed. Perhaps my impatience showed through. He stepped back uneasily.

"Never mind." I stepped to one side. "Hoi!"

The figure in the hard hat jerked upright and scowled.

I knew that expression. "Bertolucci?"

"Yeah, who wants to . . . Torvingen?"

"The same."

He took off his hat and wiped his forehead and stepped over the rubble towards me. "Been a while."

"Yes." Bertolucci had never liked me; he'd never disliked me, either. He was just cautious.

"Heard after you were kicked out you took a job in some podunk town north of here." He waited, looked at my clothes. I said nothing. "Your name came up last night. Some woman told us you were walking around here just before show time." He looked assessingly at the rubble. "You'd know how."

A compliment. It had been a beautiful job. Fast and clean. Nothing touched but the target. "I watched it burn for a while. Did it reach the garage?"

"Funny you should ask that." This time the assessing gaze was turned on me. He made up his mind. "Come and look at something. Mind your clothes."

I stepped under the tape, past a late-model Camry that took up the driveway. "I'm thinking about getting one of these," Bertolucci said. Too massive for my taste.

The garage was brick, unusual in Atlanta. The door was open. The walls were cluttered with the usual stuff: caked paint rollers; a rake and shovel, with red dirt still on the blade; a hose that had been badly coiled and was permanently kinked. Why were Americans so careless of things?

The inside was unfinished: raw bricks with mortar squeez-ing between them like cake filling. The mortar was grey and crumbly with damp and age. Spider webs smoothed all the cor-ners. Bags of potting compost that looked about fifteen years old were piled against one wall. There was a lazy humming over my head—some kind of hornet nest. It was an ordinary garage. I wondered what I was supposed to see.

"When that woman came by and talked about you, Detective Nolan laughed and said, 'Oh, Aud used to be one of us,' and sent her away. But you know he had to have wondered." I bet they'd all wondered. I knew my reputation. "He didn't wonder long, though. Not after what we found in here."

"So what did you find?"

"Coke. A lot. Six, seven keys."

"Coke?"

"What with that and the professional torch, and the guy who died, he figured it for a drug hit. Revenge, or a lesson."

It sounded plausible, until you stopped to think about it. "Recognize the torch?"

"Nope. Haven't come across this one before."

"Who died?"

"Name of Lusk. Jim Lusk. Some kind of art professor."

"Any close relatives show up yet?"

"Nope."

"He was found in the house?" He nodded. "And the coke was in here?"

"Right here." He patted the shelf that ran the length of the garage. "Interesting, don't you think?" It was, very. "I have to get back to work. Feel free to take a look around." He grinned, a hard grin that said: You owe me a favor now.

I took a closer look at the shelf. Swollen with damp, pulling away from the wall at one end. Powdery holes and termite wings. A faint outline of white powder crisscrossed with silvery snail trails. It made absolutely no sense. No one in their right mind would store coke in a damp, insect-ridden garage. And if the torch had known the drug was here, he or she would have taken it.

I knew what Bertolucci wanted: someone outside to know that he knew the obvious explanation didn't make sense. It would make him feel better when the APD accepted the obvious explanation and shelved the case. There was too much work to keep chasing after a murder that already had an explanation, even such a flimsy one. Politically, too, it made sense. Mayor Foley was fighting hard to get a special federal grant for the war on drugs. The APD, being smart enough to know that the war was unwinnable, would take the money and use it on something that might make a difference: five new cruisers, six months' worth of ammunition, a week-long training course for half the SWAT teams. Jim Lusk's death was just another ledger entry on the grant form, something to be used as a weapon in the increasingly bitter fight for money. The detective second grade who was in charge of the investigation would have four other homicides and dozens of assaults to deal with. His lieutenant would spend most of her time juggling meetings, writing duty rosters, dealing with an increasingly angry public. The precinct captain would be faced with a nightmare of budget stretching, trying to decide whether the squad room should have new terminals, which it needed, or that new air-conditioning system to replace the one that was responsible for the sick-building syndrome that meant officers on his precinct were overrunning their sick time and bringing down the wrath of the city accountants. Lusk's killer would never be found.

But that wasn't my concern. I wanted to know about the woman who thought this was something I had done, but I wasn't in any particular hurry. Let her come to me.

I was halfway to the embassy when the car phone rang. It was Denneny. "Denneny. I was just thinking of you. Made that decision between the air-conditioning and the new terminals yet?"

"Terminals this month. Air-conditioning in June. I hear you were at the scene of the impromptu Inman Park barbecue last night. I thought we could observe the formalities and get a statement."

"Do you have any plans for lunch?"

"Not so far."

"How about Deacon's at eleven-thirty?"

A very young man in button-down shirt and silk tie was waiting in the sunshine outside the consulate. He opened the Saab door for me smartly, and I handed over the leather key fob. He was practically salivating at the prospect of hopping inside.

"It has quadraphonic CD sound, too," I said.

An uncertain blink, pink lower lip caught between his teeth. "Ma'am?"

I just smiled, and hoped he would have to drive around for a long time to find a parking place. He was probably some kind of admin intern who would be spending the next three months chained to a workstation freezing to death in the air-conditioning, all to pad out his résumé. I was willing to bet he'd never parked a car for anyone but his parents in his life. Consulates don't usually provide valet parking. Most people don't ask for it. I always ask for as much as I can get. It's a matter of principle.

I hummed as I went through the heavy teak and glass doors. The carpet was a beautiful deep green. Much nicer than the cold marble of the English consulate. "Aud Torvingen," I said to the woman behind the desk. Her hair was sleek as a seal's and though she had the dark skin and eyes of Sevilla, her grooming was Southern: big nails, gold jewellery, an unnecessary bow on her blouse. As jarring as a beard on a drag queen.

I sat down in a comfortable chair. She glanced up at me once, then got on with her work: probably wondering who I was, probably also sure she would never find out. That's what life is like in a consulate. A series of closed, comfortable rooms that most of the help never get to sit in.

Philippe came to get me himself. I would have been surprised if he hadn't. He had deep gold hair and very long limbs. According to the check I had done on him after his initial phone call, he liked to play racquet sports—squash, racquetball, tennis—and was pretty good at it. I imagined he surprised a lot of his opponents who expected his arms and legs to tangle and clutter together, but his walk was efficient, fast. I rose.

"Glad you could come." We shook hands. My mother once showed me a dozen different handshakes. *This is the one that means I don't think you're worth my attention:* a quick shake, with her hand already sliding from mine before it was properly finished. *This one shows I hold you in great contempt:* a snakelike up and down, bending at the wrist, fingers stiff as though she couldn't wait to shake off my sweat. There were others. Cordova's was a mixture of reserve and haste: fast, light, whippy.

His office had a beautiful oak floor. We sat opposite each other on surprisingly comfortable Georgian chairs. He handed me a manilla folder. "Beatriz del Gato."

Consular officers love details: dates, times, places; mother, father, lovers; education, employment, illnesses. I took the folder and put it down next to me unopened. "Why haven't you informed the Atlanta Police Department of her arrival?"

He folded his hands onto his lap. "Miss del Gato will only be here for four days. She wishes to remain incognito and believes her visit is a matter of some . . . delicacy."

I smiled, understanding. "She's doing something that she would find personally embarrassing to have reported in the press, but that you wouldn't, particularly?"

His mouth gave away nothing but there was a smile in his voice. "Miss del Gato wishes to work in an advertising agency. She wishes to be offered a job without her prospective employer giving her any special favours."

"Why didn't she try New York?"

"She did."

"Ah." Beatriz was too stupid, or unimaginative, or something, to be offered a job on her own merits. "I still don't see why you can't tell the APD."

Now he did smile. "I did. They have no objection to you taking the job." Why should they? It saved them money. Besides, I doubted Miss Beatriz really was important enough for either the consulate or the police department to go to any trouble. But Philippe was only doing what the diplomatic service of any country does best: saving everyone's face.

I leaned back. "Tell me, what's she like?"

He rolled his eyes. "Earnest, boring, and unreasonably stubborn. Would you like some coffee?"

I gave the admin intern who wished he was a valet parker a ten-dollar tip because he had polished the pollen off my wing mirrors, and because it really was a beautiful day. There was still a slight breeze and the humidity was below sixty percent. Even the etiolated young birch trees that were spaced as carefully as nursery seedlings every ten yards on the concrete sidewalk looked fresh and clean.

I played Diamanda Galas all the way to Deacon's. I got there five minutes early. Denneny was already there.

Years ago, when he still wore a uniform, when his wife was alive, he would have been joking with the women dishing up the fried chicken and greens behind the counter, talking them out of a free side of cornbread, inhaling the rich steam of grits and gravy and grease until his ruddy complexion darkened to plum; but this morning he was sitting at one of the rickety Formica tables, looking around at the clientele as though he were a stranger, out of place in his city suit and silk tie.

"You look more like an executive than a cop," I said.

He stood. "I am, these days."

"Anything good on the menu today?"

It was an old joke—Deacon and now his heirs had always served exactly the same thing—but Denneny just shrugged.

We stood in line and loaded up our trays with chicken and greens and potatoes and gravy and bread and iced tea. I paid for both of us and got a handful of paper napkins. I took the seat facing the door.

"You look as though you're doing well. Watch your clothes with all this grease."

"That's why napkins were invented." I tucked two around my neck, draped one across my lap, and picked up a chicken wing. The best fried chicken in the city. "So. You wanted a statement."

He took one of those miniature tape recorders out of his pocket, put it on the table and looked at his watch. "I forgot to pick up a fresh cassette, so there's only about half an hour's worth of tape left."

"That should be plenty."

So in between bites of hot chicken and forkfuls of mashed potato loaded with enough cholesterol to stun an elephant, I told him about crashing into the woman, about the explosion, and the flames. I gave him times, descriptions, even a weather report. He didn't ask any questions, just nodded and ate. When I'd finished he turned the machine off and slipped it back in his pocket. "I'll get it transcribed this afternoon. You can come in and sign it anytime. That should take care of the formalities."

"Any leads?"

"Just the drugs."

"Surprising, that."

"I've passed the point of being surprised by anything those people do."

"I don't think it was drug dealers."

"The drugs were there, and there isn't a single other angle to pursue."

"And why even try when there's a nice, neat explanation?"

"Something like that. You know how things stand, Torvingen. If we don't get our share of the fed payout, not only won't there be any air-conditioning in June, we won't even be able to afford batteries and tapes for this little machine." He tapped his pocket. "So unless you have the address and confession of the guy who did it, butt out."

I shrugged. "Just making conversation."

He wouldn't let it go. "Do you have some special interest in the case?"

"Not particularly."

"Good, because I'd hate to get our wires crossed on this."

"Why should I care who killed whom and over what? I'm not a police officer anymore."

"And you never cared much even then."

"Oh, I wouldn't go that far."

He applied himself to the potatoes for a while. "Do you miss it?"

"No."

"Not even a bit?"

"Not even a bit."

"I still don't understand why you didn't take that liaison job I offered you when you were pulled off the streets."

"You know as well as I do that the mayor would have had kittens at the thought of me still walking around with a badge and gun in an election year." I had better things to do with my life than be photogenic for the police department.

"True. So if you don't miss being a cop, why did you take that job in Dahlonega?"

"It was work. Only now I don't need to work."

"Lucky you." It came out sounding bitter.

"Sounds as though you could do with a vacation."

"I'm taking one. Two weeks in the Napa Valley starting Saturday. Nothing but sun and the scent of the vine."

When I'd first known him, he drank only beer and bourbon. There again, he wouldn't have known a silk tie if it had bitten him. People change.

We looked at each other. I realized that his spectacle lenses were bifocals. He wiped his fingers carefully on a napkin. "Well, it's been good talking to you. Come in to sign this thing tomorrow, after you finish with the rookies."

"Anything in particular you want me to cover with them?"

He stood. "Nah. Just tell them how it works in the real world, so they don't get themselves killed the first time they step out of the car."

The real world. We had always disagreed about what, exactly, that meant. He had always believed in the rules, but rules are useless when lives are in danger. He never seemed to understand that.

two

There used to be several distinct kinds of gym. When I was growing up, school gyms—in whatever country—were sunlit and silent, the air dead and dusty with the scents of climbing ropes, ancient pommel horses sweat-soaked and bare on the handles, and a thin, greasy overlay of plimsoll rubber scraped off on the wooden floor during countless skiddings and bumpy landings. All very genteel and closed off. Working gyms in the city were meatier, more burly, with dim overhead lights, chalk dust, labouring fans, and metal everywhere: clanking Nautilus, ringing free weights, clinking dog tags. Male sweat and Ben-Gay. Hoarse huff-huff of pumping, the occasional burst of loud boy conversation: the game, the fight, the conquest. Dojos, on the other hand, were defined more by body sounds: the slap of open hands on arms, thud of bare feet on kick bags, the heavy, almost soundless impact of a rolling fall . . . and the voices, karate kiais like the cry of a stooping hawk; the very particular half-swallowed *hut-hut*, like a gun with a sound suppressor, of a whole school of people going through their katas; the endless, rhythmic susurrus of breath as half a dozen students meditate in zazen.

The precinct gym in City Hall East was less than a year old: beautiful sprung-wood floor, whispering air-conditioning, full-spectrum lighting. The sweet, cloying scent of new plastic and rubber grips on the weight machines vied with cologne and a very faint perfume. Rookies smelled different these days.

The fourteen newly minted police officers were wearing a variety of tees and shorts. I had told them to wear long sleeves and sweatpants. It doesn't matter how nice the floor is; if you miss the mat, it'll skin your knee. Two were very young but most were in their mid- to late twenties. One man had some grey at his temples. They all looked freshly showered. It was six-thirty in the morning.

"None of you are stretched out and ready. I have ninety minutes today. We don't have the luxury of using any of that time on something you could do on your own. Take five minutes now."

I watched them. How they chose to warm up told me a great deal about their experience and personalities. The older man started jumping jacks, probably what he had learned at school, which was probably the last time he had done any structured physical activity, apart from the mandatory classes at the academy. Two well-muscled men paired up and stretched each other's hamstrings. A big woman was doing what looked like the kind of thing track athletes do in the last moments before an event. None of them looked very competent.

"Gather round. The first rule of survival is: pay attention. Usually that means paying attention to what's going on around you. Today it means pay attention to me. Very close attention. I won't tell you twice. You can call me Lieutenant." I wasn't, anymore, but I found it got me a faster response time. That and the Red Dogs sweatshirt I was wearing. "This isn't the academy. Today you're here to learn how to protect yourselves, first, and how to restrain a perp without injuring him, second. You can't protect yourself from someone when you don't know where he or she is. If they're in cuffs and on their belly, you're a bit more safe. You," I said to a wiry man with red hair who looked as though he was supple enough to not hurt himself. "Pretend you're trying to pull me off balance and run away."

I held out my right wrist. He reached for it.

If this was real and I knew my attacker intended to hurt me, I would have crippled him without thinking: a kick to the knee, an elbow slammed into his floating ribs. But this was, perhaps, an elderly drunk who didn't deserve to be hurt, so as Red grabbed with his right hand, I turned my wrist, drew it back just enough to pull him off balance, stepped behind him on the diagonal, and whipped his right arm straight and against the joint. He froze in pain and I swept his feet out from under him. He went down on his belly.

"If you keep hold of his arm like this, he won't struggle, because if he does, you can pop it out of its socket as easily as pulling the wing off a turkey. Make sure you keep his palm turned up, like this." I moved it just enough to show them and Red squealed. "As soon as it starts to hurt, slap the mat and your partner will stop." Red slapped the mat. I eased off. "Your grip will be firmer if you keep your thumb on the back of his hand, and your elbows close in to your body." I pulled cuffs out with my left hand and snapped them on. "You should practice with the cuffs until you can do this with either hand. Keep him on his belly while you pat him down, and when you let him up, keep that wristlock on until you can get him in the car." I unlocked the cuffs, tucked them back into my waistband. "Questions?"

"How did you turn your hand over his, right at the beginning?"

So I showed them; in a group, singly and in pairs. Over and over. Some of them were quicker to grasp the concept than the others. Some didn't bother with technique at all. The big woman was relying on her strength to simply overpower her opponent.

"You. Yes, you. Over here." We stood eye to eye. I took her wrist. "Try with me." She tugged. I shifted easily. She tugged harder. "Don't use your muscles. Besides, what if I was a seven-foot biker on PCP?"

"I'd shoot you," she said, looking around, playing for a laugh.

"Guns are vastly overrated," I said mildly. "Go get your weapon and belt." She smiled uneasily, obviously wondering if she'd heard right. "What's your name?"

"Miebach. Linda."

"Miebach, go get your weapon." I let her see I meant it. She practically ran and came back with the heavy belt with gun, cuffs, baton and extra clips. "Put it on."

She buckled on the belt.

Everyone was watching. "The only safe place to be when someone is about to draw a gun is behind them. Everyone stand behind Miebach." They did, looking nervous. "Now, Miebach, draw your weapon. Eject the clip." She tucked the clip into her belt. "I'm glad to see you have the safety on. Now take it off."

"But—"

"Take it off. Reholster the weapon. I want you to draw and try to shoot me."

"I—"

"This is not the police academy. This is what it's like out there. Do it."

So she tried, and I took it away from her and put her down and touched the cold metal ring to her forehead. "Better not move, Miebach. You didn't check to see if the chamber was empty." A bead of sweat trickled into her eye but she didn't dare blink. I don't think anyone in the room breathed except me. I stepped away and worked the chamber. A round shot out and tinkled on the wooden floor.

There was absolute silence. "She could have shot you," someone said in a shocked whisper.

"No. But I could have shot her. Remember that. Never draw your weapon when the perp is within reaching distance. Miebach, put that belt away and collect yourself." I fished out my watch. Twenty minutes to go. "You." One of the muscle guys. "Come here." He stepped up warily. "Miebach seemed to think that her weapon would protect her from anything. Guns can be taken away. Now let's take a look at strength. This man is bigger than me." He was certainly wider. I held out my wrist. "Try manhandle me."

He didn't want to, I could tell, but he tried anyway. I slid my hand over his, sidestepped past him on a diagonal and, going to one knee, brought him down in a back-arching bow over my thigh. He breathed fast and shallowly, toes just touching the floor. "If I sneeze, I break his back. He'd never walk again. If I move him a few inches higher . . ." he gasped, "he'd never feed himself." I rolled him off and looked around the white faces. "There will always be someone bigger than you. Muscle is not the answer. All of you, try it again."

The two most inept rookies had paired up. It usually happened that way. I watched them flailing uselessly at each other and wondered why I bothered doing this.

"Break," I said. "Let's take it one step at a time." I held out my wrist. I gestured for the pale-haired one with the freckles to take it. He looked terrified. "We're going to do this in slow motion, one stage at a time. I won't throw you. I won't hurt you. Reach for me slowly." He grabbed nervously. I just smiled encouragingly and moved my arm as slowly as treacle, twisting up and over his. I stopped just as the tendons began to pull tight in his forearm, before he started to hurt. "See how I'm keeping my elbow tucked into my waist? All the movement is in the lower arm. And the pressure goes on there, on your wrist. Remember, where there's a joint there's a weakness. Again." I showed him twice more. "Now you try it." I reached for his wrist. He jerked in panic. "Slowly for now. Let's try again. That's right . . . no. Let go a second. Have you ever drawn a circle using a pin and a piece of string tied to a pencil? Well, imagine your elbow is the pin at the centre of the circle. Your forearm is the string, and you have a pencil fixed to the tip of your middle finger. Keep the elbow still, tucked in, and draw that circle perpendicular to the floor." I demonstrated. "That's the basic movement. Let's try again."

And on the third try, he got it. He smiled tentatively.

"Good. Very good. Now let's try a bit faster, about a third speed." It was still right. "Half speed." It got a little raggedy as he tensed up. "Remember to keep those shoulders relaxed. A bit faster." He did it as fast as he could and got me in a very respectable arm lock. He grinned like an idiot. "You can let go now."

He did, and swung his forearm in a circle a couple of times, as pleased as if he had discovered a cure for AIDS.

He was wearing a Braves T-shirt. "It's a bit like pitching: get your elbow in the right place and everything else follows. Now show your partner how it works."

I surveyed the room. They all seemed to have the basics, now.

"Okay, people. Now that you understand how it's supposed to work, let me tell you that it often doesn't. When you get someone who is dusted, or a certifiable lunatic, they don't care whether you rip their arm off. They don't feel it. So when you're faced with someone like that, you disable them."

I had their attention.

"Captain Denneny wouldn't approve of what I'm going to say but he's not here. If you're not sure you can handle a suspect, hit them a good one in the stomach. About here." I pointed to my solar plexus. "It won't bruise or swell so you can deny it later if you have to. Use the tip of your baton. If you're too enthusiastic you could damage them. Then you say they fell onto the corner of an open door of your vehicle as you were trying to restrain them."

Red was looking around uneasily. The two muscle guys were impassive. Miebach seemed to be listening to her internal organs.

"If you want to knock someone senseless without leaving a bruise, go for a palm strike to the forehead. Then there's the knee. They can't run after you if they can't use one of their legs. Some places you must never hit: the throat and neck, the eyes, the back of the head, the genitals. If you get hauled up on a case with the perp showing injuries in those areas, you don't have a chance. And remember this." I smiled. "Any perp could be someone important. If you hurt them, their lawyers could take your badge or maybe even put you in jail. And we all know what happens to police officers in jail. Be clear on this point: if they're not crazy or dusted and you hurt them, you're incompetent. All your fellow officers will know that. They won't want to work with you because if you're incompetent you won't be any good in a situation. So don't hurt a perp if you don't have to. And if you have to hurt them, don't hurt them more than necessary. And don't get caught."

I looked at my watch. Seven fifty-five. "Okay, people, that's it. Next time I want you warmed up by the time I arrive."

I sent them on their way. They wouldn't have time to shower before reporting to the squad room for day shift. Too bad.

When they had gone, I took off my shoes, stood in the middle of the floor and closed my eyes. Soft hiss of air-conditioning. Faraway rumble of East Ponce traffic. Slow-turning thump of my heart. I breathed deeply, in and in until my belly swelled with air, out again through my nose, in, out, letting my hands rise a little with each inhalation. Then I stretched up, and up farther, held it, came down, palms to the floor. Held it, held it, and on the outbreath bent my elbows farther.

I moved through my routine automatically, stretching tendons and ligaments and muscles, and after twenty minutes I was as flexible as a whip.

There are only four schools of Shuto Kai karate outside Japan. I had learned it in England, on Tuesday evenings and Sunday mornings in an old community centre whose concrete floors were always still sticky with spilled beer and cigarette ash from the event the night before. I had studied with five men under the instruction of a truck driver with a sturdy Yorkshire accent and a real love of the art. He taught me the way of the empty hand. I would kneel in zazen on that unheated concrete floor in the middle of winter and extend my arms. He would lay a heavy pole across my wrists, and the battle would begin, the battle of breath and pain and will. The first five minutes were easy, the next ten just about bearable, the next thirty a nightmare. Sweat would roll down my neck, and Ian's voice boomed from the walls and rattled the children's drawings pinned there. "Breathe through the pain! Breathe! With me, in and *out*. In and *out*." And my shoulder muscles, which had already taken me through two hundred push-ups and an hour of sparring, burnt dully, then sharply, then with pain bigger than the world. And the only way through it was the breath. In and out. Falter and you are lost.

And after forty or fifty minutes, the endorphins kick in and the childish drawings on the wall assume a crystalline edge, the colours deepen and bloom, and my face relaxes utterly. All there is, is a tide of breath, sweeping up and down the beach of my body, until each cell is as distinct as a grain of mica and I feel washed clean. I sometimes wondered what would happen if I just . . . stayed there; whether the endorphin high would burn itself into my cells permanently and for the rest of my life I would smile gently around the edges, even when I was breaking someone's legs. But then Ian would take the pole away, shout, and we would run around and around the hall. Twenty minutes. Two or three miles, usually. Then we would do a kata.

Katas are choreographed series of fight moves against one or more imaginary opponents. Done well, they are a meditation and a dance. They range from the most simple, railway-straight line moves against only one opponent where you use nothing but punches, to the flying, whirling battle-an-army dance of the Basai Dai. You don't learn the Basai Dai until you get your black belt.

The first few months I studied, the katas were my reward: the fluid dance, the grace, the hot whistling power of punching tight air, of using my whole body. It was only after my blue belt, the second kyu, that I learnt that the real reward of Shuto Kai was understanding my will. I learnt that pain is only pain: a message. You can choose to ignore the message. Your body can do a great deal more than it wants you to know.

And so, although for all practical purposes Shuto Kai is not a particularly good martial art, I still dance its katas.

I did the fourth, which has all those difficult kicks, and the Basai Dai. My breathing was as smooth as cream, my blood oxygenated and rich. I was probably smiling.

I moved on from karate to kung fu, a Wing Chun form, the Siu Nim Tao, or Simple Idea. I was on the second round of pak sao, the slapping hand, when the door opened. Even with my eyes closed I would have known who it was. Her scent was a little more pronounced today, even though her hair was dry. I nodded very briefly but did not stop. Ding jem. Huen sao. She started stretching. Bill jee. Moot sao, the whipping hand. She was wearing black spandex pants and an emerald body sheath. I concentrated on the form.

When I took the last slow breath and released it, she straightened. "First form?"

"Yes."

"Want to chi sao?" It was a challenge.

"Take off your shoes."

"My shoes?"

"I value my feet."

That angered her. It was meant to. Always take the advantage. I extended my right leg, and my right arm, elbow down and in, wrist level with my sternum. She did the same. The backs of our wrists touched. Well-shaped nails, no wedding ring. Her skin was dense and fine-grained, taut over smooth muscle, and her bones slender. She looked the sort of woman who has studied ballet for twelve years. Her eyes were blue, the deep blue of still-wet-from-the-dye denim, with lighter flecks near pupils tight with concentration. Her hair was in a French twist. A French twist for the gym.

Chi sao means sticky hand. The wrists stay touching. All moves are in slow motion. It's a game of chess using balance.

I moved my hand forward, the first inch of what could have become huen sao, the circling hand, but she stepped smoothly to the side and, without even moving her arm, countered. But the counter of course became her own move, which was to keep stepping, trying to lead my arm away from the centre of my body and leave me unbalanced. So far, all beginner's moves. Her baked-biscuit skin slid back and forth over her collarbone. As the pace intensified, I wondered how women got those tans. The colour was delicate, never too heavy, never too light, and they had it in February and November yet they never seemed to use tanning salons. Their eyebrows always arched perfectly and their hair was never out of place.

*Who are you?* Blank concentration for a reply.

She was good: well balanced, smooth, knowledgeable about the connections between feet and belly, wrist and elbow and shoulder. She centred well and breathed unhurriedly.

I wanted information, and stepped back, signalling a pause. "Sern chi sao?"

She merely nodded and extended both arms. Double sticky hands.

We moved faster this time, our legs bent lower, circling around the gym in jong tao, a deadly waltz. A woman's centre of gravity is generally about two inches below her navel, just where the belly rounds. No matter how fast you travel across the floor, that point should move in parallel. I was taller than her but having one's centre of gravity higher is a disadvantage, so I moved in a lower stance. We were both sweating lightly now, and our breath came faster. Her skin felt marvellously alive beneath mine. We moved back and forth, and my belly warmed, and I knew hers warmed, too, as we revolved around the gym and each other, a planet and its satellite turning about the sun.

Time to let her know which was which, to show her I didn't much appreciate having my wallet stolen at the scene of an arson and murder. I moved more strongly, breathed in great long gushes, as though my breath alone would move her aside. Her body sheath was dark under the arms. My belly burned hotter. She began to move just a little out of balance. I made a slow biu tze, the shooting fingers, up towards her eyes, with my left hand, and a going under hand with my right. Being out of balance, even so slightly, meant she had either to let me through or speed up to regain the advantage. To speed up meant it would become almost a sparring session.

She sped up.

Differences in skill become more apparent with speed. I harried her round and round the gym, in no hurry, enjoying testing her. She began to spar in earnest. She snapped a punch at my head, which I palmed away easily enough, then launched into a series of battle punches, hoping to drive me off balance. I centred, then stepped right through her with a double circling hand—and in my head, for a split second, moved over both her wrists and dumped her on the floor—but in actuality let the moment pass.

She felt it, felt the moment when I could have thrust the heat of my belly against hers and taken it all, and now the whole character of our sparring changed. I led, she followed.

It became a dance, teacher and pupil. I would ask, she would answer.

When we came to a halt, wrists still touching, in the centre of that beautiful gym, her face was as smooth as butter. We bowed to each other. I waited.

"Can I buy you coffee?"

The Beat Bean on Monroe is the kind of place I hate: seamless period decor of the fifties, orange chairs and Formica tables, the goateed servers wearing all black. The confectionery she bought for herself looked dry enough to be forty years old, too; the coffee determined and without grace. I like French roast, myself, but there are few places, these days, that serve it.

She chose the mustard vinyl sofa, I took the distorted design nightmare opposite.

"My name is Julia Lyons-Bennet."

I wasn't a bit surprised. "I gather you already know mine."

She flushed, a quick hard colouring that turned her high, golden cheeks the colour of Madeira. "I hope you found your wallet."

"Yes."

"I suppose you're wondering why I'm here."

"You want something."

"I want to know why you were lurking fifty yards from Jim's house, in the rain, after midnight, five minutes before his house exploded." It came out as a challenge. She was breathing hard with some righteous emotion and her flushed cheeks made her look quite, quite determined.

"I was out for a walk."

"That's about as informative as telling me you were breathing!"

"Like saying the cause of death was heart failure," I agreed.

"What?"

"Look, Julia, I was out for a walk. Nothing more. I understand that the deceased was a friend of yours, and you must feel terrible, but I had no more connection to his murder than the fact that I was outside his house when it went up. I'm sure the police have already told you that drugs were found on Mr. Lusk's property, that they believe his death was some kind of message to the drug fraternity in this city."

"Don't tell me you believe that garbage!"

"Not particularly. But I still want to know what you want from me."

"I found out about you. You used to be in the police, but then your father died and left you money. I read your record."

My record. Lists of deaths, the innocent and the guilty, and she had been paddling about in it. I stood.

"Please. I want your help." She pushed her coffee cup to one side and lifted a worn pigskin briefcase onto the table. "Can you just spare ten minutes to listen?"

The briefcase was old, worn and comfortable. It spoke of a real person with a real life, real feelings.

"Please?"

Ten minutes is a very small fraction of one's lifetime. I sat down.

"I run an art acquisitions and security business: buying and selling for corporations, mostly. Sometimes I set up corporate museums; on occasion I advise on the transport and security of travelling exhibitions. Two weeks ago I was approached by a man, a banker. He had a valuable painting, a Friedrich, to ship to France. Discreetly. Normally, of course, I don't do that penny-ante stuff, but he was referred by a very good client of mine—the man to whom I had brokered the Friedrich in the first place. And so, as a gesture of goodwill, I agreed. In fact, I oversaw the packing personally." She reached for her coffee, then changed her mind.

"I'm going to order some mineral water. You?"

"Thank you. Yes."

The water came, we fussed with slices of lemon.

"Now, as you can probably appreciate, I very rarely do this

kind of work myself, but I was in the building when the painting was delivered, so I went to take a look at it before it was recrated. It's a lovely painting, lovely. I watched as my assistants took it out of its old packing case. They barely glanced at the painting, but I did. As I've said, it was a lovely painting. Luminous work. I had brokered it to the client I mentioned, the one who sold it to this banker. I wanted to see it again." In this light her eyes were the rich blue of twelfth century stained glass. "I looked at it, and it made me uneasy. I brokered it two years ago. I know more now than I did then. I looked at this painting and knew it wasn't a Friedrich. What I don't know is if it was the same painting I had sold as a Friedrich two years ago."

"What made you think this one was a forgery?"

"A fake. A forgery is a piece passed off as a previously undiscovered original. I don't know. The brushwork, I think. It . . . well, it's hard to describe, but it didn't have the precision I associate with Friedrich."

"You've seen a lot of his work?"

She looked troubled. "No. More in the last twelve months than ever before, but the German Romantics aren't really my field of expertise. I'm much more familiar with work from the last thirty years. My specialty is investment. For small investments, anything under a million, you get the highest returns for contemporary paintings."

"But you brokered the Friedrich anyway."

"Its provenance was impeccable. The original seller's reputation was unimpeachable. I had absolutely no reason to doubt either."

"But now you do?"

"I don't know what to think. All I know is that I don't think the painting I was supposed to be crating to ship discreetly to France was a Friedrich."

"That's the second time you've described the shipping as discreet."

She looked surprised. "Art is almost always shipped that way to France. The French government enforces rather punitive tax laws that make it desirable for art owners to be somewhat secretive about their acquisitions."

"Ah."

"What do you mean, ah?"

I shrugged. She would not want to hear that she was aiding and abetting what amounted to smuggling, especially from someone who didn't even know the difference between a fake and a forgery.

"Anyway, seeing that painting made me very nervous. So I took it over to a friend, an art historian and appraiser. I thought about calling the original client, but decided not to. After all, I didn't know whether it was a fake or not and, besides, he had sold it for a good profit. It wouldn't hurt him either way. But I had to tell Honeycutt, the banker, that there would be a bit of a delay. Of course he wanted to know why so I told him I had some doubts regarding the painting's provenance. He was concerned, obviously—we are talking about a considerable investment for an individual—so I tried to reassure him. I told him how reliable and discreet my appraiser was; how he was doing all this on a rush basis for me; that I had an appointment at eleven-thirty that evening to get the definitive answer, one way or another."

"An appointment with Jim Lusk."

"Yes. With Jim. I was supposed to be there at eleven-thirty. But some things came up at work. And I know Jim. He's . . . he was . . . a night owl. He wouldn't mind if I was a few minutes late. But I was even later than I thought, so I'd parked and was running to his house when I bumped into you." Her back was pressed flat against the back of her chair, creating an extra two or three inches between us. Probably reliving the look on my face as I had mused on breaking her neck.

I thought about that writhing tiger lily of flame, and the

bright stamen at the centre of that flower; the burning, curling Jim Lusk.

"You walked away, his . . . the house burned, and I saw your wallet. It must have dropped when we collided." I would give her the benefit of the doubt. "So I looked through it. And I went to the police. They more or less laughed at me. 'Aud!' they said. 'Oh, not Aud! She was one of us!' The odd thing was, underneath their bluster, they sounded uncertain, as though they thought you just might have been involved somehow. Then one of the uniformed ones came running to the detective in charge, and he sighed, and he told me he was pretty sure, given the new evidence, that this was a drug killing. I said it wasn't. Jim always found . . . well, let's just say that not only did he not take drugs, he found those who did rather amusing." She shook her head. "I know people say this about their friends and family all the time, but believe me, I knew Jim."

Ah, but we never really know even our best friends. Even the spouse who snores next to us every night. We can never see behind those glistening eyes, never get beneath the skin, venture inside that shining ivory bowl to the dark dreams and slippery lusts that slide through the crocodile brain without regard for civilization or religion or ethics.

"He was murdered for a reason. If there were no drugs, it was something else."

"There were drugs. Several kilos of cocaine."

"Then they were just window dressing," she said impatiently, "a way to twist the truth."

"Very, very expensive window dressing." Which of course played both ways: why hadn't the firebug taken the merchandise?

She shrugged away the importance of several hundred thousand dollars worth of evidence. "Yesterday, Honeycutt's insurance adjuster showed up, which is normal for a claim of this size. Honeycutt had said nothing to her, of course, about the question of provenance. He would have been a fool to. I told her that, yes, everything was fine. That I had merely taken it around to the appraiser's to get a second opinion as a matter of course."

"You lied."

"Yes. And I hate that. I resent it. But I did it because I have to consider my reputation. People trust me. It's my job to be utterly reliable. I can't afford clients thinking: She was the one who muddled up that Friedrich. I just can't."

"Honeycutt won't say anything—after all, he wants his insurance. The previous owner won't say anything because as far as you're aware, he doesn't know anything. The picture can't talk because it's now no more than a few greasy atoms in the stratosphere. So explain to me what your problem might be with this."

"My conscience."

We looked at each other in the artificial fifties gloom. Conscience. Such a high-minded kind of word. In my experience, people used the word "conscience" when what they really meant was, *Oh god I shouldn't have done that it was stupid what if they find out?* "Conscience" sounds better to their internal censors. "Conscience is a matter for a priest."

She gave me an odd look. "You would look good in the old-fashioned clerical garb, the long black coat and dog collar. Those pale, pale eyes, the way you nod intently and sit so still . . ." She laughed then, a brittle vocal shimmer that tried to hide the loss and bewilderment, tried to turn it all into an amusing game. "So here I am, confessing my sins. But what I want isn't forgiveness. Or penance. It's information."

"You know as much about all this as I do. More."

"I want you to help me find out who did this to Jim, and why." Her voice was raw, believable. "You would be paid by my company, Lyon Art. You would be paid well. Not quite as well as your investments, perhaps, but surely it would be better than . . . than grubbing about in the police gym with nervous rookies. Much more exciting."

I wondered what excitement meant to her. A frisson, a brief hormonal thrill to flutter the muscles and pull tendons tight for a moment. Excitement is the product of facing something dangerous. I like excitement from danger that is carefully controlled: the bungee jump, skydiving, free diving off the coast of Belize. Danger of the uncontrolled variety has a nasty tendency to lead to people with guns or knives appearing out of the dark and a split second to live or die. Danger is that place where the space between one breath and another decides your fate, where your life and theirs are like two ice cubes sliding down a hot blade and the fulcrum is speed, where survival means the ability to move from one state to another faster than thought. It means suspending consideration and just being, acting and reacting, moving through a world where everything but you cools and slows down so you can glide between the blows and bullets and take out someone's heart. Danger is desperately seductive.

"No. Thank you. I'm perfectly happy as I am."

She leaned back in her chair, until the top of her head was almost touching the hideous orange shade on the hanging lamp and strange shadows pooled on her face. "If you're so happy, why did you resign from the police? Why do you walk the streets in the middle of the night looking haunted by demons? Why do you hang out with dangerous, filthy people in loud, foul-smelling night clubs where no one would even give you the time of day if they knew who you are, knew that your mother is King Harald's ambassador to the Court of St. James?"

My face is my most useful tool. I made it smile. "Did you practice that?"

Her high cheekbones stood out sharply in the light but the shadow hid her eyes and mouth. "I'm not a trained investigator like you, but Jim was my friend. I'm going to try to find out what happened. I'll do it on my own if I have to—I'm smart and I learn fast—but you could help me, and I'm willing to pay."

I know police work and death, I understand the intricacies of diplomacy and the strange sharp angles where performance art and outlaws, tattoos and high society meet and mingle. I also knew what she didn't: that stalking a professional killer is not a game, not a hobby you can learn at the weekend. Not when the stakes are your life.

The lamp was warming her sleek, French-twisted hair, and through the brown bitter smell of coffee I caught a quick scent of her shampoo, light and sunshiny and sharp, the way cloud-berries on the fjord smell when the sun comes out after a quick summer rain, and I saw her clearly. An innocent who believed herself a cynic, one too innocent even to understand that the timing of that incendiary device had been carefully planned; that she had to have been as much the target as Lusk or the painting. Someone had tried to kill this woman who had read my record and asked for my help, and if she blundered around making noise, they would try again. So I surprised myself, and said yes.

While I read through my transcribed statement, Denneny, immaculate in white linen short sleeves, leaned back in his chair on the other side of the desk and polished his spectacles.

"There is no 'e' in lightning."

He ignored me. The spectacles had left deep indentations on either side of his nose and he had to bring the lenses very close to check for blemishes. His expression was utterly fo-cused, as pure and concentrated as that of a boy studying the dissected body of his first goldfish.

I signed and dated the statement. "You should really pay for better-educated clerks."

He slid the spectacles back on and his face was a man's

again. He picked up the statement, looked at my signature, and put it on the top of a pile on his left.

"Your new rookies were particularly raw this time."

"I hope you didn't hurt anyone," he said, more distracted than concerned.

"You should take a session yourself."

"I've spent too much time lately sitting behind a desk—"

The lack was more in his soul than his body.

"—besides which they wouldn't listen to a captain. They'd say, 'Yessir!' but their eyes would glaze and they wouldn't really hear a word I said." Just as he wasn't hearing a word I said, not really.

I stood. "If any of them don't measure up, I'll let you know."

"Yes." He made an effort. "I appreciate this, Torvingen. The department can't afford to pay warm bodies to spend time in the hospital instead of patrolling the streets."

His rookies had once been more than entries in a ledger, cogs in his cost-effectiveness machine. I tried to remember the last time I had seen him shout or laugh. I failed. Twenty years in the police force had killed everything, bit by bit: his ambition, then his passion, then his wife.

three

I don't like being surprised, especially by my own behaviour, and I had no idea why I had taken Julia Lyons-Bennet's card and agreed to be at her office tomorrow morning at eight-thirty. When a machine acts oddly, it's easy enough to take it apart and look for the fault. If it's a computer, say, which freezes while you're online trying to read e-mail, you just shrug and hit the reset button.

My preferred reset button is adrenalin.

Revolution is not the hippest women's dance club in Atlanta, but it's the biggest, a huge building in Ansley Mall. When I slid the Saab into a parking slot, the place was already filling with the vehicles so loved by Southern dykes with money: apple-green Samurais, blood-red Jettas, peach Cabriolets, dignified gold Camrys, two silver Isuzu Troopers. It was only ten o'clock and the air was still soft and sooty with rush-hour fumes. Dogwood blossoms lay underfoot, and the parking lot smelt of rubber and asphalt and perfume: an exciting, urban scent. I made sure I was wearing my open, friendly face.

On Tuesdays, there is no cover. I slipped in unnoticed and got a Corona from the bar. There were already about two hundred people in the club: half on the dance floor, the rest drinking and talking. Two of the three pool tables were occupied. The third had money lying on the side. I put down my own quarters, looked around a little, and took a pull of my yellow beer. Lovely cold bite.

"Toss for the break," said a clear-skinned, long-haired woman who looked as though she were just off the farm.

I smiled. "Sure."

We exchanged names—she was Cathy—and played the first round amiably. I let her win.

"Another?"

"Why not?" I got another beer, too.

This time I won, and there were more women in the club. It got warmer. I got another beer.

Cathy left and was replaced by Ellie. I didn't much care. I was waiting, enjoying the beer, taking the pulse of the audience because there is always an audience. Of the women at the small tables surrounding the pool area, some were talking, drinking and watching, but some were just drinking and watching.

When Ellie was replaced by Jodie and I realized the club was nearly full, I decided it was time. I smiled at Jodie, tucked my hair behind my ears—to show my jaw and the small muscles in my neck—and opened myself to the audience. As I racked the balls I held the last one in my palm, the way you cradle the weight of a breast when your lover moves over you and your breath is searing in and out, in and out. As I leaned over the cue I let the yellow light hanging low over the table slide over the hollows in my wrist, up the long smooth muscle of my bare arms and lose itself in the dip and shadowed curve of collarbone and breasts. As I drew the cue—the long beautifully polished warm strong cue—back over the sensitive webbing between thumb and index finger, I enjoyed the sensation, and let my face show it, and then I thrust with my hips with my arm with my cue into the ball, through it, and the pretty-coloured triangle exploded into a dozen rolling pieces. I threw back my head and laughed as the balls dropped in the pockets: one, two, three. Around the table with the cue now, picking up the chalk—stroke it rub it over the tip, the rounded, velvet tip, cherish it, make sure that not a millimeter is ignored—laying my left breast plump against the felt and stroking that cue back and forth, back and forth, calculating, measuring, waiting as my breathing quickened and the moment trembled then thrusting again, and round the table and again, and again and again and again until the felt was all green and clean and I straightened, nipples hard against the silk of my waistcoat, and smiled a slow, satiated smile. And then she smiled back at me from a table and stood and stepped forward like a young deer leaving the shelter of the trees.

I ordered us a beer each. She was Mindy, up from Birmingham for two days, interviewing with Coca-Cola for a job in their budgeting department. She was staying in a nice hotel downtown but didn't know anyone and was I here on my own? Oh yes, I said, and touched her lightly on the wrist, and now I had her scent, light and flowery but not innocent, and she brushed against me with her hip, her just-a-bit-old-fashioned-from-Alabama-jean-clad hip, and she lifted her chin a little and blinked and I kissed her.

"Such pale, pale eyes," she said.

And we had another beer and played more pool and drank more beer and danced, and at one o'clock I took her back to the hotel and took off her clothes and, to the sound of a late-breaking thunderstorm, took my time. I kissed her, and stroked the soft planes of flank and thigh, teased with fingertip and breath and gaze, and when she was shuddering like a kite on a long line, when she began to whip and plunge, when she begged me, I turned her and steadied her and let her loose.

It was always the same. They flew and I flew, but to different places.

Later, she stroked my cheek drowsily. "Your eyes are different in this light. No colour at all. Like cement."

The Bedouin definition of day is when the light is strong enough to tell the difference between a black hair and a white hair. There are no colours in the dark.

Eventually she slept. I listened to the rain and contemplated the relaxed face, smooth and fine and very young. No doubt she thought herself worldly, sophisticated, but what would she think if she knew she was sleeping next to a woman who had killed for the first time when she was just eighteen? What did she know of that blank look that always touched their eyes before they spat blood or tried to rattle out one last breath?

I looked at my hands, turned them over in the tarnished shine of streetlights seeping through a crack in the curtains. They were long; strong and competent with nicely shaped nails; hard enough for a palm strike, soft enough to trace gentle arabesques on a taut trembling stomach or along a soft inner thigh. The stains did not show.

I woke up just after dawn, lying on my side, with a greasy headache and a craving for eggs and the bite of grapefruit juice. She scootched up behind me, tucked her belly against my back and ran a hand up my thighs. I stopped thinking about eggs. This time it was simpler, more straightforward, with grins on both sides. Angst was for the dark.

She moved away from me then, and I understood she was done: it was six-thirty, time to resume her job-seeking mask of brisk, detached efficiency. After I showered I was not surprised to find her encased in a business suit and hiding behind impersonal makeup. She didn't have time for breakfast, but I was to feel free to use her room number in the hotel dining room. I thanked her politely, we nodded instead of touching, and I left.

The corridor to the elevators was long. I wondered why Atlanta hotels kept their public spaces so cold.

The Saab still smelled faintly of her perfume and the after-club effluvia of smoke and beer, and I told myself I was a fool. I drove back to Lake Claire very fast, with all the windows open, and found when I returned that the clocks were blinking 88:88—there had been a power hit in the middle of the night. The thunderstorm, no doubt.

I gave the homeless man in front of the Marquis Tower Two a dollar bill that was nearly whipped away in a gust of warm April wind, and went into the lobby which was all black marble and chrome. A very good, hidden sound system played Satie. The piano notes glided around the hard walls and polished floor, warming and humanizing the space, but not enough.

Thirty-four floors up, I headed towards the Lyon Art suite, expecting more sleek surfaces, with perhaps some uncomfortable furniture and elegant but indifferent staff. Instead the door swung open to laughter, bright colours and the earthy, welcoming scent of French roast. The woman who was laughing—comfortably plump, about sixty—turned at my entrance, scooted her chair under the beautiful pine reception desk, and smiled. "Good morning. How can we help you?"

The four or five people in the cubicles to the left were on the phone or tapping away at their keyboards. I smiled back. "Aud Torvingen. I have an appointment to see Julia Lyons-Bennet."

She frowned. "Oh. She said . . . Didn't she call you? I distinctly remember her telling me she was going to call you last night." She swung her chair around again and called to a man who was munching a cinnamon bun by his computer. "Ricky, tell me I'm not losing my mind. Yesterday afternoon, when Julia got that message from InterCom, she said she was going to call Ms. Torvingen?"

"Sure did."

She turned back to face me. "Well, somebody got their wires crossed. Julia's not here. She had to go to Boston yesterday. She said she would call you and let you know last night."

I remembered the storm battering the hotel window.

"I apologize on her behalf. I hope you haven't been too inconvenienced. I know she particularly wanted to talk to you."

Her look of genuine distress made me want to reassure her. "I think I know what happened. She probably left a message but I had a power hit last night. I bet the machine reset itself, and when I got in, there was no blinking light so I thought there was no message. No one's fault."

"I get so tired of the power company, don't you? Every time there's a storm, *phht*, the power goes. Still, at this time of year it's not so bad. But when it goes in August, I just go crazy without my air-conditioning. The heat!"

"I know what you mean. When is she expected back from Boston?"

She looked surprised. "This morning. Didn't I say? No, I don't suppose I did."

"Well, perhaps you could ask her to call me." I reached for one of my not-very-informative cards.

"Oh, heavens, keep that. She's got your number. Besides, there's no need for you to rush off. Her plane lands in"—quick glance at her watch—"less than an hour and I'll page her to make sure she'll come straight here. Do you take sugar? In your coffee," she added kindly.

"No. Thank you."

She started bustling about. "How about cream? Yes? I wish I could get Julia to take some cream. Nothing but skin and bone. I tell her she could do with some padding, no one dates skinny girls, but she just gives me that look." She handed me the coffee, directed a piercing look at my ringless left hand, and nodded to herself. "Dating can be hard for career women."

I thought about Mindy, probably already smiling efficiently at her prospective employer.

She gave me a sly smile. "Well, come along, let's go see if we can find that file she wanted you to see."

I followed her past Ricky, who flashed me a sympathetic look, behind the cubicles and past a large room full of strange crates and bags of foam peanuts, into what I took to be Julia's office. "Here we go." She held out a maroon folder. I hadn't seen where she had taken it from. "Well, don't just stand there like a lamppost. Sit, sit." I allowed myself to be chivvied into a comfortable chair. "You read that and drink your coffee and I'm sure it won't feel like a minute before Julia gets here."

I felt like a seven-year-old being comforted by a friend's mother, but managed to regain my poise enough to smile and say, "I'm afraid I don't know your name."

She gave me a roguish twinkle, said "Mrs. Miclasz, but you should call me Annie," and closed the door behind her.

I sipped the coffee. It was delicious, perfectly prepared, as I imagine anything prepared by Annie Miclasz would be. One of those formidable women who felt they had to hide their efficiency behind a soft, caring front; who hid for so long that the front became real; one of the women who kept the world turning; one of the women it paid to never, ever cross.

The office was large, and obviously made for use rather than show. Two large drafting tables, one with sheets clipped down; a computer; four filing cabinets; three different Rolodexes; rough iron statuary in the corner near a huge picture window; two lush green plants that I couldn't identify; and lamps everywhere, mostly unlit. I had expected art on the walls, but they were covered with graphs and charts. No doubt the view of the city at night would be more than fair compensation.

I opened the folder. Fastened to one side were scrupulous

records of billable hours (I lifted an eyebrow at her rates); phone calls; packing materials; special transport; estimated costs of airport tax; a list of security measures to be engaged to and from Atlanta and Orly—all subcontracted; a muddy Polaroid of a strangely angular picture of what looked like a ship crushed between ice floes, with *Caspar David Friedrich, 39 x 51, oil* pencilled on the bottom. . . .

I mused on the relative value of things. The homeless man outside begging for dimes. Thousands of dollars to ship a single piece of canvas that was not even big enough to shelter a person from the wind and rain.

I looked at the photograph again. The pencilled writing was angular, too; that of a Lyons-Bennet more than a Miclasz, I decided. The items attached to the other side of the folder were more interesting: partly typed, partly handwritten memos detailing phone calls between Lyons-Bennet and the banker, one Michael Honeycutt; between Lyons-Bennet and James D. Lusk, Ph.D., ASA, ISA; between Lyons-Bennet and Paulette Ciccione, who turned out to be the insurance adjuster.

I took notebook and pencil from my jacket pocket and made notes as I read. Phone memo: on April tenth, David Honeycutt asked Lyon Art to ship the Friedrich to Mantes-la-Jolie (a careful annotation in Julia's hand read: *twenty-five miles from Paris*), to provide insurance and security, and to have the painting in France before the end of the month. Receipts indicating that Honeycutt handed the painting over to Lyon Art on the twelfth. I jotted, *Who brought? What transportation? Directly hand to hand?* and went back to the notes.

Perhaps half an hour later the door opened and Annie came in. "I've paged her. She should be here soon." She picked up my empty coffee cup, nodded with approval. "More?"

My forehead felt tight from lack of sleep and too much beer. Not something caffeine could fix. "No, thank you."

Julia's later notes were all handwritten. The prospect of the painting being a fake, of her having made a mistake, had understandably led to a desire for privacy. Handwritten notes were much more secure than any computer hard drive. I was willing to bet, though, that Annie Miclasz already knew everything in this folder.

When I had read everything I went to the window and stared out. Peachtree Street was, architecturally speaking, a virtual John Portman fiefdom. Typical of his New Atlanta, One Peachtree Center rose diagonally across from the window: arrogant, too big, erected without any consideration for neighbours, its open metalwork spire glinting wasteful and golden in the late morning sun. To the left was another of his monstrous towers with its buff-coloured stone and mean, prisonlike windows, linked—by those silly glass sky bridges that Dornan, a friend of mine, refers to as gerbil tubes—to the Mariott Marquis and the Gaslight Tower. People scurried back and forth looking nervous; below, the streets seethed with traffic even though it was not remotely near any kind of rush hour or even lunchtime. I wondered idly what kind of damage a couple of antipersonnel mines would do to those tubes and the street below.

Atlanta was a big city getting bigger every day: three million people living, breathing, working, cutting down trees and spewing out waste. This week there was one less than there had been: Jim Lusk, Ph.D., ASA, ISA. Where did he fit in the story of the fake painting, the very suspicious cocaine, and the banker? The police were no longer looking; they were only too happy to believe the soured drug deal story, but drug dealers would not leave several hundred thousand dollars worth of product lying around for the police to pick up.

Murders are committed for a variety of reasons but, given the supposed worth of the painting, and the cocaine, I would bet on money, power, or a warning—or a combination of all three. The question was, whose money, whose power, and who was being warned, and about what?

Ask any airline attendant and they will tell you that the worst passengers are always from first class: corporate CEOs who defecate on aisle trolleys and wipe themselves down with linen napkins when their third bottle of wine isn't brought fast enough; the seventeen-year-old daughters of Arab sheiks who pinch and slap attendants who can't provide Belgian chocolates. They have money and power and are used to the world conforming to their every whim. Lusk's murder, like every other, came down to the same thing: someone out there believed that the rules everyone else obeyed did not apply to them.

The door opened behind me. Julia. No coat, hair in a French braid so tidy that either the wind had stopped or she had taken the time to replait it after arriving. She was sipping from a large coffee mug: probably already briefed by Mrs. Miclasz.

"I'm so sorry you have had to wait."

I nodded over the file still on the chair. "It's been fruitful."

"I imagine you have questions."

"I do. But let's discuss them over lunch. I didn't have time for breakfast."

"Certainly, but there is one formality we should attend to first. The fee." Here on her own turf she looked different: more whole and competent; denser somehow.

I had no idea what private investigators charged. "One twenty-five an hour, plus expenses, with a three-thousand-dollar advance."

"The advance is fine, but I can't pay more than eighty an hour, and the only expenses I'll allow are travel."

"One hundred, travel and food." I smiled and added, "I'll buy lunch." I didn't need the money but, judging by the rates she charged for her own services, she could afford it.

She gave in gracefully enough and asked Mrs. Miclasz to draw up a contract. It appeared in suspiciously short order. "Do you hire investigators often?" She shrugged, which I interpreted as no. I read it carefully—it seemed straightforward enough—and we both signed. Mrs. Miclasz then cut a cheque, one of those oversized corporate things that I had to fold twice to get in my pocket.

The old Murphy's Restaurant had reminded me of the lower decks of a nineteenth century sailing ship: hot and airless, with cramped alcoves and no headroom. Five years ago, they had moved to specially built quarters just across the street, and Julia and I took a table by one of the many long, open windows where the spring air—softened, now that we were out of the canyon streets of downtown, to a gentle breeze—wafted pink and white dogwood blossom over the flagged floor, and where sunlight made me want to blink and stretch like a cat.

I ordered mixed greens with oregano garlic dressing, followed by lemon chicken and wild rice. "And please bring some bread meanwhile." Julia pondered the menu, her blue eyes the colour of faded ink in the strong sunlight. I sipped idly at my water, felt a sudden flush of desire as a bare-midriffed waitress eased by and reminded me of Mindy's pliant body under my hands.

Never mix business with pleasure. I thought deliberately about the fire, what it would have done to a human being. "Somebody out there killed Lusk for a reason. Do you have any ideas?"

"No. But the whole drug idea is ridiculous."

"Yes."

"You agree?"

"The cocaine was a plant. Did Lusk have any enemies—or any friends, lovers, ex-spouses who might want him dead?"

"No. Or at least not to my knowledge."

"How good a friend was he?"

"Good." A pause. She made a visible effort to let down her barriers. "Getting better. We met ten years ago, at Northwestern. He was one of my teachers. We kept in touch. When I moved to Atlanta six years ago, we had lunch. We had lunch regularly. Sometimes we had supper at his house when he had a rare painting or sculpture for me to look at. It doesn't sound like much, but for him it was. He was a kind, gentle man. Shy. I think it took him all those years to realize I didn't want anything from him except friendship, to share his knowledge and love of art. But he was beginning to unbend. We'd been talking about maybe going to Memphis together this summer to see that Moderns exhibition. He doesn't like to travel, but he was so excited. . . ." She looked fixedly out of the window.

I didn't want her to cry before I'd had something to eat. "Were you romantically involved?"

"No." It came out clipped and glacial. I could imagine the half-formed tears freezing across her cornea.

"What do ISA and ASA stand for?"

"The International Society of Appraisers and the American Society of Appraisers."

"That's how he earned his money?"

"Yes. As I said, he didn't like to travel very much, he hated to fly, so he told me he made his travel rates quite ridiculous, but every now and again there would be a particularly difficult identification problem somewhere like New York or Vancouver and a client would be willing to pay his huge fees plus the expense of travelling by train, first class."

"When you say 'ridiculous,' just how much?"

"I don't know, but probably something like four thousand dollars a day."

A day. "So he wasn't under any financial pressure."

"Not that I know of. But he was a very private person."

I pulled out my notebook, made a note to check out Lusk and to ask a few questions about the recovered cocaine. The salad came. I paid attention to the food for a few minutes, then flipped back a couple of pages for the notes I had made reading Julia's file.

"Tell me about the transfer of the painting from the banker

to your premises. One of your staff picked it up from an address in Marietta—was that Honeycutt's home or an office?"

"His home. He works downtown, at Massut Vere."

"Was the painting received from his hand, or from one of his representatives?"

"Ricky and Maya—that is, Ricard Plessis and Maya Hall—who have both worked for me for a long time, took one of our trucks to Honeycutt's house at ten in the morning and took delivery of the painting from his housekeeper. It was already crated. They gave her a receipt." Fast, clear, detailed: she had obviously been through all this herself before talking to me.

"Did they unwrap it to check what it was before giving the receipt?"

"No."

"Did the fact that it was all crated and covered up not make Ricky or Maya suspicious?"

"No. It's usual to protect such valuable *objets*."

"Yet you uncrated it to check."

"No. That is, yes, I uncrated it, but that's usual, too. If I'm to be held responsible for the safe transportation of a painting, I like to pack it properly from scratch in-house. Owners sometimes have very odd ideas about wrapping pictures. I've heard horror stories of Old Masters wrapped in newspapers and arriving with ghostly copies of the funnies imprinted on a stately old forehead."

"Do you think the clients know you will unpack their careful work?"

She considered that. "I don't know. Those that ask are told we carry our own packing materials to protect the work during the transfer from client to Lyon Art, but not many do ask, so I suppose they assume we'll just crate up around their packing."

"How well was the Friedrich—or the fake Friedrich—packed?"

"Very well. Clean linen wrappings. Properly measured

wooden frame crate with the correct filling. Actually, it came wrapped in the same packing I used when I first brokered it to the original owner, Charlie Sweeting, two years ago."

I made a note to ask for Sweeting's address. "Tell me about the painting."

Apparently Caspar David Friedrich was arguably the most important German Romantic. His technique was impersonal and meticulous. The picture was painted in 1824, insured for three million dollars. "It would probably fetch a little less than that at auction, of course. Two years ago, when I first brokered it to Sweeting, it sold for one and a quarter."

"And you were quite persuaded of its genuineness two years ago?"

"I was." Her pupils were tight and small.

I said easily, "I don't know as much about art as I need to for this, so if I ask questions that seem to question your expertise or, even worse, your integrity, chalk it up to my ignorance, but please answer them. I need the information." She nodded infinitesimally. "What made you so sure, then, that it was genuine, and equally sure now that it was not?"

"There is a certain quality in Friedrich's work, a haunting, prismatic loneliness." She didn't sound the least self-conscious. "It doesn't editorialise. It doesn't try to manipulate the emotions the same way, say, Turner did with his tinted steam."

"Tinted steam?"

"Something that Constable said about Turner. Anyway, when I first saw *Crushed Hope* it seemed to me that this clarity was present. When I saw it again, ten days ago, it was not."

Interesting, the way her speech got more formal as she discussed art. "So, if pushed, would you say you might have been mistaken two years ago, or that there were two different paintings?"

Our entrées arrived then and she used them as an excuse to delay her reply, but after a while, she sighed and said, "I don't know. I *think* they're different paintings, but I don't know how to prove it.''

We ate for a while longer. If it was the fake painting that had gone up in smoke, where was the real one? "When you first brokered the deal to Sweeting, did you check the painting's provenance?''

"I took a look, of course. The then-owner had had possession for more than thirty years, and he showed me the provenance he had been given by the auction house in the sixties.'' I frowned, but before I could say anything, she said, "A provenance from a reputable auction house is a bit like the deed to a house, like a bank note. You just . . . accept it.''

"Do you have a copy of that provenance?''

"Yes.''

"I think we need a division of labour. I'll check on the people, you take the painting.'' She needed to be clear about the provenance; doubt about her own judgement was eating her up. "Find out everything you can. Check back more than a hundred years if you have to. I'll need addresses for Honeycutt and Sweeting. And Julia, when I say division of labour, I mean it. Stay away from Honeycutt and Sweeting. Stick to the painting. Can you do that?''

"Why?''

"Because I'm making it a condition of working with you.'' I took the oversized cheque from my pocket. "If you don't agree, I'll tear this up now and we'll part on friendly terms.''

"But why—''

I held the cheque up. "Yes or no.''

"I don't have much of a choice, do I? Yes, all right. I'll stay away from Honeycutt and Sweeting.''

We talked some more but said nothing useful. I paid. We walked out into the sunshine, stopped by our respective cars. After chi sao, it seemed ridiculous to shake hands.

"I'll call,'' I said.

\*    \*    \*

"Benny? It's Torvingen. Yes, I know it's been a long time but why would I want to spend my days hanging around the evidence locker when I don't have to? Pretty good, pretty good. Listen, Benny, just curious: What can you tell me about the coke that was fished out of that Inman Park burn earlier this week? No, Benny . . . Benny, I don't need to know everything. Just tell me if it was the real thing or dreck cut a hundred times. It was? You're sure? Yeah, me too. How about later this week? There's a new Katherine Bigelow coming out."

Ben Heglund was a movie buff. He would do anything to get a free pass and see a film a week before the general public. He was also five-foot-eight and thin as a rail and could eat more junk food at one sitting than anyone I have ever known.

So the cocaine was pure. Hundreds and hundreds of thousands of dollars worth of it left to be found by the police. Why? It no more fit the drug killing scenario than the murder itself.

Drug killings generally fell into two categories: simple, gang-related turf warfare—who controls what parts of the neighbourhood, who decides on the volume of product; and struggles among the real power brokers which usually led to the spectacular executions of whole families and sometimes even friends and acquaintances, executions gruesome enough to serve as a dire warning to other little fish who were tempted to grow bigger. The burn that killed Lusk, though, had been surgically precise.

Three names: Lusk, Honeycutt, and Sweeting. Lusk was dead and out of the game, and it wasn't to Sweeting that Julia had talked about Lusk and her doubts about the painting's provenance. There was no hurry. Honeycutt would have no reason to think anyone suspected him of anything, and complacent people are rarely dangerous.

I mulled it over. I had spent more time as a member of the Red Dogs, the hit squad of the APD, than I had as a regular detective, but the basics were very simple: gather information, assimilate the evidence, make an arrest—or, in this case, give everything to the police so they could make the arrest. But information was the first step.

Although I had Charlie Sweeting's phone number, I looked him up in the book. He was listed under *Charlie Sweeting,* not C. or *Charles,* and the number matched the one Julia had given me. One face for all comers. I phoned. He agreed, in the kind of Southern accent that seems to embarrass the inhabitants of the New Atlanta, to see me just as soon as I could get there.

He lived ten minutes from me, on Spring Street, where the servants' cottages in the back gardens were bigger than my house. I pulled up before a mansion with a sweeping front lawn that was probably planted sixty years ago, bright with thousands, perhaps tens of thousands, of perfect tulips. They would not last much longer in this heat, no matter how many gardeners he employed. One of them was out there now in threadbare summer chinos, clipping busily.

He stood up as I approached the door and I realized immediately that he was not the gardener. "Miss Torvingen?"

White moustache beautifully trimmed, greyish blue eyes, thin, freckled arms with crepey skin, liver spots showing through the thinning yellow-white hair. Old enough to be stubborn about the ways to address women. "Yes."

He stripped off his work gloves and held out a long, beautifully kept hand that looked absurdly young and able. "How do you do?"

"A little warm." I wasn't, particularly, but I am tall and move too easily, and old-fashioned Southern men never relax around me until they can convince themselves that they are physically superior. It speeds things along a little if I help them out. He led me into the airy entrance hall and then a sunny drawing room. Air-conditioning whispered in the background. He spent some time pulling out the chair, ordering me iced tea from his housekeeper, asking me if the temperature was agreeable.

"Lovely tea," I said when it arrived, and it was: brown and strong as a tennis player's arm, and cool, with just the right touch of lemon.

"Thank you. Bessie's been making it for the family to that same secret recipe for twenty years."

I smiled, and we complacently admired our exchange of information: I had the breeding and manners to not rush, to appreciate his hospitality; he was rich and settled enough to have an old family retainer and to putter about in his own garden if he chose.

"Now then, Miss Torvingen—"

"Aud, please."

"Then you must call me Charlie. Miss Lyons-Bennet tells me there's been some unpleasant business with the painting I sold to Honeycutt. Something about a fire, and now questions about the insurance."

"Yes."

"And you think I can help?"

"I do. I'd be grateful if you could tell me first why you decided to sell."

He looked at the European cut of my clothes. "I don't know how long you've lived in Atlanta, Aud, but it's a thrusting, hot-blooded place. Fortunes to be made, even now." He knew as well as I did that Atlanta fortunes were now made by real estate reptiles with cold eyes and flickering, forked tongues. "I'm a hot-blooded man myself, and that Friedrich was a cold piece of work to wake up to, day after day, every brushstroke just so, making the ice look like a bunch of stacked bricks. I just got tired of the darn thing."

"You didn't start to wonder whether or not it was authentic?"

His face stilled for a moment, then stretched in a grin that was wide enough to draw what was left of his widow's peak an inch closer to his eyebrows. "So that's what this is about! No wonder Julia was so goddamned coy on the phone. Looks like I got rid of it in the nick of time. They think my Friedrich's a fake?"

"Actually, it depends on who you mean by 'they.'"

"Oh, let's quit fencing, shall we?" He was full of good humour now: he hadn't been skunked in any deal. He was still a top dog. "So what you want to know is: was I a dupe, or was I trying to dupe someone else?"

"That's about the size of it."

"All I can tell you is that I bought a painting from Julia Lyons-Bennet in good faith, and sold that exact same painting in just as good faith three months ago. I believed—still do, as a matter of fact—that it was genuine. No one but a poker-faced German with a high pucker factor could have painted such a humourless thing. No, no," he said genially, "the only thing I can't tell you is why I bought it in the first place."

I switched direction. "How did you come to offer the painting to Honeycutt?"

"*He* made an offer to *me*."

"How did that come about?"

"We were at one of those damn charity dinners, for the zoo, I think, or maybe it was the symphony. Anyhow, he was asking about reputable dealers in the city. I told him about Julia—how she got me a good price on the Friedrich even though I now hated the damn thing. Then a few months later we bumped into each other in Turner's box at a Braves game." He was much too well bred to wait to see if I had picked up on the fact that he had been Ted Turner's guest, but I obliged him with raised eyebrows anyway. "He'd remembered our conversation. We talked some more about other things, investments and so on. It's always good to know another banker, so I invited him to the party I give every year to pay off all my social obligations—kills about a hundred birds with one stone. Anyhow, he accepted. During that party—and I remember particularly because we were just about to start serving the food, and goose goes cold so fast—he asked to see the painting. It used to hang in the upstairs dressing room, so I told him to take a look but not to be too long if he wanted any of the bird. When he came down, he said he'd like to buy it. I told him he could have it and welcome if he paid what I paid for it two years ago, plus ten percent—art goes up all the time, you know, even stiff Germanic mistakes like that—plus any expenses. And that was pretty much that."

"When was your party?"

"January nineteenth."

"And the Braves game?"

"That would have been September or thereabouts."

"Tell me what you think of Honeycutt."

His eyes gleamed with amusement. "He speaks well and knows the right people but I wouldn't put my money in his bank, and I sure as hell wouldn't trust him to be able to shoot his own dog if he had to."

I considered for a moment. Good old Charlie Sweeting liked me, probably thought I was a smart, sweet thing. "I'd like to ask you a favour."

"Fire away."

"I'd like to meet Mr. Honeycutt, but I don't want him to know why I want to meet him. It's all very delicate, with Ms. Lyons-Bennet's reputation involved and so on. Perhaps you could think of a way?"

"Well, now, I might just at that. Give me a day to chew on it."

I gave him my card and left him feeling quite pleased with himself.

When I built the deck and the master suite, I turned one of the original two bedrooms into my work space. It is a big, square room, with a heart-of-pine floor, large windows and a skylight. Up against the two white walls farthest from the door are my benches and vises, the mitre, jig, and radial arm saws, the sanders, well machined, efficient and reasonably new. I use them when needed and forget about them when not. The wall on the right as I enter the room is where I keep my hand tools, some of which I have had since I was a teenager. I found my brad-awl, for example, in a junk shop in a small Yorkshire town; it was probably made in the 1920s; its smooth wooden handle nests perfectly in my palm. I have several planes, different sizes and types. Their handles are painted sober, strong colours—navy blue, hunter green, chocolate—their blades all gleam that particular oily grey of quality steel. The chisels, with their matching pale oak handles, are a complete set that belonged to one of my mother's uncles. I know the foibles of every single tool, how each shapes the wood to which I set it.

Wood is an endlessly adaptive material. You can plane, chisel, saw, carve, sand, and bend it, and when the pieces are the shape you want you can use dovetail joints, tenpenny nails, pegs or glue; you can use lamination or inlay or marquetry; and then you can beautify it with French polish or plain linseed oil or subtle stains. And when you go to dinner at a friend's house, the candlelight will pick out the contours of grain and line, and when you take your seat you will be reminded that what you are sitting on grew from the dirt, stretched towards the sun, weathered rain and wind, and sheltered animals; it was not extruded by faceless machines lined on a cold cement floor and fed from metal vats. Wood reminds us where we come from.

When I want to use my long muscles, feel arms and legs flex and bend, the sweat run down my neck and get in my eyes, I build something big. Framing in the master suite extension had taken me two weeks, the deck another six days. But after talking to Sweeting, I wanted something more exacting than energetic, something to free my mind.

I had been working for the last two weeks on a chair of English pine. My hand plane slid down the wood, *zzst zzst*, and buttery shavings curled to the floor. *Zzst zzst*. English pine is darker than its acid-yellow American cousin, so rich it makes you want to reach out and put it in your mouth. The grain is finer, denser, a little less spongy, such a joy to plane that when I first started working it I often took off more than I needed in the sheer pleasure of watching the blade slide through it. *Zzst zzst.* The shavings piled up. Sunlight, shivered and greened by the foliage outside the window, warmed the heaps, filling the room with the simple, uncomplicated scent of fresh-cut pine. *Zzst zzst.* I could feel my face relaxing, the muscles around my ribs letting go.

The phone rang. I listened with only half an ear as the answering machine stopped clunking and the caller started to talk. Helen and Mick, telling me about the performance artist and body sculptor who would be at the King Plow Arts Center on Thursday night, and asking if I wanted to go with them. I hadn't seen Helen and Mick for two or three weeks. I might enjoy it.

Ten minutes later, the phone rang again. "Ms. Torvingen, this is Philippe Cordova. Our client is arriving in two days and I would like to go over some of her intended activities with you before then. At your convenience."

Less than fifteen seconds. Very European: no hello-how-are-you, no extraneous information, blessedly uncluttered.

I put down the plane, twirled the brass handle of the vise, lifted the thick oblong of wood. Coming along nicely. I resecured it. Set the plane to the wood, stopped when I realized this side needed slightly less pressure, then began again until I was back in the unhurried, endless rhythm. *Zzst zzst.* This was the kind of work I understood. I knew where the wood came from, that for every tree cut down, another was planted, that I could make a chair both functional and beautiful. I was adding to the world, not taking.

Did Julia ever feel this kind of inner satisfaction? I had only ever seen her look tense or worried or irritated. I could not imagine that face in contented repose, or that the fierce competitiveness of collecting might induce such a frame of mind. But everyone has a private and joyful hobby, even if it's just bobbing about in the bath playing with yellow rubber ducks. I smiled at the thought of Julia talking to her ducks, hair pulled up in a topknot, soap bubbles clinging to the damp skin just below her bare collarbone. . . .

*Zzst zzst.*

Little Five Points is Atlanta's East Village, the hipcoolfunky heart of the city where the two most recent commercial buildings are a tattoo parlour and a leather and fetish rummage store called The Junkman's Daughter. I don't know if there's a special tenants' committee, but the uncool are not allowed. Even the pharmacy is run by a man called Ira who knows everything about everybody and flips pills and salves and prescription printouts with the pizzazz of a cocktail waiter. Here is where you'll find Charis, the city's only feminist bookshop, and Sevenandah, the whole-food cooperative. Here is where Atlanta's musicians and poets and artists hang out to reassure themselves that, yes, they really are right to starve for their art.

The two triangular patches of grass at the nexus of the five converging roads were as usual full of long-haired men and short-haired women trying to look drawn and anguished and tragic and succeeding only in looking a little muddled, rather young and tolerably well fed. Dornan calls them the Oh-I'm-so-depressed-I'll-paint-my-room-black-and-purple crowd. He takes their money with great delight.

Dornan owns the Borealis Café chain. There are seven stores in Atlanta and its suburbs but the L5P store was the first, and Dornan spends most of his time there. Today, it smelled of dark, bitter coffee, frothed milk, red wine and, very faintly, pot—as always.

"Torvingen! Luck smiles on you as usual. A second or two later and I'd be away to Marietta to pay a little visit to the newest addition to our café family. But now that you're here, perhaps I'll stay a minute or two."

He was always just about to leave, always about to pick up the phone, and he always persuaded himself to sit for a minute or two that stretched into thirty, into two hours, all night. We go back a long way.

"And what's new in your life?" he asked as we took our usual table in the corner where he could lean over and beckon a server, watch the other tables, and look through the window all at the same time.

"This and that."

"Ah, now, don't be coy. You're wearing your hunting face. Two lattés, tall, and biscotti, Jonie, if you please." The long-suffering barista was already lifting cups and spoons onto a tray. "Thank you, my dear." As always, he looked delighted, but I knew if she had not known what to prepare, those merry blue Irish eyes would have glinted cold as Galway Bay in February. He sipped, sighed with pleasure as though it were his first coffee of the day, and leaned over the table. "So tell me about your hunt."

I told him about bumping into Julia, the fire, Denneny poking his nose in, and Julia's offer. "So unless it's all one big coincidence, I'm looking for someone who can find a professional torch at six hours' notice, who thinks nothing of leaving several keys of pure cocaine behind as false evidence, and who is somehow tied in with a valuable piece of art."

"Is that all," he said comfortably.

"And she doesn't even realize that the burn was as much directed at her as Lusk, or the painting."

"You haven't told her?"

"No. She doesn't need to know. The painting was burnt, the art historian is dead, and she told the insurance adjuster she had no doubts about the painting's genuineness. She has no evidence and has already undermined her own credibility by lying to the insurance company. She's not in danger."

"So what is it that's making you think you want to be a detective again instead of a nice, boring personal security consultant?"

I ignored him but, as usual, that made no difference.

"Well, maybe it is the boredom. Ah, but then why don't you just go risk your life rock climbing or skydiving or hang gliding, in your usual way?"

He didn't really expect an answer, which was good because I couldn't give him one.

I wore a light linen suit. It was going to be a hot one today: only ten-thirty and already in the high eighties. I opened all the Saab's doors and windows and waited while the oven heat gushed out. A small redheaded woodpecker, a male with black body and white stripe across its back and wings, was thwacking its beak industriously against the siding under the eaves. No doubt the resonant drumming would sound impressive to the brown females in the area and they could take turns feeding him when he was too addled to catch beetles.

I left the air-conditioning off, the windows down, and enjoyed the fat heat that snaked through the car as I drove.

What kind of car did Michael Honeycutt, banker, drive? What did he look like, how did he sound? I wanted to see him, to weigh the fabric of his suit, smell his cologne, judge his haircut, watch his body language, listen to the way he shaped his vowels.

One of the first times I had been called on the carpet as a police officer had been back when Denneny was still a lieutenant, back in the days when he could still tremble with fury, or laughter, or worry for one of his people. I couldn't even remember the details of the incident; all I remember was him pacing up and down his office, shouting at me: "You can't just break in and start banging heads, Torvingen! Knowing isn't good enough. You need proof, because our justice is legal justice, not street justice." So I would need to assemble my proof, I would need to bide my time. Besides, while personal indicators would tell me things that no dossier could, they would also give me nothing like the whole story.

People are twisty animals. I have met unpleasant men and women whom I do not like because I suspect they are at heart cruel, or take absolutely no joy from life, or believe some sections of society are little better than vermin and should be exposed at birth; but I have trusted some of these same women and men with my life because they have learnt to bind their natural inclinations with cages of rules and ethical behaviour that I know will hold and guide them under almost any circumstance. Equally, I have met people whom I have liked instinctively, on sight, but would not trust because they have never been tested, not even by themselves, and have never had to formulate rules to get by. Think about two young adults who go to college. One is brilliant, a genius who floats above her colleagues like a cirrus cloud, the other is merely a plodder: dogged, determined, competent. Throughout their education, the genius has always been able to leap obstacles as though they're not there while the plodder has, through necessity, learned patiently to climb walls. One day, say in the second year of their Ph.D. programme, that genius will come across a wall so high even she can't jump it. But she doesn't know how to climb. The plodder, on the other hand, rubs his hands, checks his equipment, and starts hammering in the first piton. Who do you think will reach the top first?

So although there were certain things I could only learn about Michael Honeycutt by meeting him face-to-face, there was a great deal I could find out by looking at his track record, his habits, and his job.

At the Ponce de Leon branch of the Fulton County Library I parked carefully under the pathetic sapling in the middle of the lot. Better than nothing. There was a minivan four spaces down. The sliding door was open. A man was lying back in the driver's seat, eyes closed, keys dangling from the steering column. Probably waiting for his wife. It would be so easy to slip into the passenger seat, break his neck with one twist, bundle him into the back and drive away. Less than forty seconds. No witnesses. People are so stupid.

"Anthony," I said to the plump, balding man blinking in the sunshine leaking through the enormous skylight over the reference desk, "I need some information on Massut Vere, investment bankers."

He sighed—he always sighed and acted like a fifty-year-old who had been forced to get out of his cosy fireside armchair and shuffle off in his slippers on some unpleasant errand, even though I doubted he was a day over thirty—and repeated, "Massut Vere."

"Corporate structure, personnel, specialist interest, political flavour, anything that would give me a feeling for what kind of institution they are. Pay particular attention to any mention of a man called Michael Honeycutt."

"When do you need it by? Yesterday, I suppose."

I didn't smile; Anthony thought smiles frivolous and out of place in a library. "I'll be here for forty minutes or so." He would have a first cut for me in less than half an hour. The more he looked forward to a task, the more he grumbled.

At the New Fiction section I skimmed the rows of E. Annie Proulx, Anne Rice and Robert James Waller and moved on in disgust to Non-Fiction. There was a new biography of Albert Murray that looked interesting. Farther down was something called *Gender Critique in Body Modification*. Helen had said something about that performance artist being into "gendered body art," so I picked it up. I took those and a text on cults to a carrel and started flipping through. An index can tell you a book's parameters. Everything I looked up in the Murray was there: Romare Beardon, Malcolm X, Count Basie, Ralph Ellison, The Omni-Americans, Wynton Marsalis, geopolitics. The cult book, on the other hand, was less promising: Cohesiveness, Conditioning, Controlled Drinking, Conformity. . . . The body modification volume had something it called a hyperindex, no doubt put together by someone who thought they were designing a web page. I flipped through charmingly obtuse text and stomach-churning graphics.

After half an hour I took the Murray and bod-mod books to the reference desk. Anthony was presiding over a pile of books, catalogues and printouts looking sour: his version of smug complacency. "These you can check out"—he pointed to the books—"these you can keep"—a handful of still-warm photocopies—"and this is a list of files, some of them more general than I would like, that I've pulled from a quick electronic search. Just two references to Honeycutt."

I didn't thank him—he would start to stutter—but I would as usual send a cheque for the library's Children's Books fund that was Anthony's particular passion. Maybe I'd put that one on expenses.

I stared past my monitor and into the back garden. A chipmunk picked up an old, old pecan, threw it down in disgust. Two cardinals trilled liquidly at each other, bright red against the emerald green. One of the neighbour's cats slunk belly down through the grass towards them. Snakes in fur coats, Dorothy Parker had called cats. Sometimes I could see why.

Anthony's references had not been much help. I had tedious details about Massut Vere, who, despite the unlikely name, were one of the oldest and richest merchant bankers in the South, with interests in everything from tobacco, cotton and railroads to bioengineering, cable television and pizzas.

Michael Honeycutt had been with them for just under two years, coming to the company from a bank in California. There was a small black and white photograph that could have been anybody.

The cat stopped, twitched its hindquarters to and fro, and pounced; not at the birds, but something hidden in the grass. Probably a shrew. The garden teemed with them. They dug burrows all over the lawn and if you crouched motionless on the grass, sooner or later you would hear them rooting about under what was left of last year's leaves. They were always there, even in the rain. Shrews can't store or metabolize fat. If humans ate proportionally as much as a shrew, we would have to consume the equivalent of two pigs, thirty chickens, two hundred pears, three pineapples, and twenty bars of chocolate every day. Busy life.

I turned off the computer. Time to go to the second leg of my plan.

I called Eddie, the special assistant and researcher to Elaine Merx, a popular columnist at the *Atlanta Journal and Constitution.*

"Hello, Eddie."

"Aud. Good to hear from you. And how are you?"

"Good."

"Let me guess, you want some help on something."

"Of course."

"There's a new restaurant I've discovered. The Horserad-ish Grill. . . ."

"Anytime after next week." It would be expensive—it was always expensive when he picked—but the food would be wonderful, the service even better, and we would both enjoy ourselves immensely. I have known Eddie for a long time. "I want to know everything about two different people. Charlie Sweeting, who lives—"

"In his seventies? Lives off Ponce? I know Charming Charlie. And the other one?"

"A banker with Massut Vere, Michael Honeycutt."

"Hmmn." A long drawn-out contemplation as he tick-ticked at his keyboard. "Ah. Hmmn. There's a fair amount here. And some of the information on Charming Charlie isn't in the electronic archive, so perhaps you should come down and take a look. I'll be here until seven tonight."

"I'd like to come now if it's convenient."

"Of course."

I found my way around the big *AJC* building on Marietta Street and to Eddie's cubbyhole with the ease of long practice.

"Aud, lovely to see you!" There was no way to describe Eddie's voice except to call it lugubrious. He was almost six feet tall, built like a dancer, with tight nappy hair and mournful brown eyes that could light up with bright, clean joy at the slightest provocation. We hugged. "You look . . ." he tilted his head to one side, "engaged."

I lifted my eyebrows.

"As in engaged with life, rather than engaged to be married."

"I'm trying to find out who burned someone to a crisp in Inman Park last week."

"A crusader at last."

"At last?"

"Don't tell me it's for the money, or for the thrills and spills that you're taking on a drug case."

"It's not a drug case."

"The police found cocaine."

"Yes."

"But it was a white boy art historian who died and not some crack dealer."

"Eddie . . ."

"Sorry. It's a habit I get into around here, pointing out the obvious. So, you think Charming Charlie, and Honeycutt, patron of all the most boring Big Culture groups in the city and darling of the downtown gallery owners, are involved in this nondrug drug murder?"

"Darling of downtown galleries?"

"Oh, indubitably. Take a seat." Click. "Top bidder for this jade piece in November." Click. "Purchaser for an undisclosed price of not one but two Fabergé eggs." Click. "This rather indifferent sculpture by a local artist." Click. "Owner of these recently discovered Roman coins. Hmmn."

"What?"

"Remarkably catholic, don't you think?"

"Explain."

"Most collectors have a specialty, a burning passion: silver snuffboxes of the seventeenth century, British Commonwealth stamps pre-World War II, that kind of thing. These items don't seem to have anything in common."

"Are there more?"

"Many." He clicked through the rest: a ten-inch jewel-encrusted icon; a rare stamp; a pair of Judy Garland's ruby slippers from *The Wizard of Oz* ("There are at least six pairs of those floating around that I know of," Eddie said); a messy explosion of an oil painting by someone I'd never heard of. . . . "He has bought these over a period of just two years."

"How much has he spent?"

"Some of the prices were not officially disclosed, but at a conservative guess I'd say somewhere between twelve and fifteen million. That's all of them. You want to see them again?"

I nodded. Fifteen million. Fifteen million on such a wild collection that was part odd, like the painting and sculpture, but mostly precious. "What else?"

"He goes to dozens of fund-raising balls, dinners and speeches. He is a member of the Chamber of Commerce and two or three other professional organizations. Gives parties. He's not married but often photographed in the presence of beautiful young women from Atlanta and from out of town."

"Gay?"

"Don't think so. There was a rumour last year that some old girlfriend was threatening to sue him for battery and emotional abuse but that the case was settled before it got to court. He's forty-two—"

His photographs showed a lean, tanned, smiling man with short dark hair and wire-framed glasses. "Older than he looks."

"Indeed. Previously employed by California Mutual Holdings and, before that, Bay Banking. No arrests here or in California. Not even a parking ticket. House in Marietta, one on Lake Lanier."

"Tell me about his job."

"Vice president, but I don't know what of. Several articles mention meetings with foreign business managers, and I think he was involved in helping North Carolina get that BMW plant. Travels to various offshore tax havens such as the Bahamas, Bermuda, and—three times last year—the Seychelles. Also flies to Mexico and Los Angeles fairly regularly."

"Give me the names of the galleries he patronizes most."

"Easy. Cess Silverman at Hye Galleries."

I frowned. Cess Silverman. "Isn't she one of Georgia's Democratic Party movers and shakers?"

"The same."

I thought for a while but could not make any of it hang together. "How about Sweeting?"

"Ah," he said with approval, "at least he knows how to collect." He handed me a one-page printout.

"This is his obituary."

"Yes. As a précis of his life so far, it's hard to beat. We have them on file for all prominent Georgia citizens, updated every four months." I wondered if they had one on me.

I ran through it quickly. S. Charles Sweeting III. Born in Covington, Georgia, in 1922. Son of congressional representative S. Charles Sweeting, Jr. Purple Heart in World War II. Married Jonetta Marie Sturton in 1947. Three children. . . .

Worked in radio. Inherited. Bought radio station. Bought second. Bought TV station. Divorced. Remarried. Patron of High Museum of Art, Atlanta Ballet, the zoo . . . "It all looks very straightforward. What's not on here that I should know about?"

"He's said to have been a real son-of-a-bitch to his first wife. None of his children can bear to live in the same state as him. The closest is in Virginia, I think. He's on the board of the TV station still, but can't influence programming."

"Reputation?"

"Straight shooter: worked hard for what he's got, doesn't take shit from anybody, gets what he wants when he wants it, no matter who he has to run down. And he's run down quite a few. Earns a lot, gives a lot. What's not on there are contributions, the very hefty contributions I'm pretty sure he makes anonymously to the Atlanta Society for the Deaf."

"If they're anonymous, what makes you think he gives?"

"One of his mistresses gave birth to a son after she caught measles while pregnant. The son was deaf; retarded, too, as I recall. I talked to one of the ASD's finance assistants last year—you remember that piece the paper did on Southern noblesse oblige?—and he told me that every July for the last seventeen years they get a cheque for one hundred and fifty thousand dollars. They've come to rely on that money, but because they don't know who gives it, they worry about the golden goose just . . . flying away one day. So they did some research on past beneficiaries of their services, looking for rich relatives, and my friend discovered that Sweeting's son was born in July seventeen years ago. A big coincidence, wouldn't you say?"

I nodded. "You said he was a real collector?"

"He buys publicly and in a big way, always makes sure everyone knows what he paid. Representational art: landscapes and portraits. Nothing more modern than the 1920s. He displays the art on his own walls—no bank vaults for Charlie

Sweeting. He takes the same kind of pride in owning beautiful things as being a man of his word."

"Have you met him?"

"Once. Briefly."

"Would you trust him?"

He thought about that. "Sixty years ago he and his buddies would probably have spent their summers setting their hunting dogs on folks like me, but, yes, I'd trust him to do what he said he would do. Or to not do what he said he would not. His honour is who he is."

I sat on the deck sipping a Corona, watching the last bloody footprint of the sun fading from the sky, listening to the tree frogs and crickets, thinking idly that I really should cut some flower borders at the back one of these days.

A murder, some cocaine, a fake painting. Sweeting and Honeycutt.

Sweeting was ruthless, no doubt about it, but I agreed with Eddie: faking a painting did not fit his profile, nor did an anonymous murder. Which left Michael Honeycutt, as I'd known it would.

Roman coins. Unmarried. Jade carvings. No parking tickets. Fabergé eggs. The Seychelles. Democratic Party. Cocaine. I could not see a connection.

A huge barred owl ghosted silently across the garden to land in the pecan tree overlooking the deck. It turned its head this way and that, intent. Somewhere on the lawn a shrew crept through the grass in a desperate search for juicy insects to stoke its ever-needy metabolism. The owl focused for an instant, dropped into a shallow glide. It dipped once and I heard the tiniest squeak, then the soft wingspan and full talons were lifting over the hedge, blending with the darkness to the east.

That night I dreamt of a man in a bathtub. He looked dead but he wasn't, he kept sitting up. Every time he sat up, I hit him: palm strike to the nose, thud and splinter of bone slamming into his already dead brain; knife hand to the larynx, crushing it like cardboard; double fist to the temple, fingers sinking in to the second knuckle. But he kept sitting up. And then he smiled and opened his mouth, and out flew an owl, clutching a small jade statue in its taloned fist.

I woke at six with my muscles pulled tight as guy ropes and my mind flapping like a split sail in a high wind. My hands kept flexing of their own accord, remembering hitting his face. I pulled on shorts, boots and muscle-tee, took a bottle of water from the fridge, and went out into the back. The air was still and quiet, heavy with morning damp and the scent of jasmine. The shed I had built under the deck was dark. The spade hung from the opposite wall. I took it down and unwrapped it. It took a while to locate the tarpaulins.

Cutting flower borders through healthy sod is hard work but my body needed to sweat for a while, and I have never understood the wasteful American pastime of running. Why not direct your muscles towards something useful? After I had laid out four overlapping tarps, I set the gleaming edge of the spade against the damp turf, put my boot on the rim and pumped, taking great satisfaction from the slide and grit of steel through dirt. I turned the sod onto the tarp. Set and pumped and turned, set and pumped and turned. After half an hour, I switched feet.

An hour later the muscles of thigh, calf and lower back were warm and supple and the tarps full. I switched to the fork, bending my knees, letting my triceps and shoulders power the tines through the topsoil. Birds were singing now, and in the distance I heard the chunk of a car door and an engine turning over. At some point the background had filled with the hum of traffic streaming down McLendon three blocks away. I worked on.

By the time I had all the borders cut and the dirt turned, had cleaned and oiled the garden tools and put everything away, it was nine-thirty, and though my skin was slick with sweat and muscles burning, I felt calm and refreshed. I had a leisurely shower, an enjoyable breakfast of cold rice and smoked fish with hot, fragrant tea, then called my banker.

"Laurence, it's Aud Torvingen. Very well, thank you. And you? Catherine and the children? Good. Laurence, I wonder if I might impose upon your goodwill for a few minutes this afternoon. I find myself floundering for information on a subject far outside my area of expertise. I hoped I could persuade you to share some of your experience on these matters."

It was a very small branch, and my deposits were substantial. He said yes, of course, and how did one o'clock suit?

From the Spanish consulate downtown, the drive to my Decatur bank along Piedmont and then North Avenue is about twenty minutes if you ignore the speed limit. I whipped along, letting the slipstream take care of the pollen on the Saab's paintwork, enjoying the power under my hands, the smooth glide of the stick as I shifted into fourth. Traffic was surprisingly light and I cut through it like an otter knifing playfully through the water. I opened the windows. Nina Simone sang "Feeling Good" in her chocolate and cream voice. A wonderful morning to be alive.

I had Beatriz del Gato's proposed itinerary weighted open on the seat next to me. She wanted to visit a Spanish-speaking school in Duluth then go on to a community centre in Buford. Just as Philippe said: boring. Other places on her list—apart from the half dozen ad agencies downtown—included Underground Atlanta and a Catholic church. She was twenty-three, reasonably good looking if the photo was anything to go by, well educated, and all she wanted to do in the historic South was visit a mediocre mall, go to Mass, and try to get a job.

I made it to the bank in fifteen minutes.

Laurence is about fifty, one of those African-Americans from the North who heard that Atlanta, the City Too Busy to

Hate, was a paradise of opportunity. He applied for a corporate transfer and moved his whole family, hoping for big things. He had been here nine years now, long enough to realize that the good old boy network was even stronger here than in Pittsburgh. He had managed this bank for all of those nine years. He no longer expected to be promoted out of there. Once a year I met his wife and children at the stiff Christmas function the bank held for its more important customers. We treated each other with unfailing politeness.

Today he looked a little more formal than usual as he ushered me into his office. We sat in two comfortable easy chairs near the silk rubber plant whose leaves shivered in the hissing air-conditioning. "Perhaps you would like to tell us how we can help you."

He almost always said *we*. I don't think I had ever heard him say anything personal, ever use *I*. "The matter I wish to discuss is rather confidential." He simply nodded. "I need to know what kind of responsibilities and authority would be expected of and given to a particular banking position. The position I am talking about is as a vice president with a very well established investment bank in this city."

"Do you have any additional information? It could . . ." He pushed his glasses up. "Well, it's a little like you being asked by someone: What does a police lieutenant do?"

"I take your point." A lieutenant could be on a SWAT team, could be a PR person, in Internal Affairs, homicide. . . . "The banker in question may or may not have been involved in the effort to persuade a foreign automaker to build a plant in North Carolina; he flies to the Bahamas, Bermuda and the Seychelles. I could tell you what sort of authority and accountability a lieutenant in the APD would have, but I have no idea about bank VPs."

"Given that he is a vice president, he is to some extent legally responsible for the affairs of that company and can be held liable. To the same extent, he—depending on the decision-making policy of the company—would be able to commit the company to a certain amount on his own recognizance."

He wasn't giving me anything I didn't already know. I wondered what he would do if I leaned forward and said: *Larry, I don't belong here, either. It's a beautiful day outside. Let's go get a six-pack and watch the ducks on the pond.* It would never happen. He had so many defenses because he needed them. No doubt he saw armour glinting around me that I was not even aware of. He probably hated being called Larry. "So he wouldn't necessarily be checked up on a great deal?"

"It would depend on the size of the bank. If he's a VP of a large national organization, then it's probable he would have considerable personal authority. The fact that he travels frequently to the Bahamas and Bermuda is interesting." He paused. "That he travels to the Seychelles even more so."

"How so?"

"The Bahamas and Bermuda are tax havens, as you probably know."

"Aren't the Seychelles?"

"Oh, yes. But they're also eight thousand miles away. He wasn't just taking a vacation?"

"Not three times in one year."

Again, he paused, and I knew that he wanted something from me, a sign, an indication that if he offered me something he wouldn't be rebuffed for stepping beyond the bounds of manager and client.

"It might help if I told you something of the context for all this. You know I am no longer with the Atlanta Police Department, of course, but I have just undertaken to investigate a murder on a private basis for a third party because the police think it's a drug case, and the third party and I don't. It . . . I saw the victim's house burn, Laurence, I felt the heat on my face, and whoever did it is going to get away with it unless I can find him. I don't even know if this banker has anything to do with it, but he might, and I have to run every possibility, no matter how wild, to ground. So if you have any ideas, please help me."

"What's the bank we're talking about?"

"Massut Vere."

He took his glasses off, leaned back in his chair, polished them awhile. There was the faint shininess of burn scar tissue at his right temple that I'd never noticed before. He stared into the middle distance. "Apart from the fact that the Seychelles are eight thousand miles away, they aren't generally used as a haven by what I'd call respectable banks." . . . *what* I'd *call respectable banks* . . .

"Why's that?" I asked obligingly.

He put his glasses back on and this time when he looked at me I think he really saw me. "What do you know about international banking?"

"Probably about as much as you do about tactical hostage rescue."

"It's amazing what you can learn from watching TV." A joke. Well, well. "It used to be that the Swiss were the people who took money, no questions asked, and held it against all comers. Then they changed their laws so that the money of any depositor who was proved to have earned it illegally was liable to be returned. A lot of unsavoury characters switched to money laundering and the tax havens off the East Coast. Then three years ago the Seychelles declared that anyone who wanted to deposit ten million dollars or more with them would be entitled to protection from extradition and from seizure of assets, as well as . . . Hold on." He jumped up, looking ten years younger than when he had ushered me into his office, and pulled open a file drawer. He rifled quickly through a buff folder. "Here we are. Apart from the extradition and seizure protections, big depositors would also be entitled to 'concessions and incentives commensurate with the investment.' " He shut the folder, put it away, slammed the drawer shut and dropped back into his chair. There was something familiar about the way he moved. "In other words, they held up a great big sign saying, 'Welcome All Criminals.'"

The implications were staggering, especially the extraordinary entitlements. The Seychelles government had written a law that made it possible to issue diplomatic passports to terrorists, the mob, drug traffickers. . . .

"You've just made my life a lot more complicated," I said.

"You're welcome." And he smiled. The scar tissue by his eye crinkled.

"Laurence . . ." When an imago first pushes free of the binding chrysalis and unfolds its still-damp wings, anything, even something as ephemeral as breath, can deform the final, glorious insect. A crass question now could crush this fragile new understanding. I asked anyway. "Where did you serve?"

He touched his face and sighed. "Two tours in Vietnam. The Rangers."

We sat silently, contemplating the ghosts we had created between us, and the difference between our world and that of most people.

Beatriz del Gato arrived on the four forty-five flight from Madrid. I met her in the international arrivals terminal at Hartsfield Airport. Either the photograph in her dossier was a very expensive special effects shot or it had been a truly terrible flight. Beatriz del Gato was a small, ferociously plain woman. Her features were symmetrical enough, in proportion and in roughly the right places, but she seemed weighed down, pulled out of shape by a relentless dullness. Brown hair was tugged back gracelessly from a face that looked white and puffy next to the glowing tans of other passengers. Her hands hung at her sides as though she did not know where they came from or what to do with them now they were here. Her brown eyes looked very small behind thick glasses.

"Ms. del Gato?"

"Yes?" The way she lifted her head and looked at me sideways reminded me of an adolescent, not a woman of twenty-three.

"Philippe Cordova asked me to drive you to your hotel this evening and get you settled in. My name is Aud Torvingen and I'll be escorting you during your stay in Atlanta."

"Thank you." So low I could hardly hear.

I got her and her luggage—surprisingly little—to the Saab, held open the rear door for her, then got behind the wheel. As she was finding the seat belt I slid the Walther PPK from the underarm spider harness to a lap holster that I clipped to my belt, handy in case I should need it while driving. When we were both strapped in I pulled out smoothly into the streaming traffic.

I glanced in the mirror. She had slumped like a bundle of abandoned knitting. "How was your flight?"

"Quite pleasant, thank you." Four whole words. Perhaps a tightly modulated contralto, it was hard to tell. Soft, gliding Castillian accent.

"Traffic will be bad at this time of day but I hope to have you at the Hotel Nikko in forty or fifty minutes." She nodded without looking at me. "Philippe gave me your itinerary, of course, but I'd like to go over it with you to make sure there are no errors or misunderstandings."

"Certainly."

"And I would like to know how inconspicuous you want to be."

A pause. "Perhaps you could explain."

"Philippe tells me you are interviewing at the ad agencies we'll be visiting tomorrow. If I am obvious as a bodyguard, it might be a little off-putting for your potential employers."

"Yes. I see." The knitting was straightening, just a little. "What would you suggest?"

"That you call me Aud and I call you Beatriz, and we take the parts of strangers put in touch by a mutual acquaintance while you are visiting a foreign city."

"Very well. Aud." Her trace of accent made my name longer and softer.

"It would mean I don't hold doors open for you or carry your things."

"By all means." She seemed to be sagging and fading again. Probably exhaustion. I concentrated on driving.

The first thing I did when I got home was take off the gun and stretch. The next four days were going to be very, very long.

There were two messages on the machine. The first was Charlie Sweeting sounding conspiratorial.

"Miss Torvingen? Aud. I haven't forgotten your request. I think I might have something for you in a day or two."

Beep.

"Hey, Aud, it's Mick. Are you there? Oh. Well, listen, we got a call an hour ago from Helen's father. Her mother's in the hospital. I don't know if it's serious or not. Well, it's got to be fairly serious or she wouldn't be in the hospital so suddenly." Get to the point, Mick. "Anyway, we'll be flying to St. Louis first thing tomorrow, so we won't make the performance tonight. Sorry about that. I think it'll be wild. Tell you what, let's go out for a beer when we get back and you can tell us all about it. We'll call you. Bye. Oh, forgot. The thing tonight? It's been moved from King Plow to the Masquerade. Same time. Bye."

Helen's mother had been ill for a while. At least she had Mick with her.

The last time I'd seen my mother had been the three days I had spent in London on my way to Kirov. We had both been busy—she with embassy functions, me trying to get in touch with the guide who was supposed to be travelling with me to the steppes—too busy to spend much time together. Story of our lives. Not always unintentional. She's never really forgiven me for choosing to live in my father's country. "You've no one there, Aud. No family. No job. Nothing to keep you."

On impulse, I picked up the phone and dialed.

"Hello?" Clear and sharp, so unlike Beatriz del Gato.

"Julia? It's Aud."

"Have you found out something?"

"Yes and no. That is, nothing spectacular, and that's not why I was calling. How broad is your definition of art?"

"Why do I get the feeling I shouldn't answer that one?"

"There's a performance tonight that you might find interesting."

"What kind of performance?"

"You've got me there. She's a performance artist into body modification. That's all I know."

"Okay. . . . Hello? Aud, are you still there?"

"Yes, yes. I was just trying to remember what time it starts," I lied. "How about if I pick you up around nine-thirty?"

"Why don't I pick you up? After all, I know where you live."

"Fine. And don't dress up. It's at the Masquerade."

"The what?"

"Never mind. Wear something casual. And if the CD player in your car has one of those removable face plates, remove it."

She must have got the message. She arrived at nine-thirty wearing just the right clothes: wide-legged jeans with a big belt, tight low-cut button tee that exposed her flat, tanned belly, and big boots. She'd even done something with her hair, wearing it casually upswept with thick wings hanging at each side so that it didn't look quite so sleek and moneyed. Two silver studs gleamed from her left ear and her fingernails were painted a red so dark it was almost black. The effect was to make her seem both younger and more worldly. I slung my leather jacket in the back and got in the passenger seat. It had been a long time since I had been driven anywhere; door locks and seat belts all seemed the wrong way around.

"North Avenue," I said, and after a while I began to relax. The hands on the wheel were competent.

We drove in silence. The only things we knew about each other revolved around the death of a man who had been her friend and I didn't want to talk about that, didn't want to think about murder and men with money.

"So. What am I letting myself in for tonight?" Orange streetlight glided across her right cheek and disappeared through the back window.

"Diane Pescatore has spent the last eleven years of her life surgically and cosmetically altering herself to look like a Barbie doll."

"Barbie? Those shoulders and hips and legs aren't physically possible!"

"I believe that's the point. According to a book I got from the library this week, Pescatore is one of several well-known artists and/or body sculptors who try to draw attention to the way women's bodies have been objectified by the patriarchy et cetera, et cetera."

"You mean she actually does this stuff on stage?"

"Please watch the road. No. At least I hope not. I think she's put together some kind of multimedia . . . thing."

"Thing?" She sounded amused.

"Performance, then."

The car passed under a railway bridge and slowed down by a garishly lit, dilapidated warehouse. "Is this it?" She swung into the lot, parked automatically under a light. It was strange, being with a woman who thought about these things, who remembered to take corners wide, even when she was running.

The Masquerade is an odd venue in the middle of an industrial wasteland. It looks a bit like a cross between a castle and a wooden fort from the Old West, with huge, chained freight doors on the third story and a massive iron-bound front entrance. We showed ID, paid, and walked into the gloom. Julia had her hands out of her pockets and all senses on red alert.

"It's not dangerous. It just likes to pretend it is."

"If you say so."

"Let's find out where this performance is."

The Masquerade is divided into three spaces: Heaven, upstairs, for the larger bands; Purgatory, a sort of coffee hangout for those who don't get up until after dark; and Hell, down a series of ramps where the lighting gets gloomier and gloomier and music louder and more unsettling. As we headed down I could feel my face stretching into a smile and my stride loosening and lengthening. The sharp scents of dance sweat and tequila cut through the hip haze of handrolled cigarettes. Julia's eyes glittered. I had to put my mouth to her ear and shout to be heard. "Want a drink?"

She nodded, pulled my head down to her level and touched her lips to my cheekbone just by my ear. "Beer and a tequila shot."

"Aud!" A young, thin woman cut through the crowd. Metal gleamed from forehead, shoulder, nipples, even the webbing between thumb and fingers. Thin chain threaded from nose to ear to temple. "Aud, how are you doing! Helen with you?"

Julia stepped a fraction closer.

"No. Cutter, this is Julia. Julia, Cutter. An old friend."

"Hey, Julia. Nice to see you around." She reached a thin, strong hand to Julia's face, touched the corner of her upper lip. "Little topaz would look good here. Very fierce. Aud likes fierce. Think about it. If you like the idea, Aud can give you my e-mail. Gotta go get ready. Aud—later, okay?"

Julia, finger on the place Cutter had touched, watched her slide back into the crowd. She turned to me. " 'Aud likes fierce'?"

"Let's go get that drink."

Even though Hell was full, there were not many people waiting at the bar. Julia ordered, and gave me a warning look when I made a move to pay. "You've known Cutter a long time."

"Eight years."

"Eight? She doesn't look old enough."

"She was fourteen, living on the street."

"Was she . . ." She pointed to her temple and nose.

"Yes. When I first met her she had seven studs in each ear, one in her nose, a ring through her tongue. She's got them everywhere now. And scars."

"Is it the pain she likes?"

"I've never asked."

"What about her family?"

"What about them?" They wouldn't be bothering her, not anymore.

"It's just . . ." She changed tack. "All that metal, it seems a bit excessive."

"If wearing all the hardware stops her jamming herself with heroin and makes her feel good about who she is, then I'm all for it. She even makes a living at it. As you'll see tonight. From what she said, it looks as though we'll be getting a live demonstration of body mod after all."

She sipped her beer and licked the foam off her lips. "Who is Helen?"

"Another friend."

"Like Cutter?"

"There's no one like Cutter. Helen is a professor in the Sociology Department at Georgia State. She and her husband would have been here but they had to go to St. Louis because her mother's in hospital."

"So I'm here with you instead."

I tossed down my shot, turned back to the bar and said, "My turn to buy."

After midnight and we were sitting with Dornan in the Borealis. A dozen or so other customers dotted the place. Dornan and I were drinking red wine, Julia had coffee.

"But what was interesting," she was saying to Dornan,

"was the Q&A they did afterwards, how seriously they took everything. They were talking about what gauge metal to put through the penis the same way student drivers ask what kind of gas to put in their car."

Dornan blinked a little more rapidly. "Through the penis?"

"Through everything: penis, scrotum, nipples, labia, tongue, nose, eyebrows, navel, clitoris. It made me feel so . . . old. The only holes I have are the ones I was born with, and one in this ear, two in this."

"That's one more than I have," I said.

"Well, you've both had me beat since birth," Dornan said mournfully, and Julia laughed. I had not heard her laugh before. It was subtle and warm as swirled brandy.

"And then there was the cutting," she said. "I've never seen anything like it, have you, Aud? They had this stool, just an ordinary wooden stool on stage, and Cutter got this man to sit on it and strip to the waist. He only looked about twenty. She washed his pecs with surgical alcohol and picked up a scalpel. It was like watching someone cut into a radish to make those fancy patterns. Her tongue stuck out of the corner of her mouth as she concentrated. They looked like children playing with red paints. At least she wore gloves. And he smiled the whole time she was cutting this big spiral round his nipple, cutting through his lovely soft golden skin. Cutter said that skin like that is prized because you get a nice thick white raised scar. And then she taped gauze to his chest, he put his shirt back on and everyone just chatted normally. People do very strange things for kicks." She stood up. "Excuse me a moment."

She walked like a thoroughbred towards the bathroom. I turned back to the table to find Dornan smiling slightly. "Very nice, Torvingen."

"It's business."

"You've never introduced me to one of your business acquaintances before."

I shrugged. "Always a first time." We sat in companionable silence until Julia came back.

"So," Dornan said, looking from her to me, "you paid good money for the privilege of watching this primitive blood ritual?"

"Ah," I said. "Cutter was just like the previews you get at the start of a video, an unexpected bonus. The main feature was truly strange."

I told him about Diane Pescatore and her performance, about the banks of video screens showing tapes of various operations she had undergone to sharpen her cheekbones, clip out her floating ribs, remove her molars, shape her nose, fill out her lips, carve her belly and lengthen her legs. Throughout the tapes, she had chanted peculiar verse about the subjugation of women, their hopeless quest to look like the women of men's dreams, to look like Barbie. "Yes, the doll," I told a disbelieving Dornan. "She said, quite seriously, that she's trying to find a surgeon who will try to narrow her shoulders and maybe even shave her pelvis down."

"But what does she look like?"

"Crazy. As though the only thing holding her together is this fierce will to *show* people, to *make* them understand what it's really like, in the face of the realization that her audiences only come to see her because they're horrified by what she's doing to herself. I think she knows she's made a terrible, irreversible mistake but she can't stop because if she did, she'd have to acknowledge the mistake and the fact that people really don't care. They just think she's a freak."

"Do you?" Julia had her chin on her fist and was looking at me intently.

I shrugged. "Who am I to judge?"

She decided to dig in another direction. "So how long have you two known each other?"

"A long time."

"You mean she hasn't told you how we met?" Dornan shot

me a sly smile. "It was a summer afternoon, at ten thousand feet. You see, it was in the nature of a bet I had with an old girlfriend . . ."

He loved to tell this story. I excused myself and headed for the bathroom. He was still telling it when I got back.

". . . hurtling through the air and nothing was happening, nothing, and I thought, Mother of God, I'm going to die, and I was spinning around like a top, one minute seeing the ground rushing at me like a drunken rhinoceros, the next seeing the sky and all these tiny dots that were open chutes, and I was tugging on that bloody parachute cord and nothing was happening. And then I saw one of the dots . . . split, and this body came bulleting down at me. It was Aud. She'd cut her chute loose and was swooping down on me. She didn't even know me!"

"I knew you were a fool who was panicking and had forgotten he had an emergency backup chute."

"I hadn't forgotten, I don't know how many times I've told you that, but I hadn't forgotten: I'd never been told about it in the first place! So there I was, and she came bulleting at me, arms all folded in like a human cannonball, and smacked into me hard enough to take my breath away. And you should have seen her face! Lips skinned back and eyes like a demon. I swear she was laughing. She clamped her legs around me so hard she broke two of my ribs."

"I fractured one, slightly."

"It's just that the doctor at the hospital didn't look at the X rays properly. So, anyway, she had her thighs clamped around my chest like a vise but did she pull the cord straightaway? Oh, no. She had her mouth to my ear and was yelling, 'Do you feel it? Feel it, *feel* it!' and I thought I was going to die. But then she tugged on something and *flump,* we were floating. It seemed to last forever, but it was only about eight more seconds before we hit the ground, she'd cut it so close. And then we landed. She left me all tangled up like a kitten in a ball of wool and strode off to find the instructor, who was screaming at her for being a dangerous lunatic. She talked to him—"

"You were only half trained. He should never have let you up."

"—but she never raised her voice, she rarely does, you know. And that's when he made his big mistake. He smiled. She broke his jaw."

Julia's expression gave nothing away, but she did try to sip from her empty coffee cup. "And how long ago was this?"

I never got to answer that. The door banged open and in breezed a woman of around twenty-five with black hair, lips as red as her press-on nails, and an astonishingly pneumatic figure. Dornan jumped to his feet, and all the intelligence drained from his face to be replaced by an idiot grin. He held out his arms. "Tammy, darlin'!"

I sighed and stood up, too.

"Mmmn, Dornan, I've missed you. Mmmn." Then she stepped back and smiled her heavy-lidded smile—"Aud, how nice to see you"—and raised her eyebrows at the table.

"Julia, this is Tamara Foster. Tammy, this is Julia Lyons-Bennet."

Julia stood and they shook hands in that brittle Southern girl-girl squeeze of limp fingers; the one that says, *When did they start letting people like you in?* Dornan, of course, noticed none of this. His world was full of Tammy, his girl, his fiancée, the light of his life. "Sit, darlin', sit. We were just swapping stories. Aud and Julia here have had an extraordinary evening. Jonie, Jonie!" he shouted at the barista. "We'll have another carafe of this red, and bring four fresh glasses."

"No, Dornan, not for me. I'm sure you and Tammy want some time on your own. Julia and I will be getting out of your way."

Julia stood up. "I had a really good time, Dornan. Thank you. And it was lovely to meet you, Tammy."

Dornan merely beamed.

In the car, Julia drove as though she had not been drinking at all. "You don't like Tammy."

"No."

"Let me guess. She's really a multiple murderer."

"She's a manipulative schemer who picks Dornan up and puts him down whenever she feels like it. She flies hither, thither, and yon doing what she calls business development for a local company and is only ever in town for four or five days at a time. Sometimes less. Dornan thinks they'll get married one day."

"She wears his ring."

"It's worth a lot of money, and that's all that interests Ms. Tammy Foster. She's one of those women with a body like a magnet who just keeps trolling until rich fools clang up against her sides. I've seen her around town with different men when she'd told Dornan she's in Baltimore or Chicago. She'll drop Dornan like a rock the moment she has a better catch."

"You sound very certain."

"She's very good at what she does, but if you watch her long enough you'll see that she can't help positioning herself sexually for every man who walks through the door. It's an instinct. She's been trained since childhood by her rich daddy in Connecticut to believe that who she is or what she does doesn't matter nearly as much as who she marries."

"You sound almost sorry for her."

"That doesn't make me like her. And when she realized Dornan's best friend didn't like her, she tried to win me over by propositioning me."

"You mean . . . ?"

"Yes." I would rather go to bed with a python.

"And you haven't told him."

"No."

"Why haven't you frightened her off? I imagine that would be easy enough for you."

"She makes him happy, and it won't be forever."

"You do like to play god." She sounded thoughtful more than judgmental.

We drove half a mile in silence. "Turn left on Leonardo. It's a bit quicker."

When we pulled up, she leaned across me to unlock my door. "Thank you. It was an interesting evening."

"Interesting in the Chinese sense?"

"No. I mean it. Thank you."

There was a slight pause. We both just sat there, facing the velvet dark beyond the windscreen, breathing the same air, then I was outside the car leaning in, nodding, saying good night, telling her I would call sometime very soon to give her an update on my investigations. After she drove off I stood outside for a long time, listening to the tree frogs.

five

It was one of those Atlanta mornings when you step outside and the heat and humidity seal around you like shrink-wrap. The air is as thick as potato soup and you have to breathe in sips. I drove to Buckhead with the windows closed and the air-conditioning on and even the Mozart seeped limp and dispirited from the speakers.

I picked Beatriz up at the Nikko. She had replaced her glasses with contact lenses, her hair was sleek and groomed, and the unhealthy puffiness of her face was gone, or at least masked by professionally applied makeup. She wore a beautifully cut business suit, designed to show off a surprisingly generous figure, and instead of a purse carried a large leather portfolio. The way she did not meet my eyes when I said good morning was just the same, though, as was the facial spasm that passed for a smile.

Traffic moved south on Piedmont in fits and starts. Drivers in some of the cars around me began picking up cellular phones and calling in to explain why they were going to be late. Horns blared. We crept forward. With the engine at idle speed, the air-conditioning lost some of its bite. The car began to warm up. Just ahead, flickering red and blue lights across two lanes funneled vehicles past a car with its roof ripped off and a white-sheeted figure on the melting asphalt. I knew how a haemoglobin-carrying red corpuscle must feel as it squeezes through the hardening arteries of a fifty-year-old executive running about the tennis court in one-hundred-degree weather trying to impress his secretary, knowing that at any moment everything could jam up and stop forever. But then I was past the accident and traffic sped up and we all survived to hurtle endlessly along our paths for another day.

The sweat beneath the gun harness could not evaporate. With its seven-round clip full, the Walther PPK weighed less than a pound and a half, but it felt like more, an unaccustomed and unbalancing weight. Guns can be a distraction, a dangerous focus of one's authority, a crutch. Many come to depend upon them: take away the gun and you take away their identity. Once I saw a police officer deprived of his weapon stand uselessly, dazed and uncomprehending, when he could have been calling for backup, chasing the perpetrator or helping me staunch the blood pumping from his partner's thigh.

I wear a gun when the occasion demands it. I was being paid well to ensure that during the next three days strange little Beatriz del Gato came to no harm. Philippe Cordova would expect me to wear a gun. I wore one.

As we neared the centre of town and Atlanta's one-way system we travelled west for a while on Tenth. The sun poured into the car through the rear window, and in moments the interior was swollen and thick with heat. I glanced in the rear-view mirror. Beatriz did not seem affected. South again on Juniper, and into the cool shadow of the Peachtree Medical Building. The interior temperature dropped fifteen degrees. Beatriz stared out of the window and did not move a muscle the whole time.

I parked on Courtland and prepared for the long, long morning of appointments.

It was after she came out of the first office, face stiff, that I understood Beatriz del Gato was wasting her time. No one was going to employ an advertising executive who did not seem to understand the meaning of small talk and whose expression was as impervious as pottery glaze. She was utterly self-involved, did not acknowledge my presence at all but simply followed me doggedly through the hydrocarbon heat of downtown Atlanta to the sterile chill of another office tower for the second appointment. I waited in the reception area while she went off to some inner sanctum to show her wares. I tried to imagine her talking to one of these potential employers, and failed.

As the morning progressed, her expression began to change. She got paler, and there was a disturbingly gelid cast around her eyes and cheeks, as though the pottery glaze were on the verge of melting.

As we arrived at the offices of Perrin & Norrander, her fourth appointment, I found myself holding my breath, willing her to hang on. It was the usual Atlanta advertising agency: hand-knotted silk carpet, blond wood inlay (a competent assembly of ash and maple), men wearing Hugo Boss, women good jewellery, both with far too many clothes for this kind of weather; an ultimately self-defeating attempt to prove that advertising in the capital of the South was every bit as aggressive and cutting-edge as Madison Avenue. There is one thing Margaret Thatcher said that I agree with: if you have to tell people you're important, you're not.

The secretary was one of those sorority sisters from Ole Miss who didn't believe in pronouncing *l*'s when they appeared in the middle of a word. She was on the phone. "Would you please ho'd one moment?" Efficient punch of button with terrifyingly red nail followed by professional smile at us. "How can I he'p you?"

"Beatriz del Gato to see Anthony Perrin," she said, like one of those old-fashioned porcelain marionettes.

The Taloned One ran her finger down a screen, then favoured us with another artificial smile. "If you would take a seat, Mr. Perrin will be with you shortly. How do you like your coffee?"

I answered for both of us. The waiting room was frigid and the three chairs built more for looks than comfort. They were arranged under a horrible painting that looked like a television test card. Beatriz sat, portfolio on her lap; I didn't bother. Even if the chairs were worth it, the painting hung so low I wouldn't be able to lean back.

A moment later, the secretary came in carrying two cups of coffee on a tray.

I took one. She turned to offer the second, just as Beatriz stood up to take it. With a flap and squawk they collided. The secretary leapt back to avoid the cascade of scalding coffee. Beatriz didn't manage as well. She hopped into the chairs, knocked her open portfolio onto the now-sodden floor, then overbalanced and toppled into the painting, which slid down the wall and landed on the polished wooden floor with an emphatic *crack*. Glass fell out of the frame.

"Goodness," the secretary said.

Beatriz stared at her. Her eyes were like black holes burnt in stiff paper and the hand wrapped around the back of one chair was white at the knuckles. The mask had finally slipped.

The secretary took a step towards the chair. "Let me he'p you with that."

Beatriz trembled like a deer. I stepped smoothly between them. "Perhaps you could direct us to the bathroom so we can see what we can do about Ms. del Gato's clothes." I gestured at the dark splash down Beatriz's skirt.

"Oh, goodness. Of course. Two doors down on the right."

I took Beatriz unobtrusively by the elbow. "Let go of the

chair," I said into her ear. "It's all right. Everything will be all right. Let go of the chair."

"Yes, fine," she said, inanely, brightly. I led her through the reception area, through the door, down the corridor, to the bathroom.

"Here we go." I parked her between the sinks and paper towel dispenser. It would have been a waste of time trying to get her to sit. Her body felt like wood. "I don't think you need to take the skirt off. Let's try blotting it first, and soap if that doesn't work."

Her trembling turned into shaking. "I understand," I said, as I dabbed and blotted. "You're in a strange country. You have jet lag and probably didn't get any sleep at all in your hotel. Everyone is talking in a foreign language. Even the light switches seem upside down. They expect you to know what to do and you don't. But that's why I'm here. I can show you how things work and tell you where to go, and when." I talked on and on, wondering how long she had been this afraid, so afraid that she had closed herself up like a fan: nothing in, nothing out; running around inside her head frantically plugging chinks in her armour, closing openings through which she might have to reach out and the world might reach in.

"There. That should do it for now." The shaking had become long, rolling shudders and I thought she might shake herself to pieces. I took one of her cold hands. "Let it out, Beatriz, you're safe here."

An indrawn, juddering breath.

"No one will see you. No one will know. Just let it go."

And she did, in a torrent that was equal parts rage, fear, and despair. She wept bent over, gasping and whooping, then stood straight and howled, face to the ceiling. When the gate was wide open, she leaned both fists against the mirrors and coughed up great chunks of grief and disappointment and broken dreams. She wept on and on until her face was swollen, and shiny with mucus and tears. After a while she settled down to an exhausted drone. I handed her yet another paper towel, stuffed six or seven in my pocket, and picked her up like a child.

I tucked her face into my shoulder so she wouldn't see the stares, and carried her to the elevator, down fourteen floors, through the lobby, into the street, and across to the parking lot. I lifted her into the front seat, got a blanket from the trunk, tucked her up and fastened her seat belt.

"Warm," she said.

"Yes, I know, but you need to be warm and I'm going to put the air-conditioning on high." She needed the comfort more than the warmth, but I didn't tell her that. "Sleep if you like. I'll drive you back to your hotel."

"No." It was a drowsy whisper. "I hate my hotel. Hate it."

She wasn't in a fit state to be seen in public and wouldn't go back to her hotel. While I waited to pull into traffic I called Happy Herman's and ordered enough food for a picnic.

The remains of the meal lay on the blanket in the middle of my back lawn and the woman who sat like the Copenhagen mermaid in the too-big shorts and cut-off tee, peering at the base of the pecan tree trying to catch a glimpse of the turtle I'd seen, looked nothing like the Beatriz of that morning. Her eyes were alive, if shy, and the two smiles she had essayed had been quick, but not crippled. I had carried her and the blanket out to the back, fed her, and talked to her about nothing in particular, simply pointing out different birds, squirrels, naming the trees, explaining what all the different condiments on the sandwiches were made of. She'd eaten mechanically at first, then with real attention, and then fallen asleep as I was telling her quietly in my rusty Spanish about the bluebells I used to look for in the Yorkshire woods. She slept for nearly an hour, and when she woke up I showed her the bathroom and found her my smallest tank top and shorts, and now she was all clean and freshly scrubbed and watching the leaves under the pecan tree.

"You'll have to go back to the hotel barefoot."

"Yes."

"I'm sure they've seen worse. There, there's the turtle." I pointed at the blunt leathery head poking cautiously from under a pile of nature's debris.

"I see it."

I told her about shrews, about the constant war going on between the various squirrels, the chipmunks who could leap three feet straight into the air when cornered by the cat that lived next door. Sometimes I had to mime the animal with bushy tail or pointy ears because I didn't know the Spanish for all that flew and scurried in the Southeast. I'm still not sure she got "chipmunk." It's hard mimicking a tiny rodent with big cheek pouches when you're six feet tall.

"And you have no pets?"

"No. I can watch things in my garden and I don't have to feed them or take them for checkups, or worry about looking after them when I go away."

"And they don't worry about you."

A bird burst into song among the jasmine. A plane droned in the distance. After a while I said, "Do you want that job at Perrin & Norrander?"

She blinked, then turned away and mumbled something.

"What was that?"

"Yes."

"Do you really mean it?"

"Yes!"

"Then we need to get you another appointment."

"They won't—"

"I'll talk to them. Blame the secretary. After all, she spilled coffee all over you. How could you be expected to continue with a scalded leg?"

"But I don't—"

"You do now." I was implacable. "Your flight to Madrid leaves on Monday afternoon. If we get you a ten o'clock appointment, I can have you at the airport just after midday."

"They won't give me the job."

"No, they might not. But at least you will have tried."

"What about my clothes?"

"We'll go shopping."

I discovered that under her plain exterior beat a flamboyant heart. She wanted to buy dresses and blouses with puffed sleeves and high waists that would be more suitable for a teenager. Fortunately she also wanted them in blood red and flaming orange instead of the available pastels. I steered her towards more practical clothes, made the occasional suggestion. We ended up with flax-coloured linen suit, shorts and T-shirts and sandals, and one stunning sleeveless dress in brain-bursting colours. Whatever made her happy. Then it was her turn to make suggestions. Under her direction, we bought dozens of flats of just-budding impatiens, petunia, and marigold, as well as two long troughs, and sacks of potting compost. "You'll need seeds and cuttings for later-blooming flowers. These won't last much beyond June." She gave them a professional look. "We'll transplant them tomorrow."

It was a quite different woman I took back to the Nikko at seven o'clock that evening: smiling, competent, almost pretty.

At midnight I was cruising Cheshire Bridge Road, checking the parking lots of the nude bars. I spotted the primer-coloured 1972 Corvette in the lot of a low-slung building with bricked-up windows, but drove another quarter of a mile until I reached the well-lit Cheshire Strip. I parked in front of the Science Fiction and Mystery Book Shop where odd but harmless customers were happily choosing fat paperbacks, and walked back.

It was good to feel muscle bunch and stretch in my thighs,

good to thump my boots on the cement, feel its imperviousness and my strength. I checked the cars. The hood of the Corvette was cold. I looked around the back of the building. One door, unlocked. I went around to the front. The turbine in my chest began to hum. The night air felt greasy and electric on my tongue. The weather was about to change.

The front bar was shadowy. A pool table was pushed up against one wall, underneath a labouring air-conditioning unit that did not quite drown out the thump of music from the more private back room. The bartender polished glasses and concentrated hard on not seeing the three men in the far booth. I leaned against the bar near him, shook my head when he lifted his eyebrows.

Buddy Collins was the kind of man who looked as though his neck was too thin for his shirt collar, though it and the expensive jacket fit perfectly. An untrained witness would probably not be able to describe him as other than a slimeball. Buddy Collins had fooled even trained witnesses—of which he had been one, once.

Right now, Buddy Collins was swallowing a great deal. He was pressed up against the wall on the inside of the booth by a man who had his back towards me. That man had his hand resting on Collins's forearm. It was a very big hand. Equally big legs were jammed under the booth table; he wouldn't be able to move out fast. He was leaning forward, talking at Collins. The one on the other side of the booth was mean and whippy-looking. He was trying to clip the end off a cheap cigar, and listened with only half an ear to the big man. He had heard it all a thousand times before.

"I can't," Collins said. "Not all of it. Not tonight." The big man said nothing. "If you could just give me—"

The big man hit him, just a slap, but it was loud, and a bead of blood formed in the corner of Collins's mouth.

"Gentlemen," I said, moving in. They all swung around,

astonished. "Don't damage Mr. Collins too severely. He has some information I need."

"You some kind of weirdo?" the big man asked, and turned back to his conversation with Collins without waiting for an answer.

The whippy one, who seemed to have clipped the end of his cigar to his satisfaction, pulled out a book of matches. "Butt out, lady." He put the cigar in his mouth and struck the match. His eyes crossed in concentration. I hit him, twice, on the left temple, right hand left hand, and without pause stepped backwards and put all my weight behind an elbow strike to the big man's nose. It burst like a piñata and spilled brightly, and he screamed, so I let my arm follow its automatic one-two training and hit him again, this time a knife-hand chop to the forehead. He sighed and slumped over the table.

The cigar was still hanging from Whippy's mouth. "Do I need to hit you again?"

He did not seem to hear. I looked at Collins and gestured at the big man, draped all unconscious across the bench and table. "Can you squeeze past or should I pull him out?"

"I'll manage." He climbed up onto the table.

I turned to the bartender. He backed up a step. "There's nothing much wrong with them, but you might like to have an ambulance here soon, get them taken off your hands. They won't be very happy when they wake up."

"You—" He cleared his throat, then thought better of it and just nodded.

Collins jumped down from the table. "Time to get out of here."

In the parking lot, he looked around. "Which is your car?"

"We're taking yours. I'll drive."

"Look, Torvingen. That car's my pride and joy—"

I held out my hand. He stared at me then yanked keys from his pocket, slammed them into my hand, and went round to the passenger side. The car smelt of dirty leather and coffee. He watched me sideways as we pulled onto Cheshire Bridge.

"What?"

"Nothing. Just wondering why you suddenly appeared, where you're taking me, things like that."

"We're going to have a nice talk. You're going to tell me a few things I want to know."

"Jesus, Torvingen, you've screwed up everything. Those two guys won't take kindly to you—"

I pulled into the Cheshire Strip lot and killed the engine. "You owe them money. You've defaulted. They seemed about to get very unhappy. I've just accelerated the process a little. I'm sure you'll think of something." Collins had been a Vice cop until his spending had led to such excessive graft that even the APD could no longer turn a blind eye. He had been turned out when I was a rookie. Now he earned his money selling information from one street interest to another, and sometimes to law enforcement.

"You're not on the force anymore," he said.

"No. So now I can afford to pay more."

"I don't like you."

"You don't have to like me. Just tell me about the burn in Inman Park five days ago. Who ordered the job? Was the victim, an art appraiser called Lusk, known? And where does the big money go these days?" The Big Money, the money raised from the wholesale dealers who sold to midlevel hustlers.

He reached up and turned on the dome light. "You don't have the money for that last answer. And if you did, and I told you, I'd never live to enjoy it."

His eyes were still shifting, but he wasn't swallowing. A quick cost-benefit analysis of forcing him was not promising: he probably didn't know. "Fine. Then tell me who would be capable of this burn. Bertolucci didn't recognize it. How do I find them, and who have they worked for in the past?"

"How much?"

"How much do you think it's worth?"

"Two thousand."

"I'll give you five hundred." I pulled the money out of my pocket and counted off five hundreds but didn't hand it over.

"Guy from Boston. You don't know him."

"Name."

"I don't *know* his name! He's just some technician hired in, like you'd pay someone to check your brake fluid." He was getting agitated.

"Then tell me who he worked for."

"Arellano." He practically spat it out.

Arellano. The Big Money man of two years ago, the representative of the Tijuana drug cartel here in the South. Only no one had been able to prove it. "He's been dead for two years."

"This technician worked for him two years ago."

"I don't know what you're telling me here, Buddy. Did the technician work this time for Arellano's replacement?"

"Maybe."

" 'Maybe' doesn't cut it."

"This time he worked for a guy who might work for the guy who took over from Arellano. Okay?"

"What do you mean by 'might work for'?"

"The guy washes money. He washes a lot of money. He hired the technician."

"Give me his name."

"I don't know his name."

I was pretty sure I did. "Another hundred if you tell me why he paid the technician."

He hesitated, craned his neck to try to look up the road. "Another two hundred."

"One hundred."

He touched the blood at the corner of his mouth with a fingertip and sighed. "The fire was to clean up some evidence."

"And did the evidence get cleaned?"

"A guy died."

"That's not what I asked."

His eyes shifted.

"The truth, Buddy. If you don't know, just say so and you get to keep fifty."

"I heard some of the evidence is still walking around. But the technician got paid, okay? And no one is pissed off, and no one is talking about trying again. So it doesn't make sense, okay?"

It made perfect sense to me, or part of it did. Julia was no longer important: she had no evidence and, after lying to the insurance investigator, no one would even begin to believe her without it. With the painting gone, Honeycutt thought he was safe. The question is, what was a money launderer doing dabbling with fake art? It was a stupid extra risk. *That* made no sense. Nor did the drugs on the scene.

Buddy could not make up his mind which was more interesting: the road or the money I still held. "Those sharks'll be awake now, Torvingen. Just give me the money. Look, here's a freebie for you. That evidence that got burned? Two old friends of yours know where it came from."

"Tell me."

He held out his hand. "An extra hundred."

"Free."

He shook his head and got stubborn. It wasn't worth pushing. My job was to work out who had tried to have Julia killed, and now I knew. I handed over the money. "Get out of the car." I climbed out after him and tossed him the keys. He was screeching out of the parking lot before I was halfway to the book shop.

Taeko Jay has worked for the DEA for as long as I've lived in Atlanta. Longer. Her coarse black hair is streaked with grey and she wears it long, with no apology. She came over to America twenty years ago—fell in love with a member of the

CIA in Tokyo, got married, and had her citizenship papers two days later. The rules are different for some people. Her husband died ten years ago and now she lives with a skinny game designer half her age. She smiles a lot. Her teeth are white and pointed. A Japanese vixen.

Saturday morning at seven we were eating sushi. "Arellano's successor? Well, here's the funny thing, we don't even know if there is one. There haven't been any of the usual killings you would expect during a power struggle and we haven't found any evidence of an organizational nexus here in town. Though they are using the same money man."

"Honeycutt."

She paused, with what looked like raw squid halfway to her mouth. "How did you know that?"

"I hear he's not being so smart."

"Is that so?"

"Playing both ends against the middle. I think you can expect trouble at some point."

She looked thoughtful. "Two years ago, maybe. Now? Whoever is in charge is very savvy. Very, very savvy. And very low profile."

I ate some raw tuna rolled up around something cold and spicy. "You sound as though you approve."

"Well, the stuff's going to get in no matter what we do, and if fewer bodies pile up, the citizens don't complain as much, which means the people in Washington don't breathe down our necks. Though politically speaking coke is old news. Smack's the thing now, and with its traditional tie-ins with organized crime, everyone in Washington is jumping up and down and getting very hot under the collar. Smack is only just reemerging and the lines of supply are still new and reasonably clear. The politicos see this as their big opportunity, a chance to crush the drug trade—or one of them, anyway—and bang behind bars all those crime bosses they've been after since

Gotti went down. And the heroin trade doesn't use street gangs."

"Not that gangs seem to be much involved in Atlanta's coke trade."

"That's another strange thing— Are you going to use that lemon?"

I passed it to her. "Another strange thing?"

"Yeah. You look at, say, San Diego, and all the enforcers there are gangbangers, little sixteen-year-olds who see hundreds of thousands in cash and coke pass through their hands every week." She squeezed the last of the lemon over her salmon. "No, smack's the flavour of the month, and I'm glad. A smack habit is something you have to *work* to acquire, and when a user goes wild on smack, they just nod out, they don't go psychotic. Did you know that heroin is actually beneficial to the body in small amounts? Like alcohol."

"Think how much tax money the government would make if they legalized it."

"But they never will. Lot of campaign contributions these days—especially in California—being made by pot smugglers. They want it to stay illegal. They make a very nice living, thank you very much. It's all— Sandy," to a passing server, "can I get some more lemon? So, yeah, it's all becoming more or less respectable, like bootlegging during Prohibition. Hell, it already is respectable in Mexico. The Tijuana cartel owns the federal police and everyone knows it, even the politicos, but so few people are getting killed, and those mainly gringos, that none of them care. Just like no one cares here when big American corporations ship thousands of tons of baby formula to the third world and kill all the children. Deadly white powder, but this time wrapped in pretty boxes and the official cooperation of the government. So we have the commander of the federal police openly being the liaison man for the Tijuana cartel, and people down there just shrug. Blood pressures in Washington are, if you'll pardon the expression, shooting up."

We both grinned. I applied myself to the ahi.

"Hey, Aud, interesting case last month."

"Yeah?"

"We helped bust a Nigerian heroin smuggling ring run— get this—by women. Apparently it's traditional in Nigerian culture for women to run all the business stuff, and they've somehow got hooked into the opium pipeline that runs from the East, through Africa, and up to Seattle. I went up to Seattle with the task force. Got them all in one swoop. God, I love my job."

I drove through the morning traffic, trying to think. Tijuana. Low-profile successor to Arellano. Honeycutt and the torch from Boston. But where did Honeycutt get the coke, and why would he want it there in the first place?

Beatriz was wearing the new sandals and shorts and tee when I picked her up again at half past ten, and her hair was up in a loose twist. She looked young and bright and fresh. She climbed into the front passenger seat.

"It's safer for you in the back."

"But I have never really been in any danger, have I?"

"No."

"And you are wearing your gun?"

I lifted my jacket to show her the Walther. She put her seat belt on and that was that.

We ate brunch on the deck. Beatriz made pencil sketches as she ate. "The front needs some colour. If you cut another trench in front of the porch, we can plant some impatiens out there. Some around the tree, too." Then she ate a croissant with quick, precise bites and picked up her pencil again. "While you dig the new beds, I'll start on the tubs." She sipped at her coffee, stared out at the back. "I wonder if the bed at the end needs widening. . . ."

It was my job to keep her safe, and I was getting free help for my garden.

Two hours later, the new bed was dug, the old one widened, and there were bright flowers dotted around the beech tree and in two three-foot troughs beneath the front windows. Beatriz had a smudge on her left cheek. Her skin was beginning to darken after hours in the sun. It made the whites of her eyes seem faintly blue. She looked healthy, energetic.

"What do you think?"

My house had looked efficient, well maintained and clean. Now it was inviting. "Lunch," I said.

I turned on the air-conditioning and we ate at the kitchen table. Halfway through the smoked salmon, bean salad and beer, the phone rang. It was Charlie Sweeting. He was excited.

"Hope you don't have plans for tonight. Honeycutt's giving a party. Black tie. I can get you an invite."

I thought fast. "Charlie, can you hold a moment?"

I pushed the SILENT button, turned to Beatriz, who was trying not to listen. "Do you want to go to a big party tonight?"

She plucked at her T-shirt. "We would have to shop again."

"Charlie? Yes, I can make it if I can bring a guest. And Charlie, when you give our names, just say it's the daughter of a Spanish Cabinet minister—"

"Which one?"

"Luis del Gato, Minister of Labour."

"Pity it's not trade."

"Indeed. The daughter is Beatriz del Gato. I'm to be her nameless escort."

"I'll have to—"

"Just say 'and bodyguard.' And if you're going to the party, don't acknowledge me." Beatriz had now given up all pretense of not listening.

"Don't you worry about me. It's at his house in Marietta, eight until he thinks he's impressed everyone. Are you really a bodyguard?"

"More of an escort. Thank you for this, Charlie."

I put the phone down and turned to Beatriz. "I want to meet a man, but I don't want him to know I'm meeting him."

"What kind of man?"

"That's what I want to find out. The party will be a formal affair, and very public. There will be no danger to you, at least no more than in any other situation."

She looked at me steadily. "You have helped me. I will do this for you."

I picked up the phone again. "Will those flowers need watering before we transplant them tomorrow?"

She took the hint at once and went to water the flowers. I called Julia. "It's me. Sweeting got me two invitations for a black tie party at Honeycutt's tonight."

"What time?"

"Eight."

"That doesn't give me much time to get ready."

"It wouldn't be prudent for you to go."

"Don't be silly. All our business was by phone. He's never even seen—"

"I've already invited someone else."

"I see." Her tone was icy. "Well, I'm sure you'll have a lovely time." Click.

They don't sell things in bad taste at Saks, so that's where I took Beatriz. And after she had picked out a deep red silk sheath and even darker red backless pumps, I took her to the cosmetics counter where a woman like a lizard helped her select the things to go with her dress. Then it was on to Hairanoia.

While she was having her hair washed I beckoned Douglas over. "She'll want something . . . excessive. If you keep it to the merely dramatic, I'll be appreciative." He nodded politely. I would hate to be a hairdresser, always being told what to do by amateurs who think that just because they're paying they should be in charge.

\*     \*     \*

She changed in the bathroom then chattered at me through the bedroom door while I got ready. This would be her first big party.

"What about all the parties in Madrid?"

"I lived all my life in a small town called Cuenco, about a hundred miles from the city. It was only after Papa was offered the Cabinet post that the family moved."

When I stepped out of the bedroom in a tiny black Vera Wang dress, she stared at me.

"It's not polite to be too surprised."

"What? Oh, no, it wasn't. . . . It's just . . ." I let her flounder. "You'll carry the gun in your purse?"

"I never carry a purse."

"Then . . ."

I walked into the living room, put my left foot up on the couch and turned towards her. My dress rode up and exposed the black stretch neoprene thigh holster attached garter fashion, with black elastic to-the-waist strap and waistband attachment. Her blink rate went up. I slid out the little Sig Sauer P230, showed it to her, then put it away. "Time to go."

By the time we were on I-75 her excitement was back. "Who will be there?"

"Everyone who is anyone. Politicians, media moguls, bankers, that kind of thing." Money launderers, crooked politicians, murderers.

She didn't say anything to that but began to root around in my CDs. She stopped and swore softly in Spanish.

"What?"

"My purse. I left it at your house."

"Do we need to go back?"

"No," she said, and smiled. "Besides, what do I need for a party?"

A gun. Car keys. Credit card and five-dollar bill for the valet parking. Bodyguard to carry it all. She went back to sorting through the music. We listened to Skunk Anansie, very loud, all the way to Marietta.

Honeycutt lived in a neighbourhood of oversized Georgians with gravel drives and half-grown hedges that went up five or six years ago when the land out here in the middle of nowhere was cheap and you had to drive three miles to pick up a pint of milk. Now the land is expensive and stuffed with houses that all look alike and belong to neighbours you'll never meet—and you still have to drive three miles to get a pint of milk. There were people all over the lawn: women wearing little jewel-encrusted silk slippers, men in midnight tuxes with brilliant cummerbunds. Four men in white shirts and black trousers parked cars. I noted the cut of their trousers around the ankle, pocket, and waistband. No weapons.

To the smooth-eyed man with the list at the door I announced, "Ms. del Gato and escort," and we were in. A server glided past bearing a tray of martinis and Beatriz grabbed one, eyes sparkling. The roar of conversation and shimmer of diamonds was overwhelming.

A woman I recognised from Eddie's pictures as Cathie Tyers, Honeycutt's latest girlfriend, was standing before a huge wall aquarium, playing host. She greeted us with the pursed vowels of a Canadian accent, usual generic smile and Pleased-you-could-come, and unwilling handshake, then turned her attention to the sudden stir behind us. Cess Silverman had arrived, along with Georgia's Secretary of State. They were greeted then wafted discreetly by one of the staff towards the back of the house.

I glanced about at the walls, as if admiring the moulding, following the wiring, the phone lines. No sensors on the hall windows; probably specially designed glass, fitted by the security company. I edged Beatriz towards a sideboard groaning under hors d'oeuvres. "For tonight, I'm not Aud. I'm your escort, Torvingen. Treat me like hired help."

"I will try to remember."

"Try hard. You're the one with the invitation. No one here has any reason to believe I would be here except as your escort."

"No one except Charlie."

"Except Charlie Sweeting. Who is the white-haired gentleman heading our way."

He was holding out his hand but remembered himself just in time and pointed it at Beatriz. "Miss del Gato. Charlie Sweeting. A pleasure indeed." He shot a bushy-browed look at my legs. He was too well bred to lick his lips, but I could see him revising his opinion of my intelligence. Why is it that some men equate the size of a woman's brain with that of her dress?

I gave him an up-and-down and let him see my professional dismissal of him as threat. When he recoiled with injured vanity, I dropped him a wink. He recovered with aplomb and turned to Beatriz. "Ah, Miss del Gato—may I call you Beatriz?"

"Certainly."

"Allow me to advise you on some of this food. A sophisticated European woman like yourself might not be familiar with our plain country fare."

She glanced at me. I nodded fractionally.

"Very well, Mr. Sweeting. It looks quite delicious. What are those green vegetables?"

"Okra, I believe. Now, I once heard a story . . ."

I trailed after them as he exuded courtly charm and she giggled. She was in safe hands for a while. I excused myself.

I trawled the party. Music was playing in the reception room; no one was dancing, but the conversation was loud and fast, with a high laughter quotient. I beckoned to a passing server for a glass of whiskey, and sipped. Not cheap. I passed through room after room, smiling my *Goodness me, look at all these people!* smile, which always gets a response. In thirty minutes I talked to an insurance broker from Los Angeles; some drunk old photographer with a very handsome face who wanted to tell me all about her work and snarled at her husband when he came to find out who she was talking to; one of the bigger building contractors in the city; and the lieutenant governor's wife—who turned out to be a civil engineer. I asked her the usual questions about her job, and she was happy to tell me all about the design of the elevated MARTA tracks and why the support arches were the shape they were.

"Heavens!" I said, looking at my watch. "Is that the time? My poor husband will be wondering where on earth I've gotten to. So nice to meet you!"

I was drifting through the back parlour when I caught sight of a man and woman I recognized, sitting on a sofa, looking like successful executives in love. Lois and Mitchum Kenworthy. Or at least that's what they had been calling themselves last time we ran into each other, three years ago, when they were up on embezzlement and fraud charges. Two old friends. Now I knew who had provided the fake Friedrich. I edged into another room, where I could watch them without being seen.

No sign of Cess Silverman, the Secretary, or Honeycutt, for that matter. No doubt they were huddled in the treehouse with the rest of the secret club.

Parties are like life—you think that what you see is all there is, until you discover the next layer, a whole other culture that's going on all around you but you never knew existed. About three months after Helen married Mick, she called me up and we went to the Vortex. Somewhere around the fourth drink, she stopped talking and stared at her wedding ring. "It's just a piece of metal, but it's weird. It's like a funny handshake. All of a sudden I find myself part of this club that I never even knew existed. With this ring on my finger, I'm visible, I'm *real* to other members of the club. They treat me differently. Even my *mother* treats me differently. She calls up and starts telling me all this *stuff*, about her and Pop, about their marriage. As if I'll suddenly be able to understand. I was thinking the other day, my god, if I'd never married, I would never have learned all this about my own mother and father. Mind you, sometimes it's not stuff I want to know. Then again, you know, it makes me feel good. To belong. To be one of Them. I mean, I'm thirty-eight, and for the first time in my life I'm being treated like a grown-up by the grown-ups. Even my dental hygienist treats me like a real person now. It's frightening. I mean, what other clubs are there out there that I don't know about?" She wasn't looking for an answer. "My god, last time I was in the airport, some kid offered me his *seat*."

"And you liked it?"

"Well . . ."

"Mostly?"

"Yes, I suppose so."

"And that makes you feel guilty, sorry for all those people like me who'll never belong to your marvellous club." She stared. "Don't worry about it. I belong to the big bad butch club, where only dykes who have broken people's noses are welcome. Then there's the tough cop club. And the ex-pat club. Not to mention the filthy stinking rich unemployed. You should be writhing with jealousy, not guilt."

She burst out laughing. "You're so refreshing. Let's get drunk."

And what I hadn't told her was that you could be accepted as part of any club if you pretended you were already a member. The hard part was working out the fact of a particular club's existence.

But I knew all about Cess Silverman's secret club, the cronies sipping whiskey and talking about who to make or break in state politics. I'd been born into the Norwegian version, but declined to take up membership as an adult. Ten years ago, Denneny would have been at this party, fighting to gain entry to the club. He had even tried to use me. "Inside information would be very useful," he said. "With your background and smarts you'd be a natural." What he'd meant was, *You'll do well, and you'll be seen as my protégé, and then I'll do well.* And *I'll be informed.* He always had been ambitious. He'd been very bitter for a while when he was refused that promotion to commander, but perhaps that was partly because his wife was drinking herself to death. Now he no longer seemed to feel anything at all.

I waited until the back hallway was clear so no one would see me go upstairs. I cruised the upper floor. Sensors on the windows, no motion detectors in the corners of rooms. This time the wiring ran along the baseboard. He needed a new cleaning service.

I found the breaker box in the closet of what looked like a guest bedroom. I put a chair in front of the door, so anyone coming in would knock it down and give me warning, and flipped open the box.

He had made it too easy: everything was neatly labelled. I slid the screwdriver from its snug leather band on my thigh and hummed as I worked. He had what he thought was a good system: sensors on all windows and doors, battery backup in case someone cut the mains. I simply disconnected the battery from the mains so it could not recharge, and switched the alarm hookup over to the circuit labelled HALL: a few hours' extra life for the fish in that fancy aquarium in case there was a power hit. No booby-trap lines to the phone. Good.

I closed up, put the screwdriver away, and went back to wandering. The carpet in the hallway was the particular shade of deep red that men favour when there is no woman around to tell them any better. It was wonderfully thick. An elephant could probably jump up and down outside Honeycutt's bedroom and he wouldn't hear a thing. Just made to be burgled. There was a reasonable amount of art, but nothing like the quantity Eddie had shown me. I recognized a particularly ugly sculpture in one of the bathrooms, and the large Day-Glo painting on the wall. No icons, no precious statuettes, no display cases. Given the shoddy electronic security, I doubted he had anything that small and precious in the house at all. They were too easily hidden in a pocket or . . . smuggled. Of course. Part of the money would be washed that way. Use dirty money to buy art quietly. Ship art abroad where it's sold for clean money that can come back quite legally.

I opened the door to what seemed like a den, but the air was empty of the scents of use: no paper, no hot plastic from faxes and computers, no smoke or alcohol, no late-night sweat. The desk had a pile of papers on it, but they were tidy and curling at the edges. This was a front.

At the end of the hallway was a second, smaller stairway leading to the third floor. I walked up two stairs and tilted my head back. From above my head came a creak and sigh, the sound of a bored man on a chair outside a room. A guard. Another time, then.

The music from below was louder, a lot louder, and now it had a pronounced beat. People were dancing. I started downstairs.

Charlie Sweeting met me in the hall. "There you are. I think your young charge might have had a bit too much to drink."

"Where?"

He stepped back. "It wasn't my—"

"*Where?*"

"Dancing."

He had to almost run to keep up. People peeled from my path like sod before the plough.

One of those party songs from the early eighties was thumping from the speakers and the dance floor was half full. Beatriz was being whirled around by some young man. Her hair was loose, eyes brilliant, cheeks flushed. She was laughing. People were watching. But her feet were sure and her energy high.

"She's not drunk. Just having the time of her life." I smiled at Charlie, as much to make everyone in the room relax as to reassure him. He muttered something I didn't hear over the music, and headed for the quieter back parlour. I watched him walk past the Kenworthys, who were talking to someone with his back to me, then turned again to the dance floor. I watched for a long time, unseen.

Whoever Dancing Boy was, he was energetic. He was still twirling Beatriz around, and she was still laughing, when Charlie come back in with Michael Honeycutt. They were heading straight for me.

I did that subtle straightening thing that makes people pay attention, and Beatriz saw me, and waved, and dragged over Dancing Boy.

"Ms. del Gato," I said deferentially, "I believe Mr. Sweeting wants to introduce you to your host." And then Charlie was there, booming genially over the music, and Beatriz was shaking hands with a clean-boned man of about forty whose tux hung beautifully and whose gray eyes looked as guileless as a child's. He was wearing some kind of cologne I couldn't identify, a pleasant scent—not too strong, the way many men wear it—and seemed the kind of man who would do well mediating disputes: very little of that overt male body language that delineates the hierarchy. It seemed he and Dancing Boy, whose name turned out to be Peter Herrera, already knew each other, and the latter's painfully obvious drawn-in elbows and slightly lowered eyes made it plain who was the alpha male. Honeycutt's smile was affable, and he said all the appropriate things, but he was on automatic pilot, mind elsewhere, and after a minute or two, he excused himself. He moved well through the crowd, quite at home. I imagined that if someone faced him with his crimes, he would frown and say he was sorry, anything to avoid bad feeling or confrontation, but underneath would wonder what all the fuss was about. A man like that will often do what he thinks will please others; the trick is in predicting what he thinks. From the back, I recognized him as the man who had been talking to the Kenworthys.

Beatriz led Dancing Boy back onto the floor. It was nearly eleven o'clock and I had everything I had come for, but Beatriz was as happy as a child at her first birthday party, so I let them dance.

She chattered about Dancing Boy all the way south on I-75. He was ten feet tall, very kind, and could speak Spanish with *such* a charming accent. I didn't interrupt until we were on Ponce, three miles from the house.

"What does he do?"

"He is an intern"—she sounded a little unsure of the word—"at a firm of attorneys. Lawson and Walton."

"What kind of things does he do?"

"He's some sort of liaison," she said vaguely. "With a bank, I think."

"Massut Vere?"

"Yes. Is it, then, a very important bank in the city?"

"Important enough. How long has he worked there?"

"Not very long. He doesn't like it very much." A point for Mr. Herrera. "He says that after he finishes his law degree, he wants to work with poor people."

How very nice. I turned right on Clifton. She yawned.

"Two more minutes. You can stay in the car while I get your purse. We'll have you at your hotel in less than half an hour."

"Aren't you tired?"

"I wasn't dancing half the night."

She smiled again.

"Here we are." I turned into my street. There was a car parked in the driveway. Julia's. Julia was in it. As I pulled into the curb, she got out. "Stay in the car," I told Beatriz.

"There you are!" Julia said, heading towards my screen door, assuming I would let her in. "I called but there was no reply. And I remembered what happened with your machine last time. I've been . . . Never mind. I've got things to tell you. Earlier today I—"

Whatever she was going to say was lost in a thud as she walked into one of the flower troughs Beatriz had filled this morning. Julia grabbed at me just as I caught her under the arms and for a moment we were frozen in an awkward tableau somewhere between *Gone With the Wind* and a game of Twister.

I hauled and she scrabbled up my body. She froze as one hand touched the bulge at my thigh and the other the harness around my waist.

Beatriz chose that moment to get out of the car. "Aud? Are you all right?"

Tousled, flushed, shoes in hand, she looked about sixteen and well used. Julia picked my hand off her shoulder like a dead bug. "Taken to packing in public for your sweet young thing?"

One in the morning. Two strange women in my driveway with even stranger ideas. I couldn't help it, I laughed. Julia turned and walked with great dignity to her car.

"Julia. Wait. What is it you have to tell—"

But she started the car, shot me a contemptuous look, and drove off with a roar.

I woke at seven but slid back into the warm depths of sleep before I could make myself move, and then I was drifting through a slow swell of dream images: bullets bursting through flesh, skin opening like heavy silk under a cold razor, a child begging for me to help as her sister went up in flames. I finally heaved myself out of it and woke to a bedroom shimmering with morning, light and luscious as meringue. Sunlight turned the red rug into a patch of raspberry and the old oak dresser to Viking gold.

I got up, automatically began to make the bed. I straightened the ivory linen top sheet, then pulled the quilt up, folded the sheet down, tugged it taut. The quilt had been hand-pieced in the Netherlands sixty years ago and the colours were still as rich and mysterious as a nineteenth century oil painting. I smoothed it, remembering finding it, putting it on the bed for the first time. No one but me had ever seen it. No lover, no friend, no family.

I had breakfast on the deck. Everything was very distinct. Sunshine turned the deck rail into a long, continuous stick of butter. Cardinals appeared in the oak tree, bright and round. My grapefruit juice smelled like another country.

With food before me and sunshine on my skin, the dreams and strange mood faded, as they always did.

I threw a piece of bread down onto the grass. Two shrews came across it at the same time and fought, squeaking and shrilling and single-minded, like two crackheads quarrelling over a dime bag. I threw another piece. The noise stopped.

I wondered what Honeycutt was doing this morning, what he was planning to do about his money problems. He was a deeply stupid man. If you wash money for the Tijuana drug cartel and one of your pipelines is buying and selling art, you don't draw anyone's attention by faking that art. He was risking everything by splitting the pipeline in two: real art smuggling, clean money proceeds to the cartel; fake art smuggling, proceeds to his own account. But as far as I knew he lived more or less within his means, did not take drugs, did not gamble, so where was it all going? Some would be funnelled off into a secondary account in the Seychelles, but no one played both ends against the middle unless they were desperate. So what would make a man like Honeycutt desperate?

But that information was not necessary. I knew who had ordered Lusk's death, and that the Friedrich had indeed been faked after Sweeting had sold it to Honeycutt. I even knew who had provided the fake. That was all I needed because I was working for Julia, and that was all she wanted to know.

There was no proof, but Julia had not asked for the kind of evidence you could take to court. I would turn over what I had to Denneny and let him deal with it. It would be up to him to decide whether or not he tried to get admissible evidence, or just let Lusk's death go as a drug-related homicide. But there was still the question of all that cocaine.

It was almost ten o'clock. I stood and stretched, imagining the look on Julia's face when I told her she hadn't made an error of judgement over the Friedrich. Instead, all I saw was her contempt last night.

The phone rang. I picked it up. "Julia?"

"No. This is Beatriz."

Peter had invited her out for lunch and she didn't want me along and was that all right? I listened to her chatter and watched a bee humming around the forsythia bush just below me. Much more interesting than any phone conversation. "Beatriz, just call Philippe. If it's fine with him, it's fine with me."

"Are you sure?"

"Yes." The bee was gone now.

"I . . . Did I wake you up?"

"No."

"And you will drive me to my appointment tomorrow?"

"Yes." I made an effort. "I'll be there at eight-fifteen tomorrow to pick you up. Enjoy your lunch."

"And you don't mind that I won't be there to help with the flowers?"

I told her I didn't mind. Eventually she went away. When I dialed Julia's number, it rang and rang and rang. She had even turned her machine off.

To many Americans, dirt exists only to be eroded with four-wheel drive or mountain bike. The great outdoors with its fragile systems was created for the convenience of fools who tear into the heart of a wilderness area to gawk at the grizzlies, get indignant if one gets too close, and roar off in a cloud of noxious exhaust, trailing Rush Limbaugh at ninety decibels and leaving behind their sewage.

If only they looked, they would see a world in their own back garden.

Gardening, the English vice. Kneeling on the grass, I could see a microcosm in a yard of dirt. Ants, ranging from lone black soldier ants with mandibles the size of my little fingernail, to the pale streams of fire ants like tiny amber necklaces.

A glistening pink roll and wriggle of earthworm; beetles like apple seeds. Ladybugs—which the English call ladybirds—sitting like spatters of wet enamel on the underside of leaves. Black wasps with their menacing dangle of legs. A daddy longlegs trundling like some strange Mars Rover over granular soil flecked with specks of mica, then waving front legs at a pecan shell turning soft as rotting cardboard.

Sometimes I used my fingers, digging down into the rich dirt, feeling it push under my nails. No doubt I'd regret it later, but it was good to feel so much life under my hands. I dug, tapped an impatiens or marigold free of its PVC pot, dropped it in the hole, brushed dirt back around the pale green stem, pressed firmly until the young plant stood on its own. I wondered if there was a group anywhere in the state that planted trees in deforested areas. I could volunteer for that as soon as Beatriz was on her plane and I'd prepared a report for Julia.

I straightened, took a look. Bright, welcoming colour filled about half the beds. The back garden now looked a place for people as well as wildlife. I wondered if Julia liked flowers.

It took a while to clean up enough to eat lunch. I tried Julia again. Ring, ring, ring. I went back to the garden.

Evening. I called Julia. Ring ring ring. What had she found out that she wanted to tell me on Saturday night?

I tried to settle to a book by some philosopher called Roszak who declared ecology and psychology were the same thing. According to his bio he wrote fiction; god knows what it was like.

I had no way of knowing if leaving the answering machine off was one of Julia's normal habits. Maybe she had found something out and done something stupid.

Her house was in Virginia Highlands, a brick tudor with roses outside. She liked some flowers, then. I parked down the street. There were lights on, one upstairs, one down. Her car was in the drive, and I could hear music. Light jazz. I watched for a while. Eventually the light upstairs went out and another came on in what might be the dining room. I saw the swing of shadow hair against the blinds.

I drove away.

I was running around the corner in Inman Park, only this time she didn't take the corner wide, we didn't bump into each other, she went on to the house and had her flesh blown off her bones when it went up, nothing left but a standing skeleton surrounded by chunks of what looked like raw pork.

I got stuck in morning traffic a mile from the Nikko. I tried Julia's home number. Ring ring ring. I called information, got her office number. Her voice told me to leave a message for Lyon Art.

"Julia? Aud. This morning I'll be with my client, whom you met Saturday night. I drop her at the airport at midday but will be free after that. I have the information you want. Call me at home or on my cell phone." I gave her the number.

Beatriz was full of beans when I picked her up. She chattered at me all the way back to the city, and walked into Perrin & Norrander full of confidence. Afterwards, she smiled all the way to the airport.

I parked in a no parking zone and helped her carry her bags to the first-class check-in. "I think they'll offer me the job," she said suddenly as the clerk stamped various things and put tags on her luggage.

"Congratulations."

She looked down at her shoes, suddenly shy. "It means I'll be back in a month or so. Will you . . . I mean, you're probably busy . . . but . . ."

"Someone will have to advise me about what flowers to

plant." She gave me a tentative smile, and I found I was smiling back. "Call when you've booked your flight."

"Thank you," she said. "I think you are a very kind woman."

I zipped east on I-20. Honeycutt may have given the order, but he was not the one who actually lit the match that was supposed to have burned Julia Lyons-Bennet to a carbon carcass. All of a sudden I wanted that name; a little tidbit for Denneny. Perhaps it was time to have a little chat with Michael Honeycutt.

I was following the hairpin bend of the Moreland exit by the time I got through to his secretary. "I'm Katy Willis, personal assistant to Charles Sweeting," I told him in a brisk, impersonal voice. "Mr. Sweeting would like an appointment to see Mr. Honeycutt at his earliest convenience."

"Mr. Honeycutt left very early this morning for a six-day trip to the Seychelles. If it's urgent, perhaps I could help?"

"No, I believe it's a personal matter. Perhaps we could go ahead and schedule an hour for, say, next Tuesday?"

"I could manage to squeeze him in for forty minutes on Wednesday at ten."

"Thank you." At five minutes past ten next Wednesday morning Michael Honeycutt would go grey under his Indian Ocean tan. By the time I was finished with him, he would want to cancel the rest of his appointments that week, but I would have that name.

When I got home I spent half an hour watering the flowers. The cheerful pinks and yellows and violet in the two front troughs reminded me of something: the window boxes lining the smart Mayfair mews where my mother had lived the last two years. She had never seen my house.

When making a rocking chair it is extremely important for the runners to curve in exact symmetry. I hummed as I checked one against the other; shaved; sanded. Perhaps when it was done, I would ship the chair to my mother. Perhaps I would go visit her for a week this summer.

Birds sang their evening chorus. The harsh screeching of a blue jay drowned them out for a while, then I heard again the trill of a cardinal, liquid as the sunset spreading like cranberry juice along the cloud line between the trees.

When I had the runners shaped to my satisfaction, I started on the armrests. I wanted them wide and comfortable, but not so wide that they overwhelmed the balance of the piece. I went over to the far wall, ran my fingers over a few pieces of pine, thinking. Eventually I selected one, brought it back to the table vise.

The doorbell chimed. I leaned the wood against the table, knocked my boots against the table leg so I wouldn't trample sawdust through the house, and went to answer it. It was Julia, lips like sunset, hair like evening shadow.

"Will you let me in?"

I stood aside and gestured her in.

"This place is so quiet." She looked around, down at the silk Persian rug, then up. "My god. This is beautiful."

I had removed the ceiling last year and replaced the inadequate two-by-four rafters with antique oak four-by-sixes I had rescued from an old Ponce de Leon mansion and carved myself. A fan turned lazily overhead. "Thank you. Can I get you something? Iced tea? Beer?"

I got us both a beer. She was still standing in the dining room, craning upwards.

I handed her the beer. "The height makes it very practical in hot weather."

She nodded absently, then recalled her manners. "I'm sorry. It's just . . ." She took a sip of the beer, then looked at the bottle. "What is this?"

"Lindeboom. It's a Dutch lager. Would you like to sit?"

She surprised me by ignoring the couches and folding herself down onto the rug, the way I would if I were alone. "Was she really your client?"

"Her name is Beatriz. The Spanish consulate hired me to protect her while she was in Atlanta for a four-day visit. She needed a babysitter more than a bodyguard, but she was useful as cover. I went to Honeycutt's party as her utterly anonymous escort."

"You're six feet tall and were wearing a dress no bigger than a napkin. How were you anonymous?"

"By acting exactly the way each individual I encountered expected me to act, and by lying."

She looked at me curiously, at my boots and cut-offs stained with glue and varnish. "Don't you ever get . . . lost, pretending to be so many people?"

I shrugged. "It's just like being an actor."

"No. No, it's not. Actors follow other people's scripts. You follow your own."

Verbal chi sao. "Call it improvisation, then."

A beat of silence. "Do you know many actors?"

"None. Some performers."

"Like Cutter?"

"There's no one like Cutter."

She grinned. "You said that before." Then she stretched and seemed to relax. "And your . . . Beatriz has gone back to wherever she came from?"

"For a month or so. She met a harmless law intern called Peter at the party and is probably somewhere over the Atlantic even as we speak, dreaming of having his babies. So what was it you were so hot to tell me Saturday night that you drove out here at midnight?"

"The Friedrich provenance is impeccable. There's a fifteen-year gap not long after it was created, but I talked to a man who is considered to be the foremost Friedrich scholar—you wouldn't believe my long-distance phone bills—who examined the painting thirty years ago and would stake his reputation

on its genuineness. Apart from that, the provenance was perfect. And I found out from a dealer that there was a rumour
last year that Honeycutt was trafficking in fake art. Something
to do with an Anglo-Saxon armring. After a lot of discreet
calls, I've discovered there are now two armrings in private
collections—one in Argentina, one in Italy—that look exactly
the same. I got the owners to fax me pictures late Saturday.
So it was Honeycutt, the bastard."

She took a long, fierce swallow of her beer. Her throat
moved once, twice, three times.

"When I thought about those phone calls I made, assuring
him there was nothing to worry about, not really, that we were
having just a little teeny problem, I got furious. He knew all
the time. The asshole knew all the time! But what I want to
know is, how does he expect to get away with it? Does he
think we're all fools, that we'll lie down and take it?"

Her beer was gone. I held out my hand for the empty. She
followed me into the kitchen and looked around at the cherry
cabinetry, the white counters, pine floor.

"This is nice, too."

I popped the top off another Lindeboom and handed it to
her, reached into the fridge for mine.

"So, anyway, I called him. I told him—"

I paused, hand still in the fridge. "When did you call him?"

"This morning. I told his machine—"

"What time this morning?"

"What does it matter? I said . . . You look very odd."

My hand was getting cold inside the fridge. I took it out,
closed the door. "Tell me exactly what time you called."

"Before breakfast. About eight."

. . . *left very early this morning for a six-day trip* . . . What
did that mean? Five? "Tell me what you said in your message. Exactly."

"Oh, I was careful. I told him that I didn't want his business anymore, and that I was sure he knew why, that I hoped

he would avoid unpleasantness and never try to contact me again or use my name in a business context. I'm sure he got the message."

"Nothing else?"

"I told you, I was careful. I said nothing actionable."

I ignored that. "You called his home number?"

"Yes."

"Was it fuzzy, like a tape, or clear, like digital voice mail?"

"A tape, I think. What's wrong?"

"Honeycutt is the one who ordered Lusk's death." She blinked and held her beer with two hands. "He ordered yours, too. You were supposed to go up along with the painting." She started twisting the bottle. "Honeycutt left for the Seychelles this morning. With any luck, he left before you called and hasn't heard the message."

"Honeycutt was . . . Honeycutt tried to kill me?"

"Yes. I want you to call the airport and find out what flight he was on."

Her blink rate went up, and her skin colour greyed to pearl.

"Julia, it's very important that you call the airport and find out what flight he was on."

"What are you going to do?"

"I'm going to change."

As I stripped and changed, I heard her voice rise and fall and finally harden as she jousted with the airlines. When I emerged, her colour was back.

"The most likely flight was through Lisbon. It left at eight-fifty. He would have had to check in two hours before departure." She looked at my charcoal silks and black Kenneth Cole shoes. "I don't understand."

"When I break into Honeycutt's house, I don't intend to be seen. If I am, I don't want to be remembered. The best way to be invisible, unmemorable, is to blend in."

"Do my clothes pass muster?"

"You're staying here."

"No. He tried to kill me. I have to do something about that. It's me he'll be after if he gets that tape." She flushed, as though suddenly self-conscious. "I know it'll be dangerous, but I'm a grown-up. I know what I'm getting into. I can handle myself."

She stood there with her hair in a chubby braid, makeup so perfect you could hardly tell she wore it, smelling faintly of European beer. What did someone like Julia Lyons-Bennet know about danger? She knew martial arts as an art and self-defence as theory. Hers was a world of board rooms and galleries, auction houses and banks. She had lived her whole life in civilized enclaves and believed the universe to be an essentially civilized place. Danger to her was just another game that her smarts and good looks and privilege would see her through safely, but danger is not a game. Danger is a casually violent Viking. It doesn't care about motivation or intention or explanations. When it sits opposite and offers you the cup and dice, you either walk away or play full throttle. Danger, with its well-used axe and huge ham hands, is out to take you for all you're worth. Luck can work for or against you, but danger loads the dice, it cheats, and when it does you have to pin its hand to the boards with a knife, no hesitation. She wasn't ruthless enough, she didn't understand enough.

"He tried to kill me," she said again.

She was a grown-up. She wanted this. "Come, then. But don't get in my way. Meanwhile, in my office, through there, there's a pine cabinet. Key is in the kitchen, hanging below the clock. In the cabinet there's a satchel. Bring it, please."

How big was that battery? Small enough to have drained in just twenty-four hours? Honeycutt's house was laid out cleanly enough. I knew where the den was, I knew where the breakers were. Most people put their alarm boxes somewhere easily accessible. Kitchen, probably, or hallway. There should be time.

I went into the office. Julia was holding the thigh harness and holster. She blushed bright red when she saw me. I put a tape in the answering machine, then switched on the fax machine and dialed.

"That's your number."

"Yes. Did you find the satchel?"

She lifted it. I nodded. The phone rang, the machine took it, the fax whined and shrilled and beeped. I dialed again, and again, until I had nearly five minutes' worth of electronic noncommunication on tape. I slipped the tape and a Sony Walkman into the satchel.

"We should go now. Eight in the evening is the best time for breaking and entering." Our break-in would have to be traceless if Honeycutt's suspicions were not to be aroused.

I carried the satchel out to the Saab. We took Highway 280 instead of the interstate.

"Take your jewellery off and put it in the glove compartment. You don't want to lose an earring at Honeycutt's and have to go back." She complied silently.

The road surface was just-laid blacktop and we'd left streetlights behind a mile or two back. The drive was smooth; the night rushed by like water. Everything was black and white. We could have been exploring the bottom of the sea. Julia seemed to have withdrawn into herself.

"Why are you doing this?" I asked after a while.

"Jim was my friend."

"There's more to it than that. More than his death on your conscience. Most people would mourn and leave it at that. Look at your life. You have money—not as much as you grew up with, I suspect, but you're more than comfortable. You're an art dealer, a corporate art dealer. You don't even deal with the artists direct, just galleries and auction houses and agents. Yet you have studied at least one martial art; at some point you took a self-defence course that you regard seriously enough to make changes in your everyday life; you've obviously studied defensive driving. Why?"

"To be prepared. For violence."

Not nearly the whole truth. "And are you?"

She looked at me then. In the backwash of the headlights, her eyes were sheened like a Persian cat's. "I don't know."

There is never any way to know. It happens so fast. A snap of your fingers and the world is different. Most encounters are decided in five or six seconds and if you freeze, you can die. I wasn't sure there was a way to explain.

"Have you ever been in a situation?"

"No."

"Have you ever been shocked? I mean had terrible news or seen something awful happen right in front of you?"

"Yes."

There was pain in that answer. "That's how it feels when everything goes wrong. It's as though someone with a knife tried to slice your mind free of your body and everything just automatically starts shutting down. Surprise, shock, whatever you want to call it. The trick to surviving is to believe what your body is telling you, instantly, and then act. Don't stop and think. There simply isn't time. In the first split second, getting moving, reacting, is what counts." She was nodding, and I knew she wanted to understand but I didn't think she did. "Put your hand palm down on my thigh."

To her credit, after a barely perceptible hesitation, she started to lay her hand on my thigh. Without looking at her, without giving her a hint of what I was about to do, I slapped it, hard.

She whipped the hand away, incredulous.

"Your first reaction is to pull away, and glare, but imagine if I really meant it. You can't afford to stop and wonder at it, to try work out *why*, you just have to accept it and take steps to make sure I'm not going to be in any state to do it again." She sucked at the back of her hand. Her breasts were rising and falling, faster and faster. Now she was angry. Adrenalin. "That slap hurt but it won't leave a bruise. If I'd given you a black eye that *would* have hurt, but no permanent damage. A two-by-four across the ribs might crack a few but you would still be able to run or hit someone. Do you understand what I'm trying to tell you? Pain is just pain. It's a message. You don't have to listen. Sometimes you can't afford to listen."

"The Nike school of martial arts. Just Do It." Her face was perfectly smooth, unreadable, but then she huffed down her nose, half amusement, half cynicism. "Nike was the winged goddess of victory. How appropriate."

"We hope."

"Are you expecting trouble?"

"Not particularly."

We were driving through Smyrna now. I pulled into the parking lot of a strip mall. "Time to apply some camouflage."

We walked to a party store, where I bought two bunches of Mylar balloons, then to a wine shop. "What champagne do you like?"

"Why ask me?"

"I could buy something cheap and throw it away, or get something nice and you could drink it afterwards. It's a legitimate expense, so you'll end up paying, whichever way."

She chose a Mumm's brut. I paid and we bobbed with the bottle and balloons along to a pharmacy. I asked the pharmacist for latex gloves. He gave me, the bottle and Julia a knowing look. Julia blushed very, very slightly, and lifted her chin. She moved like a cheetah as we left.

We put the balloons in the backseat and draped my jacket over them so they wouldn't float about.

"In a perfect world, how would you hit that pharmacist?"

"Jern," she said without hesitation. Palm strike. "Right to the nose."

I like a woman who knows her own mind.

We left the lights of Smyrna behind and once again were whipping through the dark, the Saab following the white line like a tracking dog. The night was alive with scents: jet fuel from Dobbins Air Force Base just over the rise, fading heat of blacktop, the musk of Julia's hair. There was a sharp, smoky undertone to her scent now; adrenalin was pumping and she was beginning to tense up. My muscles were loose and warm and my heartbeat steady and strong.

"Almost there. Get some gloves on."

She shook out the gloves and her breathing quickened as the faint aromas of talc and latex filled the car. The sense of smell is the most primitive of all, wired directly into the crocodile brain that knows only the basic urges of sex and survival. It conditions very quickly.

I steered with one hand, punched Honeycutt's home number into my phone with the other. It rang until the machine picked up. I hung up. No one home, or at least no one was answering the phone. And then we were there, pulling into the driveway, crunching over the gravel. It looked smaller without all the people milling about on the lawn and dim light showing only from the kitchen and one upstairs room. I turned off the car, snapped on gloves, turned to Julia.

"Look happy, in case there are observers."

She carried one bunch of balloons and the champagne. I had the other bunch in one hand, satchel over my shoulder. I looked around, up at the windows, at the door, as if trying to work out if this was the right address for the party. No neighbours' lights were flicking on.

The entryway had two steps and was lit with soft yellow, two locks, both at waist height. He had made it very easy.

"Keep close." The lock gun's rubber-sheathed handle was slippery against the latex gloves. I had to steady it against my ribs. Using Julia's body as a shield, I shoved the prongs into the first lock.

"Pretend to ring the bell." The lock clunked, I moved to the second. "Pretend again." Julia obliged. The second lock thunked back. "When I open the door, follow me in, and smile, just in case. I'll disable the alarm. You push the door to, and stay just inside. Be very, very quiet."

I looked at my watch, pushed the door open silently, and stepped inside. The air was cool; he hadn't even turned the air-conditioning down. I listened for five seconds. Apart from the preliminary warning *beep-beep-beep* of the alarm, there was nothing except the distant hum of air-conditioning and faint burble of the aquarium. In the light of the entryway, the fish glided ghostly and golden. I put my finger to my lips and pointed at the floor. Julia nodded. I trod softly to the wall by the kitchen where the alarm box sat at chin height. Ten seconds down, twenty to go. I pulled out two lengths of black-jacketed wire, one with crocodile clips, the other with soft-tack connectors. I popped the lid off the box, took one look, clipped on one wire, cut another. The beeping stopped. I looked at my watch. Seventeen seconds. I ran up the beautifully carpeted, silent steps to the guest bedroom, opened the closet door, and opened two breakers. The air-conditioning stopped. If I had done this wrong, I only had eight seconds to find out and cut the phone lines.

From the top of the stairs I saw a faint, very faint light from the aquarium. No noise of bubbles. I relaxed. The battery was almost drained, which meant the alarm system wasn't getting any power at all. Terrible security.

I padded downstairs, put the screwdriver, wire clippers and extra wire back in the satchel, hung the box cover back on, but loosely, and beckoned to Julia.

The kitchen was clean and empty and shadowy beyond the single dim lamp. A Sony answerphone blinked greenly from a countertop. I flipped up the lid, popped out the tape, and handed it to Julia. She opened her mouth. I put my finger to my lips, then took out the Walkman, and gestured for her to use it to listen to the tape. She nodded. I pointed to myself and the doorway, to her and the floor. She nodded again.

A quick check around the ground floor behind wall hangings, in desk drawers turned up no safe, no cache of interesting papers. I hadn't expected it to, but it was always best to be certain.

Back in the kitchen, Julia was tugging the earphones out and giving me the thumbs-up. I put one plug in my ear, played the tape back. Some man talking about the lawn; another leaving a message to call Harry; then Julia; then his sister. I wound it back to the very last phrase from Harry, then played it again, timing Julia's message. I rewound back to Harry and stopped it. I pulled my tape, connector, and a piece of paper from the satchel, scribbled, *Record my tape onto his for exactly two minutes and twenty seconds. Listen to check. Wind tape to end of current messages, put back in machine.* She had to hold the note up to the light coming through the windows to read it properly. She nodded. I pointed at myself then at the stairs and before I'd finished she rolled her eyes, pointed at herself then at the floor. My turn to nod.

I ran up lightly, listened at the foot of the second flight. Nothing. What I wanted was the inner sanctum, the room where Honeycutt and his cronies had gathered Saturday night. It had to be up there.

The third floor was very dark. A short hallway and four doors. I opened the first. Cold, hard floor, scents of soap and toilet cleaner: bathroom. The second led to a dark space with the empty feel and dead air of a guest room. The next was a storage closet. Then scents of leather, very faint expensive perfume; thick carpet underfoot; utterly dark. I stepped inside, pulled the door to behind me, and *Move!* shouted my crocodile brain, just as my skin registered the warmth of a body standing to one side, the light swirl of air that was another stepping towards me.

It unfolded like a stop-motion film of a blooming rose: bright, beautiful and blindingly fast. And I wanted to laugh as I ducked and lunged; wanted to sing as I sank my fist wrist deep in an abdomen, whipped an elbow up, up, through a fragile jawbone, slid to the side of a thrusting arm and took it, turning it, levering it, letting the body follow in an ungraceful arc. My heart was a tireless pump, arteries and airways wide. I was unstoppable, lost in the joy of muscle and bone and breath. Axe kick to the central line of the huddled mass on the floor; disappointment at the sad splintering of ribs and not the hard crack of spine. Mewl and haul of body trying to sit; step and slam, hammer fist smearing the bone of his cheek. Latex slipping on sweat. Body under my hands folding to the floor, not moving. Nothing moving but me, feeling vast and brilliant with strength, immeasurable and immortal.

A bellow from downstairs and the world snapped and re-formed and I was running, running, taking the steps three at a time, four, and a woman was standing in the hall, bathed in the yellow entry light because the door was wide open. Her head was back and her eyes huge. A woman. Julia.

"I hit someone."

"Yes." I stopped four feet away.

She shook her hand at her side, lifted it, looked at it. "I hit him. He came down the stairs and I hit him. I really hit him. I've spent years wondering if I could, wondering what I'd do if it happened to me, if I'd been the one in front of that theatre. . . ." She looked at her hand again, fascinated. "I hit him, and he ran away."

The realization of what she had done, the exhilaration of her own strength rushed into her, like champagne rushing to fill lead crystal. She shimmered with it, she fizzed. I wanted to lift her in both hands, drink her down, drain her, feel the foam inside me, curling around heart, lungs, stomach.

I stepped closer. She lifted her chin. Closer still.

"Wolf eyes," she whispered, and I could feel her breath on my throat, "so pale and hungry."

A car roared into life behind the house and headlights sliced through the window and doorway, then away and towards the road. She turned slowly, blinking in their light, their undeniably real light, and the exaltation faded. My left wrist ached slightly and breath was harsh in my throat. Just under the ribs on my left side, my shirt was cut and wet.

"The tape?"

She shook her head.

"Finish it."

I ran back up the steps. The den door was open. I closed the curtains and found the light switch: thick green carpet; two men, both in dark clothes, one still holding his stained knife; a desk, under which lay the other knife and on top of which sat a computer, screen blank and dead. A drawer hung broken and empty from the middle. I knelt, felt for a pulse in the first body, found it. The second one was breathing audibly so I didn't bother. I checked them over. Gloves, clothes with brand labels cut out. In one jacket pocket a small sheaf of papers covered in strange-shaped letters. I tucked them inside my own jacket to examine later. No scars or other identifying marks. Both knives were broad-bladed, serrated on the upper edge, black composite handle: standard manufacture, available in any catalogue. I wiped the thin thread of my blood from the blade still in one man's hand.

Something bleeped, and bleeped again. The computer. A red light on the minitower flickered. I felt around for the screen switch and pushed. The cursor blinked by the c: prompt and the cheery message *Reformatting complete*. Hoping it didn't mean what I thought it meant, I tapped in *dir /p*. Nothing. All gone, wiped in the hard drive reformat. No sign of any diskettes.

I searched the rest of the room quickly but methodically. No safe. Filing cabinets full of personal papers, each hanging file carefully labelled in blue ink, presumably by Honeycutt. Two hanging files labelled BANK and INVESTMENTS were empty. Honeycutt's doing, or the man who got away? I pulled off the first one's gloves, dabbed his hand on the arm of a chair upholstered in leather, put the glove back on. Took off the gloves of the second man, pressed his hands, one at a time, against the broken drawer.

The door creaked. I whirled. Julia, swaying. "Are they . . . ?"

"No."

She watched in silence as I put his gloves back on. "The tape's clean."

"Back in the machine?"

"Yes."

I finished and stood. "Get the Walkman, the balloons and champagne, and wait by the door." She straightened. Her march down the hall was wooden but not wobbly. She'd make it.

I turned the light off and stood at the top of the steps. When she was by the door, balloons bobbing, I went back into the spare room and reconnected the battery to the alarm, checked my watch, then closed the breakers and ran downstairs. Six seconds. I stripped the wires from the alarm box, clipped the cover back on, accepted the Walkman from Julia and put everything back in the satchel. Nineteen seconds. "Out," I said. She stood there, balloons bobbing, as I closed the door behind us and relocked it. Twenty-seven seconds. Free and clear, with no sign of our passage but the two unconscious men in the third-floor study.

She was shaking by the time we got to the car. I opened her door, gave her the balloons. "Hold on to those." I pulled my jacket from the backseat and settled it over her shoulders.

I drove for about five miles. She was still shaking, though not as badly. One eye on the road, I handed her the satchel. "Use something in here to burst the balloons." She looked at me as though I were crazy. "It will be easier to dispose of them." And it would give her something to do. "There's a brown paper grocery bag in there, too. When you're done with the balloons, put them in it."

It took her a while.

"Now your gloves. Carefully."

She complied, peeling the left right down to the fingertips, then using the left to peel down the right, and dumping the whole lot into the bag. She flexed her bare hands, studied them. Graceful, clean hands. Made for holding, not hitting. After a while, she said, "How about you?"

"One more thing to do first."

I pulled up at a phone box. Dialed 911. When they asked whether I wanted fire, police, or ambulance, I just said, "4731 Fallgood Road, Marietta," and hung up.

Back in the car, I stripped off my gloves and dropped them in the paper sack. We drove in silence for a while. The wet patch on my shirt was spreading and with it a cold ache.

"Who were they?"

"I don't know."

"It might be important."

"I'm sure it is, to them. Not to you. You have the information you wanted. You know who ordered Lusk killed. You know you didn't make a mistake brokering the painting. Now that we've fixed the phone tape, no one knows you know."

Her face was pale and set. "Can you find out who they were?"

"It's over, Julia. Done."

"Can you?"

She looked small and fragile and alone. I wanted to take her hand, tell her everything would be all right, that no one would ever hurt her again because I would track them all down, tie up the loose ends, make the world safe. But there is no perfect safety. "Jim Lusk is dead. He'll stay dead whatever you do. You are not to blame. The police will take it from here. Let it go."

She looked at me as though from a great distance, then turned away.

She stared out of the window all the way back. When I pulled up outside her house, she thanked me nicely, smiled at me gently and without depth, and said she would be by to pick her car up in the morning. Just as though we had been carpooling from the PTA meeting. Partially shock, partially a need to distance herself from blood, and burglary, and attacks by strange men dressed in dark clothes. I would have gone in with her, made her something hot and sweet to drink, but I belonged to that world she didn't want to think about right now, not in her nice little house in Virginia Highlands with roses climbing up the trellis.

I drove myself and the bottle of Mumm's champagne back to Lake Claire. I put it in the pantry, not the fridge. I had a feeling it would be a long time before I drank it.

The knife wound was not too bad, a shallow four-inch gash across a lower rib. I cleaned it, pulled the edges together with butterfly Band-Aids, covered it with gauze, then started wrapping a crepe bandage round my torso. If it hadn't crusted over by the morning, I'd get it seen to. The emergency room staff would believe the fake name and a story about a mad, jealous husband with a steak knife, and a terrified wife who didn't want to face the truth and call the police. Happened all the time. As usual, the bandage finished in the small of my back, where I couldn't reach to pin it. I had to fold it back and pin it at my right side.

I swallowed some ibuprofen and broad-spectrum antibiotics, then took the papers from Honeycutt's house into my office. They were stained with my blood but in clear halogen light their nature was plain: blackmail notes. They were photocopies of messages made by cutting out words and phrases from magazines, with careful annotations—in the same blue ink, the same handwriting, I'd seen on Honeycutt's files—in the top right hand corner: date, time, and method of arrival. All but one had come by U.S. mail.

The first was from March last year. It was straightforward:

*I know who you work for. I know how much you wash: I want some. I'll call.*

Interesting. No problem saying "I." No problem with gram-
mar: the colon had actually been written in using a black
marker. Obviously not stupid: a photocopy meant no saliva,
no magazine subscriptions to trace.

I assumed whoever it was had called. The next one was
dated May last year:

*Same place, same method, same amount.*

The next dated just a week later:

*Don't ever try that again. The rate just doubled. Every time
you try something, it will double again. I know how much
you can afford.*

What had Honeycutt tried? Whatever it was, the blackmailer
didn't seem too perturbed. They obviously thought of themself
as rational, reasonable, and aimed to keep Honeycutt controlled by simultaneously reassuring him and laying down
simple rules. The next note was two words:

*Thank you.*

I had a sudden flash of a networking cynic. Grip and grin.
Be nice. Say the right thing. . . .

After that, the notes came regularly, every month; identical
copies of the *Same place, same method, same amount* note, followed a week later by the *Thank you.* Until January.

*A new year, a new rate. Fifty percent more, with penalties
for late payment.*

January, just when Honeycutt had shown interest in the
Friedrich. Say two weeks to track down someone to commis-
sion the fake, another few to paint it. . . . But obviously no

outward complaint from Honeycutt; the usual *Thank you* note followed on schedule. More *Same place* notes followed by more *Thank you*s. Until an April date two days after Lusk's death.

> *You are a fool. What would you have done if I hadn't cleaned up for you? No more independent action. I'll call.*

I would love to have listened in on that one. The blackmailer obviously didn't care for Honeycutt's creative solution to the rate hike, and seemed to understand that if the drug cartel found out about Honeycutt's playing both ends against the middle, the source of extorted cash would dry up. You can't blackmail a corpse.

That was the last note. I put them all back in order and read through them again. A smart, cynical blackmailer, apparently in it for the long haul and willing to play by clear rules. Someone who liked rules and order, liked to plan ahead but could act swiftly. *What would you have done if I hadn't cleaned up for you?* But it had been Honeycutt who had ordered the burn, so what had been taken care of?

The ibuprofen wasn't working. My ribs flared every time I moved. I put the notes in the folder labelled LYONS-BENNET, found some codeine in the bathroom, and took myself off to the bedroom of raspberry and Viking gold.

I was up early and waiting for the paper the next morning. I scanned the main section. No mention of anonymous burglars in black found hurt at banker's home. Honeycutt was a prominent citizen. If they'd been found, they would have been reported. They must have dragged themselves away before the police got there. Given how hard I'd hit them, it was more likely the uninjured one had returned with reinforcements and carried them off. The Cobb County police would have noticed the mess upstairs but that wouldn't be big enough news to hit the main section, and my local news section was all Dekalb County, not Cobb. I shrugged, and it hurt. Muscles going from rest to full output in less than a second felt sore the next day no matter how fit or ready you thought you were. I wanted a long soak in the bath but the cut on my ribs was crusting over nicely and I didn't want to get it wet. I lay flat on my back on the living room floor and did Chi Gung breathing until all I could smell was the wool rug, and I ran with sweat, and the tightness eased. Then I called the zone six precinct house.

Just like the man himself, Denneny's voice mail is pleasant, relaxed, and gives away nothing. "This is Brian Denneny, zone six captain. Let me know how I can help you and I or an assistant will get back to you very shortly." It was a masterpiece of misdirection. "Very shortly" could mean anything, and his assistant was never allowed to listen to the messages on pain of excommunication. Denneny made it sound as though he were open to inquiries from all and sundry but in fact his secretary was instructed to give the extension to no one, not even his children. He had given it to his lieutenants, and the police chief, and the mayor. Everyone else went through the chain of command or left messages with the desk sergeant—but it didn't do for one's message to sound unwilling before the great voting public if someone like the mayor called.

"Brian, it's Aud. While you've been sampling the produce of Napa Valley and basking in the gentle breezes, I've been doing your job. Remember that arson and murder case in Inman Park, corpse name of Lusk—the one you've classified as a drug case? It's not. Or at least only partially. It turns out that the torch was from out of town and was brought in by one Michael Honeycutt, a banker with Massut Vere who appears to be washing money for Arellano's successor.

"Here's what I know. Honeycutt has been laundering for a year or more. To my certain knowledge, he's washed more than twelve million in the last few months but I imagine the real total is several times that amount. Some of the dirty money is turned into art: small, precious and smuggleable. Mostly he gets this from public dealers, but recently he went to a private source, which is when things started to go wrong. It turns out that in the last few months our banker has developed a little sideline of his own, faking some of this art, then selling both the original and the fake. Proceeds from the genuine article find their way back to whoever is running Honeycutt, those from the fake go straight to whoever has been blackmailing him for the last year or so. Apparently the blackmail rate went up at the beginning of the year. He probably no longer has enough money to stash in his personal bank account in the Seychelles.

"Honeycutt acquired a fake painting from our old friends Lois and Mitchum Kenworthy. My client suspected fraud and sent the picture to an art appraiser, Lusk. Honeycutt ordered the torching of Lusk's house, Lusk, and the painting. You can add attempted murder to the murder, conspiracy and arson charges: my client was also supposed to die in that fire. However, I doubt she's in much danger at this point. The evidence is gone, and Honeycutt doesn't know she's been interested—and whoever is blackmailing Honeycutt seems to be smarter than he is. I think he'll keep him under control. At least for now. One thing that doesn't fit in all this, though, is the coke found in Lusk's garage"—I wasn't quite sure where the three men who had been at Honeycutt's house last night fit, either—"but luckily finding out is not part of my job description. Nor is it in my job description to prove any of this, so I'm not going to bother trying. Let's just say I got the information from a reliable source." He would probably figure it out. "And you could always haul in the Kenworthys. Whatever you decide to do, I'm done with this. Once I write up the invoice for my client, I'm taking off for a week or two to plant trees in north Georgia." Or the Carolinas, or anywhere where people had stripped the earth and I could forget myself, forget all this while bending and planting, forking the rich dirt back over roots, making something instead of breaking it. "Send me a case of something good from one of those wineries."

He always did. I always wrote him a cheque.

I got up and went into my office, turned the computer on, and pulled up the template I used for invoices. A warm breeze sneaked through the screened window and ruffled my papers. I typed in the Lyon Art address, *Attn. Julia Lyons-Bennet*. Denneny would not be pleased at my news, he liked things clean and clear and simple, but he was a good cop and, besides, he might see some political hay to be made by the connection of a prominent banker with the drug trade. Once he got started, he would be thorough. Let Denneny find out who had left the coke in Lusk's garage, and why; let Denneny work out who was blackmailing Honeycutt. Maybe he'd give the blackmailer a medal. Julia had the information she wanted; my job was done.

I added up dates, times and expenses, and started transferring totals to the form.

A receipt fluttered out of reach. When I reached for it the scab over my ribs stretched and cracked. I pressed the gauze tight with my right hand until the warm trickle stopped. Who carried knives these days? Someone who had reason to be quiet. Someone who had been ordered to be quiet by a man or woman who had a lot to lose. The blackmailer. Find the man with the knife and he would lead you to someone else. Someone interesting. But Denneny didn't know about the men in black who had tried to slip a knife between my ribs and I couldn't tell him anyone had even tried. That evidence was not only inadmissible, it was illegal, and he had given me a hard time about breaking rules in the past.

Who or wherever the men were now, they would be needing a doctor. I could tell Denneny to canvas the accident and emergency rooms of five counties to find two men brought in on the same night: one with displaced ribs, shattered cheekbone, and—depending on how much my fist had slipped on his sweat—compressed cervical vertebrae; one with a broken jaw, dislocated shoulder and probably concussion. But it was a lot of work, and Denneny wouldn't start for a few days, and, meanwhile, whoever had sent them probably had a good description of Julia from the man she had hit.

What could that third man say? White, five-foot-seven, a hundred and twenty-five pounds, blue eyes, long dark hair, a pale imitation of the real Julia standing there, head thrown back, glorious in her triumph. It might be a generic description, but if they worked for Honeycutt it would be enough. But why would Honeycutt employ people to sneak around his own house? It had to be the blackmailer. And one of them had seen, had most definitely seen Julia's face.

I saved the file for later and went back into the living room for the phone.

"Eddie? Did any of your reporters hear about a break-in at the Cobb County home of Michael Honeycutt, Fallgood Road, last night? Good. Give me the details."

There was little enough: police, in response to an anonymous call, had proceeded to the Marietta home of banker Michael Honeycutt only to find that the burglars had left some time before. Officers were reported as being puzzled at traces of blood found in an upstairs room. Honeycutt could not be reached for comment; he was believed to be out of the country. Convenient, but it meant nothing one way or the other.

I promised Eddie we would have that dinner very soon, then hung up and dialed again.

"Benny? I need the crime scene report on a disturbance last night at the Marietta home of Michael Honeycutt, banker. The address was Fallgood Road. Yes, yes, I know it would have been Cobb County but didn't you once say computers were born to talk to each other?" His response was definite and inflammatory. "Well, I'm sure you and NCIC between you know how to persuade them. And when you do, look for any reference to fingerprints and blood typing. . . . Yes, yes, I know Cobb County has to input the information before you can access it. I'll wait. . . . Well, how about a full pass to the Atlanta Film Festival next month?"

Eventually he agreed. He always does.

When I got up to the fourteenth floor, the Lyon Art office smelled just as strongly of coffee, the air was bright with noise, but this time Annie Miclasz knew my name.

"Aud!" Her look of surprise was swiftly hooded. She nodded back towards Julia's office. "She didn't tell me you were coming."

"No," I agreed.

She studied me, then made up her mind. "You'll want it with cream again, no doubt." She beckoned me to join her as she poured and added and stirred.

"How is her schedule?"

That hooded look again. She carried my coffee to her computer. I followed. She pulled up a screen of calendars and deleted all but *Annie* and *Julia*. She studied the mosaic, then with a few keystrokes she moved several chunks around, one from *Julia* to *Annie*, and one to tomorrow. "It looks pretty uncrowded for the next hour or so."

I smiled at her. "Isn't that lucky?"

Her voice was round with approval. "I imagine you remember the way. She'll probably want some coffee, too."

I carried both mugs in one hand to Julia's door, knocked, and went in.

She was at her desk, brilliant with the sunshine streaming through the big picture window, staring out at the Atlanta skyline. In quarter profile I could just see the tip of her right ear and the glint of gold at the lobe. A lavender shirt collar softened the grey silk suit. Her head was very still.

"I've brought coffee."

She swung around. "I thought you were Mrs. Miclasz."

There seemed no point responding to that so I just put her mug on the desk. "No sugar, no cream. Annie doesn't approve."

"No." She ignored the mug.

"I brought you an invoice."

"You could have left it with Annie."

"The thing is, I don't think we're done. There are a few more things to be said. To be considered."

"I have a lot to do this afternoon."

"I took the liberty of checking with Annie. I believe you'll have time to talk for a few minutes."

She picked up the phone. "Mrs. Miclasz? What do I have on my plate this afternoon? I see. Thank you."

I sat down in the sofa near the window and assumed an unthreatening pose, legs crossed at the knee, hands folded in my lap. She watched me, like a bird with a broken wing backed into a corner.

"I'd like to talk to you."

"So talk."

"I'd rather know you were listening. Perhaps you'd like to tell me what is disturbing you."

"You. This is my office." She seemed to realize that did not make much sense. "You walk in here, cool as glass, you conspire with my staff to rearrange my schedule. . . . This is *my* office."

"When did it happen, Julia? Who was in front of that theatre?"

She looked at me as though she hated me.

"You've spent the last few years preparing yourself for this. It happened. You responded. You did the right thing, only now you're not sure." She said nothing. "Maybe you should have let him hit you after all, then run back upstairs and help his friends to finish me off."

"He was running, trying to get past me. I should have let him."

"He might have killed you—"

"You don't *know* that!"

"—his friends were certainly trying to kill me. One of them had a knife. Very sharp, very businesslike."

She shook her head stubbornly. I sighed, put down my coffee, and unbuttoned the bottom of my shirt. She stared at the bandage.

"It's a knife wound." I unfastened the safety pin.

"Don't." Her face was dirty white. "I don't . . ."

"No. I want you to see. I want you to see what might have happened to you if you hadn't hit that man."

She watched, mute, as I unrolled the bandage. When I peeled back the gauze, she stood, took a half step, then slumped like a melting column of ice cream onto her knees. Her eyes were black, but whatever she was seeing, it wasn't me.

"It's about four inches long. If I hadn't moved, it would have slipped right into my stomach. You can bet they wouldn't have called an ambulance. I would have died, Julia. If you hadn't been there, ready to hit that man, he might have come back upstairs before I could disable the other two."

"My brother," she said. "My brother, Guy. I was nineteen. He was knifed to death in front of a Cambridge theatre. In the middle of the day." She stretched out her hand.

"No. Don't touch it." I started to cover it up again.

"Please. I have to see." She crept closer on her knees, like a child; so close I could feel the heat of her breath on the cut. "It's so thin."

"It was a very sharp knife."

"Guy was stabbed eleven times. My mother wouldn't let me see his body. His face was all cut up. There were no cuts on his arms or hands, and it was only later that I realized what that meant, that he hadn't even tried to defend himself, and I promised I would never, ever let someone do that to me. Never just stand there and let them hurt me. But I never knew what it was really like. . . ." She settled her weight back on her calves and looked at her hand, open on her thigh. "I can still feel the shape of his face on my palm. I think I might have broken his nose. And I liked the fact that I had hit him. I knew I wouldn't have died without fighting if I had been in front of that theatre. I really knew. And I spent all night wondering—why people do this in the first place, why Guy didn't fight, what makes me capable of violence and not him. Part of me wants to feel like a bad person because I *could*."

"Was your brother a saint?"

She blinked. "Guy? Not even close. What's that got to do with anything?"

I laid the gauze back over the wound and starting winding the bandage back around my waist.

"Tell me what you— Please, let me do that." She wrapped me gently, started to pin the bandage neatly at the back.

"I won't be able to reach that."

She repinned it. "You should get it stitched."

"It's already healing."

She accepted that with a nod, then kept nodding. Eventually she said, "I understand, I think."

And I think she did. Being capable of using violence to defend yourself did not make you a bad person. Being dead because you couldn't did not make you a good one. I buttoned up my shirt and she waited for me to lean back and get comfortable, handed me my coffee, then trundled her desk chair over to the sofa. "You said it wasn't finished."

"I think you may still be in danger."

"That's not what you said last night."

"No. Think. Did you get a good look at the face of the man you hit?"

"Yes. Ah. He probably got a good look at me, too. If they find out I've been pursuing this . . ."

"They'll want to know what information you have. They might be frightened. Honeycutt tried something very stupid last time he was scared. Who knows what he'll try this time?"

"We should go to the police."

"That's in hand, but given that the police think they already have an explanation for Lusk's death—"

"Jim. He was my friend. Call him Jim."

"Jim," I acknowledged. "Given the fact that they think it was a drug-related murder, they're not going to be eager to dig. The only one I trust to get things going is out of town at the moment. As soon as he returns, you can relax. Until then, you might like to think about going away somewhere. The farther the better. Do you have any jobs abroad waiting?"

"Yes." Her pupils dilated briefly; a strong reaction to a job. "There's a foreign glass-making corporation that wants me to set up a sculpture garden for them. I could call them. I'm sure they'd be delighted if I arrived tomorrow. I'd be gone a week or two. Could you get everything sorted in that time?"

Sorted out, tidied up, ended.

A hundred feet below, a siren wailed. People streamed endlessly back and forth in their gerbil tubes. Empty city.

"Aud?"

"Yes, I could get everything sorted."

She leaned forward, coffee balanced on her knees, and studied me as though I were a hieroglyph. "Why do you do this?"

"It's a job."

"You don't need the money."

"No."

"So why?"

"I'm Norwegian." I didn't care if she understood or not.

"Are you?" she mused. I had no idea what she meant by that. If she'd read my file, she knew about my mother. She sipped her coffee thoughtfully. "Do you miss it, being a police officer?"

I had no idea where she was going. "No."

"Always so definite. But if you didn't miss the APD, why did you take that job with the Dahlonega police? You resigned after thirty-eight days." Her voice was neutral. "It must have been pretty different from the big city."

"Not really. The same kind of people thinking the same thing: that the rules don't apply to them because they're special." She seemed to want me to talk. I had seen her vulnerable, now she wanted to see me. "The last man I arrested was beating a lamb. There was a show. A taut, firm body is one of the things judges look for in prize livestock. This man was beating a lamb so its body would swell and feel more firm. I arrested him. The district attorney refused to prosecute. They kept saying to me, 'Officer Torvingen, Bubba here is a fine, upstanding citizen, and you want to spoil his reputation, for a lamb?' "

"I don't blame you for resigning if your superiors didn't back you up."

"That wasn't my reason. I had to drive him back to his house, and all the way I was thinking I should have just taken him behind the woodpile and beaten him until he swelled up, nice and firm, then maybe he would learn."

"And wanting to beat him bothered you?"

"Bothered me? No. It was just that I realized I didn't want to work for people whose rules got in the way of being effective. I resigned immediately in my head, and then it wasn't my job anymore to do anything with this man. He was no longer my responsibility. I stopped the car and tossed him out in the middle of the road. I've never worked for anyone but myself since."

"You said you never wanted to work for anyone whose rules got in the way of doing your job. Will you . . . I mean, if . . . Will you work with me again?"

"This one's not finished yet."

"If I'm out of the country, there's nothing urgent, is there? So would you?"

"It depends on the job."

"The glass corporation who want the sculpture garden, they're in Norway. In Oslo. I'd need someone to translate. And we could take a few days to . . ." She went on in a rush, "What I mean is, I've never seen the country. Perhaps you could show me some of it. Introduce me to some people. You could see your mother."

"She's in London."

"We could stop off on the way, or the way back. Will you come?"

Norway. It had been eleven years. Norway: a solid world against which to lay myself and make a mark that could be examined, could be held up in comparison with who I used to be, before. Norway. And my mother. Perhaps it was time. "Yes," I said.

It was a cool day for the end of April, in the low eighties, but I drove straight up I-85 with the windows closed and the air-conditioning on because of the '90 Margaux, duck terrine, boxed sandwiches and assorted delicatessen goodies on the back seat. I put on a CD of Ella Fitzgerald who sang about it being too darned hot.

The first time I'd driven this road to my new apartment in Northwoods Lake Court, Duluth, it had been a lot hotter. The roads had been a lot less crowded. I had never seen a human body fall and spasm and relax its sphincters.

I took the Pleasant Hill Road exit, heading for Duluth. At the top of the ramp was a man holding a WILL WORK FOR FOOD sign. Thirteen years ago I would have stopped for him. I drove past. Ella sang about oysters in Oyster Bay.

I sighed, did a U-turn, parked, walked over to the man. He was wearing black pants, white shirt, and a jacket that was far too big for him. Perhaps once it had fit. His feet stayed in one place, but he couldn't seem to keep still.

"Hey, there," I said. His head wobbled as he turned. "I'm on my way to the grocery. What kind of food do you want?"

It took him a while to work out what I was saying, then he smiled. Most of his teeth were missing. I doubted he was even my age. "Yes, ma'am. Thank you, ma'am."

"I'll spend up to twenty dollars. What kind of food?"

"Just give me the twenty dollars." It was beginning to get through to him that this wasn't going the usual way. He started moving from side to side.

"No. Tell me what kind of food you want."

"Can't," he said sullenly. Even in his jacket and the sun, he did not seem to be sweating. I wondered when he had last remembered to have a drink of water. "Can't point at something that's not here."

"I'll drive you to the store, then."

"It's all white person's food. Can't eat that. Give me the money."

"I'll drive you to any store you want as long as it's within ten miles. I'll buy you food. I won't give you money."

"I need money!" Three steps one way, three steps the other.

"So you don't want any food?"

"I want money!" Now he was shambling along the verge, this way and that, in the lolloping, loose-limbed gait of the crack addict.

"If you want food, I can get you food. If you want to go to a shelter, I can drive you. I won't give you money."

He started shouting, waving his arms about. I walked back to the car, retrieved a bottle of mineral water from the cooler, and took it back. I put it on the grass two yards from where he stood.

"You should drink this." I waited until I was sure he'd seen the water, then left. A mile up the road both lanes were clogged with mall traffic and the asphalt under their tires was still streaked red with runoff from last night's rain. The strip mall developers might rip out trees and gouge the earth flat but it refused to die completely, it just bled its life away, rainfall by rainfall. Ella sang about saying goodbye, and then I was out of the bottleneck and shifting through the gears.

The park appeared suddenly, as it always had. One minute I was doing sixty, the next I was in a small, crunched limestone parking lot shaded by a stand of towering Douglas firs. The engine ticked, birdsong wove through the wood. Nothing had changed in thirteen years.

I carried my basket to the lake, where I could watch the white geese and mallards paddling around. Some were trailed by lines of tiny chicks, cutting wobbly V-shaped wakes behind their parents. I pulled the Margaux cork, picked up an enormous turkey sandwich, and ate my picnic, sunshine warming my face and wine and the grass, making my world smell like French countryside. On the far side of the lake, by a fallen tree trunk, two geese started a honking competition. I poured more wine. The honking competition ended in a flurry of feathers and a swift, sharp arc of water from one to the other that glittered in the sun like a diamond necklace.

*Why do you do this?* Julia had asked, and I didn't know. I would be better off working as some kind of park ranger or planting trees, and instead I had agreed to accompany Julia to Oslo. I was going to go on and find out more—the identities of those men, who they worked for, why they carried knives—when really I could not care less. What did it matter? They had no idea who I was and all Julia had to do to be safe was stay out of the way for a few weeks while Denneny and maybe the DEA sorted out the whole mess. But *I'm Norwegian* I had told Julia, and Norwegians were supposed to tidy away what they had disarranged, finish what they started.

And *Are you?* she had asked. In Oslo, perhaps I could find out.

I put the remains of the picnic in the trunk and had to search a minute or two before I found the head of the trail. It was laid with mulched bark weathered by sun and rain to a crumbly punk, soft enough for bare feet.

Under the trees it was another country, with sounds and scents from another age. The air was rich and still. If you stood quietly, you could imagine the trees were breathing, the soft sigh of ancient forest. But this wasn't an old wood. Through the thick foliage of mature birch and yellow poplar, the sun was bright on the fresh new green of sycamore saplings and young birches. The flash of thrush wings stitched bronze-black threads between tree trunks. A busy clutch of finches twittered, green-patched heads turning this way and that, while somewhere over my head a cardinal fluted.

Such small birds for a such a big sound. I had a sudden

vision of yellow beak opening to show startling red and pink throat and tongue, feathers swelling as the tiny creature tried to fill the world with song, tried hard enough to shatter its fragile, hollow bones, and all it was singing was, *This is my tree, my tree, my tree. Keep away or I'll break your wings.*

A twitch of movement up the bark of a white pine: a lizard with a blue belly and tiny glittering eyes that would not have looked out of place as a jewelled pin on a woman's evening coat. It skittered around the other side of the trunk.

The trail dipped. To the right the ground was boggy. Swamp oak loomed over reeds and a stand of yellow iris. Damselflies hummed in and out of the shade like tiny titanium helicopters. Some bird flashed through and snipped a couple out of the air. Beauty and innocence never saved anything.

Just past the dog violets on the right, on a crumbling log, sat a salamander: five inches long and fire-engine red with black speckles. I watched it sunning itself for five minutes before something I couldn't see or hear startled it. It moved so fast it seemed to disappear. Perhaps thirteen years ago there had been salamanders in the woods on the northeast side of the apartment complex at Northwoods Lake Court. I hadn't been there long enough to find out.

The trail was just over a mile. It came out above the lake, less than a hundred yards from where I had picnicked. Full circle.

Northwoods Lake, the first place I had lived in this country, was less than a mile up the road, but no friends, no family had ever seen it. It was only two minutes' drive; perhaps it was time to make the journey, go back, find out for myself what I had missed. But perhaps they would have cut down all the trees by now, drained the ornamental lake and leveled the brushy slopes to squeeze in a few more units. Perhaps I would find that my memory had played tricks on me. Perhaps I would find I had not lost a wonderland, that I was who I was not because I had killed someone but because that's just the way I was born. I had never talked to anyone of what had happened there. Not even to my mother. No doubt the consulate had apprised her of events, but we had never spoken of it.

I stood by the lake for a long time, through the full heat of afternoon, through a light shower of rain whose big drops felt unrealistically light, as though they were hollow. I stood while the mall traffic turned to rush-hour traffic, until the sun started to bloody the horizon. That's when a blue heron glided in over the lake. With head tucked back on the long neck and legs dangling, it looked impossibly prehistoric, a pterodactyl with feathers. It alighted on the dead limb of a white oak hanging over the water, where it immediately assumed the pose of a Japanese painting: a single vivid brushstroke, stark against the gold and orange of the sky. It edged forward a little and turned its head this way and that, watching the lake intently. It stood nearly four feet high; its beak—a dead-looking thing of yellowed ivory—must have been ten inches long. Its plumage was slate blue with a powdery pinkish undercast, the topknot of four or five head feathers—like a silly chapeau—almost white. After a while it gave a little skip and a jump and hauled itself back into the air in a clutter of legs. With a couple of powerful wing beats it was gliding once again, sure and silent. Its shadow rippled over the darkening water and it headed southwest towards the city, the opposite direction from Northwoods Lake Court.

I watched it awhile, then drove back towards the interstate. The water bottle lay broken open on the road. There was no sign of the man or his board.

A fax from Benny waited for me at home: no matches on the blood type or fingerprints found at Honeycutt's house from local files. It would take several days to run them against the FBI's enormous file but the preliminary results were interesting: professionals who were not yet known to local law enforcement. Interesting but ultimately uninformative.

I called Denneny's voice mail again. "Brian, my client and I are leaving the country for a week or two. We leave the day after tomorrow, arriving Oslo on the first of May, and will be back midmonth, depending." Depending on a lot of things. "You might be interested in the reported burglary at Honeycutt's house last night."

He should have everything taken care of by the time we got back.

I called my mother, who stayed up all hours. I talked to her secretary. It was a new one. "This is Aud Torvingen. Her daughter. Can you tell me what her schedule is like later this week? No, no, I'm in America. I'm . . . No, no, I'm Her Excellency's daughter. Yes. Aud. I'm flying into London the day after tomorrow, from America. I want to find out when Her Excellency will be free so I can perhaps arrange an overnight stay before completing my journey to Oslo. No, no, I'm not in London now." I switched to Norwegian. After two sentences she let me know that Her Excellency was in fact fully booked for the next ten days. "Then will you tell her to please call me?" I gave her the number, then repeated it just to be sure. "Tell her . . . tell her that I hope she can rearrange her appointments. That if she can't, I'll be passing back that way a week or two later and will be happy to fit in with her schedule. But I do want to see her. Please make that clear. Say I particularly asked to talk to her properly. Yes. Properly."

*Properly.* We had never really talked to each other after I was nine years old. She had been busy and I had been resentful. I had grown up independent, and then she had not known how to find her way back to me. I wasn't even sure she wanted to, or what she might find if she did.

The nights were getting hotter. The dogwood blossom was gone, azaleas in full bloom, and the air cupped my cheek as softly as a woman's hand. I strolled through Little Five Points, careful not to swing my left arm too much and pull the healing cut over my ribs. The tables outside cafés and bars were full. Four different sets of street musicians competed with traffic and the ecstatic shirring of crickets and tree frogs. One woman on six-foot stilts was trying to play the harmonica. As I crossed the street, some man with sideburns and an apron was waving frantically at Stiltwoman. No doubt he was trying to point out the power lines that ran quite low near his bar. I stepped into the orange glow of Borealis.

Dornan beamed. "Ah, Aud, don't you just love the beginning of summer? So wonderfully good for business. Lattés here, Jonie, please."

"What is that thing you're wearing?"

"This?" He flicked a finger under the gaudy purple bandanna around his neck. "Tammy gave it to me. She says it makes me look wicked."

With the red shirt, colour-blind was nearer the mark. "She's gone again?"

"Some godforsaken place in the Midwest. But she'll be back in time for the grand opening of the Smyrna café."

"Another one, Dornan?"

His beam stretched even farther. "Yes, indeed, business is good. You'll be coming?"

"When?"

"What other day is there for an opening but Saturday? Saturday, when we can snag all the young mothers going to the Y to work out; all the teenagers coming out of the mall; all the angry young things who are too young to go to a bar."

"I'll be in Norway."

"Norway? What's in Norway but a miserable wasteland of snow?"

"Blossom on the fjord, spring sunshine in Vigeland Park, a country waking up from a hard winter. I'll be there a week or two, depending."

"On what?"

"How long it takes Julia to get her business done, whether I'll fly via London on the way there or back to see my mother."

"Julia, is it, and for two weeks? And no doubt seeing your mother was her idea." He nodded wisely. "Always the first step. Tammy wanted to meet my mother, too."

"Dornan, it's business."

"Two weeks isn't business, it's a holiday."

"I'll be translating for her."

"Of course you will," he said.

There was a message from my mother when I got back.

"Aud. How nice to hear from you. I'm afraid this week I am fully booked. The embassy is hosting the acid rain negotiations." The Norwegian government was protesting about the acid rain damage to their forests caused by British power station effluent. "My government also wants me to open dialogue with regard to a touchy North Sea oil matter. Of course, if it is imperative that we meet, I can cancel one or more appointments. However, I would very much look forward to seeing you on your way back. And if you will be taking a holiday while you're over there, please remember the seter. If you see Tante Hjørdis, give her my regards." A slight pause. "Aud, it is good to hear from you. Please let me know, when you can, what date you will be returning through London."

She spoke in English.

I got changed and went to the workroom. The chair was done, but raw. It needed finishing. I studied it. It was plain and graceful and strong. Not varnish, which could be hard and brittle when dry, and not paint, which would be cold in winter. Oil, then beeswax. I hummed as I pried the lid from the linseed oil and soaked the rag. I rubbed glistening liquid onto the armrests and imagined the hands that would touch the wood, perhaps resting there between turning the pages of a book, perhaps stroking the smooth wood, absently at first, then slipping a bit as the owner slept.

Some wield money like a blunt instrument, bludgeoning their way to what they want. Others hold it up like a flashing light: *Look! See how important I am!* I prefer to employ it as a lubricant, to ease the wear and tear of daily living. The first time I had crossed the Atlantic as an adult I had spent nine hours folded up like an accordion in coach class, surrounded by children coughing up their childhood diseases into air that was changed only five times an hour. So this time, when dinner was served, about an hour into the flight, we were sitting in business class, on leather seats with footrests and individual screens. The cabin attendants were slightly older, with the expert makeup and extra pounds that come from confidence and efficiency. There was even room for our attendant to hand the tray directly to me in my window seat rather than resort to the pass-along method used back in steerage. My steak and Julia's salmon were presented on real plates, and we had a choice of wine. Julia had mineral water. Afterwards, we sipped coffee. Julia's was decaffeinated. She was the one twisting restlessly in her seat.

"Perhaps you should try to sleep."

"Yes." She didn't sound convinced.

The cabin attendant whisked away my empty cup and I pulled down my window shade, dug out blanket and pillow, and prepared to get comfortable, which was more difficult than usual because of the healing gash along my ribs.

"Won't you be too hot?"

"My body temperature will drop when I'm asleep."

"What about your sleep mask?"

"They'll dim the lights soon enough." Wearing something over my eyes in public has never struck me as particularly safe. I reclined my seat, pulled up the blanket, and listened to the muted roar of the plane as it hollowed through the night.

I woke up five hours later to find Julia looking at me. There were dark circles under her eyes. "I don't understand how you do that. I just can't relax with all these people around."

"Your body would wake up if necessary."

"At least you're not claiming it's a Norwegian thing." She looked better than the other passengers, most of whom were far gone down the red-eye, puffy face road to transatlantic hell.

I stretched, carefully, folded away my blanket, and pulled up my window shade.

Imagine a blood orange, torn open, and a highly polished mahogany desk. Smear one over the other and add a wash of light blue: dawn over Ireland; rich, unearthly colours that reached past my eyes and stole part of my soul. People were not designed to see such things. I felt the cellular hum of four hundred people as they dreamed or worried or rehearsed speeches in their head in this steel and aluminium shell thirty-three thousand feet over the sea, hurtling through air that is just that, thin air, and knew we were remote from the world, separate, aloof, supported by nothing but speed and physical laws I could recite but have never really believed.

A few minutes later lights were going on, the smell of coffee seeped back from the galley, and people woke and mur-

mured to their companions. A full English breakfast brought me back to the real world, then we started the ear-popping descent.

I joined Julia in the noncitizen immigration control line. She said nothing when I got out my American passport, though I knew she must be wondering. I was wafted through but they asked Julia a dozen questions. She was smart enough to keep her temper but by the time they let her go her eyes were snapping.

"So, do you suppose they have X-ray eyes and can see through your hand luggage to your UK passport?"

"It's the smile. Make it sympathetic but mechanical, as if to say: Jeez, bet you're as bored with your job as I am with you *doing* your job, again. Let's be quick and efficient and pleasant about this."

Her irritation lightened to amusement. "It's nothing to do with the smile. It's the eyes. They say: Nothing personal, but delay me and you die, old bean."

"Old bean? They stopped saying that a decade before the war."

"Which one?"

"Here, 'the war' means only one thing: World War II."

"You're a chameleon, you know that? Ten minutes on British soil and you're already in their mind-set." She eyed me speculatively all the way to the SAS gate. It was a three-hour layover, so we waited in the business-class lounge. I pulled out an Iain Banks novel but every time I looked up she was watching me.

Eventually I put the book away. "Give me your ticket."

"Why?"

"I want to check something."

To my surprise she didn't argue but handed it over. I wandered out to the concierge, who was very helpful and did a lot of telephoning on my behalf.

Julia contained herself until we were aboard and tightening

our seat belts. I made sure she had the window seat this time. "Okay. I give in. What were you checking?"

"The flight path. That we were seated on the left-hand side of the plane. That we could get our luggage sent on to the hotel at the other end so we don't have to wait."

"I didn't know you could do that."

"They don't offer, but if you ask, and pay, they can be persuaded." Another of those clubs that you have to know exists before you find out how to join.

The plane taxied for takeoff. The pulse in Julia's neck beat faster. "And what about the flight plan, and seats?" The plane jerked a little as the pilot braked. The huge Rolls-Royce engines turned now in earnest and one of the overhead bins began to rattle. It was an old plane. The rattling got louder and faster. Julia's nostrils were pinched and white.

"Just after takeoff, there's something I think you might like to see."

The engines suddenly roared in release and we lumbered down the runway. A bump, a lift, and we were airborne, the pilot hauling back on the stick so hard I thought he was trying for a loop-the-loop. Julia's fingers dug into her armrest.

"Look down now. It's Windsor Castle."

We flew just a few hundred yards above the now-gracious showpiece of robber barons turned monarchs: the cathedral-sized chapel; the huge hall built by Edward III to bolster his new order, the Knights of the Garter; the vast outer ward.

The plane groaned. Julia breathed very fast. "Edward rebuilt everything in stone, starting about 1350," I said. "Trouble is, that was just after the great plague. There weren't really enough stonemasons, carpenters and other artisans to go around, so Edward scoured the whole country and brought them all to Windsor. They demanded bigger wages because now demand outweighed supply. Edward outwardly railed against it, but privately paid them what they asked. Medieval inflation."

We were leaving the castle behind. Julia's breathing had evened out a little. "I've never seen a castle before."

"We'll have a couple of days in London on the way back. While I see my mother, you might like to visit Windsor, and there are numerous cathedrals, ruined abbeys, manor houses. . . ." We were up among the clouds now. She still had not let go of the armrest. I sighed. This could be a long journey.

"When I first started living in the U.S., I would drive along interstates and country lanes, along highway and freeway, and I would constantly scan the countryside. Every time there was a ridge or a hilltop or a bluff, I found myself looking up, expecting to see . . . something. It was years before I realized what I was searching for: evidence of the hand of humankind. In England, every hill is topped with the weathered remains of some Iron Age fort, of ruined manor houses, or abbeys staring naked and roofless at the sky. Sometimes it's just the faint outline of ancient earthworks, but there's almost always something, some indication that people once lived there. You can look out of the window of a plane and see fields and hedgerows that were first laid out in the ninth century. The hills have been smoothed, the rivers banked, the woods coppiced for thousands of years. And then I moved to Georgia. To Marietta, where a railway that's barely a hundred years old is trumpeted with huge signs demanding that the poor motorist visit the Historic Railroad. To Duluth, where I lived in an apartment complex called Northwoods Lake Court, surrounded by old-growth pine forest, but where an eleven-year-old child now might go and look around and ask her mother: 'Why did they call this place Northwoods, because there aren't any trees?' To Atlanta, Atlanta which they say Sherman burnt to the ground, but which is really destroyed every ten years by greedy developers who rip down beautiful buildings that have stood for decades and replace them with tissue-walled condominium boxes not even built to code. In Georgia, you drive ten miles outside the city and all you see is bare red clay and huge signposts declaring 'Land For Sale' to the highest bidder. It feels cold, sometimes, inimical and empty."

"So why do you stay?"

"Because despite everything developers are trying to do, there is still a lot of natural beauty. For instance, there's a park near Duluth. It has a lake with geese and ducks and fish, and it's fringed with duckweed and cattails. The woods are full to bursting with birds. Cardinals and three different kinds of woodpecker, nuthatches, warblers, bluebirds . . . Have you ever seen a bluebird? They're extremely sensitive to pollution. They're always the first to go. But this park has bluebirds—they're the colour of blue powder paints in the sunshine. In the woods are salamanders, lizards, mice, voles. There are yellow iris and tiger lilies, trumpet honeysuckle, swamp oak and white pine. And no one is ever there. It's always empty."

"You sound angry."

"I've lived most of my life in London and Leeds, in Bergen and Oslo, and most of the time in those cities the only birds are sparrows that cough themselves awake on phone wires in the morning, and if you see a squirrel it's a big nature day. Americans have no idea how lucky they are."

She was quiet for a while. "I was brought up in Massachusetts," she said, "with winding country lanes, blackberries that have grown along the mossy walls for three hundred years, the occasional Cape Cod that has weathered storms off the Atlantic for a hundred and fifty. I had no idea I missed them until now."

And so for the next two hours, I told her about Yorkshire—the towns there with Roman walls; the pubs in the Dales that were built as farms in the fourteenth century—and she talked about the private school she attended in Boston.

As the western coast of Norway drew near, I glanced out at the sea every few minutes. The captain announced we were beginning our preliminary descent. Then I saw it.

"Look down there," I said.

We were about two miles out from the coast but the North Sea below us, usually a steely grey, looked like an estuary: huge currents and swathes of what looked like mud.

"Oh, the assholes! What caused that?"

"It's not pollution."

"Then what is it?" She was quite belligerent.

"Herring, on their way north, lay so many eggs and release so much milt that it clogs the water." I imagined their cold, muscular bodies glinting silver in the freezing water, thrashing and ecstatic with the urge to procreate, releasing their vast, living milk tide. "There are so many eggs that they wash up on the rocky northern shores like snowdrift. Then massive flocks of birds dive in to feed. It used to be that massive flocks of people would appear to bring down the birds. Puffins are very tasty. But that doesn't happen much anymore."

"Much?"

I just smiled.

The plane turned southeast, the captain struggled bravely with the intercom but remained incomprehensible, and we made our final approach. Beneath us, at the head of the swan-shaped neck of water that is Oslofjorden, Oslo glittered in the spring sunlight like a broken-open geode.

International airports usually smell of jet fuel and stale clothes but at Fornebu, on the peninsula that pokes into Lysakerfjorden just six miles west of Oslo, those scents are swept aside by sharp sea air and the fragrance of pine trees. The scents of home.

The immigration officers were courteous and efficient and spoke English. The people striding past us on the concourse all wore bright sweaters and swung their arms as they moved.

"Why do they all walk so fast?"

"Because they're healthy. Because they don't work ten hours a day. Because it's not ninety degrees outside." It was odd, after being swaddled in Southern languor for years, to be surrounded by so many white smiles that were not strained, people moving at speed because they liked it, not because they were late or afraid. We walked past an Avis desk.

"Aren't we going to hire a car?"

"Not while we're in the city. We can take a taxi to our hotel, and everything you want to see is walking distance from there."

She looked at the striding natives. "Norwegian walking distance, or American?"

Then we were outside in the taxi line. Like everything else in this country, it moved forward efficiently. The sea breeze fizzed on my tongue like sherbet.

"It's colder than it looked from inside."

"It's sixty degrees," I said, surprised. "Warm for the season." Winter had lasted a long time this year. It seemed that nature had turned up the thermostat in an effort to make up for the late start. But Julia was from Atlanta, where sunshine on the first of May meant ninety degrees. Her eyes and her skin were telling her different things.

The driver of the cab that pulled up in front of us had the smooth cheeks and tilted eyes of someone with Sami blood. "Where to?" he asked in English.

"Hotel Bristol," Julia said. Telling him the street address would have been like telling a New York native how to get to the Empire State Building.

We drove east along Drammensveien. Julia was quiet. As Drammensveien crossed Bygdoy Alle, I pointed north to the park. "Three blocks that way to Vigeland's sculpture park. What kind of art do the glass corporation want?"

"Whatever it is, it'll have to resist the elements. How far to the hotel?"

"Another mile."

But it took a long time to get there. The streets were full of parades, people holding banners and placards, men and women marching along behind bands.

"It's May the first. Labour Day." I had forgotten. "A public holiday when trade unions and political parties hold rallies. All very dignified when compared to the seventeenth of May, National Day, when everyone runs the flag up the pole and parties to celebrate the anniversary of the Norwegian constitution." By the seventeenth we would be by the still green waters of Lustrafjord, two hundred miles from the crowds of screaming children waving their flags, smearing their best clothes with mustard from their *pølse* and spilling fizzy *brus* on innocent passersby.

The driver, who had been nosing his cab patiently through the crowds, sighed, pulled on the brake, and told us he could go no farther, and that would be a hundred thirty krone, please. We climbed out and Julia shuffled through her money, trying to decipher the unfamiliar notes. She found hundred-Nkr and fifty-Nkr notes but I leaned forward and said quietly, "Give him more. Another twenty-Nkr."

She did. He smiled. *"Takk skal du har."*

*"Ingen arsak,"* I replied.

He drove off slowly through the crowds. "I thought Norwegians didn't believe in big tips."

"He was Sami. What Americans would call Lapp. The fare from the airport should be at least a hundred fifty-Nkr. Perhaps he charged less because he couldn't get us to our exact destination, but perhaps it's because he expects to be treated badly."

"So Norway isn't perfect."

"Just cleaner. The hotel is that way." Out in the early afternoon sun, I could see that her skin was stretched and tight, and the circles under her eyes had darkened from tobacco to charcoal.

Inside the doors of the Bristol, Julia stopped and stared. Jet lag, a strange country, and now the exotic cinnamon and gold arches of a Moorish-style lobby.

"I'll check us in." I left her on an ottoman recovering her poise.

The Bristol is one of the few good hotels left where getting two rooms with a connecting door is possible without breaking the bank. I asked for two keys to each room, two for the connecting door. The clerk obviously thought I was eccentric but given the amount we were paying, he didn't seem inclined to argue. I told him to send our luggage up when it arrived.

Julia smiled at me as I approached, still looking tired but now as relaxed and unfazed as though she had spent her life sitting on Turkish couches in Moorish lobbies in Norwegian cities. Such a relief after babysitting Beatriz. I sat next to her. "This is the key to your room, this is the key to mine, here's the one that fits the connecting door, though I think we should keep that unlocked." I handed them over. "I have a complete set, too."

"Just in case?" She smiled but sounded more fatigued than amused. "God, I need to sleep."

The elevators were small, and elegant with brass and mahogany. Julia peered at the buttons, which appeared to be made of ivory. "I just hope my room's not got out like a harem or something."

It wasn't. It had a slate blue carpet with rosewood armoire and escritoire dating from the 1880s. The headboard was beautifully inlaid. Simple, elegant, warm. She opened the connecting door to my room, which was carpeted in moss green, with walnut furniture. "Very nice."

I checked the windows, then went into her bathroom. Huge tub, shower stall with faux nineteenth century hardware. Mounds of white towels. A second phone. I brought the robe out with me.

Julia was sitting on the bed, bouncing lightly. "The mattress, at least, is new. What's that for?"

"Our luggage won't be here for an hour or two. If you want to sleep, you might like a robe handy."

She held out her hand for the robe. "If I'm not stirring by five, will you wake me?"

"Five," I agreed, and left her to it.

In my room, I called the front desk to make sure they delivered both our bags to my room. Just in case they processed my request with less than usual Norwegian efficiency, I took my DO NOT DISTURB sign, went out into the corridor and hung it on Julia's door. My bathroom was blue and gold. I unwrapped the bandage around my ribs, dropped it in the bin, and looked at my ribs in the mirror. The skin was clear, not red, and when I touched the hard scab the pain was minimal. It didn't need to be wrapped up again. I dressed and went back to my room of tasteful moss and polished walnut.

From the chaise longue by the window I could see clouds scudding over the harbour. The sea would be beginning to chop, the temperature dropping by the minute. The crowds would soon start thinking about going home to eat *middag*. By five I would have the pavements to myself. I could taste the air, listen to the gulls, reacquaint myself.

There were trees throughout the city, scattered here and there on the streets, lining the harbour walk, gathering in dense growth in the parks. From up here, Slottsparken, surrounding the Royal Palace, looked like lime-green felt, fresh and vigorous with new foliage. It seemed all wrong. It should be autumn, with a gale whipping leaves from the trees, swirling them underfoot, so my strides would crunch gold and russet and brown, scenting the air with the pungence of loss and regret. But it was spring, late spring that was trying with a vengeance to become summer, and my solitary walk would have to wait for a while, because Julia was asleep and I had promised to wake her at five. And I was uneasy.

I made a phone call. I read Iain Banks.

At five, I knocked on the connecting door. A murmur. I knocked again. Nothing. I went through.

She had pulled the thin curtains closed but not the heavy

drapes. The room was in light shadow, just enough to bring the richness out of the wood and make the blue carpet deep and mysterious. She slept on her back, arms over her head, mouth open, shoulders showing bare. Her breath was short and fast and cross. How easy it would be to step closer and put a hand over her mouth, pinch shut her nostrils. She would struggle, of course, but under the duvet and hotel-tight sheets, under the slippery silk bedspread, she wouldn't stand a chance. Her heart would beat under her ribs, frantic as a bird, and her muscles would bunch like tight little apples.

All that stood between her and death at the hands of a stranger was a door, but all one had to do was bribe the desk clerk, or trick a chambermaid, or pick the lock, and then all her training would be for nothing.

But this was Oslo, not Atlanta. Honeycutt had no idea she was here. Nor had his blackmailer.

"Julia."

She turned away. The scent of sleepy, warm woman drifted from the bed.

"Julia."

"Mmmn." She turned back towards me, face soft and unfocused. Still asleep.

"Julia. It's five o'clock."

The essential Julia flowed back into the body on the bed, reanimating the flesh, sharpening the face, focusing the gaze, and I understood why some people believe in possession.

"It's five o'clock," I repeated. "Our luggage arrived. I'll go get yours." I also went back out into the corridor and retrieved the DO NOT DISTURB sign. Then I waited an extra minute or two.

She was standing by the window in her robe, curtain drawn back. Her skin looked soft and warm and alive against the white towelling. "It all looks so fresh and clean, as though people here don't even sweat." Her hair fell forward over her eyes. She tucked it back behind her ears. "What time do people eat in Oslo?"

"Early, though not as early as they used to. But there's someone I should visit before dinner. You are welcome to come with me, unless you prefer to stay in the hotel and rest."

"Someone who takes precedence over dinner?" She studied me. "A relative."

"My great-aunt, Hjørdis."

"A relative. . . . Yes, I'd love to meet her. But I need to shower, then work out my travel kinks. How about a walk?"

"Norwegian or American?"

"Norwegian. I'll dress appropriately."

"I'll be in my room."

When I looked up forty minutes later she was standing in the doorway, wearing stretch twill pants, light boots, and a thick sweater the swirling colours of sunset over the sea. "Nice room," she said, then: "I'm not a vampire. If you invite me in you can always get rid of me later."

I stood. "I'm sorry. Please, come in." It sounded wooden and overly formal. Her boots made deep imprints on the carpet. Walnut and moss, not raspberry and Viking gold. I wondered how long they would be visible.

Ulleval Hageby, where Tante Hjørdis lives, is almost three miles from the centre of the city. I walked between Julia and the road. It was a beautiful evening. The sky, cloudless now, arched overhead like a fragile eggshell painted blue so long ago it was beginning to fade, and the sun slanted across the pavement like a glass sword. Trees absorbed the traffic fumes and the world smelt deliciously of green sap and distant ozone. I walked fast, letting my blood pump through veins and wash away the travel toxins and rush oxygen to my scalp and fingertips and retina, and all the time scanned the trees automatically, listened for following footsteps. Nothing. This was Oslo. Julia kept up, moving easily, alert, enjoying herself. She seemed to have shed her city skin, or perhaps just a layer of armour. Red squirrels jumped from tree to tree ahead of us. "It's like walking through a garden."

"*Hage* means garden, and *by* is town. Hjørdis has lived here ever since I can remember."

"Do you like her?"

That surprised me. "She's my aunt."

"But what's she like?"

I thought for a while. "Older than she seems."

Julia laughed and picked up the pace and for a while we swung along in opposite step, hip to hip, her right leg moving out with my left, so I could feel her boot hit the ground, feel it through the soles of my feet, up my calves, in my pelvis. It didn't last, of course. My legs are longer.

Tante Hjørdis's house is made of wood, in a row of wooden houses painted bright colours. Hers is red. We climbed a short flight of wooden steps and I lifted the brass knocker. I'd always loved its tidy, bright *rat-tat-tat* sound as a child.

The door opened so fast Julia took a step back and there was Tante Hjørdis, still tall, still with that iron-grey hair in a short bowl cut. The sweater was brighter than usual. There was no *Hello*, no *Aud, how lovely to see you!*, but her eyes were bright, and she said, "You're the only person these days who doesn't try hammer that thing through the wood." She turned to Julia and said, in English this time, "Everyone else thinks I'm going deaf."

She held out her arms and we hugged. I remembered when she used to engulf me. Now I was an inch or two taller, though her bone and muscle still felt like granite.

I stepped out of the embrace and spoke in English. "Tante, this is Julia Lyons-Bennet. Julia, this is my great-aunt, Hjørdis Holmsen."

Julia held out her hand and they shook heartily. Hjørdis nodded approval. "Come in. I'll be in the kitchen."

The *vindskap* was dry and tidy now, nothing like the muddy, wet and cold room of my childhood winters when my mother and I pulled off boots, down jackets and sealskin hats, and leaned skis up against the wall. Even though it was dry outside, I wiped my boots carefully on the mat and Julia copied me. There was a large mirror on the far wall. I ran my fingers through my hair, more because it was expected than necessary. Julia shook her hair loose, combed it with her fingers, and tied it back again. Like Hjørdis, she looked impossibly young.

The *vindskap* led into a hallway whose walls were lined with family photographs; a painted wooden staircase lay at one end and a single door in the middle.

The sun would be up for another two or three hours but the living room blazed with candles. I smiled at the familiar warm scent of beeswax.

"It must run in the family," Julia said, pointing at the polished wooden floor and big French windows in the dining area that led to the back garden. The dining table was draped with a linen cloth and sparkled with three places of crystal and sterling flatware. I sighed.

We nearly ran into Hjørdis in the kitchen doorway. She was carrying an enormous tray. "You take this one," she said to Julia—in Norwegian, but her intent was perfectly clear. "Aud, you come in here and help me carry the rest."

I had told her we were on our way out to dinner, but she had laid out plates of *geitost* and crackers, home-cured ham and *rømme* and *lompe*, salmon and cucumber salad. . . . I followed Julia to the dining room table. Hjørdis brought homemade wine and fresh, very strong coffee.

"When did you get here?" In English, this time, directed at Julia.

"About four hours ago."

She handed her a steaming cup of coffee. "You don't look tired."

"Aud persuaded me to take a nap."

"She's good at that." They both turned to look at me and I wondered how a person could become the outsider so fast.

"So you want the key to the seter." It was still in English but this time addressed to me.

"Yes."

"When will you be there?"

"Julia will be doing some business in the city tomorrow and perhaps the day after. Then we will go on to Lustrafjorden. If Julia likes it, we'll stay for a week or two."

"Or longer."

Julia smiled and said, "No, I can't take too much time away from my business."

"Oh, people always say that, then they see the fjord for the first time, they smell the sloping fjell and taste the water, and suddenly their very important job in the city fades to meaninglessness, and I nearly have to send in the army to evict them. So let's say four weeks, just in case, and then I won't have to be cross if you stay longer than you intended. Now, Aud, why don't you explain to your polite friend what all this food is and I'll go get the key."

We watched her stride out of the room. Julia smiled. "Better do as she says or she'll eat you."

"A few years ago I believed she could. So. Pass me that plate with the cheese on it. This is *geitost*, goat's cheese. You can put it on these crackers. It has a toasty, caramel flavour. I think you'd like it. The salmon you eat with the cucumber salad. You might find that a bit sweet. This ham you can wrap in *lompe*, which is that soft flatbread over there."

"And this?"

"*Gravadlax*, buried salmon. A great delicacy." Only Hjørdis would serve it along with *geitost*. "Try it if you feel brave."

"And this?" She lifted a dish of little, pale round things.

"Rolled cod's tongues."

The dish went back on the table with a bang, but then she picked it up again. "How do you eat them?"

"With one of these." I held up a long-handled silver fork with three tiny tines. "Pass the pickle castor. That crystal and silver thing on wheels." She trundled it over. I used the tiny silver tongs to transfer a few of the silverskin onions to my plate, then skewered one with the fork, then a cod's tongue and popped them in my mouth. I savoured the texture and bite. "You dip them in *rømme,* that sour cream there."

She spooned some onto her plate and was just dipping a tongue when Hjørdis came back. Julia, wearing her poker face, put the whole thing in her mouth and chewed. After a second or two, she looked relieved. Hjørdis laughed. "Such a pleasant surprise to see an American enjoy good, wholesome food. Now. Aud." Julia heard the suddenly formal tone and sat up straight. "Here is the key. You're lucky. Your mother phoned up yesterday and told me you might be wanting it. I phoned Gudrun at the farm and she will be airing everything out for you, so you will be comfortable, but next time try give me a little more notice." She handed it over. It was big and made of black iron, and very cold. She probably kept it in the cellar. The business of the key to the family seter was purely ceremonial—the back door and windows did not even have locks— but Hjørdis took her duties as eldest family member quite seriously. "Now, eat, and Aud can tell me why she has stayed away so long, and you, Julia, can tell me all about this business of yours."

We never did get out to dinner. I listened for hours as Julia talked about art; about Atlanta and how she had come back to the city, where her mother now lived, from Boston. I watched Hjørdis absorbing Julia with those bright eyes; agreeing with sharp nods and the occasional emphatic *ha!* when Julia talked about discrimination against women in business in the South. We drank homemade *tyttebaer* wine with the meal, and Hjørdis's face flushed, and Julia relaxed and talked with her hands. As the sun went down and left candlelight wavering over brow and throat, wrist and mouth, it seemed for a moment that they could be almost the same age: two women, enjoying a conversation.

We walked back to the Bristol, but slowly. There was very little traffic, and a sharp breeze blew in from the fjord. No unusual sounds, no unusual scents. "You were quiet tonight," she said.

"Yes."

Sound of breath and boots. "I liked Hjørdis. And she seems to mean a great deal to you."

"She's my aunt." Hjørdis had always been part of my life, always there in her wooden house when my mother was busy and my father out of the country. When I was in England, I wrote to her every week, and every week she wrote back. "My father told me once that she had fought in the Resistance during the Second World War."

"You've never asked her?"

"If she had wanted me to know, she would have told me."

"Is everything in Norway left so . . . unspoken? I'm glad you'll be with me tomorrow when I go to Olsen Glass. You can tell me afterwards what each particular silence really meant."

"Nothing is unspoken in business. It's all very straightforward. Telling the truth, and nothing but the truth, is the cardinal rule."

"What about the whole truth?"

"That, too."

A momentary silence. "And do you believe in that, Aud Torvingen?"

"It depends on who I'm talking to."

"You're doing it again. I don't think you've lied to me, exactly, but you keep information back."

"What do you want to know?"

"You've been tense all the time we've travelled. I hadn't even realized that until this evening when I saw you relax at Hjørdis's house. Do you think I'm in danger even here, in Oslo?"

"I don't know." And that was what filled me with deep unease. "Reason tells me you are safe."

"But you don't believe it, do you?"

I had no idea how to explain that behind every tree, looming beyond every building I sensed the shadowy outline of Honeycutt's puppet master, the blackmailer.

We were walking a little faster now, and Julia's shoulders were hunched. "Ever since Honeycutt's house, you've been different. I've seen the way you eye the doors, gauging their sturdiness, the way you check shop windows as we pass to make sure we're not being followed. I've noticed that you always walk on the curb side of the sidewalk, and you make sure cars have fully stopped before you cross a street. Especially here, even though you told me I'd be safe in Norway."

Reason dictated that I say, *You are*, but what came out was, "I'll protect you," which puzzled me, because it was not the same thing at all.

nine

It was only a mile and a half from the Bristol to Vigeland Park but it was a sunny morning and our route along Bogstadsveien was lively with galleries and art shops. Julia seemed to find them amusing. Even so, we still had to cross traffic and tram tracks every few meters to look through yet another shop window: "If I'm going to design a sculpture park for a Norwegian corporation I have to get some idea of what Norwegians like."

She looked at the displays, I scanned the crowd.

"A lot of Neo-Romanticism," she said.

"You should look in museums, not these tourist traps."

"That's where you're wrong. You need to look at both sides. I couldn't learn about Americans' taste for art, and that art's history, by touring MoMA. To explain sixties pop art, for instance, I'd have to know about Disney World and Coney Island and network television as well as the formal canvases that hang on museum walls. That's what helps me understand what will become valuable in a few years, what will be a good investment." And then she was distracted by a collection of dolls dressed in *bunad*, bright red traditional costumes with tiny silver buckles and earrings. "They're all different."

"Each region has its own traditional dress."

"Do people really wear them?"

"Sometimes. On national holidays." I didn't like standing here with people brushing by on both sides.

"Did you have one?"

"Yes."

"Did you wear it?"

"When I was confirmed." She wasn't going to move along until I gave her what she wanted. "I was thirteen. I wore it once. Lutheran church though, no, I'm not particularly religious. It was and is more of a cultural event. I have no idea where the *bunad* is now."

"Did you have long hair?" She fingered the doll's braid.

"Yes."

"And did you wear it in braids, with ribbons?" She was grinning.

It took us ninety minutes to reach the massive wrought-iron gates of Vigeland Park. Julia stood there for a while, just looking. "I'd like to look at this on my own for a while, I think."

She was wearing a peach shirt; easy to keep track of in all the green. "An hour, then. Back here."

The centrepiece of the park is the monolith. Standing before it, I understood why, when Vigeland was first working on these monuments, half of Oslo hated him. It is huge, made of whitish granite probably sixty-five feet tall, and depicts more than a hundred human figures twined and writhing about each other, some standing on and others clambering over their neighbours to reach the top. Not a very Norwegian sentiment. Around its base, on plinths on the steps leading up to it, are Vigeland's vision of humanity teaching, playing, fighting, loving, eating and sleeping: a woman combing another's hair; a man with children; a child having a tantrum. Massive figures, all naked, all gazing down at Norwegians with truth in their eyes.

I was still there when Julia climbed the steps. "I've just read in the museum that that piece of granite weighed two hundred and sixty tons and in 1926 took three months to transport to here from the harbour through the streets of Oslo."

"Another reason for them to hate it."

She gazed up at the figures, shading her eyes from the sun. "Hate it?"

"The primary tenet of Norwegian social life is something called the Jante Law: Don't believe you are better than anyone else. We're all equals."

"I don't see what's so bad about egalitarianism."

"You didn't go to school here in the early seventies. They were ruthless: Don't do better than anyone else. Coming here was such a relief to my eleven-year-old self. Vigeland may have been an egotistical monster, but at least he sometimes showed the truth."

We studied it silently for a while. "The earlier work in the museum is quite different," she said. "There's one particular wall relief of emaciated figures. It's disturbing, very powerful."

"I like this better. You can see emaciated, tormented people anytime, in any city, especially the civilized ones."

"Why do you suppose his work was so large?" she said to herself as we descended the steps slowly. She stopped before the woman washing another woman's hair. "It's intimate, almost sexual, and yet quite ordinary. I suppose that's what he was trying to say: everything is ordinary."

"He was saying everything in life is special. Every moment is a gift."

She looked at me for a long, long time. Her eyes were sunlit, the colour of bluebells, and still shadowed very faintly with fatigue. She turned away. "We should get moving."

We caught the number 2 tram back down Bogstadsveien.

\*     \*     \*

The meeting with Edvard Borlaug of Olsen Glass was on the ninth floor of their new corporate building in the heart of the revitalized eastern side of Oslo. I briefed her on the way up.

"Don't ask about his family. That will be seen as intrusive. He probably won't indulge in small talk but will want to get right down to business. He will speak English, but may not always understand what you're saying, though he'll be too proud to admit it. I'll do my best to step in when I think that's happening."

It was an austere office, good furniture but quite plain. Borlaug was younger than I had expected. Even though she had been warned, I think his briskness took Julia aback. He strode out from behind his desk, shook Julia's hand firmly, and announced in basic English that he was a vice president of the corporation and fully empowered to make final decisions and that the corporation hoped to open the park next spring. I suspected he had been made vice president last week.

Julia introduced me as her "associate." He stepped back behind his desk and gestured at the two chairs in front of it. I sat between Julia and the window, and turned my chair to have a view of the door.

Now it was Julia's turn. She became grave and deliberate. "I don't know if it's possible to open the park by spring. A lesser project, perhaps, but if as you indicated in previous communications you want a lasting monument to the corporation's importance and achievement, it may take longer."

He seemed to relax: she was not some silly American out to make impossible promises. "How much longer?"

"I think we should leave estimates about time and money until later in the discussion. Right now, we need to know what ideas you have had about what you want."

He pulled out a file folder. Opened it, closed it. Nervous behaviour, for a Norwegian.

Julia became even more steady and deliberate. "Why don't

we run over several possible avenues of approach and see if any of them seem appropriate?" He assumed the half smile people do when they don't want anyone else to know they've missed something, especially when they think others might think they are too young for their job.

I cleared my throat. "Perhaps," I said in Norwegian, "you will allow me to translate the more abstruse concepts." He appreciated "abstruse." No one would speak to him that way if they thought he was stupid. I repeated it in English. They both nodded. I translated.

The meeting lasted two and a half hours. Julia was very patient. She explained to Edvard Borlaug the various options: monumental outdoor parks, like Vigeland; indoor installations; traditional or interactive; representational or abstract.

A great deal depended, she said, upon their client base. "Who is it that you want to come and see the sculpture?"

"Everyone. All of Oslo."

"Fine, very commendable. But let's start from the beginning. We'll need information on who uses your building—corporate clients, the general public, others?—and how they use it—which doors and so forth. Where would the most natural installation be? How would we funnel people there? How long would you like them to stay? We'll need to know if the park is intended purely for enjoyment or whether its proposed function is more educational. For example, would you like to see schools bringing busloads of children to trample through the installation"—her prejudices were showing; I changed "trample" to "wander"—"or would they be under the feet of your corporate clients?"

I translated with half my mind, and used the rest to assess the room. The chairs were solid Norwegian pine; awkward as weapons, not strong enough for a shield. The desk, though, was probably a good inch of heart-of-pine, which would offer some protection from a small-calibre handgun.

He pulled pieces of paper from his folder: plans, columns

of figures. Julia read them with approval. He started to warm up. After forty minutes he seemed quite enthusiastic. They started to talk about glass—how a vitreous sculpture might hold up under the extremes of the Oslo climate. They got into maintenance questions: long-term care of the individual items of the installation; short-term care, such as keeping the grass mowed—if they decided they wanted grass because they could, of course, go with gravel. With glass and granite sculpture a gravel surface would be very evocative of the ruggedness of the Norwegian landscape. If he wanted representation of Norwegian sculpture, then, naturally, he would want something from the abstract pioneer Haukeland. And what did he have in mind for children?

He became almost animated. Perhaps representations of figures from myth and legend—a bridge, complete with troll and billy goats Gruff; Sampo Lappelil, the little Lapp boy who defeated the king of the trolls, with his reindeer; The Woman Against the Stream. I obligingly gave Julia condensed versions of each tale. Edvard drew sketches. They were surprisingly strong-lined and clean.

"Edvard," Julia said suddenly, looking at one, "where did the idea for this sculpture park come from?"

He blushed, and spoke in English. "The company made a big, a large profit last year. Which is good. But it was so large, it felt . . . it was felt we should not keep it all. We talked about giving it to a charity, but there are so many. And then we thought we could . . ." He pulled his thoughts together. "This part of the city is being built again. For a long time it was . . ."

"Desolate," I supplied.

"Yes. Desolate and empty. We can help to make it better, to give the people something good. And it will help to make more money, too."

He glanced at his watch and his face fell. "It's five minutes past four o'clock." He stood abruptly. "Thank you. Thank you. Perhaps we can meet again tomorrow?"

Julia looked surprised at his haste but she stood. "Certainly. The same time?"

"Earlier," I suggested. "Perhaps the morning."

"Yes," he said. "Eleven o'clock?"

The corridor was crowded. There was a queue for the lift. We took the stairs. Unlike an American stairwell, it smelled fresh and well ventilated; often used.

"So what happened?" Julia asked on the way down. "It all seemed to be going so well then suddenly, *phhtt*, he wants to get rid of us."

"Norwegians finish their workday at four sharp. He probably considered it very bad manners to have kept you past that time."

"Ah. Did you see how he blushed when I asked whose idea the park was? He seems a bit young to be in charge."

"He'll live or die by this project. If it fails, his career fails."

"Then we'd better make sure it doesn't."

We. How odd.

Outside, the streets were busy with home-bound office workers. "Would you like a walk before dinner?"

"Only if it's an aimless American stroll. And only if we get a taxi back to the hotel first so I can change out of this corporate drag."

When we got to the hotel, Julia suggested I wait in the lobby: It wouldn't take her a minute. I read *Dagbladet*, a name that translated pragmatically to *The Daily Newspaper*. Julia came back down in jeans and the sunset-coloured sweater.

We wandered up Karl Johansgate, now almost deserted, to Slottsparken.

We walked under the trees. "In winter this is all white, and crisscrossed by ski trails." Strangers are easy to see. "Tante Hjørdis bumped into King Haakon, literally bumped into him, over there near that statue."

"No security people?"

"The royal family are very informal."

"So how old is she?"

"In her seventies, I think. And she skis every day in winter."

"You come from good genes. How about your mother—is she like you and Hjørdis?"

"And how is that?"

She looked me up and down slowly. "Tall. Strong. Hidden. But Hjørdis's eyes are more blue. And she is less complicated, I think. Still very Norwegian. I don't think you are."

Under the tree shadow, I couldn't read her face. "My mother's eyes are more blue, also. She's shorter than Hjørdis. About your height, but wider. She is . . . subtle."

"You must have learned it from her." We reached the statue, which was surrounded by an ironwork fence resembling bare winter branches. Before I could stop her, Julia climbed over it and strode to the bronze statue. "Camille Collett," she read from the plaque. An early Norwegian writer. She beckoned me over. There was no English translation, but instead of asking me to tell her what it said, she touched my arm and said, "Aud, I want you to be less like your subtle mother and more Norwegian. I want you to tell me the truth, the whole truth, and nothing but the truth—everything you know about Michael Honeycutt. Tell me what he's up to, who those men might have been in his house. I need to know why Jim really died and if I'm . . . if they're likely to come after me when we get back to Atlanta. I need to know." She stood straight, unconsciously graceful, utterly serious.

"Let's find somewhere to sit."

The bar was only half a block from the Bristol. It had a Wurlitzer jukebox, a reasonable-looking menu, and table service. The music was loud, and the server had a sneer due more to a pierced upper lip than essential attitude.

"*Ol,*" I said, "and *akevit.*" The shots and beer chasers came

swiftly. "Just bring us refills when you see our glasses empty."
I picked up the *akevit*. "*Skal*." We drank it down.

Julia breathed heavily through her nose, and her eyes wa-
tered. "Not unlike grappa." She folded her hands together before her on the table. The formal effect was spoilt by her
having to shout above the music. "I know you've told me what
I paid to find out, but I would like the rest, with no evasions,
no elisions, and no sugarcoating."

"I don't have all the pieces."

"Then give me what you have."

I sipped my beer, considering. "When you first asked for
my help, you were adamant that the arson and Jim's death
had nothing to do with drugs. You were right in that Jim was
just an innocent bystander, but you were wrong in that the
case has everything to do with drugs. No, just listen. Honeycutt has been laundering money for the Tijuana cocaine cartel. Don't confuse the Mexican cartels with those from
Colombia. They don't produce or process, all they do is ship
or sometimes simply allow passage."

I used the salt shaker to pour an outline of central and
north America onto the formica. I put my thumb across Mexico. "The Mexicans, here, are middlemen: the Colombians can't
get their product to the western U.S. if the Mexicans don't
allow it." I lifted my thumb. "The Tijuana cartel employs Federal Police, U.S. border inspectors, local police on both sides
of the border, and San Diego and Los Angeles gang members.
For U.S. drug enforcement, it used to just be a western and
border states problem, but according to the DEA and the Georgia Bureau of Investigation the influence of both Tijuana and
Sinaloa cartels has been marching steadily east." I drew a salt
arrow. "Atlanta passed quietly into the hands of the Tijuana
people three years ago. And I mean quietly."

The server brought us more *akevit*. I brushed away the map
and sipped the icy liquor.

"These cartels have a lot of power and influence. They are

almost immune from the law. They own the Mexican Federal Police, and they own the politicians, and the Mexican voters think that's fine because the only people getting hurt are Americans—and the few Mexicans who don't play ball. They are smarter, more attuned to the rest of the world, and higher up the business evolutionary tree than the Colombians."

"What?"

The music was getting louder. "I said, they're a leaner organization. There's no Tijuana guy in Los Angeles or San Diego, just his consultants—gang members who act as enforcers and hit men without any of the usual benefits, like protection. The key to the success of these cartels is their relatively low profile: the bloodshed can be passed off as gang warfare; which means the bribes are easier for those in authority to stomach. Money moves to and fro smoothly. Only there's a great deal of money, and unless the cartel's bankers can clean it up sufficiently, the heads of the cartels can't really use it."

"Money laundering."

"Precisely." Behind Julia, someone was smoking hash. I wondered if there were Moroccan cartels. "Honeycutt is laundering tens of millions a year. Some of it must go through his bank, probably in shell accounts, but some gets cleaned up by buying artworks, selling them overseas, then banking the sale money quite legitimately."

"Like the Friedrich. But that was a fake."

"This is where it gets interesting. Honeycutt uses dirty money to buy one legitimate painting or sculpture—"

"Or Anglo-Saxon armring."

"—sells it for clean money, and banks it openly. But then he sometimes also gets a copy, a fake, made, and sells that, too. This time, the money goes into his own personal account. I suspect he was using the money to pay off a blackmailer. When you spot the fake, he panics: tries to have you, your colleague and the evidence all go up in smoke. But the good

the blue place / 191

news, the very good news, is that the cartel doesn't know about it." Just the blackmailer.

In the dim light, surrounded by swirls of sweet hash smoke, she was as clear as a cut-glass figurine. "Explain."

"Honeycutt hired in someone used by the man who *used* to run the drug trade in the Southeast—not someone who the Tijuana cartel would employ. Besides, the cartels pay a lot of money for good, quiet, loyal service. They don't want their employees or consultants drawing attention to themselves by silly stunts for personal gain."

"So Honeycutt is terrified the cartel will find out. . . ."

"And we can assume, for now at least, that they know nothing of you, or me." And I would dearly like to keep it that way.

"Then if the cartel doesn't already know . . ." She tapped her fingernail on the table while she thought. I couldn't hear it. "Who planted cocaine in Jim's garage?"

"I don't know."

"Could it have been Honeycutt?"

"I doubt it. He is strictly a money man. He probably wouldn't have had access to the drugs. And that coke was worth a lot of money. He would rather have pocketed the proceeds."

"Then who?"

"The blackmailer. Those three men at Honeycutt's house were there to remove any evidence of a link between him and the blackmailer. They didn't succeed. It might have been better for us if they had. I have no idea who the blackmailer is, or how much they know about you, or what they might do about that. The whole operation smells of calculation and organization and money." Which, of course, made absolutely no sense: where would someone who was blackmailing for money get the cash to pay for several kilos of cocaine? Assuming that it was, in fact, the blackmailer who planted those bags.

"They're going to come for me, aren't they?" She could have been talking about a taxi pickup.

"I don't know."

"How would they do it?"

When I had been three months in the APD, my partner and I had pulled over two men on a routine traffic stop. Officer King had stepped up to the car and asked for some identification. They had backed up their car and run him down. I still remember the crunch the tires made going over his left arm. I shot out the perps' rear tires, called in their license plate, and drove King to the Piedmont emergency room. He had sat there, perfectly composed, while the doctor and nurses clipped away his uniform, cleaned up torn flesh and muttered over X rays. When they told him they were going to have to operate, to put all the bones back inside the flesh and then screw on a steel plate, he had pursed his lips, nodded, and said curiously, "What size screws do you use?" Partly shock, partly genuine curiosity, partly a need to drown the reality of the whole in a flood of incremental and essentially useless details.

"There are as many different methods as there are killers."

"I thought we agreed no evasions, no elisions, no sugar-coating." She folded her hands again, a neat, tidy package between the empty glasses, beer rings, and salt.

"I would be guessing."

"Then guess." Her gaze was unwinking.

"Death is not something I like to play guessing games with."

"I don't consider obtaining information in order to stay alive a game." Her voice was suddenly savage. "I feel as though I'm spinning in a greased barrel here, with nothing to hang on to!" She picked up her brimming glass of *akevit*, swallowed it down in one gulp, and slammed the empty glass down. "So help me out."

"If I were the mystery person who sent those men to Honeycutt's house, I would kill you in Norway. Less chance of it being connected back to Atlanta. There again, no one knows you're here, so that's unlikely."

"I gave Mrs. Miclasz the name of the hotel. But she promised not to mention it to anyone else."

Promises were useless in the face of torture. "You might want to give her a call, just to make sure everything's all right."

Her hand tightened around the glass until the webbing between her thumb and index finger was quite white. "They wouldn't!"

"Probably not. Just a precaution." But I was still uneasy. Why? What had I missed?

"Go on."

"Supposing he knew you were here, it would be child's play to bring you down from a distance with some kind of scoped hunting rifle, and those would be easy to get hold of in Norway. You were a perfect, stationary target in the park." I imagined her folding down in surprise, eyes wide, hot red blood splashed on bronze. "But it's not hunting season, there's no way to make such a shot look like an accident, and that's what he'll want this to look like. He might shoot you, but if he did it would be with a World War II relic, an old Lahti pistol maybe, and it would be set up to look like an accidental discharge while you were cleaning it." No. A tourist wouldn't be cleaning a gun. "That's unlikely." I sipped at my beer. So much depended on how much time he had, what kind of person he was. I had a sudden image of an iceberg: cold and unwinking, nine-tenths hidden. "If he thinks he can afford to wait to bring in professional talent, then it would be an elegant accident: a drowning in the harbour"—*Julia, hauled blue and swollen from the cold fjord, winch chains dripping, onlookers gawking*—"maybe electrocution in your hotel bath"—*thrashing water, hum and sizzle, stink of sphincter letting go.* "But if he was in a rush, then it would be local talent with less finesse. A mugging gone wrong might be the way to go. Have you ever seen a body that has been bludgeoned to death?" Her face was pale and set but I couldn't stem the flood of words. "The body is remarkably resilient. Take skin, for example. It has to take a blow over a bone before it will split." *Those lovely cheekbones, gaping wide.* "And you can live with a dozen broken bones, with the loss of a kidney or lung, pierced by one of those splintered ribs." *Hiss of air like a punctured tire.* "The surest method would be a blow across the throat, then the larynx swells and death by asphyxiation follows in two or three minutes. Most likely they would just beat you around the head for a while. The skull, though, is designed to take punishment. If they hit the wrong places you'd be conscious for quite a while. . . ."

She watched me, eyes soft as a doe's, and I imagined a hand lashing out, a fist reddened by working on an offshore trawler, pulping her cheekbone, tearing open her cheek, ripping loose one of those eyes, and my throat tightened around the ugly words.

". . . there's always fire. The way Jim went. Only if it's a fool doing the setting it will be in a place where it won't be fumes that take you but the flame itself. . . ."

My voice went on and on, harsh and brutal, and the pictures in my head flickered like a series of Technicolor slides: Julia, blackened like charbroiled steak, bits of clothing sticking to raw muscle; Julia, butchered like a goat; broken like a painted doll on the rocks. . . . I couldn't stop talking, and I couldn't stop the pictures. Those beautiful hands, folded so neatly before her on the table, would lash out but he would have her from behind in a garrotte. When she fell she might have five seconds' strength left, which she would spill out scrabbling against the pavement, tearing out her nails.

" . . . or they could smother you in your bed. Is it real enough for you yet? Is it? Because this might be a foreign country for you but people still die here. They still leak blood." *Their bright eyes still fade.* Her nostrils were wide and although her fingers were still folded, they were white around the knuckles.

"It's real," she said. The words were squeezed out, the way you squeeze air from a Ziploc bag before you seal it. I wondered if she might faint.

"Julia . . ."

She breathed for a moment. "If you were trying to scare me, you succeeded."

"I wasn't trying to—"

"Yes, you were." She stood. "I'm going to call Annie. I can find my own way back to the hotel. It's only half a block. Good night." Her back was straight; she moved with enormous, fragile dignity.

Had I been trying to frighten her? Yes. Yes, because she had to *see*, she had to *know*, because she had to stay safe, had to, because someone—someone I didn't know, someone I couldn't see or hear or smell—was waiting back in America, and maybe their reach didn't extend across the Atlantic and the North Sea to Norway, but maybe it did. I watched through the window as she entered the Bristol. "Another *akevit* over here!"

The corridor was quiet, the lights muted. The hotel hummed in shut-down, nighttime mode. There was a tray outside Julia's room. I squatted down to look: the remains of a hamburger and fries. Upset enough to revert to familiar food, but not upset enough to lose her appetite. I touched the bun. Stone cold. Not surprising. It was two in the morning.

The door to my room seemed narrower than it had been. I clipped the doorjamb with my left shoulder as I went in. I did not turn the light on; there was enough illumination coming through the gauzy inner curtains to make out the tightly made, impersonal bed, the chaise longue, the connecting door. I stood for a while and listened. I was breathing heavily through my mouth. I shut it. Nothing.

I took off my jacket and threw it on the bed. Sat down. Stood up again. Still no sound from Julia's room.

I eased the connecting door open. It was warm, much darker than my room. I closed the door behind me, listened. Nothing. I crept towards the bed. Still nothing. My heart began to pound like an asymmetric crank. There was a shape on the bed, very still.

My eyes were adjusting. I could make out her head, the spill of hair across her pillow. I reached out, held my hand, palm down, just above her face. Warm breath, steady and strong. I blinked hard. She slept on.

She knocked on the connecting door just before eight. "Aud, are you awake?"

"Come in."

She was still in her robe, hair tucked behind her ears. She seemed surprised to find me still in mine, drinking coffee on the bed. She smiled tentatively. "That smells good."

I picked up the phone, talked to room service.

"What did you say?"

"They're bringing more coffee, another cup, and breakfast. I asked them to hurry." She hovered. "Please, sit. Or we can sit over by the window if you would be more comfortable." I felt ridiculously formal. "Julia, I want to apologize. Last night—"

"No. I came to apologize to you. I asked."

"There was no need for me to go into such detail."

"No, it was me who— Oh, give me some of that coffee will you?" I handed her my cup. She took a sip, then a gulp, made to hand it back but I made a *keep it* motion. She finished off the coffee, despite the cream. "That was good. You know what frightened me more than the details? The way you talked about it. Your face was . . . I've never seen anything like it, except maybe some African sculpture. All implacable planes. Almost inhuman. And your voice, harsh as a broken engine.

And I looked at you and thought: Oh, that's what he'll look like when he comes for me. I'll just be a thing, a problem to be solved, and it doesn't matter that I've eaten cod's tongues, or that I really don't much care for *akevit*, that I like roses even though they have too many thorns, and hot coffee in the morning. I felt inconsequential."

Room service rapped on the door before I could say anything and I had to attend to the usual ceremony of pointing out a table—by the window—signing the chit, wishing him a good morning.

"Come and eat." In the light by the window her hair was more sable than black, rich as a bear's winter pelt. I wondered how it would look flung back in pleasure. We sat opposite each other at the tiny table and though they did not touch, I felt the heat of her bare leg on mine. We pulled off lids.

"Bacon!"

And eggs, and juice, and toast. "I thought you might like something familiar and comforting. It's Danish bacon—more like Canadian than American. Less fatty." I realized I was in danger of babbling and poured coffee for us both. We ate quietly.

"I called Annie. She's fine."

"Did you tell her to be careful?"

"I didn't have to. As soon as she worked out I thought something might have happened to her, she pestered me with questions. I told her I'd explain everything when we got back. She said she'd be careful."

"Good."

We ate some more. "I was looking through the What To Do In Oslo pamphlets. The National Gallery sounds interesting. I thought we could go this morning. That is, I'd like to go, and I hope you'll come with me. And maybe later we could get that dinner we should have had last night. Oh, unless Borlaug wants to take us out to celebrate the finalization of the park contract."

"He won't. In Norway one never mixes business and plea-sure." Dornan smiled at me from the back of my mind, and raised his eyebrows.

Early morning shoppers sipped coffee in the outdoor cafés of Kristian VII's Gate. Along Universitetsgata, students in bright colours stood on the grass talking in groups of two and three. Everyone looked splendidly healthy. They had probably had more than three hours' sleep.

We had to wait outside the gallery for it to open. Julia was restless. She was wearing another silk shirt, this time in deep blue. It pulled to and fro over her shoulders and breasts as she shifted her weight from heels to toes and her briefcase from one hand to the other. Her hair was in a fat braid, tied back with brown velvet that matched her pants, and hanging over her right shoulder. She looked at her watch. "How long will it take to get to Olsen Glass from here?"

"Fifteen minutes if we take the tram, but allow thirty."

The doors opened. In the lobby, she checked her briefcase and looked at the signs. "So the question is, do we do a light-ning tour of the whole place or concentrate on one area?" She nodded decisively. "We'll just do the section on Norwegian painting. This way."

We were the only ones in the Norwegian gallery. The first thing that caught her eye was one of J. C. Dahl's huge paint-ings of fjord light and water. She stood before it and her rest-lessness dropped away. She became as still as the deep dark waters of the fjord. Her chest moved gently as she breathed, her eyes unfocused. I knew that if I put my hands on her shoulders, they would be soft and relaxed. This was a Julia I had not seen before: distant, analytical, expert. The minutes passed. Suddenly she cleared her throat and moved on, walk-ing past the works of Tidemand and Gude with a quick glance and a nod, as though confirming a theory. She spent a little longer with a series of etchings depicting barn dances and summer village scenes. "Well, here are some people at last." She leaned closer, then stepped back, looking from one to another. "I can understand that Dahl wouldn't want to put people in his paintings—they would be dwarfed by the scenery—but these artists seem to think people do nothing but dance around and put flowers in their hair."

She was not really talking to me.

"Now look at this," she said, in front of a big abstract canvas of purples and greens. The nameplate read WEIDEMANN. "Even this is about nature." I wondered how she could tell but I kept my doubts to myself.

More paintings.

"Full circle," she said. "Neo-Romanticism. This painter may as well have been a Romantic who watched television." We went back to the Dahl that had so interested her. "It reminds me of Hjørdis."

Mountainside, cloaked in fir, falling straight into water as smooth and reflective as glass. You knew, looking at it, that it was a mile deep. Lush spring flowers, laughing sky. But changeable, and everywhere bones of rock. Good country in summer, but dangerous if approached without caution and, in winter, utterly isolated from the next valley by mountains suddenly cloaked in ice and mist. Troll country.

"I'm beginning to understand." She reached out as if to touch the painting, then drew back. "So . . . untrammeled. Uncompromising. This is how you all like to see yourselves, isn't it? The consensus of the national psyche: clear, uncomplicated, immovable as granite." She looked at me with the same concentration she had directed at the painting. I felt her gaze on my bones, the cant of my eyebrows; weighing the line of jaw and length of neck; noting colour and shadow. "But these paintings don't tell your story, do they, Aud? These paintings don't have bad dreams."

We stood there for an age, facing one another. A light above one of the paintings began to hum.

"These paintings show sunshine," I said. "They show spring and summer, and when there is snow it glitters white and bright." I held out my left hand. She gave me her right. It was cool; I held it carefully. Neither of us said anything as I led her from the room, down a corridor, through a door.

"This is the Munch Room."

Self-portraits of Munch bleeding from gunshot wounds. Paintings of the sick and dying. And *Skrik*, with its sky swirling lower and lower, a long bridge whose planks aren't quite clear because there's not enough light to see, to make out anything clearly, but that doesn't matter because the world is grey and you don't care; wavy lines of nightmare; the face of one so utterly alone they scream to shake the world.

"This is how it is during *mørketiden*, the murky time, the lengthening nights of winter. The sky is so low you feel as though you could reach up and touch it, but even if you could, you couldn't, because everything is so grey you can't tell where the ground ends and the sky begins. There is wind, but it can't get through the unreality, the knowledge that it will get darker and darker, day after day. You go to bed at night and pray that tomorrow the cloud will clear and the sun will shine, just for a little while, but you wake up and it's dark, and it's raining, and it's only the first of December."

Her hand stirred in mine, then she had my hand in both of hers, was lifting it to her cheek for a moment, letting it go. Neither of us said anything.

A sudden gaggle of noisy children clustered in the doorway while their teacher marshalled them into pairs. They held hands and giggled and pointed at the paintings. The Munch gallery was once again just a room in a museum.

"Ask them whether they would prefer an abstract or figurative sculpture park," I said to Julia in an undertone. She huffed with quiet laughter. The teacher gave us an apologetic look as we left. We smiled at her with sympathy.

Outside, the students in their bright colours no longer seemed so gaudy, and I found my fatigue was gone.

The meeting with Borlaug went well but they were still mired in details at one o'clock. They agreed to a forty-five-minute break for lunch. We wandered down Dronningensgate. She stopped outside Café Tenerife. "Do you suppose it would be the act of an Ugly American to eat Spanish food in a Norwegian city?"

"Have you ever been to Spain?"

"No."

"Then think of it as a two-for-one experience."

We ordered a mountain of food.

"There's still so much to be decided," Julia said as she divided the tapas onto two plates, neat as a cat. We both ate ravenously. I was careful not to let my leg touch hers under the table.

"Do you need me this afternoon?"

She tilted her head, considered. "No. I think he's past the shy stage. He'll ask if he doesn't understand."

I walked her back to the building—she swung the briefcase, the way an adolescent, caught between girlhood and womanhood, might—and stopped outside the plate-glass entrance.

"I'll return at four. Please wait in the lobby, even if you finish early. If you're ready very early, call the hotel. I'll check for messages."

The concierge at the Bristol had bulging, oyster eyes and an encyclopedic knowledge of business in the city. I told him what I wanted and in ten minutes had a confirmation number for a four-wheel drive Audi and a cellular phone, to be delivered tomorrow at eleven-thirty. I tipped him and asked him to tell the front desk that I might be expecting messages but would be calling in for them from outside the hotel.

The harbour smelled of sunshine on cold water, the wet

wood and diesel fume of boats, and the shrimp the crews cooked and sold from the deck in little white paper bags, heads and shells still intact. When the breeze changed direction it brought the scents of warm city stone, flowers bursting into bloom in the hills and the wildness of spring. I walked faster, drawing the heady mix deep into my lungs.

Two buskers with guitar and electric violin played some folk tune with fierce underpinnings, careless of the fact that no one seemed to be listening. I stood there awhile, letting the music prod at me and work its way under my skin. They nodded when I tossed some coins in the hat, and launched straight into an idiosyncratic reworking of Grieg.

Away from the harbour, the streets turned to neoclassical nineteenth century buildings and glass and steel towers built in the last two decades. Fire had done as much damage to Oslo over the years as Sherman did in Atlanta. I wandered, paying no particular attention, just absorbing the city through the soles of my shoes and the taste on my tongue.

I am used to being alone, used to autonomy, the freedom to stop when and where I want, be as I please. I could walk into a shop, like this one—chat earnestly to the girl behind the counter about a friend's birthday, and which were the *best* chocolates she possessed, how much was *that* gorget; pay for them; ask for them to be wrapped—and the other customers would remain untouched by my presence, I by theirs. No one knew me; there was no one to compare my behaviour in the shop with my behaviour at other times. I could be fluid and responsible only to myself.

In my imagination, Julia snorted: *Very Norwegian!*

The image made me smile as I angled north and east. Half a mile or so from the Olsen Glass building the pavement was torn up and cordoned off. Below street level, a handful of people in cut-offs and work boots sweated away earnestly with pickaxes and shovels. They were young, and all cut from the same mould: plump tan muscles, fair hair, soft cheeks. Archaeology students. What looked like rotting foundations were partly exposed. One man was using a trowel to slice away clay, rasher by rasher, from what looked like a support post. He stretched, saw me watching, and nodded.

"What is it?" I called down.

"Remnants of the old city. Fifteenth century, we think."

It would be good to jump down into the pit, roll up my sleeves and swing a pickaxe on a spring day.

"This was a large building—look at the size of this post— perhaps with some kind of ritual or civic function."

He seemed hopeful rather than sure. *Ritual or civic function.* He made it sound so alien, but the men and women who had cut the trees, dug the post holes, woven the hangings, would have had the same concerns as us: hunger, love, irritation. It was probably something utterly prosaic: the fifteenth century equivalent of public toilets, or a tavern, or—given the unchanging nature of humanity—a combination. I could almost see a local burgher, drunk from celebrating the return of some trading ship and a handsome profit, staggering outside, twitching aside his velvet and pissing against the corner post.

The archaeology student went back to his task, nose just an inch away from the wood.

The western side of the Olsen Glass building looked like a slab of gold in the slanting sunlight. The entrance and lobby were on the south side. I was five minutes early. I stayed on the pavement.

When the lift doors opened and Julia stepped out, I watched her through the plate glass. It must have been warm in Borlaug's office; the top buttons of her shirt were undone, the sleeves rolled above her elbow and her hair pulled up into a topknot. She looked alert and lithe, a dancer with a briefcase in the wrong building. When she turned her head this way and that I saw the movement of smooth muscle under her skin. I stepped inside the door. Her face lit, softly, like a candle.

"All settled?"

She patted her briefcase. "Signed, sealed and delivered. The preliminaries, anyway. Ah," she said, as we hit the pavement, "what a lovely afternoon! I want a bath, a drink, and dinner. Followed by another drink. I feel like celebrating. It's the start of my vacation."

We were sipping our coffee and contemplating a liqueur. Well-fed, well-bred conversation hummed round us lazily. Julia sighed and leaned back. Light poured over her face, dividing at her nose and spilling over her bare shoulders and arms. Her dress, of a heavy grey silk, gleamed like oiled chain mail, and the tiny hairs on her forearms could have been made of platinum.

"This is when I would kill for a panatella." Her laugh was low and rich and adult; it fumed under my nose like a fine Armagnac. "No need to raise your eyebrows like that. I gave up smoking six years ago, but this is when I miss it most. And the smell of cigars is delicious."

"But, like coffee, they never taste as good as they smell."

"True."

I lifted my jacket from the back of the next chair and took a flat box from the inside pocket. "Your native guide decided you ought to have a souvenir of Oslo." I laid it on the heavy linen tablecloth in front of her.

She touched the velvet lightly. I imagined how it might feel against her fingertips. The moment stretched, then she opened the box. She said nothing. I couldn't see her eyes. She tilted the open box this way and that so that light ran over the polished pewter. "Aud, it's beautiful."

"Then it should suit you."

She lifted it out, draped its supple links over her forearm. It was as though someone had turned woodsmoke into metal and laid it against her skin—which suddenly seemed darker, more mysterious and infinitely alive. "It's heavy." She ran it up and down her arm, playing, enjoying the sensation.

"The maker assured me that it's been designed for comfort as well as beauty. The swan's neck is also meant to represent Oslo." The lines were simple and dramatic, the swan more suggested than actual.

"I have to try it on." She stood.

"The bathroom is that way." I pointed behind me.

While I waited the waiter came and asked if there was anything else we wanted. I ordered brandy for me, more coffee for Julia, and the check. I waited some more. No other diners were missing. She was just admiring herself in the mirror.

The check and brandy came. I paid one and sipped at the other, let it hang a moment at the back of my tongue until it seemed I would swallow more fume than liquid, and then Julia was sliding back into her seat, the gorget lying around her throat: swan's neck around swan's neck. She was right, it was beautiful.

She leaned forward until I could almost have kissed her. Her eyes were brilliant. "You have to tell me why. No flip answers. Why did you buy me this?"

"I don't know." I had said I *don't know* more times since I had met this woman than during the rest of my life put together. "I saw it in the shop. The sunlight caught it. I saw it and thought of you." Thought of you in Borlaug's office, the way your lip sometimes almost catches on your bottom incisor when you smile, how much I wanted to *see* you smile. "I thought of how it would look on you. I bought it." She listened with an odd, patient expression on her face that I could not interpret. I had not given her what she wanted to hear. I did not know what that was.

She stood suddenly. "Finish your drink. I want to go dancing."

We walked the long way round, south along Akershusstranda, the last glimmers of twilight on our faces. The sky was indigo and ink and the people walking laughed with a shiver of excitement: it was spring, and Friday night in the big city. Julia's dress slid back and forth over her hips and her gorget gleamed. She seemed on the edge of something—restless, unsettled. As we neared the club, the bass thump thrust a hand in my belly and stirred. My heart accelerated.

There was a line. The flashing neon sign over the doorway caught on piercings and leather and smooth faces. The music was a wall of sound. Julia lifted her face to it, as though it were the sun. She smiled, then laughed aloud.

The line moved slowly. Julia hummed to herself, moved with the music. The air felt wild.

When we reached the head of the line, the man at the door held out his hand.

"How much?" I asked.

"Sixty krone. And ID."

I reached for my wallet.

"What did he say?"

"He wants to see ID." I found my driver's license.

"What do you mean, he wants to see ID?" She turned to him, and suddenly all that restlessness was focused. "Oh, come on. Just how old do you think I am?"

He just held out his hand a bit more emphatically. I gave him my license. He scrutinized it carefully.

"Oh, that's just great. How old do you think *she* is? Sixteen? And I suppose you think we've flown all the way to this country and faked ID just so we can get into this club!" Her voice was fierce.

"Julia, he's just doing his job. This is an over-twenty-six club."

"A what?" Now it was my turn under those unwinking eyes. I looked right back at her.

"You have to be over twenty-six. How is he to know you're twenty-nine?"

"Indeed," he said, with a formal little half bow, "you look much, much younger."

I thought for a moment she would hit him. She restrained herself visibly. "That, I suppose, is meant as a compliment. I don't take it as such. Here is my license. If you won't let us in here, just say so. Now give me that back and either let us by or not."

He gave back the license and she brushed past him. I paid and followed. The music was like a living stream, pulsing between bodies, collecting thickly in dark corners, vibrating bone so hard it might have been cartilage.

She was already at the bar. "I ordered you beer." She tossed down the shot next to the two glasses of beer and lifted a finger to the bartender—a big woman, all fat and muscle and chipped front tooth—who brought her another. "That pompous bastard." She drank half the second *akevit*. "God, I hate this stuff," then finished it anyway. "Why do people do that with ID? They make me feel . . . It's the way they look at you, as though you're trying to *cheat* them somehow. Look, look at my face. Is this the face of a twenty-four-year-old? No. Of course it's not. It's all bullshit, this show me your ID crap. Do I look like the kind of person who would lie just to get into this lousy club? I *hate* being accused of being a liar, of trying to get something I don't deserve. And as for that crap about, 'Oh, you look so young, ma'am . . . ' Ha! Compliment my ass. Why do you suppose anyone would think it was a *compliment* to be told you look young and unmarked by experience, that is, naive and an easy mark? Well, I am not flattered. I've earned this face!"

The gorget rose and fell as she breathed through her nose; the long muscles in her bare shoulders slid over each other as she reached for her beer.

"God, I hate this, too. Bartender, bring me a glass of chardonnay."

She was fierce and wild as a hawk. I could imagine her wheeling between cliffs, sun glinting from her talons, harsh *skree* echoing down the canyon.

"So. You're very quiet."

She would lift those wings, thrust herself from the ledge to beat the hot air, rise and rise, and when her marigold eyes caught tiny movement down below she would stoop: crack of wind under the pinions, tiny rodent squeak of terror, snap of vertebrae, then the beat-beat-beat upward, hare hanging warm and limp from her talons. And suddenly I understood all those *I don't know*s. Understood why I had come with her to Norway and taken her to visit Tante Hjørdis; why I had stood in that shop and bought the gorget; why I had shown her the Munch Room. I knew how the hawk's mate felt when she returned with the hare and they ripped its flesh from its bones and swallowed the raw muscle and skin and stared into each other's eyes. I understood why when she had asked *Am I safe?* I had said *I'll protect you*, because I would protect her, from anyone, anything. The realization was shocking, like the taste of a copper penny in my mouth, like the taste of blood.

She laughed. "You have the oddest look on your face! Forget my pissing and moaning, ignore it. We're here now. Drink some of your beer!"

The music was sinuous, insistent. She was moving with it again, swaying silver like a sleeping fish in its current.

"Dance with me," I said, and held out my hand, and when she took it, it was not like before, not like the Munch Room; it was like closing a circuit and the current ran straight through my bones and began to heat my belly.

"Ah," she said, and a flush bloomed under her cheekbones.

The floor was small and crowded with dancers, each their own private country as they moved belly to back, or wildly, like dervishes. Julia danced more with her body than her arms, more with her hips than breasts, and I could almost see the heat gathering below her navel, heat to match mine, like the molten core of a planet. This time we moved around a common centre of gravity that was suspended between us. It pulled us in, closer and closer, until the swell of her silver dress moved nine inches from mine, eight, seven.

"Aud," she whispered, "Aud . . ."

I put my arm around her waist and swept her through the crowd. She stumbled once, legs uncoordinated and uncaring, all attention fixed on the heat gathering between my arm and her back, between the flats of my fingers where they curled over her hipbone and brushed her belly. I thrust two hundred kroner at the man at the door. "Taxi," I said.

It appeared between one moment and the next and though the cab drove fast on empty roads, inside everything was still. We hardly breathed. My arm was still about her waist but neither of us moved as the heat built.

I must have paid him, must have ridden up in the elevator because suddenly we were in the familiar corridor and she was reaching for her doorknob and I was saying, "No, my room, it has to be my room," and we were inside and I was locking the door.

She stood in the middle of the room and waited. I stopped two inches in front of her and reached out with my fingertips, fluttered them across her lips, down her throat where a great pulse beat, across the bare skin above her dress, and she began to moan, a deep rhythmic moan with a huff, until I stepped closer and my thigh pushed against her belly and she spread her feet wider and groaned into my mouth. Holding her to me with one hand behind her head, I used the other to slide down her zipper. When I stepped away an inch, the dress began to slip and she started to writhe. With the same hand, I unbuttoned my shirt and unzipped my trousers and now it was like trying to hold down a hurricane, and then she was straining against me and we were on the bed.

She was strong, lithe and fit and wild past civility. I stripped her naked and she literally tore the shirt from my back, and when I pushed her down and straddled her she had my pants yanked down to midthigh and her arms around my neck, and we were breast to breast and I could feel the muscles in her stomach flexing under mine. Her eyes were black as basalt. I ran my hands down her flank, bumping over ribs, curving over her hipbone, and then she was pushing herself up against me and the cords in her arms and shoulders stood out as she pulled me down against her, and we were moving over each other, sliding skin to skin, spinning a cocoon of wet trails, breathing each other's breath, gazes locked, and the heat between us built, and she was muttering, "In me. In me." And we moved harder and faster, and the heat built and built and now she was shouting and her arms were knotted behind my back and the heat was a blast furnace, red yellow white hot, and then it came roaring out over us, filling the world with hot air, hot metal, and flesh and bone dissolved to nothing in its path.

Julia lay on her back, smiling. I stroked her head, still tasting the shock of realization. It was just like that time when I was nine years old, and I had been playing in the autumn-wild gardens of Horley House, running and jumping for the sheer joy of being alive, and my mother had leaned from one of the big sash windows and called for me and I had run and run, full of joy and energy and vigour, leaping over rocks, over low gorse bushes, over the pile of deadwood and brambles that the gardeners had pulled together for a fire. I remember the smoky Yorkshire air, the heat of my cheeks in the rushing cool twilight, the way they burned as I finally skidded to a halt in the hall, eyes bright, and my mother looked at me, went white, and said, "What have you done to your leg?"

And I looked down and thought: *Oh*. My left leg was sheathed in red from the knee down, as though I were wearing a bright red sock. Then I could smell it: sharp and coppery. Blood. I twisted and peered at the back of my leg. One inch below the fold of my knee was a gaping cut.

"Lucky you didn't hamstring yourself," said the young,

acne-riddled doctor at the hospital as he put in the final stitches.

I still have that four-inch scar today. I still wonder how it was that I got a wound like that—from the brambles, perhaps, or the nail in some old fencing—and not *feel* it, not feel the skin part, then the fat beneath it, and the plump, pink muscle beneath that.

Julia sighed and smiled some more. How had she managed to get inside me, slip between my ribs and rest against my heart, without me feeling it?

I stroked her up and down; so long and slim and fine. My stiletto. This is where the fear had come from, the unconscious knowledge that I was vulnerable. "I love you," I said. Her smile broadened: she had known all along. I laughed, and it was my laugh, not one designed to cover anything. I laughed again at the sound. She laughed at my pleasure. The world is a strange and splendid place.

We were packed and eating our second breakfast, this time in the hotel dining room, when the hire company delivered the car and phone. I had the driver bring the papers and phone to our table. I finished the smoked salmon while Julia called Edvard Borlaug to give him the number and tell him where we'd be, "Just in case." When she was done, I talked to Tante Hjørdis, who said she would be delighted to see us on our way out of the city.

I pushed the food aside. "We should leave room. She said we can't be there for an hour. She's making *koldt bord*."

"Does that mean what it sounds like it means?"

I nodded. "She always makes the same things, and always the same amount—whether she expects a horde or just two people."

While Julia oversaw the transfer of our luggage into the car, I checked us out. I had the absurd urge to lean confidentially towards the desk clerk and tell him what a marvellous day it was; to tip everyone obscenely; to sing. I restrained myself.

The sun was hidden behind low grey cloud, but the world was still a bright and exciting place. The Audi was about two years old but its four-wheel drive did not seem to have been much abused, though the sedate drive to Ulleval Hageby at the prescribed fifty kilometers per hour was not an exacting test. Julia's hand rested on my thigh as I headed into the suburb.

We parked just down the street. Julia climbed out of the car and looked up into the trees. "Is it my imagination or have the leaves grown in the last three days?"

They were bigger. Julia was beautiful beneath them.

I knocked. Tante Hjørdis opened the door and hugged me. Just as she was stepping back she stopped and held me out at arm's length to study for a while. Then she let go and shook hands vigorously with Julia. She gave Julia the same extra moment's scrutiny, then opened the door wide, and said over her shoulder as she headed for the kitchen, "The sauce needs watching." Inside, the table groaned with food, and the scent of fish and sauce drifted through from the kitchen. We followed it to find Tante Hjørdis stirring a tiny saucepan with a wooden spoon that had been old before I was born, adding flour, pouring cream. In another pan, round white balls bobbed in boiling water.

"*Fiskeboller*," Hjørdis said to Julia. "Pass me the cream, please." Then, in Norwegian, "Aud, you can unload the tray in the dining room and bring it out." I did. "Coffee," she said, which is coffee in any language. I filled the kettle and put it on the modern halogen stove to heat.

Julia was now stirring the sauce while Hjørdis fished the fish balls out of the water with a slotted spoon. "Norwegians make good spouses," she said out of nowhere. "Tidy, sensible, efficient. If you plan and budget and work hard—but not too hard the way you Americans do—life is steady and pleasant. There! We're ready to eat."

We started with the *spekesild*. Julia seemed to enjoy it. She told Tante Hjørdis her idea about a children's enclave at the Olsen Glass sculpture garden. Hjørdis put her fork down.

"Now, if he and his family were proper Norwegians, they wouldn't be making so much profit that they had to spend it on gardens. Money, everything is money these days. Oat flour costs twice as much today as it did two years ago. Twice. And do you know how much these Greenland prawns"—gesture to the shrimp lying abjectly in their mayonnaise—"cost? And work! Work, work, work. I call your mother, Aud, and I say, 'When do you come to visit?' and she says, 'Oh, Hjørdis, there's no *time* for a visit,' as though it's *me* who is being foolish. No time for family. Imagine that. But at least you have come to visit. And you have brought Julia."

We ate salad and thinly shaved reindeer meat. Julia asked Hjørdis what she did with her day when she wasn't preparing delicious lunches for guests. Hjørdis snorted. "I work with young people—and not so young—who should know better. Those who . . ." She looked to me for the English phrase.

"Drug addicts."

Julia looked only mildly surprised, but her right leg, lying close against mine under the table, jerked.

"I help with the . . ." Another look.

"Needle-exchange programme," I supplied.

"Yes, and facts about AIDS. Though they know more than I do, I'm sure. Personal knowledge." For a moment, her ruddy face stilled but then, with native pragmatism, she shook the sympathy away. "And I represent them, no"—this to me, as I opened my mouth again—"I *advocate* on their behalf with social services and so on. A lot of work, though less in summer. All this is since I retired, of course. Before, I used to work in a chemist . . . a pharmacist's."

"She was the pharmacist at Jernbanetorgets Apotek."

"Yes. It stayed open all night. I didn't have to work at night, of course, I could have asked one of the younger people, but it is only fair for everyone to take their turn sometimes.

That's when I met all the young people, so thin, so pale. So sad. . . ." Again, that head shake. "Come along. The *fiskeboller* will be getting cold."

We ate the fish balls. Soft and milky, so unlike anything else.

"You used to get that look on your face when you were only as tall as this table," Hjørdis said, smiling. She turned to Julia. "She and her mother used to come here every Saturday for my *koldt bord*, and every holiday." Sometimes my father came, too, but not often. "And Aud, who was sometimes not a well-behaved child, would try to steal some *fiskeboller* before we'd even eaten our salads. Eat, eat. I made enough for two helpings. But save some room, there is still the cheese, and dessert."

We started on the cheese. Julia and I sat so close our arms rubbed together when we reached for the crackers or the nuts. Her leg was still against mine. I retold the story of the Nigerian heroin ring I'd heard from Taeko.

"Now, we need berries for the dessert. Aud"—I stood; it had always been my job, from the time I was seven or so and strong enough to carry up the big glass jars from the cellar— "a jar of . . ." she looked from me to Julia and back again, "the *molte,* I think. Yes, the special *molte,*" she repeated with a certain satisfaction.

I hadn't been in Tante Hjørdis's cellar for years. As a child it had been a wonderland: past the laundry with stone troughs, which I imagined might have been used during the war to cut up captured Nazis; past the mysterious sheeted shapes in the storage room; to the cavern of treasures, a long room, narrow and dry, lined with row after row of shelves, each bending under the weight of pickled gherkins and canned tomatoes, of sauces and preserved berries, that glowed with muted colour— red and gold and emerald—like precious jewels under the dust of centuries. I ran my hand along the shelves, remembering being eight, fourteen, nineteen. . . . It was different. It took me a moment to work out that the difference was illumination: the single, swinging bare bulb of my childhood had been replaced by two halogen floor lights. It only made the colours richer.

The last four jars of special *molte* were on the top shelf. I'd heard the story of their picking: during the war, when there was no sugar to be had, she had picked them and put them whole into two-litre jars with fresh water only, sealed them, and put them in a cold stream to chill. I expected to have to stand on tiptoe to reach the big jars, but that was a child's memory; the top shelf barely came to my chin. I lifted one down, held it to the light. Fifty years old. They looked like golden raspberries. Perhaps Hjørdis exaggerated for effect and they were indeed preserved in sugar or some kind of syrup, or perhaps there was just a kind of magic in her cellar, where time and dreams stood still. I would not have been surprised to find myself three feet tall again, with both front teeth missing.

When I got back upstairs, Julia and Hjørdis were in the kitchen; Julia poured coffee into cups, Hjørdis whipped the cream.

"You always did spend a long time in that cellar, even as a child," she said, when she saw me standing there with the jar. "Bring that through to the dining room."

I put the jar on a placemat. Hjørdis, still standing, put one hand on the glass lid and the other around the wooden handle on the wire fastening. She pulled, then pulled again more firmly. "You have to seal them tight," she said. She had told me when I was a child that sometimes the rubber lining between lid and jar started a chemical reaction with the fruit and fused to the glass. She was having none of that. She put her strong back into it, and the lid came free with an audible pop. I shut my eyes and breathed. Lazy late summer sun, warm grass, the cold, bitter scent of the glacier half a mile away. Hjørdis ladled a good pile into a metal bowl and took it back into the kitchen. Over the sound of the food mixer, I said to Julia, "These are *molte*. Called cloudberries in English. Families guard the location of their favourite patch as closely as national secrets. More closely." I dipped one out with a spoon. It lay, still and golden and perfectly formed in its pool of liquid. I held it out. "This is how your hair smells."

"Ah-ah," said Tante Hjørdis from the doorway, "don't eat that. The only way to taste cloudberries for the first time is in Angel's Stew." She put the bowl of sweetened whipped cream and berries on the table and plucked the spoon from my hand. "Aud, dish that out while I go get the coffee, as Julia seems to have forgotten to bring it with her."

We sat. I dished the delicious mixture into three small bowls. "The last time Tante Hjørdis brought out her special *molte* was when my cousin Uta brought her fiancé to lunch with the family and then announced she had already married him that morning. She brought out a jar, too, when my mother married my father, though she told me once she should have known he would leave her and regretted ever letting him taste them."

Julia's hand was cool and soft on mine. "She will never have cause to regret this." A statement of fact. *She will never have cause to regret this. The sun will rise in the east and set in the west. Two and two is four.*

We took E16 north. Julia drove. "At least they drive on the same side of the road we do, even if we do have to keep to this snail pace."

"You can go up to eighty a little farther on, and past that, ninety."

"What's that in real money?"

"Fifty and fifty-six miles an hour."

Pensive silence. "How far is it?"

"About two hundred and fifty kilometers. But the last fifty are on very small roads."

"The road gets *smaller?"*

As she got used to the car, and traffic thinned, she relaxed. "So, now I've eaten Tante Hjørdis's cloudberries."

"Yes."

"She's pretty smart."

"When I was little, I used to believe she knew what I was thinking."

"That's just guilt. I used to think that about my mother whenever I'd done something wrong." The city was behind us now and we began to gain altitude. The speedometer needle inched forward. She looked at me sideways. "When we get back to Atlanta, I'll have to introduce you properly to my mother."

"Properly?"

"You've met her, you know. Twice."

Sitting in Julia's office, feeling like a child in a friend's house, waiting for them to come out and play. . . .

"Annie," I said. "Annie Miclasz . . ." She nodded. "I wondered why you never called her Annie. Always 'Mrs. Miclasz.' Did you know she asked me if I was dating?"

"No! Did she?"

"More or less. Told me carefully how you liked your coffee. Just in case I needed to know, I suppose. Watch the road, please. So, what's it like working with your mother?"

"Good, usually. She's been working for me for about four years. She used to be an office manager with GE but when she remarried six—no, god, it's more like ten years ago now—she didn't have to work. But she got bored, so when I left Boston and moved back to Atlanta to start my business, I offered her a job. It was more to prod her into getting a life, you know. I never dreamed she'd actually say yes and work for me."

"She's very good at her job."

"Do I hear the word 'formidable' lurking in the background?"

"Maybe."

"Well, you charmed her socks off."

"It was quite deliberate." I put my hand on her thigh. Muscle bunched and relaxed as she speeded up to pass an ancient Volvo then slowed again to eighty kph. We passed a sign for Hønefoss. "The road is going to fork in a kilometer or so. Highway 7 on the left, 16 on the right. Take the right."

I tried the radio. There was a lot of jazz, of course, two classical stations, and a Norden pop station pumping out thin, metallic stuff like recarbonated generic cola. Then I found Radio Norway. They were playing a folk tune I remembered from my early childhood, with simple words and handheld percussion. It was the first time I'd heard it sung by adult voices. I sang along.

"What's it about?"

"A troll who lives under a bridge." I translated as I sang. Julia laughed at the troll's stupidity.

Now that we were past the fork in the highway, Julia's interpretation of the speed limit was liberal. When we drove the twenty miles along the vast lake of Sperillen, I turned the radio off. Unlike a fjord, it was not sheltered by the steep plunge of mountains, and its gray-green waters were choppy. So different from the artificially flooded valley that had formed Lake Lanier just north of Atlanta—where during dry summers the stumps of trees and drowned homes occasionally ripped the bottom out of pleasure boats driven too fast by their too-young, too-stupid owners who saw a water as a surface, a water road, unaware of depths and currents and the life that dwelt there.

North of Sperillen, we started to climb. The river on our right, the Begna, began to tumble and show white here and there.

Julia glanced from the road to the river. "Does anything live in there?"

"Trolls. Trolls live everywhere in this country. There are homes here where if you say, 'Faen tar deg'—'The devil take you'—or *'Fy faen'*—which is 'Shoo, devil!'—you won't be invited again, nor will your friends. Words associated with the devil are *trollskap*, trollmagic. They open the boundary between this world and magic, and no good will come of it. These days, city people will laugh if you talk about trollmagic—but only if it's during the day and it's summer. Away from the city, they don't laugh at all. When you see the fjells and the fjords, you'll understand. This country's bones and flesh are made of rock and its blood is the ice-cold water of glacier melt. The world is a dark place, and three of the four seasons are winter: autumn winter, high winter, and spring winter. The summer, with its green trees, lush grass, flowers and berries, is a very thin skin over the realities. During *mørketiden*, when candlelight flickers on the walls and half the country hasn't seen the sun for a month, trolls walk the streets and grin at sleepers in their dreams."

"Tell me a troll story."

"The Billy Goats Gruff is a troll story."

"Tell me another one."

I considered. "When I was eight, I had tonsillitis. I had a fever that came and went and I didn't sleep well. The line between reality and dream was strange and wavery. One night, when I felt as though I had been awake for years and my throat hurt so much I couldn't swallow, my mother came and sat on my bed in the dark. She stroked my head. 'A thousand years ago,' she said, 'in Oppland there was a family, a hardworking man called Tors and his strong-minded wife, Astrid, and their sandy-haired daughters Kari and Lisbet, better off than most. . . .'"

I was surprised at how easily the rhythms of that long-ago night came back, how drenched through it was with all things Norwegian, complete of itself and needing no adapting. Julia was a good listener. It began to rain. Julia found the windshield wipers and the headlights. I settled back and, in my mother's words, told her how Tors had hired a man named Glam as winter shepherd.

Glam was a master of herding: the sheep seemed terrified of him, and all he had to do was call out in his terrible hoarse voice and they huddled at his direction. One night, while Glam was out with the sheep, the snow flurries became a blizzard. No man could step forth and live. That night, Lisbet had strange dreams of dark shapes battling in the snow on the fjellside.

In the morning the family woke to find that Glam had not returned. They walked up the mountain and found him in a bloody, levelled place. His skin was mottled and bloated, as though he had been dead a long, long time. Huge tracks, the size of barrel hoops, filled with frozen blood, led off to a deep and narrow gully. "Troll tracks," said Astrid. She peered into the gully, looked at the blood, and said, "Nothing, not even a troll, could have survived that."

They tried to move Glam's body, but it was as if his bones had turned to stone and he would not shift. In the end they covered him with stones where he lay.

Three days later, Lisbet woke in the middle of the night and ran to her mother. "Glam walks in my dreams!" The next morning, they found a dog—or what was left of a dog—on the stoop.

Astrid went to Tors. "Glam is not easy in his grave. You must burn him, husband."

But upon toiling up the mountain with faggots and tallow, and heaving aside the stones, they found nothing. Astrid said, "The troll lives in his bones and walks abroad wearing his skin, even under the sun."

And as the nights grew longer, Glam spread terror: running on the rooftops until the beams buckled, rolling great boulders down the fjell, crushing the spirit of men and driving cattle mad.

Now, it happened that at this time, a ship came into the

fjord and Grettir the Strong, who was tired of adventuring in foreign lands, heard of Tors of Torsgaard and his dead shepherd, Glam. He went to Torsgaard and saw Kari milking the cow, saw how her sandy hair turned to gold in a shaft of rare winter sunshine, and agreed to stay and deal with Glam, for he was curiously unwilling to leave Kari Torsdottir to the anger of the troll.

On the eve of his first night, Astrid gave him a plan.

And so, as the sun went down that evening, Tors found himself strangely sleepy and he snored. Astrid directed Grettir to pick up her husband and bundle him into the bed at the far end of the hall, away from the passage that led to the door. Then she dressed Lisbet in her warmest clothes, and the two of them stole out to hide in the barn. Then there was only Kari and Grettir. They stood opposite each other by the hearth. Grettir, forgetting himself in his fear for her, took her by the hand. "It's not too late to hide with your mother and sister."

"You will need me," she said. "We must bring Glam inside."

When the embers began to die, Kari lay down on the wall-bed by the inglenook. Grettir wrapped himself like a sausage in an old, heavy fur cloak and settled himself on the wall bench opposite Kari's bed. In front of the bench was a bench beam, a huge ancient thing set into the floor when the farm was built. He set his feet against it and straightened his legs so he was firmly braced between the beam and the wall. And then they waited.

Sudden as an avalanche, something leapt onto the roof and thundered about, driving down with its heels, until the new beam buckled and splintered and the roof almost fell in. Glam. The walls shook and Glam jumped down, and the earth trembled as he strode to the door. A sharp creak as he laid his huge horny hand on the door and suddenly it was ripped away, lintel and all, and moonlight briefly lit the hearthroom before Glam blocked out all light as he thrust his huge head through. The whites of his strange eyes gleamed like sickly oysters, and Grettir felt his heart fail him.

"Glam," said Kari. "If you want me, I will come with you, but I must have a bearskin to lie on. Bring that old cloak on the bench by the fire. I'll wait for you outside."

Glam strode over to the sausage-shaped bundle of fur and tried to pick it up with one hand. Grettir was braced and ready. He made no sound and the fur did not move. Glam pulled harder, but Grettir braced his feet more firmly. Glam grunted, and laid two hands on the bundle, and now a titanic struggle began. Grettir was dragged towards the door. Finally, with a furious wriggle, he eeled around in Glam's grip until his back was to the awful face and bull-like chest. He dug his heels against the threshold stone and with a strength that was equal parts fear, determination and desperation he leaned in towards the last breath of warm, indoor air. As Glam hauled backwards with all his might, so, too, did Grettir thrust *backwards*, and his last strength and the inhuman force of Glam's heave hurled them both outside. Glam, with Grettir still clutched to his breast, landed spine down across a rock. The loud *crack* of his backbone parting would live in Grettir's mind for the rest of his days. And then Glam spoke, hoarse and horrible in his ear.

"You will live, Grettir the Strong, but you will never be the same. You will always look into the dark and see my face, hear my voice, and know I will come for you. You may kill me, but I will live on in your mind." And the troll laughed, dark and full of wickedness. At the laugh, Grettir sprang to his feet, pulled free his sword, and swung. Glam's head, like some vile rock, rolled free, and Grettir did not laugh, but wept.

They burnt Glam right there, outside the hall. And then they burnt the ashes. And when the ashes were cold they were gathered in the torn cloak and wrapped tight, and Astrid saw to it that it was thrown into a chasm, and huge boulders hurtled down on top of it.

Torsgaard celebrated all day and into the evening, but eventually the fire dwindled and the torches were doused. Everyone slept. In the middle of the night, Kari was woken up by a strange noise, like a child crying. It was Grettir, trying to light a torch and rocking back and forth. "He will come for me. He will come for me."

"He is dead, beloved."

"I am all alone and he will come for me!"

"You will never be alone again." But he would not hear her, he just rocked and rocked, back and forth.

And the story goes that though Kari stayed by his side every living minute and married him not long after, his fear grew worse and he began to rock back and forth and light torches even in the daytime. In the end, they say he ran out, barking mad, and Kari was left without a husband and the hall at Torsgaard gradually declined. No flowers ever grew in the chasm where they had thrown Glam's ashes.

"Kids around here must have strange dreams," Julia said finally. "So the moral of the story is that the troll will always get you in the end."

"Even if you think you've won. Just like the land itself." I peered through the rain, which seemed to be easing. "We're in Oppland now."

"It certainly looks like troll country."

Just to prove her wrong, the rain stopped, and above and ahead wind thinned the clouds, sending them fleeing in tatters over the endless coarse grass and wildflowers. "The road gets narrower here."

"Your turn to drive."

We stopped the car and got out. The air was as cool and fresh as dew-laden grass. Julia stretched by the left-hand side of the road and I put my arms around her from behind. I kissed the back of her neck and she rested against me and we looked out over the uplands. A perfect rainbow arched over the undulating ground.

"You can see both ends," she said.

"There are fairies as well as trolls in this country."

We got back in the car. I rolled my window down. "It reminds me of the Yorkshire Moors," I said as I drove. "They stretch like this for miles. Every mile or so, in the wilder parts, there are these waist-high stone walls that form a circle with a section cut out. When I was eight years old, I thought they were windbreaks the farmers had built for their poor sheep. I had visions of little friendly groups of the woolly creatures huddling behind the walls while the world turned white with snow, and the nice farmers driving along in their wagons and unloading hay and turnips and other sheep treats. When I was a teenager, I found out they were hides for pheasant hunters. Beaters walk the moor in a line, whacking at the brambles and heather while His Lordship and his weekend friends crouched behind the wall with their matched Purdeys and silver hip flasks, waiting for the birds to burst out in a rush of frantically beating brown and cream feathers. In spring and summer it's green and dotted with tiny wildflowers. Autumn turns it into a haze of purple heather. Then the farmers burn it off and it turns into a blasted heath, desolate and destroyed. It stays that way all autumn and into the first hard frost of winter. Then there's the wonderful, softening white blanket, and by spring it all starts up again. It can be hard to believe that anything could come to grief in such a lovely place, but every year hikers die there. They forget that the world can hurt them. They wear silly little English T-shirts and street shoes and think a bar of chocolate is all the emergency equipment they need. Norwegians don't die out here, because they understand. They know about trolls."

"Do you think hobbits are the tame English version?"

The sun was bright now, and the air seemed thinner. We were the only car on the road. As Julia talked, I watched her.

I could not imagine driving this road without her in my car. I could not imagine going back to Atlanta without her turning restlessly in the plane seat next to mine. I could not imagine how things would have been if I hadn't turned that corner in Inman Park.

At Tyinkrysset I turned off the highway and five kilometers along the unmarked surface I pulled off the road.

"Where are we?"

"The lake below is Tyin."

"My god, it's green."

"Glacier water." But that was not why I had stopped. "Look north." We were above the tree line, and ahead lay a vast range of peaks, studded with green lakes and moraine-strewn flats. Jotunheimen, home of the giants. "This is my country. Before we enter it I want to tell you that I was wrong. If we were back in Atlanta, we might have something to worry about, but not now, not here. I think I was so uneasy because I didn't know what was happening." I took her hand. "I didn't understand just how much I needed to be sure you were safe, or why. I just knew I felt vulnerable. Well, now I do understand. And we don't have to think about Atlanta, about Honeycutt or his blackmailer anymore. They don't know we're here, and by now the police will have the situation well in hand. It's time to leave it all behind."

Her eyes were as blue and mysterious as the bottom of the ocean, her smile like the sun. "I left it all behind in Oslo, stepped out of it and left it in a crumpled heap on your bedroom floor."

eleven

The boat was old—Hjørdis had said she remembered the same carved prow from when she was a girl—and with the oars shipped it floated motionless in the middle of the glassy waters of Lustrafjord. Julia slept in the bow; I held a fishing line, utterly relaxed, mind as still as the water. There was no traffic, no machinery, just the occasional warble of the little dumpapers nesting on the far bank, and the creak of sun-warmed oak. It could have been another millennium.

The family seter was not quite that old, but Hjørdis thought its basic design dated from the fourteenth century. It and the loft were all that were left of a rambling farm, and our family had owned all the land I could see on the east bank of the fjord. We still owned a great deal, but the working farm had moved north and a little downslope, and instead of sheep it was now cows and pigs and, in the summer, berries. Old Reidun and her daughter Gudrun, and Gudrun's husband, ran the place. They also owned half of it. Once or twice a year when Hjørdis called, they would make sure there was fresh linen and firewood at the old seter, that the power was turned on, and the cupboards bulged with staples. We had driven to the seter, unloaded our bags, and found a note from Gudrun asking us to go down to the farm for *middag*. I thought it was more likely that Old Reidun wanted to meet Julia, but we went.

We were greeted by Gudrun and her husband, Per, who were about forty. *"Velkommen til Norge,"* they had said to Julia, and we had been ushered into the huge farm kitchen, where Reidun was supervising. We all shook hands, then she told us to go get a home-cured ham from the *stabbur*. "It's her way of saying we're family, not her landlord," I explained to Julia on the way to the curing house.

"But you own half the farm and don't put in any labour."

"We also don't take out any profit, which in some years is considerable. This farm is one of the prime spots for *molte* cultivation. But our side of the family, who owned the farm originally, moved to the city more than a hundred years ago. In return for half ownership and all the profits, Old Reidun's father agreed to work the farm and keep up the seter for our use."

Even after so long, it worked well. The two sets of honorary cousins regarded each other warmly but with a shake of the head that said: *They're not like us.*

*Middag* eight days ago had passed pleasantly with fiery homemade redberry wine, trout, the ham, *rømme,* new potatoes and salad. We had left loaded down with fresh milk, cream, butter, eggs, bacon and bread. Gudrun promised to resupply us every three or four days.

Julia, since we had been here, had eaten an astonishing amount. "It's just so good," she always said when she served herself seconds. We had walked, and napped, and eaten, and talked, and walked more, and now we bobbed about on the fjord because she hoped we could catch some perch.

She slept on. I cast again, watched the lazy ripples. If I squinted, I could just make out the flowers growing in the sod roof of the old loft half a kilometer away on the east bank. The seter itself was hidden by an outcropping of the fjell that plunged straight into the fjord and formed its eastern bank. Beyond the fjell was Jostedalsbreen, the largest glacier in Europe. When the wind was right you could smell the almost chemical bite of the ice but today all that filled the air was the scent of Julia's skin, like dusty, sun-warmed violets, and, even two kilometers beyond the bank, the pagan smell of the earth's skin: millions of hectares of birch breaking into leaf at the same time. There was nothing like it; it woke parts of me that usually slept.

"You look pleased with yourself." Julia was awake and watching me, her eyes a startling, sheened blue against the green lake.

"I'm breathing air like wine, I have money and good health, and I'm in a boat on green water with a beautiful woman. There's nothing I can't do."

She gave me a lopsided affectionate look. "Except catch fish."

I twitched at my line. Nothing.

"Let me have a go."

We traded places carefully. She cast expertly.

"Where did you learn how to do that?"

"Massachusetts. Guy taught me." Her mouth stretched in old grief and her eyes glittered. A bird sang from the woods far away on the west bank. Its call was heartbreakingly pure.

I held out my arms and, careful of the rocking boat, she came to me.

It never ceased to amaze me how she could feel as wild as a living hurricane one minute, and delicate, almost bird-boned, the next. I cradled her to me, felt her heart beating through her ribs. So fragile. I stroked her hair, over and over, and hummed a lullaby. Eventually she sat up and wiped her eyes.

"It's been nine years. I used to weep for him every day. It's less often now, and sometimes there are days, even weeks, when I don't think about him at all. Then I'll think of my other brother, Drew, or Carmel, my sister, and I remember I'm the eldest now, and I feel . . . They live so far away now, but I feel so responsible for them. And then I miss him. Missing him is like a hole inside me, a gaping wound, wider than the hands of anyone who would try staunch the bleeding. A hole so big it could swallow the world."

"I have big hands."

"I know." She tried a smile, and it worked pretty well. She took a deep breath and I could almost see her step aside from her grief and thrust it behind her. "There don't seem to be any perch biting in this part of the lake."

"Then I'd better row you to another part."

It was good to bend my back to the oars, to watch the boat scooting over the fjord and see Julia laugh in delight at the miniature bow wave I managed to throw up.

At some arbitrary spot that seemed no different from the one we'd left, she told me to stop. I shipped oars and watched her cast, and cast again. I lay back in the thwarts and listened to the sing and plop of the line.

The sky teemed like the Serengeti: herds of cloud antelope, springbok, even rhino with cloud horns, racing in the same direction; with a bit of imagination I could make out a warthog and a line of anteaters trundling nose to tail. Farther down, a cautious tortoise couldn't decide whether to creep north or south, and right at the horizon, three pearly gray porpoises seemed to leap from the water.

"I don't miss the Atlanta sky," I said.

"No?"

"No. You get up in the morning and the sky is blue. Later in the day you glance up and it's blue. While you eat dinner, you look out of the window and it's . . . blue. There are occasional days when you get up and it's blue, you eat lunch and it's blue, but when you have dinner there's a thunderstorm, and, admittedly, those skies are something, cloud as pink as an alligator's mouth, that gorgeous violet around sunset if the storm is on its way, the occasional green flash of a transformer going out—taking the power with it, of course—and it's nice to have the road freshly washed, but when you get up in the morning, it's blue again. You can't lie on your back and watch another world form and dissolve and dance minuets over your head. Unless you count contrails."

"Do you?"

The cloud tortoise was slowly being ripped apart by its own indecision, or maybe some haematovirus of the African plains. . . . "Um?"

"Do you count contrails?"

"If they have had the time to evolve. Sometimes I think of planes as seeding the skies with new life. . . ." We contemplated the clouds for a while.

"It's odd," Julia said at last. "You talk about life so much, yet you've been around a lot of death. I asked you before why you did this, and you said it was because you're Norwegian. So now I've seen Norway. It's a land that doesn't know compromise. It's snow, ice and darkness in the winter; and endless midnight sun, bright meadow flower and sweet green grass for two months in the summer. Black or white. On or off. Yes or no. It explains some of the way you react to what life throws at you, the pragmatic immediacy, the readiness—you never forget that there are trolls in the hills. But it doesn't explain why. Why you keep throwing yourself into the path of the pain in the world."

"No."

She waited.

"The pain of the world doesn't follow paths. It blunders all over the place. It ran smack into my bedroom, carrying a gun, when I was eighteen years old." She waited again. "It's a long story."

The antelope still galloped overhead, the dumpapers warbled, Julia seemed perfectly happy to sit there with that rod, waiting, until the Ice Age came again and we travelled around the world on a tongue of green ice. I sighed, and started at the beginning.

"I was born in England, where my mother was a consular officer, and didn't see Norway until I was two. The bit of English I spoke was a strange cross between the Chicago accent of my father and the south London of my nanny. We split our time between Oslo and Bergen until I was six, when we went back to the U.K. My mother was now an attaché. My father was busy with his business, flying back and forth between London and Chicago. I was either at school or up in Yorkshire, spending vacations with Lord Horley's children. I hardly ever saw my mother but I learnt not to miss her. I learnt to expect her to be a long way off, a presence who always came on the important occasions—birthdays, Christmas, school sports days—but who moved to a holy schedule arranged long in advance and never to be interrupted." The boat creaked as I leaned forward. "My mother is one of those people who always knows how to act, how to dress, even how to do her hair. She never, ever looks out of place. She could be at a bonfire night party in an ancient Berber jacket, cutting up parkin and treacle toffee for my friends, pulling charred potatoes out of the fire embers with hair all tousled and nose just the right shade of red from the cold November air one day, and the next she would be in cashmere and pearls, hair in a chignon, taking tea with Lady Horley. Everyone thought she was a perfect mother. But we were strangers to each other. Perfectly polite, perfectly willing to try to be a model mother and daughter, but unsure how. I think it upset my father."

"Did it upset you?"

"No. Not really. It's just the way my world was."

"But you want to see her when we go back through London. What changed?"

My whole life. "I'm curious. I think she is, too. And I think we're both ready to treat each other as real people, not some personification of a role. We went back to Oslo when I was eleven, then back to London, then back to Oslo. That is, my mother and I went back. My father left and went to Chicago when I was thirteen. I went back and forth between England and Norway until I felt that both were my home, and neither. I hardly ever saw my mother. I finished school when I was seventeen. That summer my father wrote and asked me to visit him in Chicago. I didn't want to spend summer in Chicago, but his invitation set me thinking. I was an American citizen who had never set foot in that country. And I thought: I could go to university there. So I applied to all kinds of schools, and I chose Georgia Tech."

"You're smart and well connected. You could have gone anywhere: Yale, Harvard, Smith. Anywhere. So why Georgia?"

"Because they said yes first. And because it's warm. So I made a few phone calls, flew to London, told my mother where I was going, and caught the plane to Atlanta the next morning."

"The next morning, just like that?" Her hair shimmered as she shook her head, then cast again. Hiss, plop.

"I flew economy on Delta, landed at five in the afternoon, local time, and got into a broken-down taxi whose driver had no idea where he was going."

"None of them ever do," she said, one eye on her float. "Should have rented a car."

"I was used to English and Norwegian airport taxis."

"Rude surprise."

"Yes. Anyway, the only map I had was the one faxed to me in Norway by the manager of the apartment complex in Duluth where I had decided to rent—"

"Duluth? That's a forty-minute drive from Georgia Tech."

"I know that now. All I knew then was that . . . You've got a bite."

She began to reel in. "It's a big one."

She landed a glistening perch, and while it flopped, cast

again—and immediately got another bite. "Fish convention. Here we go. And another."

"I'll smoke them over an alderwood fire," I said, and my mouth flooded with saliva.

"Do it now," she said, and I rowed us back.

We built the fire near the back door and sat on the stoop to eat them out of the pan, hot and oily. We wiped the oil up with bread. Julia stood, pan dangling from her hand. She smiled, and the line of her back, the crumb of bread at the corner of her mouth, struck deep. I caught her free hand and pulled her back down, kissed that slippery mouth, felt her breathing quicken under my hands. We were the only people for miles. I slid her shirt over her head and her pants down around her ankles, and when she came she tore out a handful of daisies with the grass and her cry was fierce as a hawk's.

She lay in my arms and smiled her slow, creamy smile. "More. But this time in bed."

This time it was slow, slow as the fall of night in northern latitudes, as the unfurling of a leaf in spring. My north, my springtime.

We drowsed for a while, sun streaming through the southern windows onto the rugs below the sleeping gallery. I stroked her long, tanned fingers. She pulled the quilt up around her shoulders. "I can't get used to the fact that seeing sunshine doesn't necessarily mean it's hot. Does it ever get hot here?"

"It gets warm in July and August, but not hot, and not humid."

"Not like Atlanta." She settled more comfortably against my shoulder. "You were telling me how it was when you arrived in the U.S. Duluth."

I buried my face in her hair. Cloudberries and frying fish. "Well, for one thing, before I came to Atlanta, I didn't know what humidity was. I'd read about it, and Christie Horley told me how awful it had been in New Orleans when she'd been there the year before, but verbal information isn't the same as somatic. You have to feel it on your skin, touch it, smell it, run your fingers lightly through the sweat that never evaporates to understand." I felt her nod against my shoulder. "So I got to Atlanta and took a cab for Duluth in August. The cab had no air-conditioning and the air was thick and sweet, like peach juice. I knew I wasn't in Norway anymore. I was alone in an exotic foreign country at the start of a fine adventure. Anyway, the cab driver couldn't seem to understand what I was saying half the time. Even though I'd told him I was Norwegian, he insisted that I was German—then wanted to know if I knew his son, Dan, who was in the army in Germany, in Mew-nick. I told him I was very sorry but that I didn't know his son, and would he please head north on I-85 here, instead of south? His driving worried me."

Eighty miles an hour without seat belts, windows open to scoop up the viscous air, him steering with one finger and leaning back to talk to me about his son in Munich, careless of the fact that the other drivers hurtling along the interstate seemed as oblivious as he of the rules designed to keep people alive on the road.

"The apartment complex was called Northwoods Lake Court. It was brand-new, frame units built around a lake. I don't know how many buildings because they were all hidden by trees, but according to the manager there was only me, at the northeast end, and one family due to move in the next day at the extreme south end. The rest wouldn't fill up for a month or so. The lake had fountains. The only luggage I had was two suitcases. I'd intended to take another cab into Duluth and buy necessities—bedding, kitchen things, lamps, because it was one of those apartments with no overheads—but the place was so beautiful I just wandered around until it was dark."

I couldn't begin to describe to Julia the wonder of that

place: swamp oak and bluebirds, swallows and bullfrogs, white oak and birch, my own private playground for a month.

"My apartment was built on a slope so that although the front door was at ground level, the only possible access to any of the windows would be via ladder. And the apartment complex was empty. Besides, this wasn't real life. This was the start of a grand adventure, like sleeping on the beach in Mauritius. All I had in my two suitcases were clothes, an old flashlight my father had had as a boy and had given me when I was seven, and a few books. That night I slept naked on the bedroom carpet, flashlight by my head and screened windows open to the sound of the fountains below and the chirring of tree frogs." I had felt perfectly safe, cradled by air so soft it was tangible.

"I fell asleep early; it must have been about ten o'clock but it seemed a lot later because of my six-hour jet lag. I don't know what time it was when I woke but all of a sudden I was lying there, staring at this strange ceiling, lit by sodium light slatted by the window blinds, listening to the fountain. I was absolutely still, rigid, and I knew something was wrong. My heart ratcheted like an asymmetric crank. I listened hard, but all I could hear was the creaking chorus of tree frogs, the scratch of crickets across the velvet night, and the endless fountain. But I knew I had to keep still, there was this little voice in my primitive hindbrain whispering, *Don't move, don't move*, so I tried to look around the bedroom without turning my head but all I could see was shadow the colour of lead and those strips of yellow light. I was sweating, slick with it, and my heart felt like a vast, runaway engine, but I tried to think."

I could still remember the faintest metal touch of the flashlight against the middle finger of my right hand, the sudden itching of the carpet as I sweated, the way a car changed gear in the distance, the voice in my crocodile brain saying, *Don't move, don't move,* and the restless red turbine in my chest beginning to whine and overheat.

"And then a man's voice said, 'Don't move, I have a gun.'"

"Jesus!" She sat up.

"It was an unremarkable sort of voice, very quiet and steady, but I couldn't see him. The voice was so ordinary and the whole thing so surreal I thought that maybe he wasn't there at all, that maybe it was a dream, but then there was a faint, oiled clicking from the shadow, and I knew it wasn't a dream, my breath started to come in great gusts, and the muscles in my arms and legs coiled so tight and ready my bones hurt. Then he stepped forward, and suddenly in the slatted light there was a gun, ugly, clumsy looking. He kept coming forward and the light inched along a bare forearm, a white-shirted shoulder, up a lightly muscled neck to a reddish gold moustache." I closed my eyes. "I can see it now, like a series of photographs. And that's when it happened. It was as though this veneer fell away, as though I stepped aside from a mask, and it felt as though my heart slipped its bearings and hurtled loose. I came off the carpet without thinking, without even blinking, holding the flashlight—and it must have weighed three pounds—like a piece of kindling. It was so light in my hands. I *surged* off that carpet, muscles whipping like hawsers, swinging that flashlight up and out, and I was so sure. It was so easy. I swung up and out, unstoppable. He started to blink—that's how fast everything was moving for me, I even noticed that the whites around his eyes looked bluish in the light—he started to blink but then three pounds of bright steel travelling at brutal speed caught him under the chin. His head snapped back and he fell. His body made a sort of lolloping thump on the carpet, like a big sack of potatoes."

I opened my eyes. It was odd to see the bedroom loft, the seter, the cool sunshine. I could remember the sweat on my skin, the blood roaring in my ears; humming with a sense of power; feeling huge and pure and fierce and filled with a wild, hot joy at being alive.

"I was still holding the flashlight. I flicked it on. It worked.

The gun was in his hand, his left hand, but it wouldn't do him any good. He was staring at the ceiling, head bent side-ways—the expression on his face was odd, a kind of gentle amusement. All of a sudden I couldn't get my breath. There was a dead man in my bedroom. My first night in a strange country and there was a dead man in my bedroom. I'd killed him, and I didn't even know his name. I remember staring at the flashlight, at the light streaming through my fingers, mak-ing them blood red. I turned the flashlight off. He disappeared. I turned it back on again. He reappeared. This time he seemed a long way off. 'This is *my* apartment,' I told him. 'You had no right.' The light shining on the carpet began to wobble. I was shaking. My breath came in little pants. There was a strange noise coming from the living room. Ringing. The phone. I walked across the carpet of the bedroom, the tiny hall, the rug in the living room."

I could still feel the carpet on my feet, the different textures of the two acrylic weaves, and the new smell of rubber carpet pad and harsh, foreign cleaning fluids.

"The phone was on the pass-through counter between the dining room and the kitchen. It felt slippery and big, difficult to hold in my left hand. A voice at the other end said, 'Is this Aud Torvingen?' and I said yes, and he went on to say that he was Lieutenant Wills, of the Duluth Police Department." I closed my eyes again. " 'Please listen carefully,' he said. 'We are aware that you are probably speaking under duress. We are in control of the situation. Please remain calm.' It was a very soothing voice. 'Now, if you can, ask him to talk to us on the phone.'

" 'He can't talk to you,' I said. I felt dizzy. Blinding light filled the apartment. Then there was another voice from out-side, with a bullhorn, harder, eager, you could hear the adren-alin in it, shouting that the building was surrounded, that he should pick up the phone. 'No, you don't understand,' I said, but then realized I wasn't holding the phone anymore. The receiver dangled from its cord, near the floor. I picked it up. 'You don't understand. He can't talk to you because he's dead.'

"There was silence, then a faint muttered conference on the other end, then, 'Ms. Torvingen? There have been no reports of gunshots in the last half hour.'

" 'What?' I said. I had no idea what that had to do with anything.

" 'Ms. Torvingen, if he shot himself we certainly would have heard it.'

" 'He didn't shoot himself,' I said.

" 'No,' said the soothing voice, only now it was full of the *there-there* syrup of a parent talking to a child. 'Ms. Torvingen, can you speak English well enough to understand what I'm saying?' I said yes, then thought: Haven't I just been speaking English? 'Good,' he said. 'Now, are you all right, Ms. Torvingen? Can I call you Aud?'

" 'No,' I said, and then he got all urgent.

" 'How are you hurt?'

" 'No,' I explained, 'you can't call me Aud because I'm eighteen and you're treating me like a child and not listening to anything I'm saying. The man is dead. I killed him with my flashlight. He had a gun and I killed him. He's in my bedroom. He had no right. He still has his gun but he's dead. I'm fine.'

"This time the silence on the phone was longer and I wondered if I'd been talking in Norwegian after all. 'Aud, Ms. Torvingen,' he said, then sort of trailed off. He cleared his throat and started again. 'You say he's dead, that you killed him. Are you quite sure?' At least he didn't sound patronizing anymore.

" 'Well,' I said, 'his eyes are open and his neck's bent, and he hasn't moved from my bedroom floor,' but all of a sudden I thought: What if he isn't dead? What if this is like one of those horror films and he's lurching to his feet, covered in blood, and bringing his hand up with that gun, with an evil

lopsided grin. I dropped the phone and ran back to the bedroom. He was still there, of course. Still dead."

Julia's hand crept across my stomach to find my hand.

"The police arc lights had bleached his face white and a
pool of urine and faeces spread under his body. The whole
scene was grainy, like an old black and white newsreel. I noticed that his hair was thinning on top but in that light I
couldn't tell the colour of his eyes. It bothered me. Then I
thought: the gun, they'll believe the gun even if they don't
believe me. So I squatted by his gun hand, but the weird thing
was I couldn't make myself let go of the flashlight first. I tried,
but my fingers wouldn't move, so I had to fiddle for a while
with just my left hand before I could pull the gun away. I
went back to the living room, all bright now with the police
lights, put the gun down on the pass-through and picked up
the phone. 'I've got his gun,' I said. 'I'm going to open the
sliding glass doors in the living room, step onto the balcony,
and toss the gun down onto the grass.'

" 'Aud, I think—'

"This time I put the phone firmly back in its cradle—I was
getting sick of that syrupy voice—and picked up the gun. I
walked towards the sliding doors and would have stepped out
there naked if I hadn't seen my reflection in the glass. Oh, I
thought, I'll have to do something about that. The police lights
didn't reach inside the bedroom closet and I tripped over one
of my suitcases just inside the closet door. I had to put the gun
down on the floor to pull on jeans one-handed. The flashlight
wouldn't fit through sleeves, so I chose a vest. When I was
done, I stuck the gun in my back pocket. It felt good. The
flashlight felt better.

"The glass doors slid open easily. The balcony was one of
the reasons I'd chosen that apartment. Three hours earlier the
night had been quiet, soft with fountain spray drifting over
the lake. Now the night gleamed with light and metal and
well-polished boots. I stood up there and looked at the revolv-

ing lights, at the trees and lake beyond them, and thought: This is my new country, new apartment, new life; all stained, like my bedroom carpet. I took the gun out of my pocket and threw it into the crowd below. Then I leant over the rail and vomited on their heads."

Julia put on a towelling robe and made us blackberry tea. I drank mine in the bath, she sat on the floor and stroked my arm, shoulder to elbow to wrist to fingertips and back again.

"You've never told anyone about this before, have you?"

"No one. I suspect my mother was briefed on the situation via the consulate, but we've never spoken of it." I remembered the ambulance ride, being met at the hospital by overly polite administrators, and knowing that someone somewhere had gone beyond the call of duty and found out who I was, or at least who my mother was.

"Take me there."

"To Northwoods Lake Court?"

"Yes. Take me there when we get back."

It was such a private thing. No one even knew I had ever lived there, never mind what had happened, or how it looked. Such a beautiful place. "I was only there a few days."

"Take me anyway." Her hand came to rest just below my triceps. "Promise me we'll go when we get back."

"Very well. I promise."

Her hand resumed its stroking. "So who was he? How did the police know he was there?"

"The police had had a call from the apartment complex half a mile down the road, an intruder. Apparently they had a car in the area and followed him to Northwoods Lake Court. They did a foot search and saw my front door ajar. His name was Tim Schultz, an out-of-work carpenter. Married, two children, but separated. He was thirty-four years old. No one could tell me why he did it."

I soaped myself thoughtfully.

"I thought knowing the details was important, but it isn't really, because the important part wasn't what happened at the apartment, it was what I realized later, on the way to the hospital. The police and EMTs came bursting into the apartment and bundled me up in a blanket without so much as a by-your-leave and threw me in an ambulance. I was in a daze. I remember the police sergeant and EMT were arguing about the flashlight—the sergeant was saying it was evidence, the EMT said I was in shock, that if holding it made me feel better he wasn't going to take it away from me. That's when I realized: the shivering and vomiting had stopped, and the strange detachment I felt wasn't shock but the dawning realization that this was real, that I had killed someone. I had taken a life. He had had a gun, I had had a flashlight, but I had taken him, and in the moment of doing so I'd felt faster, denser, more alive than ever before. Killing him had burned me down to a pure, uncluttered core, to my essence. It was all real and it felt . . . Well, you tell me how it felt when you hit that man at Honeycutt's house."

"Good. It felt good. I felt . . . bigger."

"It's the adrenalin. When everything slows down and my muscles are hot and strong and the blood beats in my veins like champagne I feel this vast delight. Everything is beautiful and precious, and so clear. Light gets this bluish tinge and I feel like a hummingbird among elephants, untouchable."

She reached out and flicked water against the pink welt that ran over my lower ribs. "But you're not."

"I've played with adrenalin, almost every dangerous sport you can imagine, but that's not the same as violence, not the same as coming up against someone who wants you dead, where there's no room for one misstep, where it's all or nothing. Feeling that bungee cord whip you up just two seconds from the ground is one thing, looking into the eyes of a man with a knife is another. It's the ultimate competition—there's one life between us, and it's *mine*. You feel how *fine* life is. It's a sort of possessiveness. A bit like sex. Just as you can't suddenly rip someone's clothes off in public when you have the urge, you have to train the urge to violence. It's like always singing *sotto voce* when all you want to do is take a great breath and let it rip. Violence feels good. It's so simple and clear. There's no mistaking the winner. I like it, but I avoid going there, going to the blue place, because I think I could get lost, might not find my way back, I wouldn't *want* to find my way back because it's seductive." I dabbled my fingers in the warm water. "I said before that I left the police force because I didn't want to work for anyone else. That's true, but it was also because the blue place called too strongly. It had become all I wanted, all there was."

She sat back on her heels and studied me with cool, slatey eyes. "Past tense?"

I thought about the blue place, about my life then, about Julia. "Past tense."

She kissed me. I unfastened her robe. My cup fell in the water. We ignored it. I wanted to be inside her.

Later, when she was sitting between my legs and I was soaping her back with the washcloth, she put the soap back on its sturdy wooden shelf and said, "So what happened in the ambulance with the flashlight?"

"I hefted it in my hand—"

"Bet they edged away."

I smiled, remembering the EMT's undignified scramble to the back of the ambulance. "Yes. I hefted it. It was heavy and smooth and, Oh, I thought, so is the oxygen cylinder by my stretcher, so is the drip stand, the officer's baton. I was surrounded by objects I could use as weapons. I told the sergeant he could have it. And I've never worried about carrying a weapon since. They're everywhere."

"Mostly, anyway."

"Always." I dipped the washcloth in the water, folded it over and over on itself lengthwise, doubled that in on itself and twisted it, but not hard enough to get rid of most of the water.

"That?"

"Instant blackjack." With one flick of the wrist I smashed the wooden shelf off the wall.

She grinned. "Now you'll have to fix it."

"There's still soap on your back," I said, and changed the blackjack back to a washcloth by dipping it in the water.

I woke in the dark with Julia's hand on my shoulder. "Aud, it's all right. It's all right. Wake up. It's just a dream."

"I'm awake." The dream images began to drain away.

Her breath was soft and sleepy on my face. Her hair fell across my throat. I breathed in the scent of cloudberry and violet and warm woman. "Do you want to tell me about it?"

"It's a recurring dream. About a dead woman in the bath. Her eyes are like unpolished marble and she is still. So very, very still. The water is still, too, and cold. And then I realize I'm not breathing, my heart is not beating. I'm still, and I'm cold, frozen. I'm dead."

Julia slid on top of me. "Feel. That's my heart. It's beating. Yours is beating. Wrap your arms around me. There. Feel my ribs move up and down. I'm breathing. You're breathing. It was just a dream. We're alive. Just listen."

I did. I listened to the fist-sized muscle that beat valiantly in her chest, *lub-dub lub-dub*, atrium-ventricle atrium-ventricle, pumping thick red blood through her arteries, sucking it back tired and thin, sending it out again refreshed, over and over, like some comfort-station cheerleader at a marathon handing out water and banana chips to exhausted runners and sending them on. Alive.

twelve

The stave church of Urnes, the oldest in Norway, lies five kilometers south of the seter. We tramped along the grass and through the flowers, water glinting green and glassy below and to the right.

I pointed down the slope. "There, between that rock to the left and the treetops, that's the spire. We can either walk round, which is another kilometer or so, or we can head straight down."

We scrambled down like children before they realize they are mortal, when the worst thing they can imagine is falling down and someone kissing everything better, maybe the smell of antiseptic and a Band-Aid—or, even better, the glory of a white bandage—but nothing permanent, nothing *real*, and like children arrived at the bottom red-cheeked and feeling physical, in charge of the world. There was no one else there, not even anyone coming or going from the handful of village houses clustered west of the tiny churchyard.

"It's smaller than I expected."

The church, even without its spire, was taller than it was

long. The churchyard, bounded by an ancient stone wall, was a lopsided rhomboid half the size of a soccer field. The grass was smooth, as if cropped by sheep, and two large birches shaded part of the northwestern wall. Three or four dozen headstones on the north and south sides were all very plain. One was quite recent. It was quiet enough to imagine the soft hiss of worms gliding under the turf and old bones settling. It was the perfect place for a church, high above a headland that jutted out into Lustrafjord, and before Christianity it had probably been the site of the village *hov*. In the ninth and tenth centuries, womenfolk would have gathered on the headland, looking south, eager for the boat bearing their menfolk returning from a-viking. They would have seen the sail first, a faded yellowish white where once it had been bold blue stripes, taking the left fork from Sognefjord and into Lustrafjord, perhaps parting from a companion boat that would go on up Årdalsfjord to the women of Naddvik and Ofredal. Then the whole boat would be visible, and you would count the shields, look for the familiar crimson boss or the green rim, and you would run with the others down to the jetty, hoping some brother or son would bring back a fancy armring, or a bolt of fine Irish linen, but mainly just that he would be there with his familiar laugh and smile, not the awful strained blinking and bloody stump like poor Unn's son, the winter before last. . . .

"Aud?" Julia, on the bottom of the five steps leading to the door. I joined her.

Urnes church smelt of wood, old but hale Scotch pine, beeswax, and fresh flowers. Light shimmered through windows three stories up, drenching the upper tiers of wood, turning them to gold, softening the second tier to rich honey, and dimming on the dark, massive uprights of the bottom tier. Here and there red or yellow or blue or green paint caught the light where centuries ago craftspeople had painted the carvings for the greater glory of god.

"I had no idea wood could be so beautiful," Julia said. "So simple and pure. And it looks . . . well, it doesn't look a thousand years old. I can't see any cracks or woodworm."

I laid my hand on one of the massive staves. "The people who built these churches understood wood, and they were not in a hurry." Carpenters would have gone into the forest to select several Scotch pines, but they didn't fell them, just cut off the tops and branches. While the trees still stood, the outer sapwood was scraped off. The trunks were left standing for five to eight years. The trees died gradually and the remaining heartwood became impregnated with resin—proof against damp and pests and aging. They built to last, which is why everything is made from wood. The brackets between stave and plank are made of birch. Most of them are taken from where the root joins the stem, so the curve in the grain is natural, and very strong. All the pins and other connectors are juniper, a dense softwood. There is no iron to rust and to rot the wood. I thumped the stave. "This church has stood for a thousand years and there's no reason it should not stand for a thousand more."

Julia looked at the flowers, at the new hymnal someone had left on one of the pews. "It's still used."

"Hjørdis brought me here to services several times."

She sat at the end of a pew. "I can't imagine how it must be to grow up with history all around you. To walk the same path your fifty-times great-grandmother walked, to baptise your child where you were baptised, and your mother, and her mother. To see life continue so clearly, to know that your child will see the same tree, fish in the same fjord, pick the same flowers at the same time of year." She reached for my hand. "Most of us stumble along, making up the rules as we go along, but we're missing so *much*. . . . When I was little, the Tutankhamen exhibit came through Boston and I went to see it. Wow, I thought, look, those pieces of jewellery are thousands of years old! I couldn't even touch it, but it thrilled me to know that people whose bones turned to dust and blew away and was maybe reincorporated in some tree that died hundreds of years ago to make some boat or other, had made something I could look at. But this, this is something else. It's part of the everyday, it's part of ordinary life." She turned my hand palm up, traced the lines there. "I'm beginning to understand, I think. All those things that make you you, your clarity and solidity and certainty, come from this. You can actually reach out and touch your past. It's in the wood, in the cold, clear water of the fjord and in the hard rock of the mountain. And the wood and the fjord and the mountain are in you, clear and strong and massive." She looked at me then, reached to trace the line of my cheekbone, my nose, my jaw. "Aud, Aud, Aud."

A shoal of clouds, faintly violet on their undersides, swam slowly up the fjord behind us as we walked back to the seter. At this time of year I didn't know if that meant rain.

Over a lunch of salad and cold cuts, Julia asked me what my name meant.

"Haven't a clue. But I was named after Aud the Deep-minded, who was born not far from here, in Sogn, in the ninth century."

"Oh, good, another story."

The phone rang. We looked at each other blankly. There had never been a phone at the family seter. The noise was so alien it took me a moment to identify, and then another moment to find the phone. It was up in the loft, in my jacket pocket. I answered it.

"It's for you," I called to Julia, then walked it down and handed it over. "Edvard Borlaug. He sounds rather agitated—for Edvard."

She took it. "Edvard, how are y— Slow down, slow down, I don't understand. Wednesday? But— No, of course I can be there. Of course I understand." *What day is it?* she mouthed at me. *Monday,* I mouthed back. "It will be— Edvard, take a deep breath, please. I'll talk to them, I'll be more than happy to talk to them. Once they understand the general concept I'm sure everything will be fine. I'll drive in tomorrow and we'll cook up a plan of action. Tomorrow. Yes. Oh, about two o'clock. Yes, I'll come and see you then. Yes. Don't *worry,* Edvard. Tomorrow at two. You're more than welcome."

She clicked off. "He was practically hysterical."

"For Edvard."

"For Edvard. The board met yesterday and he's heard that his proposal might not get approval."

"So I gather we'll be going back to Oslo for a day or two for some hand holding."

"You don't have to come. I'll drive down, see Borlaug tomorrow afternoon, stay at the hotel, have an informal meeting with one or two of the board in the morning, and be back early afternoon Wednesday." She slid onto my lap. "Will you miss me?"

"No. I'm coming with you."

"Don't be silly. It's an easy drive. I know the route, know the city and hotel, know my way to Olsen Glass, know my way back. I'll be busy the whole time and all you'd do is sit around in waiting rooms. You'd be crazy to do that when you could be here. If you come with me I'll feel selfish, spoiling your vacation." She hugged me, then held me at arm's length. "Is that okay?"

She was my hawk, built to soar above it all. You don't chain hawks. At some point you let them go and watch them rise, and stand there with your fist out hoping they came back, that they don't run into a keeper's gun, or a bigger hawk, or a vast shadowy hand stretching across the ocean from Atlanta. No. A hawk's job is to fly, not be afraid. I made my face smile. "I'll just have to walk that glacier on my own tomorrow."

"I'd forgotten about that. We could call Gudrun—"

"No need. I'll go on my own, and when you get back, I'll

be able to show you the wonders of the ice. Just . . . come back quickly. And take the phone with you, just in case." She felt so light on my lap. So precious.

"If I take the phone, I can't call you."

"Very true." I kissed the side of her neck where the pulse fluttered. Skin was so thin, so fragile. One nick and her heart would pump that thick red blood all over the floor.

She arched and the pulse under my lips thudded. "Just think of the reunion," she whispered, and outside the grass began to bend under fat raindrops.

Julia wore a grey-blue cotton dress and tucked her rich hair up behind a matching bandeau. I wanted to tear it off, let her hair fall over my hands, and carry her inside to bed. Instead, I held the door of the Audi while she climbed in, and closed it behind her. She poked her head through the window, kissed me on the cheek and started the engine. In two minutes, all that was left was a curling trail of dust up the track.

I shouldered my backpack and walked down to the farm. The veal calves in their wooden pens were fractious, and Gudrun when she appeared was distracted.

"I didn't hear the car," she said.

"No. Julia's taken it to Oslo until tomorrow."

"You're still going to the glacier."

"Yes."

"I don't know if I have the time to drive you—"

"I can walk to Nigardsbreen. It's a lovely day."

"Nigardsbreen?" She gave me a dubious look. "Walking tours have been postponed until June, because of the late spring." When spring came late, so did the thaw, when the ice is at its most unpredictable. The small tongue of the great Jostedalsbreen glacier would be less stable and so more dangerous than its more massive parent. I just waited. Eventually she waved a hand towards the south sheds. "The equipment's in the usual place. I looked it over."

"My thanks. Don't let me keep you from the work."

She gave me a quick nod and disappeared in the direction of the feed sheds.

The south sheds were cool and dry. Skis, boots, ropes, ice picks, skates and a jumble of other equipment took up the whole of the north wall. I selected a coil of blue nylon rope—it smelled of must but was essentially sound—an ice pick with a bound handle, gloves, a folding ice probe, and crampons, and stowed them next to the water, cheese, chocolate, flask, and thermal compresses in my pack.

The rains of the night before had washed the whole fjell clean. Flowers poked through the glistening grass: bright gold, vivid red and lush purple; birds twittered happily from clean-scented aspen and birch as though it didn't matter about the washed-out nests; even the stones that began to litter my path seemed fresh and new again, even though for some it had been tens or even hundreds of years since they were plucked from their beds and scoured clean by the glacier. I crunched over the silt and gravel of till washed out by recent melt and began to kick my way through the bare, fist-sized rocks still unclothed by moss, enjoying the solid *chunk* against my boots. Julia would still be bumping along the track towards the one-lane road that would take her to another track, and then the highway.

There were no trees now, no flowers, just hectares of sliding scree, the glacial moraine, a jumble of pebbles and stones and boulders; unsorted, unstratified rock of every colour and age, but all round, all smoothed by the action of ancient ice. Here and there moss clung bravely, and insects whirred over puddles formed in rock dimples that would be gone by late afternoon, but the barrenness overshadowed the life around it. I imagined the moors of Yorkshire when the Roman engineers first arrived: the heather and gorse, the pheasant, grouse and harebells flattened by the road builders who lay down a straight arrow of crushed stone in a straight path that sliced from one camp to another, the stonemasons following with the carefully cut limestone blocks, building so well that even today if you walk up to Goathland you can see a line in the turf stretching to the horizon, where nothing bigger than buttercups and daisies grow. Foss Way, the locals call it.

These stones had not been here that long. Most of them only dated back to the Little Ice Age, the deterioration in climatic conditions that had made Jostedalsbreen grow, sending its tongues, like Nigardsbreen, thrusting down the valleys, licking up farm and field and fjell. The Little Ice Age had culminated 250 years ago, and when the tongues shrank back, they had left behind ridges of the moraine deposited at the tips and sides of the ice. Every year the moss crept farther up the old path of the tongue; every year the tongue shrank back even farther. But now I had passed the moss and was among stone deposited thousands of years ago by the ice sheet that had covered the whole country, the ice sheet that had gouged out the fjords connected by the North Way, the sea path that made life possible in this part of the world, that had created Norway.

I could smell it now, the bite of green ice, sharp as the cut a blade of grass can make across an unwary tongue. The sun was bright. I took off my sweater, folded it into my pack, and scrambled up and farther up the scree.

Julia would have run the twelve kilometers of real road and be turning right to drive south and east along another track, passing the massive Skagastølstindane, one of the highest peaks of Jotunheimen. I wiped the sweat from my forehead and kept climbing.

Now my boots rang on bedrock, raw, bare, the colour of pâté, and there it was: the side of the glacier tongue.

Old ice looks like meringue, folded and layered by a giant's wooden spoon over air pockets; fluffed egg white standing ten meters over my head and tinged here and there by different berries. But these weren't the beautiful, true ice colours, just a surface layer of pollution, a grey pretending to be pink in the late morning sun, brought by last winter's snowfalls.

I studied the ice. I wouldn't need crampons yet. I put on gloves and began to climb. It was almost midday and I was sweating lightly, but when I bent low to the ice for handholds, my breath plumed. As I spidered diagonally up the side of the tongue, the only sounds were the crunch of snow like spilt sugar under my boots and the rush of air in and out of my lungs. Most years at this time there would be small parties of expert climbers training the less expert to be guides for the tourists who would arrive in droves at the end of the month, and the ice would be dotted with figures in bright red Gore-Tex and Day-Glo orange nylon, figures who sported lime-green and hot-pink plastic logos on boots and gloves as they planted flags to show safe paths; crisscrossed with ropes in designer colours, like brilliant, unnatural snakes. Today when I reached the top I was alone with the sky, the rock, and the ice stretching ahead of me like a photographic negative of a giant's broken twelve-lane freeway.

Glaciers start from the snow that falls above the snowline and collects in depressions in the rock. Some of the snow melts and refreezes, recrystallizing to form a granular aggregate called névé. More snowfalls compact the névé to ice. The ice builds. Eventually the weight of the ice squeezes the lowest level out of the depression and gravity forces it downhill. It takes the path of least resistance, following valleys if there are any, forming them if there are not: gouging wide U-shapes from the rock, smoothing the huge chunks to vast round boulders, or crushing the softer sedimentary rock to sand that is washed out at the tip and edges, spilling out nutrients and fertilizing the lower valley, leaving behind strange rocks sometimes balanced precariously one atop the other. But the rock over which they grind is not uniform, and some parts rip out more easily than others. Over time, the moving glacier falls into pits it has dug itself and deep cracks form in the ice. These crevasses or *sprekker* are often hidden by recent snowfalls and most people who die on the ice fall down one of these cracks, especially in spring before the snow has melted. But the *sprekker* are why I come here, the *sprekker* and the ice caves and the lake.

Before the end of the Little Ice Age, the snow that fell would have been pristine, not like today, but if you find a fresh *sprekk* and the sun is at the right angle, you can look down through time and see the glacier as it used to be, the clean, brilliant colours deep in the ice.

Sunlight bounced off a thousand white and almost-white surfaces. I took off my pack, found my sun goggles, ice pick, a small bottle of water, a banana, and the ice probe. I put on the goggles, drank the water, ate the banana, put the peel inside the empty bottle and the bottle back in my pack, and shouldered it, then snapped out the probe. Probe in left hand and pick in right, I started walking. It had been nearly three years, but the automatic step, diagonal probe, two step, probe came back easily. It wasn't foolproof, of course. That's what the pick was for: if I started to fall, I would twist and swing it back at the ice and pray it held.

Sometimes the walking was easy, sometimes I had to put away the probe and use the pick to scale ice cliffs and, once, a sheet of ice like a frozen waterfall. When I started to step up the slope diagonally I sat down in the snow and clipped crampons to my boots. Judging by the sun, it was about one in the afternoon. Julia would be on E16, driving above the speed limit by the grey-green waters of Sperillen not far from the junction with E7, and Oslo, windows open and the radio on, slapping the steering wheel with her right hand in time to the music. I stood up and kicked myself another foothold on the glacier.

thirteen

As they are heated, most molecules become less dense and expand so that the solid that barely fills half a cup will, as it melts to form a liquid, overflow that cup. If heated enough to vaporize, the gas will take up half a room. Water is different. For one thing—unlike, say, nitrogen—it has different names for all its states: water when liquid; steam when a vapour; ice when solid. And when water freezes, it doesn't contract but expands. Against all reason, ice will float upon water. Ice has always fascinated us.

Climbers, when asked why they want to climb, say, Everest, reply: *Because it's there*. A more true answer might be: *Because it's got ice on it*. Ice is alluring, mysterious, alien. In the Western world, ice and science are regarded in the same light: cold and clear, ordered and deeply rational, apparently plain yet ultimately unknowable. I doubt that it's a coincidence that the very first science fiction novel, *Frankenstein*, mixes both: the monster is brought forth in cosmic fire and marooned on ice. Ice cannot bring forth life but, used properly, it can preserve it. Think of all the food in our freezers. Think of all those

kidneys and livers and hearts thrown in coolers and helicop-
tered out to save the lives of transplant patients. Anyone
knows that if you happen to cut your finger off when peeling
potatoes, you should keep the finger cool—but not frozen, because then water molecules inside the cells of skin and connec-
tive tissue and blood will begin to form tiny ice crystals that
will expand and expand and eventually rupture the cell mem-
brane, spilling protoplasm to the wind, destroying it. Those
who believe in cryogenics are dreaming. They have seen too
many rump steaks come out of the freezer as solid as hoary
planks and yet two hours later sit luscious and red and mouth-
watering on the countertop; but when something living is frozen, it dies. Only those organisms frozen before they are fully
formed—gametes and embryos—can be brought back to life
by thawing.

Ice is dangerous, but people keep climbing those mountains
and walking the glaciers because, beyond all else, it is beautiful.

The *sprekk* lay open at my feet, exposing jewels unseen for
thousands of years. I put my sweater back on, went down on
my stomach, and squirmed to the edge. The Grand Canyon
carved from ice. Inches from my nose, the top layer, sooty
with hydrocarbons, gave way to one of dirty yellow, then one
of heavy cream. These layers glistened, slick and icy, melted
and refrozen several times by the spring sun. Below that, beyond the reach of both my arms and direct sunlight, the true
colours began. The crevasse was over fifteen meters deep, and
further down the light was milky and subtle, shaded and height-
ened in strange places by irregular outcroppings from the ice
walls. Here, a bulge glittered blinding white, while the edge of
the shadow it cast shimmered pale mauve, and the deeper
shadow dusky indigo. Down, and down, and now the colours
lost all hint of the organic and the crevasse became stern and
ordered, a cathedral of ice. Striations of amethyst and aquama-
rine, deep, deep strata of pale emerald. My body heat and the

slanting afternoon sun ricocheting down warmed the ice and lifted the biting, mineral scent of water that had fallen as snow eighteen thousand years ago, when mammoths still walked and breathed and scooped aside drifts with their tusks, millennia before human beings even set foot upon the land that would be Norway. That water would not be good to drink. Every year, there was always some stupid tourist who decided to drink from the lake or dip themself a handful of meltwater and came down with violent diarrhea, and mouth sores that lasted for ten days. But there was nothing wrong with smelling it, and for a while I lay lost in the scents and interplay of light and colour.

I had to get up when my thighs got so cold I could no longer feel them. Too long, I'd been lying down too long. Careless. My pants and sweater were damp, but they were made of wool and beneath that I wore silk, which, unlike cotton, dries fast and still traps heat while wet. Where the snow was level, I did some katas, slowly at first, then faster, and faster still, until the movements were mere lightning sketches of killing blows and someone watching from a distance would have thought there was a whirling dervish on the ice. When I stopped, I was warm, but I sat on my pack and poured myself a cup of hot, sweet coffee and ate some cheese and nuts. Staying safe was a matter of prevention.

I munched peacefully. The sun warmed my back and the sweater began to steam. It was about three o'clock. Julia would be in Oslo now, being very American with poor Edvard Borlaug. I got out my map. It was not a good idea to stay on the ice once the sun was slanting enough to send strange shadows stretching out from even small hillocks of snow. There was no longer time for the ice cave, but if I planned a careful route I could still spend a few minutes by the lake.

It was a fair hike north to the lake, but it was along the edge of the glacier, where in some places the moraine was almost nonexistent or so old that it had long since been invaded by moss and lichens, then grasses and the nodding heads of the rare pale Pasquale flower and the delicate cinnamon rose, by birch and aspen and pine and all that flew and hopped and crawled in and on them. The transition from white to full colour would have been impossibly abrupt but for the silvery trunks of birch and carpets of white-petalled mountain avons.

The lake, its surface brilliant with long, late afternoon sunshine, lay in a vast basin carved by the glacier ten thousand years ago. Nigardsbreen now lay at a tangent to the irregular circle of tarn, and its moraine formed the pebble and rock shore on which I stood. On the other side lay sedge and moss freckled with purple saxifrage and, behind that, woodland. Birds sang, an endless weave of bright trill and warble.

The lake itself was glacier melt, barely above freezing, and it was so still it seemed to be holding its breath, thick and green and mineral. I touched the surface with a fingertip, very gently, and the water dimpled but didn't break, only heaved slightly, turning parts of the surface gold in the sun, part almost black in shadow. Grendel might have lived somewhere like this, deep and gelid and secret.

I sat on a rock and shut my eyes.

There is nothing like the smell of glacier and fjell in April and May, the fecund earth, rich and dark after a long winter, the warming, papery birch bark, and leaves unfurling new and tender in the depths of the wood. I lost myself, utterly relaxed, until the light began to fade and birdsong changed to evensong.

The birds stopped singing.

I opened my eyes and listened harder. Footsteps, crunching up along the glacier behind me and to my left, between me and the setting sun. I turned, preparing to give him or her my *I'm just leaving* smile, but there was no one there. My breath came fast. No rock, no trees I could use as cover. The footsteps stopped. My heart changed up a gear. He or she had to be on the glacier, but I couldn't see anything.

I stood up and waved. "Hei!" Gave a big grin. Stood on tiptoes to stretch my muscles, flexed my hands, turned my face slightly so the fattening, setting sun didn't blind me. In the heartbeat of silence took two steps toward the glacier—cut his line of sight.

A slide and scuffle of snow overhead.

"Hi there!" American voice, male. He came to the edge of the glacier and waved. Medium height, snow on his chest, gloved right hand, bare left. "Wait there, I'm coming down." He stooped for something but I was already turning, already running the three steps to the lake, when I felt a punch on my back. I heard the *phud* of a suppressed rifle at the same instant I leapt out along the sunpath on the lake, and the water closed over my head. Blind, I stroked deep.

Ice water stops your breathing, sends your diaphragm into spasm, and convulses every muscle, but the choice was simple: remain hidden, or die. He would be scrambling down the glacier, rifle in hand, padding to the edge of the water, sights trained, ready. I spasmed downward to avoid thrashing at the surface. I'd been in the water five or six seconds, but could fight to hold my breath another two at most. Think! Sun. Setting sun: dazzled water. It might be enough. I let myself rise gently. A quick fin of my right hand sent me into a roll, and I broke the surface for a split second, like a floater, exposing only my shoulder and lower face, but long enough for one huge suck of air, blessed air, then back down. My eyes stung with the minerals and the cold, but I could see the cloud of blood, brown in the green water, trailing from my shoulder. The cold would soon stop the bleeding. He would think me dead. I dived, but slowly, gently, and stroked towards the shore. He had the gun, but I had the sun: he wouldn't be able to see beneath the surface reflection, but I would see his shadow. Gloved right hand for the barrel, bare left for the trigger: he was left-handed. I felt along the lake bed until I found a smooth round stone that fit my palm.

The blood had made him careless. He was standing right at the edge of the water, one foot actually in it, rifle held only loosely to his left shoulder. I finned my way gently to his left, counted to three, and roared up out of the water, stone swinging—

—only it was more of a stumble than a roar, and the rock that should have slammed into his temple crunched into his left knee instead. He went down with a splash, face first. I was on my knees, heavy and useless with water. I swung the stone at his head, but slipped and thumped him between the shoulder blades. He thrashed and convulsed in the cold. I couldn't summon any strength; it was as though someone had pulled the plug and everything had just drained away. I dropped the stone and shoved him, boatlike, out into the lake, only just retaining the wit to hang on to his rifle. He spasmed, swallowed water. I pulled out the clip and put it in my pants pocket, jacked out the round he had already chambered, then used the rifle as a crutch and heaved myself to my feet. I was so numb with cold I couldn't tell where I'd been shot.

Think. Think fast. I swayed and closed my eyes, opened them again. He was definitely moving more slowly now. Very well, then. I tossed the rifle alongside my pack.

The water was just as cold when I waded back in, but I only had to go up to my thighs. He was barely conscious. It affects some people that way. I caught the neck of his jacket—some quilted cotton thing, sodden—and dragged him to the shore. Hauling him up was hard. I got him most of the way out and his eyelids started to flutter. I dropped him, found my stone, and hit him on the forehead, but not too hard. I wouldn't need long. I dropped the stone back in the water, which rippled heavily, the murky brown cloud of my blood still clearly visible, and finished dragging him out onto dry ground. A quick search gave me his wallet, keys with Volvo logo on the fob, and sodden cigarettes and lighter. I flicked the lighter. Nothing. I held it up to the failing sun—half full of liquid—flicked again. Nothing. His driver's license said John Turkel; so did the Blue Cross Card. Careless. No rental papers for the car. I pushed the keys into my pocket and everything else back in his.

My muscles were like lumps of wood stuck haphazardly onto cardboard bones. Nothing worked right. My fingers hung from my hands like thick, stupid bunches of bananas and I kept falling down because I couldn't feel my feet. It took five tries to strip off my sweater, more for my pants and shoes, and then I half stumbled, half ran to the glacier, where I rolled in what snow I could find to absorb most of the excess water from my bare skin. Patches of bright red stained the snow here and there but it wasn't too much. I stretched and flexed and staggered in circles until feeling returned to my torso, to thighs and wrist, and then I ran some more while I squeezed as much water as I could from the sweater and undershirt and pants. The trot back to my pack was reasonably steady but the shadows were so long I shied at pebbles, thinking they were boulders.

When I got to my pack, all I wanted to do was sit down, but I didn't dare. I fished in it, standing, tilting it this way and that until the slippery plastic compresses slithered out into my clumsy hands. They were cold as eels, but two quick twists started the catalytic reaction and they began to warm. I held one compress against my chest with my right hand and tried to use my left to wrap the other tight inside my wet sweater and pants but my arm wouldn't work properly, just flopped about. Try again. Slowly. I managed, one inch at a time. The bullet had hit something important. No time to think about that; there were more urgent things to deal with: getting my body temperature back up, warming the wool sweater and pants enough to put back on and trap what heat I could coax my body to produce.

In the gathering twilight the rocks near the lake looked like comfortable brown cows settling down for the night. I walked from one to another, found one that was still warm from the sun, and spread my undershirt out on it. An inch at a time.

I put the compress between my teeth and dragged my pack over to another rock, sat down, and dropped the compress across my thighs. I had to balance the plastic thermos cup on the turf to pour the hot, sweet coffee, and it wobbled precariously. I drank a whole cup, poured more, dug out some chocolate, chewed and swallowed, chewed again. My hands ached around the hot cup, the right just with cold, the left with more. Another ache bloomed high up on my back. Later.

More chocolate, the last of the coffee. Put it all away in the pack. Walk to gunman. Turkel, John Turkel.

Walking felt strange, as though someone had removed my arms and legs and then reattached them using odd connections. I squatted a few feet from the man, who was shaking convulsively with his eyes closed, and tossed a pebble at him. When he opened his eyes and saw my nakedness, his pupils dilated, then contracted.

"Talk," I said in English.

He stared at me.

I didn't have time for this. "I imagine your knee hurts, if you can feel it at all. You'll need several hours' surgery before you walk on that leg again. You are soaked through with freezing water and are in the first stages of hypothermia. Perhaps your thought processes are becoming cloudy. Let me make it clear: you will tell me everything about who sent you to kill me and why, or you will die out here."

I watched him gather his pitiful resources—two quick breaths, flare of nostrils, tightening of muscles around his mouth—and when he lunged, I swayed to one side and hit his already bruised forehead with the meaty side of my fist. He went down like a punched-open inflatable doll.

This was taking too long. I rooted around a bit in the grass until I found another rock.

While he was still groaning, I smashed his other knee. He screamed. I waited until he had finished. "I'm in a hurry. Can you understand what I'm saying?"

A groan. I slapped his knee lightly. Another scream.

"John, answer me. Can you understand what I'm saying?"

"Yes. Yes."

"Listen carefully. Both your knees are smashed. It'll be dark in a few minutes. The only way you will survive tonight is with my help. I will only help you if you help me. Where is your car?"

His shaking had changed to long, rolling shudders and he didn't seem to care about his car. I lifted my hand. "No! It's . . . it's . . ." He had to clench his jaw to stop his teeth from clacking together. "Miles, three maybe, valley."

"In the Nigard Valley?" There was still enough light reflecting from the water to see his nod, or what seemed to be a nod amid all the jerking and shaking. "North or south?"

"North."

The compress was cooling. My muscles began a light, internal tremble and the pain high up on my back grew, sending out shoots, twining like a liana down my left side, up my shoulder and down my arm. I backed away, looked around in the dark for a cow with a white coat. Found it. Lovely, lovely almost dry silk. "Tell me where you got the car." Cautiously, I reached around my ribs with my right hand and touched my waist with my fingertips. Dried blood but whole skin. I worked my way up slowly, had to fight to silence a hiss when my fingers met the ragged furrow along my shoulder blade.

"Gothenburg," the man said, and it took me a moment to remember what I'd asked him.

"Who told you to get the car in Sweden?" I felt along the bony top of my shoulder, nothing; around the back of the top of my arm. Ah. So the bullet had hit the bone at just the right angle and ploughed along skin and bone and along the top of my arm as I dived. Felt as though it had chipped the elbow. The nerves would be damaged, but perhaps not irreparably. Lucky. But I had lost blood, and the pain was going to get worse. "John, who told you to get the car in Sweden?" I plunked my left hand like a piece of meat on the cuff of one sleeve and used my right to wind the other sleeve over the first into a knot. I had to use my teeth to pull the knot tight. As soon as I dropped the improvised sling over my head I realized my mistake and took it off again.

"John?" No sound. No movement. He had passed out. I hurried.

My sweater was still damp but it was warm, and warmth was more important now than avoiding pain. I rested my left arm on my left thigh, spread the sweater over my right thigh, then threaded my left arm through the sleeve as though it were a stick, nothing to do with me. *Pain is just a message*. It was easy to get my right arm in the sleeve. I felt the wool dragging over the open furrow, sticking to clotting blood. Deep breath, *just a message*, pull sweater over head and down. Breathe. Just breathe. I didn't even pause with the sling: over my head, pick up left arm, shove it through. Pants next; socks, boots; check car keys and clip in pocket, tuck compresses inside waistband. Good for another few minutes. Moonlight seeped from behind heavy cloud.

Back to John. His cheek felt cool and solid, like clay. I slapped it. He whimpered. I slapped him again. Faint glimmer as he opened his eyes.

"You're not shivering anymore. You've entered the next stage of hypothermia. Unless you get warm very soon, John, you'll die. I'm all that stands between you and death. Tell me what I need to know. Who sent you?"

"Man." He looked surprised: talking was easier without the shivering. "Man in Atlanta."

"Who?"

"Don't know. Really don't. Just sent us money, wired it to the bank."

"Us? How many?"

"Three."

Julia. I had to get to Oslo. But even if I could protect her there, what then? I needed information to stop this at the source. "How did you find me here?"

"Edvard Borlaug. Called him from Gothenburg. He said other woman, Julia? Julia." The sound of her name in his mouth made my fingers stiffen with the need to punch through his eye to his brain. "Said that Julia was coming in. That you probably coming too, but not sure. So. I drove here. Asked at . . . at farm. They drove . . . Oslo. Kill her."

Three. "What do they look like?"

"Ugly." He thought that was funny and laughed, hoarse and high.

"Describe them. Tell me their names." Hurting him would not help at this point.

"McCall's tall. McCall's tall." He seemed quite taken with his little rhyme. Typical hypothermia confusion.

"How old?"

"Forty?"

"Tell me about the other one."

"Ginger. Because of his hair. Don't know his real name. Medium. Thin. Young." Not the ones from Honeycutt's house.

According to his license, John Turkel was thirty-two.

"Early twenties?"

"Younger."

"Tell me again who sent you."

"Don't know. Man. From Atlanta."

"How do you know he was from Atlanta?"

"I feel real bad."

"How did you know?"

"Asked him . . . how know where to find you. He said. Call us from here, from where he was. Then he yelled . . .

someone. In his office. 'What's time difference between Atlanta and Sweden.' Something like that. Atlanta.''

"What did he say? What did he sound like?''

"Said: kill art bitch. Julia. Kill her. Kill you.''

"Did he want it to look like an accident?''

"Didn't care. Just make them dead. That's what he said. I feel real bad. Weird.''

"And that's all? Do McCall and Ginger know where Julia is staying in Oslo?''

"Didn't. Might now. Help me.'' He tried to lift his hand but the hypothermia had him now and only a couple of fingers twitched. The air smelt like rain.

"Help me,'' he said again.

I ran through events in my head: all my possessions, anything to link me to a body, were in my pack, and the bootprints would wash away in the rain. Just my prints on the rifle, then.

"I'll need your jacket.''

It was sodden, and he couldn't even move an arm to help me. In the end, I just tore off the collar and took that over to my pack. I had to grope around for the rifle. I wiped it free of prints and used the collar to carry it to the water. It made a thin, flat splash.

"What?'' he said.

The clip followed. I knelt by John Turkel and put the torn collar in his hand. I don't think he even felt it.

"Please. Help me.'' Barely a whisper.

I picked up my pack. "There isn't time.''

The clouds parted and I stood up into a suddenly monochrome world: water sleek and black; sedge leached lithium grey; moonlight lying like pools of mercury on the upturned faces of graphite flowers. Nature, thinking there was no one to observe, was letting slide the greens and blues, the honey yellows, and showing her other face: flat, indifferent, anonymous.

Only trolls, fools and desperate people walk the fjell at

night when all is shadow and deeper shadow. I knew that I could not walk down a mountain along a trail I didn't know with muscles already cold and screaming with toxins and fatigue after the icewater of the lake, expecting my foot to twist on an unseen stone or skitter down scree, to any minute tumble into a gully or thump into a tree; knew I could not carefully place one foot in front of another for three or four miles with a hole punched in my back and a slow leak. So I ran.

Cloud closed over the moon and the rain came down, gentle and light, almost like mist. I ran like a deer, snuffing the scents lifted by the rain, veering away from the pine or wet stone that warned of danger and towards the safety of wet grass and opening flowers, relying on the tiny sound of a pebble rattling under my boot and tumbling away down to my left to warn me of a gully, ran like a deer that ignores a bullet through the shoulder because the wound is not the urgent thing, the urgent thing is the adrenalin stride, the run, covering the ground, the need to keep going, to never stop, to leap brooks and low-lying branches, to crash through brush, to weave through trees and skitter and fall on loose stone and get up without pausing, without thinking, without missing a beat. The branch whipping across the face, the slow hot leak of blood down the back and deeper tear of skin where the pack pulled open the wound, did not matter, because pain is just a message. I ignored it, washed it away with adrenalin and endorphins and the rhythm of breath and blood and bone.

Three miles, Turkel had said, but that was in daylight with map in hand, when you could plot the perfect diagonal. I was going to have to run farther; to get down into the valley, then run north. Five miles, perhaps. More. The rain came down harder, the underbrush thickened. My boots began to slide in mud. I shortened my stride a little and ran on.

Breath whistling in and out through nostrils and mouth, thigh muscles pumping—contract, relax, contract, relax—toes gripping inside boots and wearing raw against wet wool. Sweat running down my belly.

It was when each stride started coming shorter than the last and the pressure was on calves, not quadriceps, that I realized I had reached the floor of the valley and was starting up the other side. I turned left and ran north.

The valley trail under the trees was so dark I would have missed the place but for the suddenly alien scent of tires and good-quality leather getting wet. Then there it was, windshield streaming in the rain, both front windows open.

It was when I sat down on civilized leather, when I turned the key and the dark and the rain were outside, that the pain snapped like a gin trap on my back, biting down so hard it seemed to drive its teeth into my lungs and tear my breath apart. The headlights shining into the rain started to recede, as though I were on the back of a train heading into a long tunnel.

I slewed the Volvo to a stop outside the seter and stumbled in. It was two o'clock in the morning. The phone was on the table. I couldn't remember the phone number of the Hotel Bristol. I called information. They could not understand me.

"Oslo," I repeated. It sounded muddy and slurred. I shaped the next words carefully. "Hotel Bristol. Kristian VII's gate."

They gave me the number. It sounded like surf crashing in my ears.

"Again. Please. Give me the number again."

"22 41 58 40."

I had no pen, no paper. 22 41 48 . . . no, 58. 22 58 . . . I called again. The same woman. She gave me the number again. 22 41 58 40. I tapped it in carefully. It rang and rang and rang. Blood dripped down my back.

"Hotel Bristol." Bright, young, male.

"I need to talk to one of your guests, Julia Lyons-Bennet."

"Perhaps I could take a message." His voice started to slide away. I breathed deep.

"No." I had to hold on. Just another minute, another two. "I have to speak to her, now."

"It is after two o'clock. In the morning."

"I am not drunk. I am not in a different time zone. This is an emergency. Please put my call through."

"After ten p.m. it is our policy that guests—"

"I wish to speak to the night manager."

"Ma'am, the—"

"Get the night manager."

He put me on hold. Pain pulsed like a candle under a glass sucking in oxygen and flaring, using up the oxygen and dying, sucking more and flaring; heating my nerve to a white-hot wire. I walked, very slowly, very upright, to the kitchen. Hold on. Hold on for just another minute, another two. I had to tuck the phone under my chin while I opened the cupboard and pulled out half a loaf of bread and a pot of sweet jam. I couldn't cut the bread with just one hand, so I jammed it between my hip and the counter and tore off chunks, which I dipped straight into the jar. It tasted like dirt, but I chewed and swallowed, chewed and swallowed. Still on hold. The refrigerator yielded a wedge of yellow cheese wrapped in wax paper. My hearing came back in a tumble of discrete sounds: the prickles in each exhalation as it left my lungs, the creak of bone in my elbow as I shifted slightly, soft slap of white paper against cheese. The clarity of delirium. Just another minute, another two.

The phone suddenly seemed to open out as the night manager punched the hold button to off and the myriad hums of a computerized office on standby filled the earpiece. He—and I could tell it was a he from the harmonics of his inhalation—drew breath, but I spoke first.

"My name is Aud Torvingen. To whom do I have the pleasure of speaking?"

"Rolf Lothbrok, the night manager."

"Rolf, if you check your records you will find that Ms.

Lyons-Bennet and I stayed with you two weeks ago. It is vitally important, urgent, that I speak to Ms. Lyons-Bennet now. Not later, or soon, but now." The carbohydrates were metabolising now, hitting my bloodstream, and everything sparkled. Even my words seemed clear: cool, measured, precise. Rolf must have thought so, too.

"Very well, I'll put your call through."

A click. Purring electronic ring. Another. Again. On and on. Endless. The carbohydrates were cascading through my system. I disconnected, pressed the redial button.

"Put the manager back on," I told the flustered young night clerk. "Rolf, she must have turned off the ringer. I want you to go knock on her door."

"Ms. Torvingen, it is absolutely against our policy to disturb a guest."

"This is an emergency."

"Then may I suggest you call the police?"

He had reached the place where the officious become immovable, and the telephone was not a sharp enough tool. I switched tactics. "Rolf, this really is terribly urgent, but I think I know a way you can help me, if I may presume upon you for a favour." Julia was safe in bed in a well-run hotel. I could be there before breakfast. "If you're not too busy, perhaps I could persuade you to take down a note and slip it under her door where she will see it as soon as she wakes in the morning." Where she would see it, bright and incongruous against the carpet if she got up to answer the knock of a strange man in the middle of the night. "Please, Rolf, could I ask you to do that?"

"I . . . well, perhaps I could do that."

"Oh, thank you. The message is to read: 'Very urgent, take all precautions, call Aud immediately, repeat, immediately.'" He scribbled industriously. I was very, very thirsty. I wanted to say more, but I knew the Rolfs of the world. Any mention of blood, of danger or bullets on the fjell would prompt an immediate withdrawal because it would mean I was a crazy woman: such things did not happen in Norway. "Please add . . ." What? Don't talk to two men called Ginger and McCall who have been sent to kill you? "Please add my love. Please underline the words 'very' and 'all.' "

"Very well."

"And . . . Mr. Lothbrok"—make him feel big and clever and in charge—"you will see to that right away, won't you? I just couldn't sleep until I know she's got the message. You'll put it under her door?"

"As soon as I put the phone down, Ms. Torvingen."

"Thank you, thank you very much."

*Then I suggest you call the police.* Oslo police are typical Norwegians—everything one at a time, in the right order, by the book. They would show up at the hotel, ask a few questions, maybe wake Julia and talk to her. Julia would be safe—for tonight. The police would also show up here. They would surround me. They would want to know how I got shot. They would ask whose car it was. They would not let me talk to Julia. And when they stopped surrounding Julia because they thought I was crazy, I would be in a hospital cell, unable to protect her. No, not the police. Julia was safe for the night; Rolf and his staff were sticklers for protocol, wouldn't tell anyone her room number; and she would see the note when she woke up in the morning.

I needed water, painkillers, heat, more food, in that order, but they would have to wait. I needed to think. A man from Atlanta had hired three Americans to kill Julia. It had to be Honeycutt, or his blackmailer. If it was Honeycutt, he had to be acting on his own; the cartel would have used their own people. Locals. But how had Honeycutt—or the blackmailer—known we were in Norway, and how had he known where to start looking? I should call Annie, but she would have questions and I had no answers. Nothing made sense.

Think about it later. What mattered now was Julia, and for that I would need help. Local help who were not too fussy about the law.

It was nearly three in the morning, an hour earlier in London. I picked up the phone again and called a number my mother had given me when I first left home, one I had never had to use. She answered on the third ring, alert. "Yes."

"It's Aud. I need your help." I could almost see the lightening then sudden stilling of her face as she understood that it was her daughter, not World War III, but that I was in trouble. There was a click on the line.

"A tape," she said, "so you don't have to repeat anything." Norwegian. I couldn't remember the last time we had spoken our native tongue together.

"I'm at the seter, on a cell phone." I gave her the number. "I need the phone number of the Federal Police commander in Tijuana. A private number, or home number if possible. And the number of someone else, someone he might know, whom he could call to confirm my identity."

She must have had a hundred questions but she asked only one. "How urgent?"

"It . . . Julia, a woman I love, it might mean her life."

"I'll call you back within an hour."

Until she called, there was nothing more I could do. Now was the time for the water, painkillers, heat and food.

I took the old tin box that was the seter's first-aid kit down from the bathroom shelf and ministered to myself with grim efficiency. Strip off damp pants. One syrette of morphine in the upper quadrant of right thigh. Pull on clean, dry pants. Drink water while that takes hold, fill kettle with water and put on to boil. Lay out compresses, antibiotic cream, peroxide, bandages. Think how I want to appear tomorrow in Oslo. Find clean dry knit silk tunic. Strip off damp, bloody sweater. Pick up peroxide.

It was messy, it hurt, I passed out twice. I ended up having to use a doubled-over pillowcase as well as the compresses: I could not afford to bleed in public tomorrow. I made instant coffee, very strong, and wished I had some soup that was not in cans. I ended up tearing chunks of ham from the bone with my teeth, and pulling the rest of the loaf to pieces. The morphine was laving my torn muscles like warm milk, swaddling my nerve sheaths in cotton wool. I could move my left hand well enough to steady a hot-water bottle, which I filled from the kettle in my right. It took four trips to assemble writing paper, ballpoint pen, coffee, hot water bottle and phone on the table in the living room.

The embassy in London would be a hornet's nest, my mother rousting everyone out of bed, having them in turn rouse people in other embassies who owed her favours; tracking down the information I needed. I had seen her work before.

The pen was an old one, its clear octagonal plastic barrel chewed at the end, and when I put the tip to paper, it left a blot. I wrote the date, then paused. This must have been how Vortigern the High King felt when the last of the Roman legions withdrew, leaving fourth century Britain open to the prowling Saxon seawolves, and he had gambled, had picked a few from the pack and befriended them, gifted them with land along the south shore in return for a promise to defend the country from their hungry, landless cousins. Classic strategy, divide the enemy and hold the two opposing camps in perfect tension, only Vortigern had not known the sheer weight of numbers pressing up against the Saxon shore; the tension was unequal; his gamble had failed. The might of the Tijuana cartel and of Honeycutt were decidedly not equal, but when the cartel crushed Honeycutt and wanted to turn on me, this letter would be my Roman Legion in the hole.

I wrote steadily.

The phone rang. It was my mother. Fifty minutes. "The Tijuana Federal Police commander's name is Luis Palma. I have his home number, his private work line, and the general office number. The name of the man in Tijuana who can confirm your identity is Hector Lorca, a television anchor. I have already called him, and he has agreed." He must owe her a tremendous favour. Well, now so did I.

"Thank you."

"Bring Julia to London to thank me."

Four a.m. Still yesterday in Mexico, where Luis Palma would be sitting down to dinner with his family while outside the sky turned red.

I dialed. It didn't have a chance to ring before it was picked up and a smooth male voice said, "Palma residence."

"I wish to speak to Señor Palma." My Spanish had been learned in England and Spain a long time ago. It was slow but, thanks to the few days' practice with Beatriz, reasonably good. The European accent, too, would stand me in good stead.

"Señor Palma is a busy man and this is his family time. No doubt he would be delighted to speak to you tomorrow, from his office." Unctuous as guacamole.

"Tonight I do not wish to discuss police business. Tonight I wish to impart some information about the cartel's money launderer in Atlanta."

"But that, of course, would be police business. However, as you have been kind enough to call with this information for Señor Palma, I will take a message."

"No message. I need to talk to Señor Palma. Now. Tell him Michael Honeycutt is deceiving the cartel and stealing money."

"If you will give me the details—"

"I will speak to Señor Palma only. Tell him my name is Aud Torvingen, that my mother is Else Torvingen, Norwegian ambassador to London. Tell him I am to be trusted, but that if he needs to check that I am to be trusted he may call Señor Hector Lorca at his home. Señor Lorca awaits his call. I will call back in twenty minutes."

The knuckle bones were cast, the game with the bloody-handed Viking begun.

I wrote faster.

I covered three more pages with terse, blotched writing, then called again. The same smooth voice answered.

"Señor Palma will talk to you, Señorita Torvingen."

"Thank you."

"This is Luis Palma." His voice was smooth, too, but smooth like a Rolls-Royce, secure with power and money and the kind of arrogance that does not even have to display itself. "You have some information for me."

"Information and a request for your help."

"I am of course happy to help a young lady if it is in my power, but I am just a humble policeman in a poor country."

"Of course, señor. You have no doubt heard of the Tijuana business cartel and their business of shipping the produce of certain people in Colombia. No doubt it is already common knowledge to you, as a policeman and well-informed citizen of the region, that a portion of the revenue from this business is administered in Atlanta. Some of the money is put to work immediately, investing in works of art which are bought and sold in this and other countries. The proceeds of these sales should of course find their way into the bank accounts of the Tijuana businessmen who brokered the product, and naturally the banker who oversees these deals should be a very prudent man. He is not. Quite by chance I have discovered that the Atlanta banker, Michael Honeycutt, is"—I didn't know how to say *playing both ends against the middle* in my rather formal Spanish—"deceiving these businessmen. He is also drawing attention to himself and therefore the cartel through various illegal activities, including the forging of these works of art, so that he may pocket money for himself."

"I am sure that these businessmen would like to hear proof of their colleague's disloyalty."

"I have proof. I know the names of the people who supplied the forged art to Honeycutt; I know about his accounts in the Seychelles. So does someone else. Señor Palma, I believe someone in Atlanta has discovered Honeycutt's activities, including his work for the Tijuana businessmen, and is blackmailing him. Honeycutt has made many, many mistakes. Many innocents have become entangled in his web. Many innocents, including myself and a friend whose name is of no importance."

"And you, of course, have spoken to no one about this."

"No one. But I have taken the precaution of writing down all that I know and mailing it to my lawyer, to be opened in the case of my death or disappearance."

"A very foresighted precaution."

"Thank you. I am now, of course, worried that this banker in Atlanta, Michael Honeycutt, may succeed in his attempts to kill me and my friend, and that this information, this confidential information, may be loosed prematurely and damage the reputation and livelihood of this Tijuana business association. Today, one of the banker's men came very close to succeeding, and there are two others in Oslo, just waiting for me. I thought perhaps that if these businessmen understood my predicament, they might be willing to put me in touch with some associates. They might offer some local assistance, and perhaps the temporary use of some of their office equipment."

"A reasonable request. But I am not sure if the business association has an office in your area. Perhaps I could find out and telephone you in, say, one hour?"

"That is acceptable."

"I will need your phone number." I gave it to him. "In one hour, Miss Torvingen."

By five-thirty in the morning I had finished my long letter. I put it in an envelope, which I sealed carefully, then wrote a note to my attorney, which I put, together with the sealed envelope, inside a second envelope, which I addressed to the law firm of Spirkett and Clowes in Atlanta. I had no idea how much international postage was, but ten domestic stamps should be plenty. One little envelope. It wasn't enough insurance. I started another sheet of paper.

This time it went faster. When I'd finished, I addressed it to myself, in care of Dornan, at Borealis. For the first time in twelve hours I was not cold.

The cotton wool around my nerves was wearing thin and

the milk that lapped my muscles evaporating. There were two syrettes of morphine left. It would have to wait.

Outside, the rain had stopped and the sun was coming up. I smeared mud on the Volvo's license plates, just in case it had been stolen and reported to the police, and drove like an old woman to the post box three kilometers down the bumpy track. The first pickup was at seven-thirty. I slid the envelope addressed to my attorney through the slot, then drove another five kilometers to post the second.

The phone rang as I pulled up outside the seter.

"Miss Torvingen." It was Guacamole Voice, the assistant. "Señor Palma has asked that I pass on the phone number of a business associate in Oslo who will be waiting for your call." He gave it to me. It was another cellular number. "Señor Palma also asked me to tell you two things. First of all, that the banker of whom you spoke, Señor Honeycutt, was shot to death at a New York airport ten days ago."

Honeycutt was shot ten days ago. Ten days ago.

" . . . association was of course most upset at the time, but given your information, they are not as upset as they had been. They do, however, wish they knew who had set such a thing in motion."

Someone unknown to the cartel had killed Honeycutt. Honeycutt was dead. The man from Atlanta had killed Honeycutt. Honeycutt was not the man from Atlanta.

" . . . second item to convey is that despite the death, Señor Palma will honour his agreement. And, of course, should you discover who might have intended harm to Señor Honeycutt, Señor Palma would be most grateful for that information. He also hopes that given your diplomatic contacts, you might be persuaded to act as a goodwill ambassador in the future. Good evening, Miss Torvingen."

A silky threat. *You owe us. We will collect.*

fourteen

I drove like a berserker up the track to the secondary road at the tip of the fjord. Honeycutt was not the man from Atlanta. Honeycutt was dead. I should have paid attention to my unease. I should have listened. The morphine sliding slick as ice through my system could not dim the fear that kept my foot down on the accelerator even though the Volvo was already fishtailing on the loose grit and holding the wheel steady was agony. Someone hidden in the shadows was reaching out with a pair of shears to cut the strings.

I skidded onto the secondary road and brought the Volvo up to a hundred and fifty kilometers per hour. That lasted for ten minutes, then I was back on another twenty kilometers of track but it was a straight stretch, and it was empty. I risked taking my good hand off the wheel to punch in the Bristol's phone number and tuck the phone under my chin. It was nearly seven in the morning. The desk clerk put me through to Julia's room without demur. The phone rang and rang and rang. I disconnected and called again. When the desk clerk answered I asked for Rolf.

"Ms. Torvingen. What can I do for you?"

"There's no reply from Ms. Lyons-Bennet's room and she hasn't called me. Did you leave the note?"

"Indeed. I took it up personally."

"And you're sure she's there?"

"A moment." Ticking of keys. "Yes. She came in late last night and told the desk clerk she would be checking out after lunch."

"Thank you, you've been most helpful. But if you see her, please tell her I've been trying to contact her. Please also tell her to stay in the hotel. I should be there in under two hours."

"I will pass on your request."

There was nothing more I could do.

I took the hard left onto E16 without slowing and as soon as all four wheels were on the highway, I pushed the accelerator flat to the floor. Like the secondary road, the highway was deserted. My heart was a sledgehammer, driving the car forward. Without taking my eyes off the road, I punched in the number of the cartel's local contact.

"Hei." A coffee-grounds voice, dark and used.

"Torvingen."

"You can call me Sampo." Sampo Lappelil—the Little Lapp Boy who saves the world from the king of trolls and permanent winter. A bitter man.

"I'll be there in two hours. Less. You have something for me."

"Yes." He gave me an address near the Akershus. "Be here before nine."

I called the Bristol again, but here in the Oppland my signal just bounced from rock to rock.

I tore south, never easing up, letting speed and adrenalin flense away dread and pain and all feeling until I was bone clothed in muscle moving forward with deadly purpose.

As soon as I hit the outskirts of Oslo and saw the flags fluttering from every flagpole, I understood why the roads had been empty. It was May 17, National Day, a public holiday when proud Norwegians flocked from their houses to commemorate the anniversary of the constitution of 1814, clogging the streets with processions and ceremonies and celebration.

I cursed steadily and aimed the car for the city center.

It was eight-thirty. The boulevards and avenues were empty and silent but for hammering as carpenters put the final touches to speaking platforms, and the shrieks of microphone feedback as techs tested the public address systems. The workers all swung around, astonished, when I screeched by. Good Norwegians all, at least one would call the police.

I pulled up in a no-parking zone in front of the Bristol and brushed aside the doorman and his protests. The man behind the desk literally stepped back a pace when he saw me.

"Tell me what room Julia Lyons-Bennet is in."

He swallowed. "She's . . . I'm sorry. She checked out half an hour ago."

"Where is Rolf?"

His eyes bugged like boiled eggs. "Rolf?"

"The night manager."

"His . . . his shift ended twenty minutes ago." But his eyes shifted towards a door marked STAFF ONLY.

I vaulted over the counter and slammed open the door. Rolf was a big, soft thirtyish man who leapt out of an easy chair and spilled his tea.

"Where is she?" He shook his head. His left hand cupped his genitals. I don't think he even knew he was doing it. "Tell me what you said in that note."

"I kept a copy." Such a small, tight voice for a soft man.

A copy. So Norwegian. "Show me."

He edged past me as though terrified I might rip his guts from his belly with my bare hands. He pulled open a drawer under the counter and extracted a sheet of paper. He checked it carefully. What he saw gave him confidence; he blinked but did not shake as he handed it over.

It was written in Norwegian. I crumpled it slowly in my fist. Rolf stepped back. Stupid. I was so stupid. I should never have let her go. So many mistakes. I fought to keep my voice level. "Did you speak to her before she checked out?"

He shook his head. Once started, he couldn't seem to stop. "No. But don't you see," he pleaded, "it was after my shift. After my shift!"

"Give me the phone book." I looked up Olsen Glass. Dialed. After seven rings a cheery recorded voice told me to call again tomorrow and to have a happy National Day.

When I slid into the car, the phone was still hanging from the counter, the two men standing like figures from a tableau.

Ten minutes to find Sampo.

It was a modern warehouse building. Sampo opened a loading bay and motioned the Volvo inside. He was compact and brown and much younger than I had expected. A man and a woman emerged from the concrete corners.

"Your army stands ready to serve," Sampo said. He spared me the ironic salute. From the bench that ran around half the bay, he picked up something wrapped in dirty cloth and handed it to me. I unwrapped it. A massive old Lahti, nine millimeter. Full clip. "It's old. Unregistered." He held out his other hand. It clinked. "Extra rounds but no extra clip." I dropped them in my pocket, tossed the Lahti onto the front seat of the Volvo, and took Julia's passport from the glove compartment.

"This woman is Julia Lyons-Bennet." Unsmiling, hair pulled back. Beautiful. "She was registered at the Bristol Hotel. She has an appointment with the board, or some members of the board, of Olsen Glass this morning at ten o'clock. It's an informal meeting, and this is National Day, so it may not be at the Olsen building." They passed the passport around. "There are two men who want to kill her. You will stop them. Their names are Ginger and McCall." I gave their descriptions.

"Find them. When you find them, get information on who sent them, then kill them. Protect this woman. That is your first priority. That's all."

"That's all," Sampo mused. "And we don't even know where to begin."

"You're not a fool. Check the Olsen Glass building. Find out who is on the board, find out where they live and check there. Find the woman. You have my phone number. Keep me informed."

I was going to find Ginger and McCall.

In the bathroom of the Rainbow Hotek Stefan I flexed my face a few times and studied it in the mirror. A slightly nervous and rather young woman looked back. Good.

At the reception desk I smiled shyly. "Hello?"

Answering smile. "How can I help you?"

"Well, it's . . . it's silly, really," I said in a rush, looking over my shoulder, "but, you know the Internet? I'm expecting to meet . . . well, to meet a man. He's called Ginger. At least that's what he tells me. He's from America. We talked such a lot online. He *says* he's young and unmarried and has ginger hair and, I don't know, I said last week we could meet here this morning. 'On National Day,' I said. Only now, now that it's the day . . ."

"You think you might have been a bit hasty." She was only in her early twenties, but she was stern, playing the older and wiser woman of the world.

I nodded, shamefaced. "I thought maybe you could tell me if he's here. Then I could get a look at him first, before I introduce myself. Just in case."

"Much more sensible," she said approvingly, and opened up the guest register screen.

"He was supposed to come here with his business partner, a man called McCall," I said helpfully.

She ran down the names. "No. No, I don't see anyone of that name."

"Have you been on duty all week?"

"Yes."

"And you haven't seen a thin man with red hair?"

"No."

I let my face fall.

"Perhaps it's for the best."

"I suppose so. Well, thank you."

On to the Majorstuen, on Bogstadsveien. This time the desk clerk was an older woman who told me bluntly I was a fool and if I knew what was good for me I'd go home to my parents and forget this foolish nonsense. But she did tell me there was no one called McCall and no thin young man with ginger hair. When I left I realized how close I was to Vigeland Park and for one wild moment I thought: Julia will be in the sculpture park. But she wouldn't be. She would be meeting with Edvard Borlaug and one or more members of the board. Somewhere. It was Sampo's job to follow that trail.

The phone in my pocket remained obstinately silent. I pulled it out and called information, called four different Borlaugs before I heard Edvard's brisk voice telling me to leave a message. "Edvard, it's Aud. I need to talk to Julia. If you know where she is, call me. Immediately. It's very important. You have the number."

I had a sudden vision of Edvard lying on the carpeted living room floor, neck broken, while blood leaked from his eyes and my voice echoed from his machine. Perhaps Julia was lying next to him. . . .

I called information again, this time gave them Edvard's name and number and got his address in exchange. I called Sampo. "Send one of your people to this address. Break in if necessary. Make sure she's not there. Check any schedules or calendars or address books." It was ten-thirty. How long would the meeting last? "If you haven't heard from me by eleven-thirty, put someone on E16, just past Nordehov." She might come to it via some scenic route, but it would have to be very circuitous to join the highway north of Nordehov. "It's a dark blue Audi." I gave him the licence plate number.

This was all wrong. We were in too many places, like four people standing in the corners of a vast field full of horses with our hands spread. Too many gaps.

The second syrette of morphine was wearing off.

On to another hotel. McCall and Ginger had to be staying somewhere.

After I had exhausted the least expensive places, I started in on the moderately priced. Time was running out and the streets were beginning to fill with holiday crowds.

At the Continental on Stortingsgaten I gave the doorman two hundred Nkr to leave my car right by the entrance. The desk clerk was a young man, so this time when I gave my story I was a slightly older woman who had seen just a bit too much of the world and hadn't liked the way it had treated her.

"Why, yes," the young man behind the counter said. "They checked in this morning. I remember. They were here very early. They seemed tired. They were most insistent that they be given a room immediately. I thought they'd sleep. They certainly looked as though they needed it, but"—tapping of keys, nod of head at screen—"all they seemed to do was make a lot of phone calls."

"Are they still here?"

"Oh, no. They left about twenty minutes ago."

I beckoned over the doorman. "The two men who left here twenty minutes ago, what were they driving?"

"Dark green Toyota 4Runner."

I nodded my thanks and he resumed his post by the door.

The only other person in the lobby was a fifty-year-old woman sitting on a couch with her eyes closed. I slid a hundred-Nkr note over the counter towards the clerk. "Can I see who they called?"

He pocketed the money and turned the screen slightly. Olsen Glass at 8:08. Edvard Borlaug at 8:09. That call had lasted ten minutes, too long for a message. What had Borlaug told them? Then information, followed by a local number I didn't recognize. I tapped the number into my own phone, disconnected when the machine told me I had reached a sporting goods shop that was closed for the day. Short of ammunition? If so, they would stay short. Everything was shut on National Day.

Outside, the pavement was drenched in sunshine. The warmth on my arm and shoulder, even swaddled as they were, was almost unbearable. The Volvo was stuffy. I rolled down the windows and nosed out into the road, which was clogged with people in the bright red and white of national costume, all beaming in the sunshine, happily eating *pølse* and drinking fizzy *brus*, heading good-naturedly towards the square for the speeches that would begin at midday. I called Sampo— "They're in a dark green Toyota 4Runner"—and concentrated on not running down any of the herd.

It was eleven forty-five. Julia's meeting would be over by now.

Think. I tried to put myself in her head, imagined stepping out of an office or home, pleased with myself because I'd persuaded Olsen to fund the sculpture garden. The sun would be warm on my hair, my dress light around my thighs. Stepping to the car, thinking of the drive back, of the beautiful day. People having a good time. Celebrating. Being with family. . . .

And I knew where Julia would go, knew what Borlaug had told McCall and Ginger, knew where I must go.

I dialed the numbers. The phone rang and rang and rang. The sound was quite unreal. Eventually I was answered by a rather cross and breathless, "Hei."

"Tante. Is Julia there?"

"Aud? No. But she will be any minute. I was just in the cellar. I have to go back there now. She's coming for lunch

before driving back to the seter. There's a note she wants me
to translate for her. It might be personal, she says. She tried
to read it out to me over the phone but the line was bad and
she makes Norwegian sound like German, and then that man,
Edvard, came and told her the meeting was about to begin.
Would you like me to ask her to call you when she gets in?''

"Tante, listen. I'm in Oslo. I'm on my way to your house.
Don't let anyone in. No one except me or Julia. No one. And
if you see a dark green four-by-four on your street, call the
police."

"I don't understand."

"Two men are on their way there to kill Julia—"

"Julia? In Oslo? Why should—"

"One of them shot me yesterday on the glacier. Two are
on their way to your house. They are armed. Keep the door
shut. Keep a lookout for Julia. When she gets there, leave.
Head straight up E16. Use your Saab. Do you understand?"

"But why do they—"

There was a roaring in my ears like the sea. "Do you understand? Will you do as I say?"

"Yes."

"I'll be there very soon." Click. Dial. "Sampo? Tell your
man on E16 that he's now looking for a red Saab driven by
an older woman. Julia will be with her. When he sees them,
he's to keep them both safe. I know where Ginger and McCall
are heading. I'm going there now. Meet me." I gave him the
address, disconnected, and put the phone down gently on the
soft leather of the passenger seat.

My shoulder no longer hurt. My mind was stropped clean
and sharp as a razor. The muscles in my face were perfectly
relaxed and the world outside hardened and slowed until I
saw everything with crystal clarity and there was time to notice every detail: the untied lace of a three-year-old's sneaker,
the beautiful deep amber of the traffic light I ignored. My heart
was no longer a combustion engine, thumping with explosions

deep in its chambers: it was silent, smooth, and I was a maglev train flying effortlessly down its single track, my only purpose the journey, my destination fixed.

Buildings got smaller and moved back from the road. Stone became brick and wood and now there were fences, and front doors, and trees. Each clean, shining window, each green leaf with its delicate tracery of veins filled me with joy. I moved through it all like a ghost, as easy as a breath.

Hjørdis's street appeared magically on my left and I turned, and there it was, events unfurling like a brightly coloured pennant: Julia in her blue cotton dress walking back up the street on the right-hand side, towards Hjørdis's door—the car keys are still in her hand and she hums to herself; the doors of a dark green Toyota opening and two men stepping out, guns in hand—guns suddenly held close to their thighs and hidden as they hear the Volvo engine.

Unhurriedly, smiling slightly, I drive sedately down the street. Level with them, face to face, past them. They flick me a glance, dismiss me, relax. I flip on the cruise control, open the door, and roll out into the street. They don't notice. They are watching Julia, one crossing the street behind her, one staying on this side. Time slows and stretches, and I glide like butter up behind the man raising his Glock. The grey polymer barrel doesn't even gleam in the sun as he lines it up on the woman in the blue dress.

It is too easy. My elbow flashes out and docks perfectly with the soft spot at the base of his skull just as he squeezes the trigger, and he hits the pavement, dead, at the same time as his bullet hits the steps that lead up to Hjørdis's front door. Then we're all moving: the woman in the blue dress turning, mouth open, the man across the street to look at me, then back at the woman. His arm rises, a tiny tongue of light like a second, little sun jumps from the tip of the barrel, and I laugh as I sweep him off his feet, laugh as I land with my knees in his stomach, laugh as I take his fist in mine and turn it, laugh at the shock on his freckled face as I squeeze that tight warm hand and the freckles disappear in red ruin.

I stretch and smile. All done. I am still smiling as I walk over to the woman, who is lying on the pavement, one arm stretched up the steps. From the waist down, the blue dress is red. She begins to writhe and mewl. I kneel, touch the brown hair coming loose from the bandeau, then frown and start to get up when I realize I'm kneeling in something wet, but there's something about the smell of the woman's hair, something . . .

Cloudberries. Julia. This woman in the blue dress gushing her life out on the pavement and insane with shock is *Julia*.

I ripped off my tunic, wadded it, pressed it against her abdomen. It turned red immediately and she was moving so much I couldn't keep the pressure on. I knelt on her shoulders. "Julia. Don't die. You can't die. Julia. Stay with me! Julia."

Footsteps. Hjørdis, cradling her hunting rifle. "I called an ambulance. It was so fast! Oh, dear god, Aud."

"Come here. Hold this down. Press hard." She did. I started unwinding the bandages from my shoulders and arm.

"But you've been shot!"

I stripped off the bloody mess and wadded it. Blood trickled freely down my back and arm. "When I count to three, lift your hands and put them straight back. One, two, three. Press hard."

Squeal of tires. Slam of car doors. Running feet.

"They're dead," I said to Sampo and the woman. "Drag that one"—McCall—"across the road. Put him over here by the other one." Ginger. "Make it look as though they killed each other. There's a gun in the Volvo with my fingerprints on." The gun I didn't use. The gun I should have used. "Get rid of it."

"Aud, I can't hold her."

Julia was thrashing like a wild thing, as mindless and limber as a beast in her shock, throwing off Hjørdis, who was a big woman, long enough to twist over onto her stomach. No exit wound.

"Sit on her legs." I wrapped my arms around her head. "You," I called to the woman with Sampo, "come and pin her shoulders. Tante, I'll take over the compress."

" . . . *a gaping wound, wider than the hands of anyone who would try to staunch the bleeding. A hole so big it could swallow the world.*"

"*I have big hands.*"

She writhed, like a run-over kitten with a broken back.

"Julia. The ambulance is coming. Just stay alive a few more minutes, then they can do it for you. Stay alive."

Everything under my hands was red.

fifteen

She stayed alive until the ambulance arrived. I had to help the EMTs keep her still so they could get shunts in both arms. When one suggested I ride in the second ambulance that was pulling up, spilling red light over Hjørdis's street—red the exact colour of the bunad—I took him by the throat and shook him a little.

She stayed alive until we got to the hospital. She was still alive as they wheeled her into surgery.

"She's strong," I told the three nurses and one doctor in surgical greens who stood with me by the swinging doors. One of the nurses held a hypodermic. "Shouldn't you be in there, helping her?"

"We're here to help you."

"Oh, no," I said gently. "I'm fine," and I plucked the needle from the nurse's hand and squirted the drug onto the floor, but then something bit through my pants and three of them were nodding in satisfaction as the fourth stepped out from behind me and capped her own syringe.

"We need to take a look at you," one of them said. I backed up against the wall.

"Julia."

"There's nothing you can do to help her now."

The wall was cool and solid against my skin. It also seemed to be moving upwards. All I could see were four pairs of green-clad legs and white scrub shoes.

"Go get a gurney."

One of the pairs of green trousers walked away down the corridor, then all I could see was the floor.

The room smelled of clean sheets and the lemons Hjørdis had left.

"The police are accepting the story that those two American men were fighting over a woman and you got hit in the cross-fire," said Sampo.

"Not easily."

"No. But what other explanation is there? Especially as your prints were on neither weapon and you are such a re-spectable citizen. The wound helps, of course."

"Yes."

We measured each other. If it wasn't for my letter insur-ance, I would never have woken from that sedative.

"What's your real name?"

"Harald."

"Like the king."

"Just like the king."

We didn't shake hands before he left.

A nurse came in with a tray full of needles and scissors and bandages. She worked quickly, with that lack of tender-ness endemic to the profession. "You have another visitor waiting to see you. I told her you had already talked to too many people today."

"Who is it?"

"I didn't get her name. She's American."

"Tell her she can come in when you've finished."

It was Annie. No longer laughing, eyes circled with jet lag

and worry. She took a chair by the bed but did not seem to know what to say.

"When did you get here?"

"Two hours ago."

"Are her brother and sister coming?"

I thought for a moment she didn't understand me. "Oh. No. Drew . . . well, Drew can't come. And Carmel is at the U.S. Research Station in McMurdo Sound. In the Antarctic. I haven't been able to get through to her." She sat there helplessly.

"You've talked to the doctors?"

"Yes. They tell me she's critical but stable. A lot of internal damage. Her liver—" She stopped abruptly. "I was going to say it's shot to pieces. A figure of speech. But it really is. It really is shot to pieces. They had to take out four inches of colon, too. And one of her kidneys. It was the bullet, they said. A special bullet that bounced around inside."

"The only irreparable damage is to her liver."

"She . . . she's strong, isn't she?"

"Very strong."

"And a liver transplant would make her as good as new again, wouldn't it?"

"Almost."

"Why won't she wake up? She just lies there and there's no sound but that beep beep beep of the machines."

"It's her body's way of focusing its attention on what's necessary. She's fighting to stay alive the best way she knows how. When she regains strength, she'll wake up."

"You're sure?"

"Absolutely. You know Julia, she can't bear to miss anything that's going on."

She started to smile, but the stretch turned into a quiver. "I can't do this."

"You're tired. I bet you didn't sleep on the plane. Julia

doesn't sleep on the plane, either. A few hours' rest will work wonders."

"But I have to see to her things. Insurance. Her clothes. Make arrangements."

"Hjørdis, my aunt, is already dealing with getting our things from the seter—the farm where we've been staying. Everything is being taken care of. And Julia is safe now. She's in good hands. Get some sleep, Mrs. Miclasz."

"Annie." A ghost of the former roguish smile, gone in a moment. "You saved her life." I should never have let her go. "You love her, don't you?"

My hawk with broken wings and matted feathers. "Yes."

"So do I. If we join forces, she'll have to live."

"She'll live." She had to.

"The doctors tell me you were hurt, too."

Cracked scapula, chipped elbow, nerve damage. Infections had meant they had snipped away bits of skin and muscle; I had had a blood transfusion; and there were enough stitches to make my arm look like that of a child's clumsily sewn-up teddy bear.

"Nothing that won't mend."

She stood. "When I come back tomorrow I'll bring some vitamins. I want you to get well quickly. Julia is going to need us both."


A nurse brought in a phone. It was my mother.

"Hjørdis has told me what you told her happened." A diplomat's nicety of language. "I take it your trip to England will be postponed?"

"Yes. I've chartered an air ambulance and will accompany Julia and her mother to Atlanta tomorrow. They've found a donor they can keep alive until we get there."

"Will she survive the operation?"

"The odds are about even."

"Keep me informed. And if you need anything, anything at all, call."

I held Julia's hand all the way across the North Sea, across the Irish Sea and the Atlantic Ocean, even though this was one flight during which she would not be afraid. When I had to release a hand to let the nurse be about his business, I rested my palm against her thigh. Somewhere deep down in her crocodile brain I wanted to register the fact that she was not alone, that she never would be.

Annie sat on the other side of the bed. Sometimes she held her hand, too; mostly, she just looked.

Over the Irish Sea, the plane lurched a little.

"I hate turbulence," she said.

"It must be genetic."

"You should be resting that shoulder."

"I'm fine."

The plane droned through the arid reaches of the afternoon sky.

"She's lovely, isn't she?"

"Yes."

"She's too young, too beautiful to die."

"I won't let her die."

"I saw it from the beginning, you know."

"Saw what?"

"That you two were right for each other. She was so upset about Jim's death, all to pieces. It was quite unlike her. I haven't seen her like that before, well, not since . . ."

"She told me about her brother."

"Oh. Well, I couldn't understand it, why she fell apart like that. Almost as if she was blaming herself. And then you came along, out of the blue, and suddenly she wasn't in pieces anymore." She smiled. "Did she ever tell you she thought you'd done it at first?"

"The police told me."

"She went to the police about you?" She shot Julia a star-tled glance.

"It probably seemed like a good idea at the time. He was her friend. I was there when it happened. But the police didn't take her seriously."

"Well, I'm glad she didn't get you into any trouble."

Any trouble. Any trouble. I wanted to laugh, but did not know if it would escape as a howl.

Annie said softly, "But what am I saying? I'm not a fool. The Norwegian police don't really believe your story about two men attacking each other and Julia getting shot by mistake."

"Do you?"

The engine note climbed as the pilot tried to find his way out of the turbulence.

"I'll believe that rather than believe Julia might have been at fault somehow." Her face was set and so pale that the blusher seemed almost garish, the kind of work mortuary beauticians do.

"Julia was simply at the wrong place at the wrong time. No, not just in Oslo. It started in Atlanta."

"When Jim died."

"Before then." I told her what I knew, up to breaking into Honeycutt's house and taking information to Denneny. She didn't need to know about that, or my deal with the cartels. But as she had said, she was not a fool.

"So you killed them. No, don't say anything. I'm glad. If I thought asking you to kill a hundred times would keep Julia safe, I'd ask you to do it."

And I would. A hundred times. A thousand times.

"But we don't need to worry about that now, do we? The Atlanta police will take it from here. They called, you know, while you were away. They have some new evidence. They wanted to talk to Julia again. I told them she was in Oslo, consulting with Olsen Glass."

"What did they say?"

"They wanted the name of the person she would be seeing. I gave them Edvard's number. He came to the hospital, you know."

I nodded. He had visited me, too.

"He was so young, and he seemed to take Julia's injury personally—kept apologizing on behalf of his country. I didn't know what to say, so I just hugged him until he shut up. He cried. I had to mop up his tears. At least it gave me something to do, something that made a difference."

We both looked at Julia lying still and silent and beyond our care. The engines resumed their steady hum. We were above the turbulence.

"That sculpture garden he and Julia were planning, are planning, sounds lovely. All those story characters and settings for the children. The adult version sounded challenging and exciting, too, but I think it was the children's garden he really wanted. Wants. Oh, god, Aud, I'm talking about her and the garden in past tense."

We landed just before six in the evening, Atlanta time. The air was thick and hot and flavoured with diesel fumes. The ambulance drove to Piedmont Hospital along streets crowded with convertibles full of tanned people in shorts and pastel polo shirts, eyes blank and anonymous behind shades. The trees were heavy and green with full summer foliage, the sky an impersonal, bland blue. I insisted that the EMTs give Julia a second blanket; the air-conditioning was fierce. By seven, she was being prepped for surgery.

The surgeon came to talk to us in the visitors' suite before he scrubbed. "The operation will take several hours, and you won't be allowed to see her for hours after that, but I don't suppose there's any point telling you to go home and get some sleep? No. Well, I'll call in again after the operation and let you know how it went."

\*     \*     \*

I pulled two armchairs together for Annie, and two for myself, and found us both blankets. We curled up. When I woke at two in the morning, Annie was staring at the ceiling.

"Would you like some coffee?"

"May as well," she said.

Hospitals at night are strange places. The floors gleam in the dark and the air is too dry and hot. In a few hours, gurneys trundled by hospital porters spiriting away those who had died in the night would squeak down these corridors, past doors behind which frightened people lay awake, listening. I passed a vending machine on the way to the nurse's station, but ignored it.

Annie sat up when I came back with fresh coffee. "Where on earth did you find this?"

"I told the nurse that if she let me into the nurses' break room to make some fresh, I'd not only make a generous dona- tion to the hospital children's fund, I'd bring her a cup, served any way she liked. You'll be pleased to know that she takes cream and sugar. And she likes cookies." I passed her the plate.

The coffee was long gone and we were playing backgam- mon when the surgeon returned. He was one of those men who needed to shave three times a day. He was wearing slacks and sports jacket. On his way home.

He was frowning when he came in, but smiled when we stood up.

"Let's all sit down again, shall we?" Always *we* with doc- tors. "You'll be pleased to know that the operation went smoothly and the patient is stable. But as you know, recovery can be a slow process." He couldn't remember her name.

"When can we see her?" Annie asked.

"She's not conscious yet."

"When?"

"In the morning? Yes, in the morning. A quick peep around

ten o'clock. But very briefly. Yes, I think that would be best."
The man was so tired he was talking more to himself than to
us. He started to get up.

"But someone will let us know how she's doing?"

"The nurses' station just down the hall will have all that
information. Just ask. As I've said, the operation went very
smoothly."

Annie just nodded. He left. I got up. "I'm going to get
some more coffee."

I caught up with him at the nurses' station, where he was
commenting on some blunder on a TV hospital show the night
before. They both laughed.

"Doctor."

"Ah?"

"Another question, about Julia Lyons-Bennet, the woman
you just gave a new liver. When will we know if she will reject
the liver or not?"

"At least twelve hours. Tomorrow afternoon. Perhaps even
later." He just wanted to go home.

"It must have been a complicated operation."

He made a vast effort and dredged up a smile. "Well, yes,
she'd been shot and there were one or two things that we
don't normally encounter but, given that, everything went very
well. Very smoothly. As I said."

"But she's still not conscious. What were the one or two
things?"

He let his smile fade. "We had to resection her colon, and
there are indications that her remaining kidney is under strain.
But I can't stress enough that she is currently stable and doing
very well under the circumstances. It was a good organ match.
We have high hopes."

"How high?"

"High," he said firmly. He was lying.

When I got back to the visitors' suite with more coffee,
Annie was crying. "She's going to be all right, Aud. She's

going to be all right. I know it. Oh, please god she's going to be all right." She wiped at her eyes and sipped her coffee. I had put extra sugar in it. "He was very thoughtful, changing out of his bloody clothes before he came to see us, don't you think?"

More likely he had needed the time to think of the phrases that would reassure without actually lying.

"Ah." She put her cup down. "I think I can sleep now."

I stayed awake, thinking. Julia, facing me that first time in the street in the rain. Julia, telling Dornan about penis piercing. Julia, in my arms at the fjord. Julia, Julia, Julia. So many mistakes.

After I had seen Julia, I took a cab back to the house. The flowers were all dead from lack of water and the house smelled of air-conditioning. The chair sat empty in the centre of my workroom. I called Benny. "I hope you don't have any arrangements for lunch because I need some information, and I need it now. Anything you can find on the death of Michael Honeycutt in New York. The Bridgetown Grill at twelve."

I showered, changed, unpacked, and dumped the dirty clothes on the floor by the washing machine. I knelt to sort them. Hjørdis had packed; Julia's clothes were jumbled in with my own. I held a soft blue shirt to my cheek, remembered Julia's sly smile as I had unbuttoned it at the seter one afternoon, remembered her laugh and wave as she drove off down the track, beautiful in her blue dress. I couldn't bear to wash away her scent. I left the laundry on the floor.

I drove with the windows down, and the humid, sinewy heat fisted down my throat and fattened the ugly thing that pulsed under my sternum like a feeding leech.

The Bridgetown Grill was hotter still, flaring with the spit and sizzle of Jamaican cooking in the open kitchen that ran the length of the narrow gallery painted with palm trees and crowded by fast-talking dental hygienists whose glasses kept steaming up, and by white rastas whose dreads drabbled through their blackened fish and hot sauce unnoticed. Benny, skinny as a rail, was already eating, Adam's apple bobbing up and down like the red bauble on a blood pressure monitor.

"Jamaican jerk chicken," he said by way of greeting.

I beckoned the waiter and ordered the first thing I saw on the menu. "Tell me about Honeycutt."

"Gee, and how are you, too, Torvingen? I gut NCIC in fifty minutes flat and get out here in fifteen more and all the thanks I get is—"

"Honeycutt."

"Shot clean as a whistle in the back of the head in the men's bathroom at Kennedy with a .38 at about three-thirty p.m. on May eighth. No one saw anything, no one heard anything. Best for last: he hadn't even cleared customs and immigration."

"Someone with access knew his schedule." Someone with access to privileged information; who could get inside international airport security.

My food arrived just as Benny finished his. He looked from his empty plate to my full one. I pushed it at him. "Help yourself."

"Not hungry?" He was already cutting the fish into bite-sized pieces, the better to shovel it down in record speed. "By the way, that coke from the Inman Park arson that you were interested in? It's gone. Um, that's good."

I felt as though someone were squeezing my head. "When?"

"Not sure. Oh, this fish is delicious!"

"Then when did the department find out?"

"Well, they haven't, yet. But I like to check on things that interest me. Sort of look at them, like trophies. Well, not look at them exactly, just sort of test them. Every now and again. So I went to check on the coke—and it's gone. Well, not gone.

Changed. The bags are the same, and the seals, but it's not the same coke. It's not coke at all, anymore."

"But it was before?"

"It was what the lab report said: ninety-nine percent pure Colombian coke. It's not now, though."

"How do you know?"

"I just, well, you know, tested it."

"Before and after?"

"I just took a bit. Really. Just a bit, to see. It's not like it's a habit or anything."

"Never mind that. You're sure, absolutely sure that what came in was pure, but that what is there now is not?"

"Yes."

He'd never swear to it in court—why should he lose his job and risk prosecution?—but I didn't need a court. The leech under my sternum swelled. I stood.

My phone rang. "Torvingen."

"Aud?" It was Annie. "Aud, you'd better get here. She's rejecting."

Annie was waiting for me outside ICU. "The doctor says she isn't rejecting. They say she has to have another operation. No one will explain." Her once-round cheeks sagged, and she looked like a sad caricature of the Annie Miclasz I had met just a few weeks ago.

"Is she in the theatre now?"

"No, they're about to prep her."

"If she's not rejecting, why are they going to operate?"

"The liver's stopped working, and her kidney. And she's got an infection. But I thought she was getting better. I don't understand it. She woke up, and—"

"She woke up?" I went utterly still.

"Just for a minute. I'm sure."

"I have to see her." Before they prepped her and she ran away again into coma.

"I'll go get coffee and be back in fifteen minutes."

"If you see the doctor, send him to me."

In ICU everything—the walls, floors, bed linen, even Julia's bedspread—was white, against which crystal red and green lights blinked on and off, slowly, like lizards' eyes. The air was full of the hiss and suck of oxygen, the peristaltic pulse of IV units squeezing god knows what into her veins, the hum of a dozen machines.

Julia's hand in mine was mustard yellow, like her arm, like her face. I lifted it to my face. It smelled strange, of drugs and pain. The scent of one who has met that cheating Viking with the great ham hands. One who has played and lost.

"Your nails need trimming," I told her.

Hiss, suck, blink.

"They must have grown a quarter of an inch in the last few days." I sounded like a fool. "Julia, I want you to listen to me. You're ill, but you mustn't give up. I want you to start thinking about what you want to do when you get out of here. Have I told you about Whitby Abbey, on the Yorkshire coast? There's a ruin there that dates from the twelfth century, very haunting, very gothic, but the first abbey there was founded in the seventh century by Hilda. There's a power there. You wouldn't think to look at it from the outside. But then you cross the track and walk over some turf, and . . . ah, Julia, it's suddenly there before you, and it's as though the breath of the earth drives up through the soles of your shoes and into your bones. I want to hold your hand, this hand, and watch your face when you step onto the turf at Whitby Abbey."

Hiss, suck, blink.

"Or we could take a boat to the Lofoten Islands in late June when even at two in the morning the sea is silver, like ghost water, and you can read the newspaper without a light. Or if you'd rather go in autumn, we could make troll cream from whortleberries."

I told her about crushing the berries, about whipping up

egg whites, folding the one into the other; how it would feel in her mouth.

Hiss, suck, blink.

"But it might take a while before you can travel far, so before we sail to Lofoten, before you see Whitby, I'll show you Northwoods Lake Court. As I promised."

I had also promised I would keep her safe. I touched her cheek, very gently, with my fingertips. Dry now, but still soft. Her eyelids flickered.

"Fuck," she whispered.

"Julia?" I touched her cheek again. "Julia?"

"Fuck. It hurts."

"I'm here. I'm right here," I said, squeezing her hand with both mine, then stroking her hair from her forehead.

Her eyes opened. The whites were pink, but her irises were brilliant as a clear evening sky. She blinked quickly, like a camera shutter. "I'm here," I said again.

"I'm dying, aren't I?" Her voice was light and dry, an insect running over a newspaper.

"You've had a liver transplant. It's not going too well. They're going to operate again this afternoon."

"Promise me you . . ."

She shut her eyes.

"Julia?"

She tried to lift her hand. I lifted it for her, put it against my cheek. "When we met," she whispered, "you were frozen inside. Empty. Now you're not. Don't go back. Even if I die. Stay in the world."

I could not imagine a world without Julia. "You will not die."

She opened her eyes. This time she didn't blink. "My mother . . . she's not always brave. I hate machines. Don't let machines keep me alive. Don't let them."

"I won't."

"Stay in the world, Aud. Stay alive inside. Promise me. Stay alive."

I whipped through the night as the ice crept through my veins. I stopped once at a strip mall, where I called Denneny's office number, disconnecting as soon as he picked up. Then I filled my spare can with gas and bought some gloves. My mouth tasted of copper and blood.

At Cheshire Bridge Road I cruised the sex bars until I found the car I wanted, a dark, late-model Volvo with multiple airbags and antilock brakes. This time I parked in the lot of another bar and walked back. A quick thrust with a shim and I was inside.

I understand Denneny. He works late because he has nothing to go home to and when he looks inside himself, there is nobody there. I parked a block down the road from the precinct house, adjusted my headrest for maximum safety, and waited. I watched the stars. Tonight I didn't recognize any of them; they were cold and alien. I thought of abbeys on headlands, of Norwegian islands in a sea breeze, of Northwoods Lake Court, where the air would be utterly still but for the creak of tree frogs and the endless patter of fountains. Then for a while I thought of nothing.

He emerged just after eleven p.m. I let his Lexus get a block ahead before I pulled out.

When we first met, he had lived in Candler Park. When he made captain he moved to Morningside, a neighbourhood where all the houses were built of dusty rose brick on winding little streets and fronted by velvety, floodlit lawns. No doubt he had thought he would soon be promoted up to commander and the giddy heights of the Prado mansions.

At an intersection I tightened my seat belt and turned my lights off before following him up a long, empty hill. He had been driving the same route for eight years and took it faster than was really safe in the dark. Half a mile from the top of the hill, the road would take a wide curving left, then a sudden right alongside one of those pretty rose-coloured walls. His speed picked up. Fifty, fifty-five, sixty.

He took the long left curve without slowing down, as I'd known he would. Time for me and the Viking to play one last round. I smiled, shifted, and punched the gas. The nose of the Volvo touched his right rear bumper just as he would have been thinking of feathering the brakes and threading the wheel through his hands to take the car to the right.

Brake lights flared and stained the night red. I eased my foot down a little more. Tires squealed, metal screeched. My heart was an anvil. The Lexus wobbled, then slewed, then seemed to straighten. I hummed to myself as I floored the gas and drove him into the wall at sixty miles an hour.

The noise was huge and seemed to last forever and then the night turned white as airbags bloomed and the cars bounced and my head walloped back into the head restraint. The wound along my shoulder pulled at the stitches. Nothing I hadn't anticipated. I slashed the airbags and kicked my way out of the Volvo. The night smelled of honeysuckle and gas and hot rubber and seemed to turn very slowly.

His airbags had inflated, too, and like a good policeman he had been wearing his seat belt, but the impact had been a surprise, and he was still stunned. I pulled open his door, felt around his belt for his cuffs and gun. I shot the bag, then clipped his hands to the wheel.

"I never liked you, Denneny, but I trusted you. You had rules. What happened? Was it the death of your dreams or that of your wife? Nothing to work for, no one to go home to, nothing inside. Nothing except your rules. You should have clung to them, Denneny, they might have saved you."

Metal ticked. Somewhere an owl screeched.

"You know why I'm here, don't you?"

He turned his head slowly. Blood trickled from his left nostril. I pulled back the hammer.

"Don't you."

He closed his eyes and nodded.

"Good." And I shot him in the abdomen.

The frame of the Volvo had buckled a little with the impact and it took me a moment to get the trunk open. My head hurt. When I got back with the gas can, he had started to go into shock.

I unscrewed the cap and laid it carefully on the grass verge. I sloshed gas inside the car, over his body. Judging by the way he squealed and thrashed, it stung on that wound.

"I was stupid, Denneny. Who warned me off this case in the first place? Why would someone leave all that coke at the scene of a crime unless they could get it back from the evidence locker whenever they wanted? I should have known, but I trusted you. Trusted your rules. But you broke all those rules, for money. When did you stop caring, Denneny?"

The can was heavy; my shoulder burned.

"Who could have called Lyon Art to get the information about Olsen Glass? Who took his holidays in California, where Michael Honeycutt used to work? Who knew where to find three men who would kill for money?" He choked on the gas. "Who might be expected to find out Honeycutt was laundering cartel drug money? So simple. All I had to do was put it all together, Denneny, but I didn't. I didn't ask that last question: who was the only person—the only one, Denneny—that I trusted to help me with this?"

I should have remembered: the Viking never plays by the rules.

"Did you laugh when you pulled the strings? Did you think I was funny, running around like a dumb but faithful dog, bringing you bones? No, because nothing amuses you anymore, does it? And nothing annoys you. Nothing fills you with joy. It's all gone. You're dead inside. Empty."

I stepped back and looked at him. Drenched to his skin. I tore off his shirt and twisted it, then knotted it into something I could throw. My head pounded, and when I bent down for the gas can the grass verge swooped. The cap got cross-threaded when I tried to screw it back on. I had to take it off and start again. I carried it back to the Volvo and returned with matches.

I tossed his gun into the backseat, then pulled a penny from my pocket. It was warm in my hand; bright and sharp. I held it up between finger and thumb. In the headlights it could have been gold. "All for this, Denneny. All for money." I put it back in my pocket. My fare for the ferryman, not his.

I stepped back and struck a match. It burned electric blue at the centre but its wavering tip was the yellow of every torch ever used to light a pyre, that most human of fires that roars against the night to keep the ice from our hearts. I touched the match to the shirt, which I whirled over my head until it was a great orange wheel. I threw it into the car.

At Little Five Points, the night was full of the noise and laughter of people who don't know that the trolls always get you in the end, who when they look up at the night do not understand that the beauty of the bright stars turning over-head, though vast, was created by a universe utterly indifferent to their fate. These young, healthy innocents understand only enough to be a little afraid, so they fill themselves with pot and beer and in the light of a myriad cafés listen to inept street players trying to drive back the dark.

I walked into Borealis. The tables seemed to get in my way, and the chairs were not where they should have been. *Don't let machines keep me alive,* she had said. *Don't let them.* And I had promised.

"Aud! What in the world is the matter?" Over his shoulder, he called, "Two lattés over here, Jonie, please. Sit, Aud. Sit, for the love of god." He led me to a corner table. "What is that terrible smell? Gas, is it? You've been in some accident? No? Well, never mind. You'll live. How's Julia?"

Julia, with the indigo eyes and the laugh like Armagnac. Julia, who had thought she was ready. I took the penny from my pocket. Fare for the ferryman. But *Stay in the world*, she had said. I spun the penny on the table and, while it turned, stared past him, past the innocents with their light and their noise, and out into the night.

"She died."

She died, but *Stay in the world, Aud,* she'd said. *Stay alive inside. Promise me.* I closed my fist around the spinning penny. Just a coin. The world fractured; meltwater ran down my face.